GUARDIAN'S
RETURN

DARREN SIMON

DIVERTIR
PUBLISHING
Salem, NH

GUARDIAN'S RETURN

Darren Simon

Copyright © 2018 Darren Simon

Cover design by Kenneth Tupper

Published by Divertir Publishing LLC
PO Box 232
North Salem, NH 03073
http://www.divertirpublishing.com/

ISBN-13: 978-1-938888-20-5
ISBN-10: 1-938888-20-0

Library of Congress Control Number: 2018939851

Printed in the United States of America

Acknowledgements

I would like to thank my wife and two sons for their continued support of this dream of mine to be an author. I'd also like to thank my editor, Jen, for her tireless work to make my book the best it can be, my original editor, Jill, who worked with me on this book so many years ago, and finally Divertir Publishing for its ongoing support.

CONTENTS

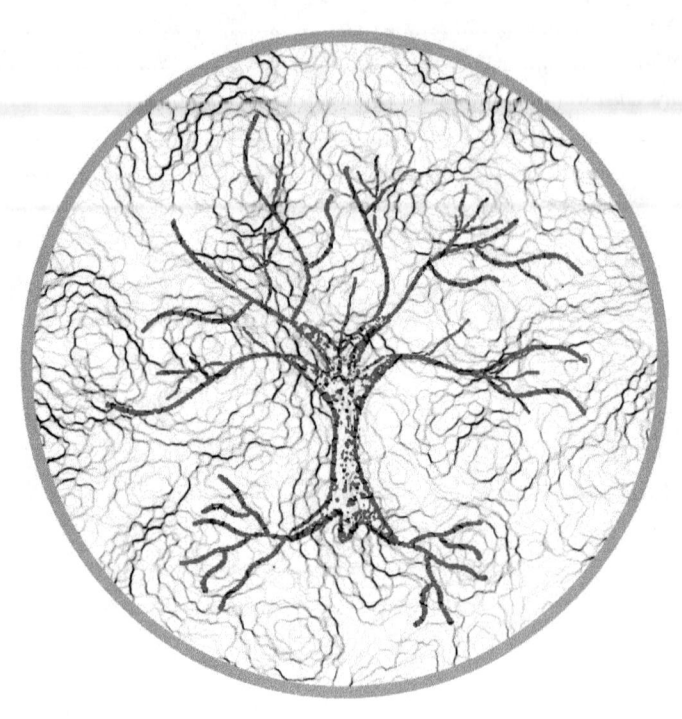

CHAPTER 1

The Awakening

FROM HER THRONE room's observation deck, Empress Theodora lifted her black hood and grinned. Below lay the ruins of her dead sister's kingdom. "Latara has become such a glorious sight, sister," Theodora mused.

Decimated townships spread across a withered, cracked landscape where grasslands and trees once flourished. Factories belched columns of choking black smoke into a murky night sky. Theodora folded her arms over her chest as fire spewed from twisted, pointy towers built from the charred remains of schools and places of worship.

"Magnificent," she uttered. Inside these massive constructs, engines rumbled, fashioning steel into the weapons her Horeng army needed to dominate the lands. The entire world of Janasara was hers. Her grin faded.

"I am meant to rule worlds. I am to be a goddess," Theodora's voice echoed through the chamber. "Yet I am stranded here—marooned by an insolent child, my own great niece, who will suffer for what she has done to me."

Theodora's porcelain-white face reddened. Her thin lips curled back, revealing yellow teeth clenched together as she grasped a round, black object with the word *Frisbee* stamped on one side.

It was supposed to be her medallion—a magical force conceived from the darkest arts—able to grant endless power and immortality. Instead, that treacherous human girl used the thing to deceive Theodora into abandoning her siege on Earth.

"She used her magic to send me back here with this false medallion, and here I will remain imprisoned until—"

Crimson energy erupted from Theodora's palms, melting the black object until it formed a misshaped clump. Her body vibrating, skin scalding hot, she hurled the black mass from the observation deck.

"Never again will I be made a fool. Before long, that child will bring me what is rightfully mine." Theodora glided from the observation deck into the dimly lit chamber, her long robe trailing along the marbled floor. She passed over a heap of bent and broken crowns, crusted in the blood of the fallen kings and queens from the Unified Kingdoms. "Then, whether she is a guardian or not, she will die—just as my sister did so many years ago. When she falls, I will begin my conquest of worlds."

1

She slithered to her throne, forged from the bones of those defeated in battle, and placed her hands over the skull armrests. With a deep breath and the slightest movement of her right forefinger, the floor beyond the dais gave way. White smoke curled from the gaping hole in the floor where a glass sarcophagus rose and hovered in front of her.

"Oh, what a joyful moment." Theodora placed a hand over her heart. "The birth of my daughter has come."

The smoke drifted away. She circled the sarcophagus, her bone-like fingers caressing the glass. Tears fell from her ice-blue eyes. Inside an infant submerged in green liquid slept.

"Wake up. Wake up, little one," Theodora's voice cooed. Tilting her gaze toward the chamber's ceiling, a chant formed in her throat and softly snaked its way from her mouth. Her words intensified, piercing the silence. A red glow encircled her hands and then swelled to engulf her body.

Theodora trembled. Her long hair faded from flowing golden locks to strands of ashen gray. Crevices formed under her eyes and around her mouth. Already gaunt cheeks receded even further into her skull. Still, she chanted in a booming voice. Her crimson magic spread through the throne room.

With a final shout that resonated through the kingdom, she stopped. The red glow vanished, and Theodora collapsed to the floor. Her heart raced and chest convulsed. Sweat dripped from her forehead. "So tired, but it was worth it to give my child life!"

She stood on wobbly legs. Her ears rang from the magical strain, but the clamor gave way to a new sound—a baby's first cry.

"Yes!" Theodora embraced the sarcophagus, razor-like fingernails clawing the smooth surface.

The green liquid was gone. Her daughter's fussing sobs bounced off the walls and grew into a wail. Little arms and legs thrashed wildly.

"Yes, my child, I hear your anger." Theodora tapped on the lid. "I will unleash your rage on the world and on the one who still holds my immortality. You will help me destroy her."

Her daughter's brown eyes shot open. Shrieks gave way to a toothless smile. It didn't last. A scream penetrated the glass. The child's eyes bulged as her body contorted. Limbs stretched and hair formed on her bald head. Her face aged, shifting from infant to a toddler. She panted, writhing inside the tomb, as the transformation added years from one heartbeat to the next. Her cheekbones nearly ripped through skin. Fingers grew in length. Eyes spread farther apart. The toddler became a young girl.

Theodora laughed. "Grow, my child. I am so very proud of you."

Her daughter's hair lengthened beyond bulging shoulders. Arms and legs gained muscle. Chin became more pronounced. Eyes showed increasing clarity.

The child moaned and twisted. She grabbed her head and kicked at the walls. One word erupted from deep inside her throat. "Mother!"

"I'm here, child," Theodora nodded. "Don't fight what is happening to you. It is...natural."

She stopped fighting the metamorphosis. With her eyes fixed on Theodora, she lay still as her body completed its journey. With one last shallow breath, the process ended. The cover to the sarcophagus opened.

"Rise, my daughter, for it is a new day for both of us." Theodora extended a bony hand.

A teenage girl with long brown hair and deep-set eyes emerged. When her feet touched the slick floor, her legs buckled. On her knees, she reached for Theodora. "Mother, I can't stand. I feel so weak, and I am so cold."

"In time you will gain strength." Theodora motioned for her daughter to rise.

"Mother, I cannot. Can you help me?"

"No."

"Mother?"

"You are a warrior, a general to rule at my side. You cannot show weakness. I will not allow it. Now rise and prove yourself worthy."

The girl closed her eyes. She tightened her hands into fists and swallowed a lung full of air.

"I am a warrior." She stood on her newly formed legs, her body trembling. Once at full height, she thrust out her chest and lifted her head. Lips parted in a slight grin, she declared, "Look at me, Mother. I'm doing it. I feel...alive."

"I know, daughter." Theodora removed her robe, approached her daughter, and placed the raven black garment over her shoulders.

"Mother, who am I?" The teen grasped her mother's hands.

"You are my child." Theodora stepped back, slipping from her grip.

"Do I have a name?" The young one tried to take a step but stumbled.

Theodora caught her. "In time you will earn your name."

"Why am I here?" She pushed away from Theodora and stood straight.

Theodora placed an arm around her daughter, guiding her to the observation deck. "You are here to help me right a terrible wrong and bring an enemy of our world to justice. Soon that enemy—a young girl not so different from you—will come to harm me. You must stop her. When I command it, you will make her suffer by killing the ones she loves. And when she begs for mercy, we shall make her suffer all the worse. I have endowed you with the heart of a warrior for this very purpose. Come, it is time for your training to begin."

The girl turned to Theodora, her eyes wide and bright. "I will kill anyone who tries to hurt you, Mother. I promise."

"I know you will."

3

CHAPTER 2

Fire!

SEEMS PEACEFUL TONIGHT, bike." Charlee stared down at the residential streets of San Francisco from the banana-shaped seat of her flying bike. Straight ahead, the Bay glimmered under a sparkling array of lights along the piers and wharfs. The Golden Gate Bridge, its massive frame jutting high into the night air, glowed in the distance.

If she never stepped foot on the Golden Gate again, that would be fine with her. Jumping from its columns high above the sea in a last-ditch bid to defeat the sorceress, Theodora, had been the scariest thing she'd ever done. If her mom hadn't used magic to save her, she would have died in the icy waters. Probably smashed to bits. She shuddered at that thought.

A month had passed since they battled the sorceress, forcing her through a portal back to Janasara before she could conquer Earth. Since turning fourteen two weeks ago, Charlee and the bike started patrolling the city.

It was a way to use her newly discovered magic.

She breathed in the crisp spring air and tingled as she drew energy from a flock of seagulls passing below. Charlee's pulse quickened. She breathed deeper. Senses heightened. This new ability to harness energy from living sources—plants, animals, people...even Earth itself—gave her great strength, superior hearing, and enhanced vision, but the powers never lasted. When they faded, she still needed her glasses, which right now were tucked in her pant pocket.

Her changeling protector soared above the city with its glimmering feathered wings extended from the white frame. The shape-shifting being from Janasara could take any form it chose, but the '60s era Schwinn Stingray, with white-walled tires and upside-down u-shaped chrome backrest, seemed to stick.

She gripped the handlebars. An electrical current rose through her fingers, up her arms, and spread throughout her body. Muscles expanded. Her heart beat with the force of a sledgehammer pounding concrete. The bike—whose life force seemed limitless—multiplied her abilities like none other.

Charlee brushed away her wind-swept brown hair from her eyes and studied the bike's giant eagle's wings. What a sight they must be. So far she had avoided being photographed or filmed by some onlooker's phone, but rumors spread on Facebook and Twitter of a mystery girl on a flying bike who helped those in need. They called the stranger—*her*—a hero.

After her birthday, her parents allowed her out a few nights a week for a couple of hours…but only with the bike. Her mom, a healer, kept a mental lock on Charlee during these excursions. Their connection felt like a ghostly finger constantly tapping her shoulder. *Be careful, honey. Be smart. I'll know if you need help.* Annoying and comforting at the same time.

Charlee tightened the knot on the black bandana over her eyes. Two slits had been cut into the cloth so she could see. Her dad's idea. Disguise herself. Protect her identity. The family's, too.

"Let's head to the Bay. Maybe we can get ourselves into something there," Charlee directed. "What do you say?"

She didn't expect her protector to answer. No matter what shape it took, the creature never spoke. That didn't matter. They were linked in a way that made words unnecessary, but she still spoke to the changeling anyway.

With one thrust of its wings, the bike dove toward the waterfront.

A light flickered to the right. Charlee glanced in that direction with her magnified vision. *Fire!* She shifted her weight to guide the bike toward the blaze. Orange flames, just beginning their wild dance, had begun to swallow a two-story house across the city near Russian Hill. A plume of smoke rose into the night. The stench of charred wood tickled her nose.

"Bike, go!"

Like a jet, the bike raced toward the burning house. Charlee leaned her face into the wind.

Black smoke billowed over the neighborhood. In the distance, sirens blared as the Fire Department chased down the blaze.

At the bike's velocity, she would arrive before the firefighters. How could she stop a fire? Could the bike transform into a giant water hose? Probably better to let the firefighters save the home. If there was anyone inside…anyone in danger… maybe, she could help.

"Daddy!"

With her enhanced hearing, Charlee pinpointed the child's cry long before she reached the scene.

The bike landed in front of the engulfed house. Crackling flames burst through the windows and licked at the roof. Neighbors already gathered a safe distance from the burning inferno. Some fought with fire extinguishers. A small crowd clustered around two crying children.

"My daddy's still in there," a little girl in her nightgown, face smudged, cried. She clutched a teddy bear as a woman stroked her ponytails. "He went in after my puppy. Why hasn't he come out?"

A few spectators tried to find a way into the house, but choking hot smoke blocked all the doorways and windows. There was no way in or out, except…

"Look! It's the girl with the flying bike."

"It's true!"

"She's real!"

As the crowd turned to Charlee, she focused on a broken window that might lead to an attic. A gray mist poured through. The flames had spared that corner of the house. So far.

"Bike, I need a lift."

The bike responded. With outstretched wings, it gained altitude, fighting against the expanding barrier of heat.

Charlee closed her eyes, absorbing as much of the bike's energy as possible. "I need all the power you can give me."

Her soft arms and legs bulged with new muscles. Her heart beat like the thunder of a horse's hooves pounding the dirt. Opening her eyes, she willed a new power—kind of like an invisible protective force field—to form around her. It would have to be enough to shield against the heat, smoke, and flames.

Charlee peered through the window shards. Black smoke replaced the gray mist. A fiery breeze rippled against her cheeks. Sweat formed under her bandana. Were they too late? She still had to try. If that girl's father was trapped inside, she had to find a way to save him. This was as good a place as any to make her entry.

Her mom's thoughts replaced her own. *Stay out of there. It's too dangerous. You don't need to do this.*

"I have to, Mom." Charlee leaned closer to the handlebars. "Now, bike—give me some breathing room!"

On her command, the bike gave one powerful flap of its wings. Like an unseen barrier, the blast of wind drove back the billowing plume past the jagged pieces of glass. As a pathway cleared, Charlee steadied herself on the bike's seat. She trembled and hesitated for just a heartbeat and then jumped through the window into the attic.

She landed on her hands, rolled once and came to a stop on her knees. Her body crunched over pieces of glass, but her super strength kept the shards from puncturing skin. Smoke crept up through the wooden floor. The blaze screamed below, exalting in its destruction. The house seemed to cry out in agony as its timbers gave way against the onslaught.

Red flames peeked through cracks in the floor. Smoke slithered toward her. The energy field surrounding her served as a protective layer, shielding her from the growing inferno and provided a pocket of breathable air. Still, searing heat bathed her in sweat. Her clothes clung to her as if glued against her body.

Panting like a dog, she tried to convince herself to escape. "I have to get out of here. Too hot! Baking! Can't do this." She paused "No, get a grip. I have to find the little girl's dad."

Stepping over flames licking at her feet, she crossed the attic and found a stairway to the house's lower levels. Each stair creaked as if it would give way under her weight, but she pressed forward until she reached a door.

What would she face on the other side? What had she gotten herself into? Fighting bad guys was one thing, but a burning house was quite another. Would her powers hold up? Would the bike be there to save her if she got in real trouble? Right now that was looking like a real possibility.

"All right, Charlee. Enough talk. Now do something," she said out loud.

Heat from the door pushed against her like an invisible blockade. She grasped the doorknob but recoiled. "Ouch! Jeez, that's hot!" Her palm might have been scalded if not for the layer of protective energy that cocooned her.

"What now?" she asked out loud. "I have to get to that little girl's dad. Time's running out. For him. And for me."

Calling on her magically heightened strength, she kicked the door. It didn't budge, but the timber around the hinges cracked. She struck a second time. The door broke from the frame and fell forward.

A wall of fire rushed through the opening, engulfing Charlee. She dropped to one knee and shielded her eyes. The blinding flash muzzled her cries. Somehow, though, the layer of energy kept her alive—a glowing barrier between her flesh and the inferno. She could breathe, too, but the air had become thick. She could only manage short breaths.

"I have to move. Can't fail."

Peering through her fingers, a swirling vortex of oranges, yellows and reds prevented her from seeing beyond a few feet in any direction. Her mom's thoughts returned. *Get up! Run through it! Straight ahead!*

Her body trembled, and her heart pounded so fast it might burst from her chest. Her skin baked despite the protective shell. Blinking sweat from her eyes, she charged through the firestorm. *Don't stop...don't stop until you're through*, her mom urged.

Overhead, the house creaked in protest. *Oh no!* Burning timber plunged toward her. Diving out of the way, she broke through the flames. Behind her the fire roared. Ahead, the second-floor hallway lay darkened by charred mist.

Coughing, Charlee clutched her chest to quiet her wild heart and slow her breathing. Her legs wobbled and her head drooped. Hot tears formed. She couldn't help it. *I'm alive. Still have a chance. Must press on.* Standing tall, she lifted her head. *You're not going to beat me, fire.* "Sir, where are you?" she called to the little girl's dad. "Can you hear me? Sir..."

Charlee cocked her head to listen for a response. A faint cough echoed down the hallway, followed by a puppy's high-pitched bark.

Three doors lined the hallway. Charlee ran into the first room. Empty. Flames snaked through the ceiling. In the second, fire spread along the walls, but still no sign of life.

"Sir! Sir! Are you here?" Charlee shouted through the third door. No response. She wheezed. The air supply within the protective layer was leaking away.

"He has to be here." Fire leaped through a vent near the ceiling, bathing the room in black smoke. Burning embers dropped onto the bed, igniting a pink bedspread and a gathering of dolls.

A man groaned from the far side of the bed beyond her view. *Yes!* She rushed to his side. He lay sprawled on the floor, a fallen piece of timber next to him. Blood seeped from a gash in his forehead.

The puppy darted from underneath the bed, yelping and jumping on Charlee.

"Move it! That little girl is not going to lose her daddy tonight...or her puppy, for that matter." With her super-strength, she lifted the man onto her shoulders with one hand and grabbed the puppy with the other. Her legs shook under the strain. Would her powers hold up? What if they didn't? They'd all burn to death. No, she couldn't think like that. She couldn't lose hope.

Stay calm, Charlee, her mom interrupted. *You can do it.*

Taking a step, her knees nearly buckled but she steadied herself. With a grunt, she lumbered through the doorway. "Have to get out of here."

Her words were lost in the inferno. The blaze spread to the stairway. Down the stairs came the shouts of firefighters. They had to be trying to clear a way, but with the stairs engulfed, there was no way out. She also had no route back to the attic. Falling timber ignited the floor behind her.

The protective energy surrounding her flickered. A mad dash through the fire wouldn't work without that layer.

"We're in trouble." Her shoulders sagged under the man's weight. Sweat dripped from the bandana into her eyes, nearly blinding her. She tried to blink away the stinging sensation, but it didn't help. "Mom, what do I do?"

Try drawing energy from the firefighters or people outside, her mom answered.

She concentrated, blood crashing around her head like waves, but for some reason she couldn't focus her ability.

She still had one power to call upon.

I can open a gateway!

Charlee closed her eyes and clenched her teeth. *Concentrate.* Already weakened, her head pounded like someone banged together cymbals inches from her ears. *Focus.* She envisioned the neighborhood just beyond the burning house. As she did, a small blue orb of energy formed in front of her.

The ball grew.

When she opened her eyes, the gateway was large enough for her to enter. Would it lead where she wanted…to the safety of the street? Too hard to tell. Her gateways never worked quite right. "Anything would be better than here."

She had no time to hesitate. The fire crept toward them from behind. The roof rumbled. It could cave in any moment. Holding her breath, still clutching the man and the puppy, Charlee jumped into the portal as a wooden beam fell on the spot where she had been standing.

Charlee leaped out of the gateway and right into the open sky above the burning house. *Wrong! This is worse!*

"Bi—"

Before Charlee finished the word, her winged friend soared out of the night sky and swooped down to catch her. Just as it had been so many times before, the bike was there to save her.

Charlee wrapped her legs around the frame. Her heart did cartwheels inside her chest. The mysterious being always found a way to snatch her away from death. She would have thanked the bike, but at this point in their relationship it was unnecessary. The bike simply knew.

Once safely seated, with the man still slung over her shoulder and the puppy held tight against her chest, the bike flew to the ground and landed behind the fire trucks. Firefighters and ambulance crews pulled the man from Charlee's shoulder. She watched as they laid him on a stretcher and fixed a bag over his mouth to help him breathe. The man coughed. His fingers moved. She hoped these signs meant that he would be all right.

"We'll take good care of him," a young paramedic, her face covered in ash and sweat, said to Charlee. The paramedic smiled. "Are you all right? Do you need medical attention?"

"No," Charlee wheezed.

"So you're the one, huh?" The paramedic's eyes were blood-red from the smoke and heat but friendly.

Charlee wasn't sure what to say. She checked the bandana. It remained in place.

Just in time, the little girl in ponytails rushed up to her dad, followed by an even smaller boy.

"Daddy," she whimpered.

"He'll be all right, little one," the paramedic reassured. "We're taking him to the hospital. You and your brother can ride along with us."

The girl smiled.

"Wait," Charlee added. "I think this little guy belongs to you." She handed the little girl the puppy.

"Thank you." The girl, her doll tucked under an arm, nestled the puppy to her face.

As they were placed in an ambulance, the paramedic turned back to Charlee. "You know, I just heard from the Red Cross their father is all they have. Their mother died last year. It's sad for one family to go through so much, but it could have been worse. You did a good thing. I just thought you should know."

The paramedic then stepped forward. "I just can't believe what—"

Charlee retreated. "Take care of that family."

The woman extended a hand toward her then stopped and nodded. Climbing into the ambulance, she closed the doors and the vehicle sped away.

Charlee felt tears as she watched the ambulance race to the hospital with four special lives…a father, his two children, and their little puppy. Back at the house, firefighters gained ground. Black plumes became a chalky mist. The night air stunk of scorched wood as the charred remains of the house sizzled.

All eyes were on her. Those gathered pointed at her. They held out their smart phones to take a picture or video. Finally, some evidence of their city's hero.

"Time for me to go." When she reached for the bike, applause spread along the street. She paused and gazed at the crowd. No one had ever cheered for her. Ever. "Wow."

The moment quickly faded. Behind the onlookers stood her parents. Her mom wiped away a tear. Her dad crossed his arms. His brow furrowed. Without approaching her, they climbed into their old Skylark and drove away. "Not. Good. I'm dead. They'll never let me out of the house again." Charlee climbed onto the bike. "Let's go. We're done here."

CHAPTER 3

A Teen Guardian's Daily Struggle

STANDING ON THE front porch of her family's home, Charlee reached for the doorknob but recoiled. Her parents would be on the other side waiting with one of their lectures about taking too many risks with her powers. Or they'd ground her for the next year.

"Well, let's get this over with." She pushed open the door.

Her mom, sandy blonde hair loose over her shoulders, greeted Charlee with a hug. "Oh, honey, what you did tonight is inspiring. You saved a life, and that is a worthy use of your abilities."

"What?" Suddenly aware how tired she was, Charlee collapsed into her mom's arms. "I thought you'd be mad."

"Concerned is all." Her dad placed one hand on her shoulder. The other rubbed his thin brown beard and then pushed up his round wire frame glasses. "But you were truly heroic, sweetheart. Yes, what you did was dangerous, but heroic."

Charlee studied her parents. This couldn't be them. They should be tearing into her right now. "I don't get it."

"We're just thankful you are all right." Her mom, blue eyes as comforting as always, ushered her to the couch and then stroked her hair. A familiar healing embrace, her mom's magic, surrounded Charlee. A pulsating chill washed over her like a cool breeze on a winter morning along the Bay, soothing her baked skin.

"So you're not going to ground me?" she asked.

Her dad lowered to one knee. He frowned at first, deep lines embedded in his forehead, but a grin quickly formed. He offered her a bottle of soda. "We'll save the grounding for tomorrow when the morning news has coverage of the fire and the hero who swooped in on a flying bike to save the day."

Charlee removed the bandana from her pocket. "At least they won't know it was me."

Her mom placed a hand on Charlee's cheek. "Your skin still feels so hot. A bit more healing magic is needed, and then you need your rest."

Charlee took a swig from the soda bottle. The icy fizz tickled her nose. "Can I finish my drink first?"

"Of course." Her mom nodded. "And Charlee, about that grounding—it will be coming. You are not to try anything that dangerous again. Understand?"

"I understand." That was a lie. Soon she would cross over to Janasara to face Theodora again and kill her. She hoped her mom couldn't hear her thoughts, otherwise all would be lost.

Charlee gazed at her mom. Tall with chiseled features, her mom was a strong, loving woman who gave up her career as a librarian to raise her daughters. She put family before everything else. A parent always there with a warm embrace whose soothing words provided clarity to a teenager's mixed-up world. When she offered advice, it centered on telling the truth.

Yet up until a month ago, she had kept a life-changing secret from Charlee.

Her mom's life began on a world called Janasara, the child of Queen Assara and the Guardian Michala, heir to the Crown of Latara. Powerful magic conjurer. Niece to the sorceress Theodora, who killed Assara—her own sister—in her quest to rule that world. Charlee's mom survived because her father, Michala, sent her through a portal to Earth, then sacrificed himself to keep her hidden from Theodora. Her mom planned to journey back through a portal, which she wanted Charlee to open, to stop Theodora and free Janasara from the sorceress' evil reign.

Charlee had other plans. She was the one who blew it, who let Theodora live. She, not her mom, had to stop the sorceress.

"Sweetheart, what are you thinking about?" Her dad once again lifted his glasses father up his long nose.

"Oh, nothing." She swallowed another mouthful of soda. "I guess I'm just really tired. Mom, can that healing session wait? I just want to go to bed. You know, school tomorrow. I should really get some sleep."

Her mom kissed her on the head. "Sure, I'll check on you first thing in the morning."

Hugging them both, she staggered up the stairs to her room. Without undressing, she plopped onto her bed. Sleep overtook her until her cell phone, sitting atop her dresser, buzzed. She reached for it. A text message from Sandra. "Check out this posting on Facebook, hero."

Charlee blinked away drowsiness. "I'm not going to like this."

She clicked on the attachment Sandra sent. A grainy video of the house fire streamed across her phone's screen. In the image, a girl on a winged bike jumps into the second story. A little while later, the girl magically appears above the house with a man and an animal in her arms, and the bike flies up to catch them before they all fall into the blaze.

"Well, we didn't have to wait for the morning news." She dropped the phone onto the bed and slid under the covers. Sleep came quickly.

§ § §

Myron Applebee Middle School didn't feel the same anymore.

Once a frightened newcomer to the school, Charlee now walked the campus with her head held high. Maybe because of her newfound powers. Maybe because she now had friends.

Something else bothered her, though. Did she even belong here?

Who was she? A guardian, like her grandfather, Michala? A clumsy, goofy, middle-school kid? Or a princess?

The questions hung over her like a storm cloud. She wrestled with competing desires—did she want to be a normal fourteen-year-old girl, or did she want to realize her role as the last guardian of a distant world?

"Charlee." Sandra, her best friend, appeared from the crowd of students. "You're all the rage on the Internet. I mean, the masked-girl is...not you. I guess Channel 12 News ran some of the video, too."

"Don't remind me." Charlee raked her fingers through her long hair and adjusted her green glasses. "My parents weren't happy this morning about all the coverage. They were cool last night. Said I did a good thing. This morning, well, the bike and I won't be flying anytime soon."

"You had to do it." Sandra smiled wide. Lifting a purple band from her denim jacket, she wrapped her brown hair into a ponytail.

"How are you doing, Sandra?" Charlee decided to risk the question.

"What do you mean?" Her friend grasped the quarter-sized golden cross, her grandmother's, hanging from a thin chain around her neck.

Charlee shrugged. "I just mean...you know...Theodora kidnapped you before I could stop her."

"It's fine." Sandra's gaze shifted to her feet. "I told you before, I'm over it."

"I know. I just want you—"

"Drop it, okay." Sandra's smile faded for a moment. She took a deep breath, kissed the cross, and her grin returned. "I know you're concerned about me. My parents, too. I'm fine, really."

Charlee nodded. "I'm glad you're okay."

She knew Sandra wasn't really. She would never, ever forgive herself for letting her friend be hurt by Theodora. *The witch took her and placed her under a spell just to mess with me. How could I have let that happen?*

The two of them walked through the school hallway side by side until they reached Sandra's locker. Charlee tried not to gaze at the scar under Sandra's right eye where she was struck by Theodora. She wanted to say how sorry she was for allowing that to happen. Sorry for making the mistake of opening a portal that allowed the sorceress into this world. Hopefully, one day they'd be able to share their feelings about the kidnapping and their fight with Theodora, which took place not that long ago. For now, it was still too fresh... too painful.

15

Charlee knew what it felt like not to share feelings. She kept most of her thoughts bottled up until they became a weight on her chest. It hurt so bad sometimes she wanted to scream.

Sandra reached into her locker and retrieved a pre-calculus book. They were among a handful of students in the advanced math class. "One of these days you're going to have to let me join you on your nightly missions to help the people of this city." Sandra shut her locker. "You don't realize it yet, but you need me."

Charlee tugged at her sweater, which felt snug against her slightly rounded stomach. "I don't doubt it, but can we talk about it after school? This is not the place to talk hero stuff. The walls have ears."

"I'm serious, Charlee." Sandra touched her golden cross pendant again.

"I know, but—"

The morning bell rang. Students shuffled off to their classes.

Charlee, lifting the straps of her backpack higher on her shoulders, retreated a few steps. "See you at lunch."

"All right, but we're not done with this conversation. See ya." Sandra turned and walked away.

Charlee sighed. Whenever she was with Sandra, the little hairs on the back of her neck rose. Why? The witch couldn't hurt Sandra again, could she? Whatever danger might come, Charlee would always protect her friend.

She often thought about letting Sandra fly with her on the bike one night, but it couldn't happen. It would be great to have Sandra by her side, but that would place her in harm's way. If Sandra's dad found out, there'd be hell to pay. If he had it his way, he'd probably prefer they not be friends anymore.

Walking into her morning history class, Charlee plopped down into her seat three rows from the front. Reaching into her backpack for a notebook and pencil, she readied for the day's lesson. She yawned and stretched her arms.

Mr. Velez strolled into the room, placed a briefcase on his desk, and immediately launched into his lecture.

Charlee's eyes flickered. Her head drooped. *Don't fall asleep.* She breathed deeply. Sat up straight. Forced her eyelids open. She wrote every word Mr. Velez said, but when she peered at the writing, the words blurred. The pencil slipped from her fingers.

"Miss Smelton, am I boring you?" Mr. Velez stood over her.

Charlee nearly jumped out of her seat. "N…no sir." Her heart raced. A cold sweat covered her brow. Her stomach felt like she'd just been kicked in the gut. "Sorry, Mr. Velez."

Giggles spread across the classroom. Mr. Velez cleared his throat and the class hushed. "Miss Smelton, I'll do my best to hold your interest, but if you feel the need to sleep, be my guest and use the hallway outside."

Charlee lowered her head and slouched in her seat. Her cheeks burned. "No, sir. I'm fine."

Mr. Velez raised an eyebrow and then continued with his lecture.

A drop of sweat dripped from Charlee's hair onto her desk. She wiped her forehead with her sleeve. A few faint giggles lingered from behind. She wanted to tell them to shut up, but she'd just get in more trouble. Besides, she's a guardian. What did it matter if students laughed at her? If Charlee chose, she could wake up by drawing the energy from every student in the class. Take too much, and they might be the ones falling asleep.

"Yeah, why not do that?" she whispered. "Let's see them squirm as Mr. Velez yells at them." Charlee bit her lip. *Whoa, where had that thought come from?* A guardian didn't use their power to hurt others. Just to help. "Get a grip, Charlee."

Thirty minutes later the bell signaled the end of class. "Miss Smelton, may I see you for a moment?" Mr. Velez leaned against his desk.

Charlee waited as the other students piled from the classroom. A couple of the girls, friends of Tina Lomeli, self-designated leader of the popular crowd, pointed at her and laughed.

When everyone was gone, she dragged her feet along the scuffed linoleum floor, stopping in front of his desk. "Mr. Velez, I need to get to my next class."

"You'll make it." He folded his arms. "Miss Smelton, I have to ask…what's gotten into you this last month? You're one of my star pupils, but lately you've been falling asleep in class. You've turned in assignments late. Your last test was not your usual quality work. Is everything all right?"

Rocking back and forth on her feet, she rubbed her forehead before answering. "I'm okay. I guess I just have a lot on my mind. I'll do better."

Mr. Velez slid around his desk and sat in his chair. "You have a great ability, young lady. However, now's not the time to let your studies suffer. I will be watching and if things don't improve, I may contact your parents."

"No…please!" Charlee placed her hands on his desk. If he called her parents, they'd know she's slipping up in school. They had already conditioned use of her powers on keeping up her grades. Who knows what they would do if they found out the truth. Then again, what did it matter? She'd be on her way to Janasara soon.

"Just stay focused." Mr. Velez stood. "We'll see you tomorrow."

Charlee nodded and then left the classroom. She avoided run-ins with her other teachers through the rest of the morning, even though her grades in most classes had dropped. At least she stayed awake.

Finally, the lunch bell rang

Charlee made her way through the hallways of Myron Applebee to meet Sandra in the cafeteria. She scanned her fellow students as they walked by. She wondered how many had seen the video of the masked girl on the bike.

No one would suspect Charlee was the hero. Most students ignored her. Just another uncool kid. Invisible. Though she walked with her head high, most students didn't bother to make eye contact.

A few of Tina Lomeli's cronies spotted her in the hallway. They never knew when to quit. Tina made life so miserable for her when she first moved to Myron Applebee. She first pretended to be Charlee's friends but soon started flinging fat jokes. It took Sandra to make her stop. Even now, Tina and her friends tried to bully her, but it no longer mattered. They couldn't hurt her, but that didn't stop them from hurling insults as she passed by.

"Smelton's such a loser." Patty, Tina's closest friend, a girl with a perfect tan complexion and long auburn hair, held her finger and thumb in the shape of an "L."

"Maybe you should skip a lunch or two, fatty," declared Tim, a jock who spent most of his time in remedial classes.

Charlee brushed off the comments, but her hands formed into fists. She should slug them. Shut them up for good. *No, those jerks don't matter anymore*, she reminded herself. Besides, she couldn't draw attention to herself. Better to remain quiet.

She finally reached the cafeteria. Sandra sat at their usual table. However, she wasn't alone. Dean Polinar and Amy Shinn sat beside her. New friends in their little group. Dean was a thin, short Hawaiian kid who could run like the wind. He already ran marathons with his super-athletic dad. Amy's family recently moved from Korea. Charlee smiled. Though she had been in this country just a short time, Amy was already mastering the English language. Her hard work had made her one of the best students in all her classes.

Amy nodded to Charlee while rhythmically drumming on the table with her fingers. She was an excellent drummer—so good she had earned the lead spot among the percussion instruments on the school marching band.

In a world of school cliques, Charlee wondered if her friends were drawn together by the fact that they were all immigrants to Myron Applebee in one way or another. Amy was the only one from another country, but Dean's family came a long way from the Hawaiian Islands. Even Sandra spent five years in Mexico while her dad took part in a law enforcement exchange program. Then there was Charlee. She had only come from a rural county outside San Francisco, but she still felt different. Perhaps because part of her family came from an entirely different dimension.

Charlee stopped in the lunch line. She grabbed a cold hamburger, soggy French fries and a warm apple juice before joining her friends. Though glad to see Dean and Amy, there was no way she could have any real conversation with Sandra in front of them.

"What's up, guys?" Charlee slipped onto the bench next to Amy. She gave Sandra an awkward smile.

"Charlee, I heard Mr. Velez caught you sleeping. He hates that." Amy continued to drum on the table. "How bad did he yell at you?"

Charlee laughed softly. "Not too bad."

Sandra huffed. "Velez is a bore. I sleep in his class all the time."

"Says the straight 'A' girl who can't stop asking questions in history." Dean poked Sandra.

"Don't you have to go run somewhere far away?" Sandra frowned at Dean.

Amy laughed so hard milk almost came out of her nose. Despite herself, Charlee laughed, too.

Dean was a little hurt. "You know what—"

He never had the chance to finish. Another voice—an all-too-familiar one—cut him off.

"This is great, Smelton. You're building quite the loser gang, aren't you?"

Charlee sighed. It was Tina. Her long blond hair flowed perfectly over her shoulders, covering a bit of her designer blouse. A wide, wicked grin crossed her face, revealing brilliantly white teeth. Her eyes were ice. Four girls dressed similar to Tina stood to her right. That was a bit of a victory for Charlee. Tina no longer came over to the nerd table by herself. She brought friends—a lot of friends.

"Tina—" Sandra began.

"Oh, here we go, Smelton." Tina bent down to Charlee. "It looks like your little friend is going to have to defend you, like always. You know what, Smelton? It's time I prove to everyone what a loser you are. I think you're afraid to fight me. What's it going to take? What if I take this milk and pour it over your drummer girl's head?"

Tina snatched the milk carton in Amy's hand and held it over her. Charlee bounded out of her seat and knocked the milk out of Tina's hand. It went flying and spilled onto the floor.

"Enough, Tina." Charlee moved close to Tina, their faces just inches apart. "You're not going to do anything to bother my friends."

"Yeah?" Tina spit back. "Do something about it."

Charlee's body tensed. She wanted to fight Tina—she had wanted it ever since Tina first began her campaign of intimidation. Now, though, a fight would be a mistake. She took a deep breath. Slowly releasing the air, her anger eased. Muscles relaxed.

Her next move hushed the cafeteria.

Charlee delivered a punch—a fake punch—to her own stomach. Then she feigned a punch to her face and one more to her stomach. With each punch, she pretended to fall back. The students in the cafeteria—all of them waiting for the fight they hoped to see—laughed. At first the laughter was soft and uneasy, but it grew stronger.

19

"Ahh! Uhh! Ouch! You got me, Tina," Charlee moaned, pretending to be hurt. "You win this round."

Tina gazed around the cafeteria. There would be no fight today—not with everyone laughing.

"Jeez, Smelton! You are a doofus." With a flick of her hair, she and her friends disappeared through the cafeteria doors.

"Cool," said Sandra.

The single word was the best response Charlee could have hoped for. She stood tall.

Then Amy spoke up. "Uh, Charlee, you owe me a milk."

CHAPTER 4

The Healing Powers

ON CHARLEE'S WAY home from school, a white dove brushed against her hair as it flew by and came to rest on a tree branch towering above. From that perch, the winged creature scanned the neighborhood of two-story Victorian homes packed tightly together before fluttering down to Charlee's shoulder.

She couldn't help but chuckle at her protector.

"You don't have to follow me everywhere, you know. It's perfectly safe here." She waved off the changeling. The tiny bird hovered overhead, then soared to the top of a light pole. As a dove, the changeling kept watch over her. At night, in a tree outside her window. During the day, on classroom windowsills.

"I don't know what's worse…having my mom in my head all the time or this overprotective creature tailing me everywhere I go." She gazed at the tiny bird. "I can take care of myself. I do have some magic of my own."

Was this how her life would be from now on? Never a moment of privacy. Always watched. Charlee sighed. If this is what it meant to be a guardian, maybe life would be better if she'd never learned the truth. Thanks to Theodora, she never had a choice. The sorceress invaded her mind, forcing this new life on her.

Rounding a corner, she reached her house. Still in dove form, the changeling circled high above before disappearing from view. She'd probably find the magical being in the shape of the old Schwinn Stingray two-wheeler in the backyard. That's how the changeling first appeared to her. In that form, they fought Theodora side by side.

Maybe it was good to have a protector.

"Thanks for being there, bike," Charlee muttered as she opened the front door and walked inside.

Her mom sat in the living room, rocking her little sister, Megan. Late afternoon sunlight spilled in through the front window, circling them in a beam that set her mom's long sandy hair aglow. Specks of gold shimmered through each flowing lock.

Megan's crystal blue eyes sparkled. Her porcelain cheeks reflected the light. A mop of blond curls blazed brightly in the sun's rays.

"Charlee, I'm glad you're home." Her mom motioned for Charlee to sit. "It's time for our session."

"Mom, can't it wait? Enough already, I'm fine."

21

"In here…now." Her mom placed Megan on the floor among a gathering of books. Though only two, Megan could sit on her own and scan through picture books. Sometimes she seemed to read them, but that was impossible.

"Mom—"

"Now." Her mom stood and arched an eyebrow.

Charlee threw up her arms. "I really don't need this."

"Yes, you do. Though your body has healed from your encounter with Theodora, a few wounds remain I think my magic can help. Not to mention the harm you did to yourself last night in the fire. Now sit down on the couch."

Charlee rolled her eyes but did as she was told. It was true she still had lingering injuries from her battle with the sorceress. A scar on her shoulder. A tiny burn mark on her back. A scratch in her side that ached from time to time, though that could be a phantom sensation. Her mom's healing magic helped, but maybe some magical wounds would never fully heal. She could accept a scar or two.

On the couch, her mom began to chant in the Lengoron language—the language of Latara, one of the Ten Unified Kingdoms of Janasara.

Listening to her mom's soft chanting, a protective, comforting warmth embraced Charlee. Her mom might be annoying, but how many teens can say their mom is an *alien* from a world across a dimensional divide and a powerful magic conjurer?

Before the battle against Theodora, her mom never revealed her true identity. Maybe if she had Theodora never would have made it across a portal to Earth in the first place. Charlee shook her head. The past was the past. Her parents made a choice. Maybe the wrong one, but they had their reasons. To shelter her and Megan. Then, there was that little prophecy of the Last Guardian having to discover the truth of their identity and powers without help. *Whatever.*

Her mom's voice broke through the healing cocoon—cutting off Charlee's thoughts. "I think we're getting close to the end of the treatment, Charlee. Your internal organs are functioning properly, and, with one more session, I can knock out those scars."

"Like I said, Mom, I'm fine."

Charlee rubbed her scarred shoulder. Indeed, new skin—soft and smooth— replaced the rough red flesh. Maybe she wouldn't have to live with scars after all.

She embraced her mom. "Thank you."

Her mom kissed her on the cheek. "Don't thank me. It's my fault you were hurt. I should have done more to keep you safe. I should have told you the truth instead of letting some ancient scroll guide my actions. The Last Guardian would awaken in a time of need but only if allowed to discover the power alone. Just stupid. I was foolish, and for that I'm sorry. Now, since you're healed, the time is near— "

"For what?" Charlee broke from the hug. She knew the answer but didn't like it.

Her mom bent down and picked up Megan. "I've been waiting until I felt you were completely healthy. Now that you are, the time nears for you to open a gateway so that I can return to Janasara and free it from Theodora."

Charlee shook her head. "Mom, we need to talk about this."

Footsteps creaked over the stairway.

"Yes, we do need to talk." Her dad, the history professor, reached the bottom of the stairs. His tie hung loosely from the collared shirt hidden under a tan sweater vest. He'd probably been grading papers upstairs, judging by his red eyes.

He took a seat on the sofa adjacent to the couch. Charlee covered the grin she couldn't suppress. Her dad was a good man. Unlike mom, he belonged in this dimension…on Earth. They'd met and fallen in love. Long before they married, she revealed her true identity to him.

Her dad removed a pipe from his slacks' pocket. He turned it over slowly in his hand as if studying it from one angle, then another. "You know our plans, Charlee. As a guardian, you are the only one who can open a portal. While I'm not in favor of anyone crossing over, your mother's mind is set."

Charlee's grin faded. She stood and paced the room. "It should be me, not you. I'm the guardian, right? Maybe the last one. Let me go."

Her mom grabbed her hand. "We need you to remain here to take care of Megan. Cryton can't do it alone. Yes, he raised me here, but at his age it's too much to ask him to care for her alone. He needs your help. Your sister needs you."

Charlee pulled away. "She needs you, too…both of you."

Her dad cleared his throat. "We all need each other, and we should all stay together, but that world is no place for Megan. Quite honestly, it's no place for you either, Charlee. You've only begun to understand your magic. You might have tricked Theodora here, but over there she's stronger. If anyone is going, it will be your mother and I. Hopefully, when it's all over, we'll be reunited as a family."

"But we have the medallion." Charlee pointed toward the basement where the dark creation lay inside a safe.

"Yes, and I will use it against Theodora." Her mom rocked Megan in her lap.

"No, the medallion should be mine." Charlee's body tensed. *No one should touch the medallion but her. It belonged to her. Wait, where had that thought come from?* She cringed, remembering her vision. Her face, scarred and twisted, etched into the dark object.

"What did you just say?" her dad asked.

Falling into the couch, she hesitated before answering. "I'm just saying I should use the medallion against Theodora."

"No, Charlee." Her mom's brow furrowed.

Tapping the carpeted floor with her foot, Charlee scratched her head. She had to come up with something. Anything to change their minds. "I have another idea. Maybe Cryton can take care of Megan with the help of the bike. That way, the three of us can stop Theodora together."

That made sense. After all, Cryton and the changeling both crossed through the portal with Charlee's mom when she was an infant. He raised her like a father, while the shape shifter watched over her.

Her mom stood. "This issue is settled, Charlee. I know you want revenge. I know you feel responsible. You have fought bravely and are becoming stronger every day, but this is my fight now as it always should have been. Soon, you will open that portal for me. Unfortunately, I cannot talk your father into staying behind, so he will accompany me."

Her dad jumped up from the sofa and then placed his arm around his wife. "Your mother and I began this adventure together, and we will finish it together. We know we're leaving Megan in good hands. Now let's say we forget about this for the moment and start thinking about dinner."

"I have some homework to do." Charlee stepped toward the stairs. "I'll be up in my room."

"All right, baby. Later, if you wish, we can talk more," her mom offered.

Charlee watched her parents stroll into the kitchen. When they disappeared, she slunk to the basement. Switching on the light, which cast an eerie yellow glow throughout the subsurface room, she tiptoed to the safe kept in a corner.

She shivered as an icy chill blanketed her, stealing her breath. Was the basement really freezing, or was she scared?

"What am I doing? I need to stay away from this, but I can't. I need to see it. I need to know."

She knelt by the safe, an iron black box the size of a suitcase. Her dad hid the combination, but Charlee found the numbers on a folded napkin inside his wallet. She had to touch the medallion. Hold it close to her chest. Her parents had no right to keep her away.

Turning the dial one tick at a time, the lock finally popped. She shouldn't do this. It wasn't too late. She could lock it again and run back upstairs.

Over the past month, she had learned from Cryton that to wield this medallion was to fall into insanity and evil. Sure, it had the power to grant its user immortality—but there was a price. The user gave up their soul.

Sometimes at night, Charlee dreamt of the black, light-swallowing medallion. Her face—warped, twisted, evil— was etched on one side of the object. Was she destined to become like Theodora?

Holding her breath, she slowly opened the door of the safe.

"Charlee, what are you doing?"

Her dad's voice stung like a slap against the cheek. Her stomach churned, and her heart pounded wildly. All the blood seemed to drain away from her body. She froze.

Charlee glanced at the ground, anything to avoid her dad's glare. "I…uh… thought…you were in the kitchen."

"Charlee, I asked what are you doing in that safe?"

"Nothing."

"Charlee."

"I…I just wanted to know the medallion was safe."

Standing over her shoulder, her dad bent down and then closed the door with a thud. Charlee gasped as the safe's locking mechanism engaged with a click as loud to her as crashing thunder on a stormy night.

Her dad placed an arm around her. "Sweetheart, I know what you're feeling. I know you want to face Theodora, but you've done your part. It's now up to me and your mother."

"But you're not even from there, Dad. Why…why do you want to go?"

"Because of the pain Theodora has caused this family. Because of all she has taken from your mother. Because she almost took you from us." He motioned for her to follow him. "Look, Charlee, I know I have no magic, as you and your mother do, but I am a warrior inside. I'll use my strength to protect your mother."

"And what should I do?"

"You need to use your powers to keep your sister safe."

"Dad…" Charlee lowered her head. She wanted to tell him so much more but couldn't. The visions. Her compulsion to hold the medallion. A sense of failure so great it pressed against her chest like a chunk of concrete she could never lift away. How could she tell him that sometimes when silence filled the house she heard Theodora calling to her?

She couldn't tell her dad…or her mom, for that matter…anything. They might think she was losing her mind from the stress of her battle with Theodora. Maybe she was.

"Charlee, it's cold down here." Her dad led her up the stairs. "Let's forget what lies ahead and just enjoy this time together."

She glanced into her dad's hazel eyes. "Okay, but first I really do have some homework to finish."

"Well, you have an hour before dinner." Her dad opened the basement door and nudged her into the living room.

"Thanks for the talk, Dad. It helped." Charlee lied. Better to make him think he had changed her mind, but he hadn't. She would cross through the portal on her own. Her mom said it herself. She was healed. The time had come. First, though, a little sword practice with Cryton.

25

Charlee bolted upstairs. When she reached her bedroom, she opened her window and signaled for the bike.

The white dove on a nearby tree branch immediately changed into the bike, its wings outstretched to stay aloft. Charlee climbed from her window onto the changeling. She felt the being's energy flow through her.

It felt good.

"Bike, to Cryton's," Charlee directed.

The changeling responded with a mighty flap of its wings.

CHAPTER 5

The Lesson

CHARLEE TIGHTENED HER grip on the long steel blade. Both hands grasped the sword, lifting it high as if a baseball player about to swing. Her arms shook from the strain; sweat rolled down her cheeks. She could have absorbed extra strength from her bike parked nearby, but that was not the point of the exercise.

Cryton rubbed one side of his long white mustache between his thumb and forefinger. The few patches of gray hair on the sides of his bald head fluttered under the air flowing from a ceiling fan just above him. He expertly twirled a blade in his other hand. "To wield a sword, you cannot depend on magic. You have to build your natural strength, and that means learning to control the steel without magic."

He circled her inside his pizza shop, closed early for Charlee's training session. Grease-stained drapes over the windows hid them from view. The day's last sunlight streamed in underneath the curtains. The strong aroma of garlic, cheese, and marinara sauce baking filled her nostrils.

Charlee's stomach grumbled. One small slice couldn't hurt. "Cryton, can we take a break? You promised me a cheese pizza. My arms are really sore, and I have to get home soon. My mom—"

"Knows you're here." Cryton studied his own sword, his gray eyes partially hidden under bushy eyebrows. "She called to alert me you were on your way."

"I should have known."

"She said it was all right for you to stay here a while." He lowered his weapon. "That you needed to blow off a little steam, so I figured we'd work a little harder this evening. Thought maybe afterwards, we'd talk a bit. Your mom is worried about you. I am, too."

Charlee wiped sweat from her forehead. "You don't have to worry about me. Let's just finish this training stuff so I can eat."

Cryton pointed his blade at her. "Okay, Guardian. Attack me, but focus on your balance. Don't give up too much of yourself. You must understand that attack and defense are no different from each other. One cannot exist without the other, or you will surely die."

Taking a deep breath, Charlee swung her steel. She trusted in the teachings of this aging warrior from Janasara who had become her mentor—and more.

27

Feeling the weight of the blade in her hands, she lunged forward to cut the old man in half.

As part of Cryton's disguise on Earth, he went by the name Mr. Levenstein, a pizza shop owner who walked with a limp. As a sword-wielding knight, he easily parried Charlee's attack with a sidestep. Agile for his age, he grasped his sword in dough-crusted hands and blocked her strike, their weapons colliding with a clink that could have been heard outside.

Charlee spun, slashing her blade at Cryton's left side. Again, her teacher gracefully dodged the move. The white apron tied around his waist flowed with him. He countered, driving the razor sharp tip toward her torso. The move came more swiftly than she had anticipated, but she leapt back and blocked with a downward slice.

One maneuver after another, Cryton forced her into an awkward defense. *Can't keep up. Too fast.* Her hands throbbed. What little muscle she had in her rubbery arms melted away. With labored breaths, she tried to keep up with him.

Must...control...breathing. Willing her lungs to suck in air, she tried one last defensive stance, but Cryton swept his sword down. She brought her blade up to block, but her strength failed.

When their steel clashed, her legs caved. She dropped to the floor, her weapon falling to the side. Cryton stood over her, holding the tip inches from her neck.

The lesson lasted only minutes. Charlee's heart sank.

Cryton lowered the sword and dabbed his forehead with his stained apron. "Good," he said. "You lasted four or five moves this time. You're getting better."

Charlee rose to her feet and wiped the sweat from her face. While moments ago she enjoyed the garlicy smell inside Cryton's restaurant, right now it made her nauseous. A slice of pizza no longer sounded good.

"What do you mean, I'm getting better? I suck. I'm supposed to be a guardian...a warrior...and I can't handle a sword. It's been a month, and I'm not getting any better."

Cryton lifted her sword and held it close to his face. He'd given it to her as a gift. With his apron, he wiped the silver T-shaped handle and cleaned the slightly tarnished steel before handing it back.

"On the contrary. You're getting much better. Swordplay takes years to learn and decades to master. You expect too much of yourself."

"I have to do better." She dragged her sword across the tile floor until she slumped into a booth.

"Why?" Cryton sat beside her. "Why do you have to do better?"

"Because I'm the last of the guardians."

"Oh, I see." He rubbed his bald head.

In many ways, he was still a stranger to her. He'd only come into her life when she tried to ditch the bike—an ugly gift from her dad—in his alley before the craziness with Theodora began. Before she knew the bike was special.

"You know, Charlee, when your grandfather Michala entrusted his daughter to me and ordered me through the portal with her to this world, I didn't know what to think. My duty was to fight at his side, not become a nursemaid to an infant girl. He and Assara knew they would not survive Theodora's conquest, and they wanted their daughter to be safe by sending her to Earth. Leaving my friend to face death was the hardest thing I'd ever done, and I knew it meant the rest of my life would be spent caring for their daughter."

Charlee tapped the table with her fingers. "I've heard this before, Cryton."

"Now wait a moment. I want you to understand something." He grasped her hand. "I did my best to raise your mother, with the changeling's help, of course. I taught her the ways of our people and made sure she knew the sacrifice her parents had made. She vowed to someday return to Janasara, but she did not inherit her father's guardian powers as you have. Still, I knew she carried a longing to return to the kingdom she'd really never known. I proudly watched her grow into a young woman, become a wife and then a mother, but her desire never faded."

She placed her free hand on top of his. "I know how she feels, but—"

"When you were born," Cryton continued. "I chose to watch your family from afar. Figured I could protect you better from the shadows, but I was always near. Even though you've only known me a short time, I've known you your whole life. Watched you grow up. In many ways, I see you as my own granddaughter. I knew one day you might face a dangerous destiny. Never could I have imagined what a strong girl you would become and what courage you would show in facing that destiny."

Charlee wanted to say he had become a grandfather to her but didn't. Her cheeks felt hot and her stomach tied up in knots. Where was this conversation headed? "What's your point?" She slid her hands away and then leaned back in the booth.

Cryton frowned. Maybe she'd hurt the warrior by not letting him know how she felt about him. Either way, he quickly recovered. "Listen, there is no doubt that you have begun your journey bravely. Your battle with Theodora shall be recorded in the annals of our people. And yes, it is likely that you have more battles to come. I have no doubt that you will face them bravely, as well."

"Yeah…but…"

"Now, let an old man finish. You asked for my point. Here it is. The fact is, you are still just a kid, and you deserve to be a kid a bit longer. You seem to think you have to rush to face your destiny. You seem to think you have to be a hero. That's why you're out flying around on that changeling when you should be focusing on your education."

29

Charlee felt a twinge of anger. "But you don't understand, Cryton. I feel her every day."

"Who?"

Charlee stepped away from the booth and paced the floor. Should she tell him? Might as well. She'd already said too much. "Theodora. I can't sleep most nights because I can feel her rage. It's as though when she entered my dreams and tricked me into opening the gateway here, a part of her remained in my head."

Cryton stood and placed a hand on her shoulder. "In all the talks we've had, you've never mentioned this."

"She wants her medallion, and she wants to destroy me." Charlee raked her fingers through her damp hair. "I can feel her lashing out at her world in some kind of twisted revenge. I don't know what it is, but I have this feeling of pain and death. It's worse when I sleep."

Cryton was quiet for a heartbeat. "I take it you haven't shared this with your parents."

"No." She paced some more.

"Why?"

"I don't know. Because they'd think me crazy. They wouldn't let me ever leave the house."

"And you have decided you have to face Theodora now?"

Charlee hesitated. "Yes."

Cryton thought for a while. "One thing I want you to remember is that you come from a strong family. Your family is your source of strength. No matter what choices you make, always remember that."

"Cryton, I can't let them risk their lives."

He removed the apron and lifted his sword. "Then grab that weapon. We both have more training to do."

"What?"

"I've been thinking that it's time I returned home, anyway."

"Cryton, no."

"Oh, yes!" He unleashed a bellowing laugh and thrust his sword at her. In reply, Charlee raised her own and blocked the blow. As night fell, the clang of their swords filled the tiny restaurant.

CHAPTER 6

The Voice of the Empress

GUARDIAN, CAN YOU *feel my presence? I know that you can. Yet you proceed with this charade of ignoring me. Why?*

Theodora's icy voice, barely a whisper, cut through Charlee's subconscious mind. Most nights she avoided sleep as long as possible to maintain a mental block against her great aunt. Tonight, she caved to the darkness—allowing the *Empress* dangerously close to invading her thoughts. Theodora called to her through the shadowy layer of dreams like a murky fog rolling in off the Bay.

The sorceress' bony fingers probed inside her head like tiny spiders crawling through her brain. Though it may have been a phantom sensation, nails as sharp as daggers carved away at her thoughts like a searing laser until Charlee had no more defenses.

Charlee's eyes shot open. Her head pounded as if an unseen force squeezed her temples. She screamed, rolling out of the bed onto the carpeted floor. "Leave me along, witch!"

The shutters over her window flew open. The glass shattered, crashing to the floor. Ferocious winds whipped her hair and mashed school papers against the walls. "None of this is real. Just a dream. I'm still asleep. Stop it, Theodora."

A swirling vortex of thunderclouds and lightning formed around her, swallowing the floor, sucking everything in. She jumped onto the bed, grasping the headboard. "Mom, help me!" How could she? This wasn't really happening. "Wake up, Charlee!" she urged herself.

"*Come to me, Guardian.*" Theodora's voice rose above the howling squall.

"Leave me alone!" Charlee's bed plunged into the vortex.

She fell into darkness as if falling into a black hole. Farther and farther, she plummeted into the void, thrashing her arms and legs wildly. Theodora's cackling laughter surrounded her. When would this chasm end? When would she awaken from this nightmare?

"Bike, I need—"

Charlee crashed onto a rocky surface hidden by a murky fog. The wind knocked out of her, she rolled onto her back, grasping her chest, forcing her lungs to breathe in the dank air. *I have to be calm. This isn't real. Can't be real.* Shallow breaths gave way to deeper ones. Her heart, at first thudding loudly, quieted.

She slowly stood, her vision limited to a few feet in every direction by a thick gray mist. Above, a ceiling of shadows hid any route back to her bedroom, not that there would be any way to climb out of this pit.

Theodora's laughter, a constant annoyance, subsided, but the sorceress' icy breath brushed against her neck. A chill spread between Charlee's shoulders. *This may not be real, but stay alert. She's going to mess with your head.*

Theodora's disembodied words returned. "Young Guardian, I see your thoughts. You think you have become strong enough to keep me from penetrating your subconscious, but I am always with you. Since our first encounter, a part of me remains within you."

"I know you're always there, Theodora." Fists clenched, Charlee inched her way forward, trying to pierce the blackness. She fought back tears with no intention of letting the witch see her cry. Yet having her thoughts invaded sapped her strength. The scared girl she thought long gone returned. Charlee shivered. "Please let me wake up," she whispered. "Bike, if you can hear me, slap me, shock me... anything to free my mind."

"*Are you frightened, child?*" Theodora's voice carried a touch of amusement.

"No." Charlee lied. "Theodora, what do you want? We have nothing to talk about."

"*Don't we?*"

As if someone flipped a switch, daylight swept away the darkness. Under a gray sky, she stood on a familiar cobblestone path facing the Castle of Latara. She'd seen it in earlier dreams. Stone steps led to the massive archway. Cathedral-like towers rose on either side. The entire structure was cast in glowing white marble despite the gloom overhead. Built into the side of a mountain, a waterfall flowed from the cliffs vanishing into the courtyard, strangely without a sound. No thunderous flow of a river. No crash of water against rocks. Nothing.

Lightning exploded in the distance. Charlee flinched, turning her attention to the skies. When she gazed back at the castle, a crimson liquid streamed down the steps and pooled around her feet.

"*Turn around and see what has befallen the people of Latara because of your foolishness.*"

Charlee did as she was told. Bodies lay bent and twisted along the pathway. Some were charred as if roasted alive, while others were torn in half. Closest to her, a woman sprawled on the walkway embraced a toddler, probably no older than Megan. Most of the skin had been torn from the woman's back, revealing muscle and bone. Charlee gritted her teeth. It had to be the Horeng, those awful wolf creatures. How terrified the woman must have been in her final moment. How about the baby? What kind of a monster could slice through a child?

Gasping, Charlee dropped to one knee. "If this is real, I'll make you pay."

She forced herself up and lumbered through the smattering of bodies. The dead stretched to the outer walls of the kingdom. The stench of death, putrid and thick, washed over her.

"What did you do, witch?" she shouted. Her blood, scalding hot, pulsed though her like a wave rushing to shore. Was this a vision, a glimpse into the devastation the sorceress caused upon her return to Janasara, or was this the distant past? Or something else entirely? Real or nightmare, Theodora had to die. Now! This couldn't go on. "Show yourself and let's end this."

"Child, as you have pointed out, this is but a dream." Theodora manifested along the path a stone's throw away. Young. Flowing blond hair. White dress. Golden crown. Just like the first time she came to Charlee in a dream.

"Killer!" Charlee charged her, throwing wild punches. Each blow passed through Theodora as if she were a ghost.

"We cannot do battle in this dream realm, Guardian." Theodora smiled wide. "If you wish to kill me, you must come to me through a portal. I humbly await your arrival in this world of your ancestors."

"Maybe I'll just leave you in Janasara, Theodora—stranded without your medallion." Huffing, Charlee stepped away from the sorceress. That was a lie. Charlee couldn't leave this world unprotected. No, she would cross a portal. The day was coming…soon.

Theodora circled her. "Oh, I don't think you'll hide from me on Earth. Not when I have taken so many lives to avenge myself for your act of treachery—for keeping me from my immortality. If you do not come, more will die."

Charlee cringed. If only she'd killed her before. "You're right. I'm coming for you. I'll beat you with your own medallion."

Theodora knelt to the body of a young girl who lay face down just off the walkway. The sorceress stroked the girl's hair. "Pitty. Unlike you, she was such a pretty young creature. Do you think in her dying breath she called out to a guardian when none was here to save her? How does that make you feel?"

Charlee wiped away a tear. The girl was probably the same age she and Sandra were. The memory of Sandra under Theodora's spell flashed through her mind. Eyes gray and dead. Like a zombie. Charlee failed her friend and now this girl, too. How many more people would suffer? "You're going to pay for this."

"Our reunion shall be most joyous." Theodora released the dead girl's hair and hovered an arm's length away from Charlee. "After all, we are family. Keeping me from my medallion all this time has been oh, so rude of you. But then I know you desire it as much as I. Its darkness fills your heart. You feel it, don't you?"

"All I know is you're going down." Charlee's thoughts returned to the vision of her face on the medallion.

Theodora crossed her arms. "Silly girl, your warped sense of good and evil will soon change. Come to me and perhaps we will share in the medallion's glorious power. Come to me and you will see mine is the just path. You will understand, then, why the death of these weak creatures means nothing. Join with me and the conquest of dimensions will be within our grasp. I will be a goddess and you… my immortal servant."

Charlee turned away from the sorceress. "Don't listen to her," she uttered to herself. "You're nothing like her." The image of the medallion lingered in her mind. Her warped face chiseled in the black stone glared back at her. That wasn't her. She wouldn't let it happen.

"You just wait, aunty. I kicked your butt before, and I'm going to finish the job." Charlee spun around but Theodora vanished. The bodies faded away and the Latara landscape gave way to the black void. Her subconscious mind reestablished its blockade. She slipped back into an uneasy sleep.

Somewhere in that shadowy realm between being awake and asleep, Charlee remained aware of her dream encounter with her great-aunt.

She awoke back in her bedroom. Her eyes slowly fluttered open, and she gazed in each direction. Night time lingered outside. A soft orange haze from the back porch light filtered through her curtains. Everything remained in its proper place from her bed to the unbroken windows.

Charlee released a lungful of air and sat up in bed, covers pulled up to her chest. A new thought formed. "Theodora may know I'm coming, but she doesn't know everything. She thinks she killed the changeling back on Alcatraz, but she's wrong. Together, we can end her. If I have to, I'll use the medallion. If I start to change…to turn…I'll do what I have to."

She would even take her own life if necessary, though that declaration kept her awake the rest of the night.

CHAPTER 7

It Must Be Now

CHARLEE HUSTLED TO school, her head shrouded under a hood. The changeling—in dove form—clung to her shoulder. Last night's dream, if she could call it that, played over and over in her mind. The blood… bodies…Theodora's words. What was she supposed to feel? Sad? Angry? Scared? All three?

Storm clouds above cast the morning in murkiness. Thunder rumbled in a rage, and lightning shouted its hate. Or was it her thirst for vengeance that set the heavens ablaze?

"Bike, we have to go now—tonight." Charlee extended her forefinger to the changeling. The dove hopped onto it, and she lifted the bird close to her face. "My parents may think they're ready to go, but I can't let them do it. It's my responsibility." First, she had to say her goodbyes, especially to Sandra.

She reached Myron Applebee Middle School, and waved away her shapeshifting protector. It didn't take long to spot Sandra. Her friend leaned against a Sycamore tree just inside the front gate with a book close to her face. Other students filed past her engaged in their own conversations.

"Hey, you." Charlee removed her hood and forced a smile.

"Hi, Charlee .You want to hit the mall this weekend, I mean if you can take time away from your hero thing." Sandra nudged her. "Just kidding about that last part, but let's do it—let's do some girly stuff at the mall."

"I…I can't."

"What…why?" Sandra's pursed lips revealed her disapproval.

"There's something I have to do. In fact, that's the only reason I didn't skip school today. I wanted to talk to you." Charlee fidgeted with her backpack straps. Should she tell Sandra the truth? No, she didn't need to know. Or worry. "You may not see me in school for a…few days. But when I get back, we can go to the mall for sure."

Sandra dropped her book. "You're going after the witch, aren't you?"

Stepping back, Charlee's gaze shifted to the crowd of students milling close by. Sandra said that a little too loud. How could she know that? *Because she knows you too well, stupid.*

Charlee placed a finger to her lips. "Not so loud."

Her friend cringed. "Sorry…but I'm right. Don't lie to me, Charlee." This time, Sandra whispered.

Twisting her hair, Charlee strolled around the tree. No point in trying to lie. "Yes, it's true."

Sandra grabbed Charlee's arm. "Stay here. You don't need to go."

"Yeah, I do."

"Why? You did what you were supposed to do. You saved us all. Isn't that enough?" Sandra raised her voice again.

"Shhhh." Charlee tapped a foot and adjusted her glasses. She spoke in a soft voice. "I have to do this. It's…like…my responsibility. Theodora hurt you and many others. She is doing worse to those in *her own world*. And it's my fault." She flashed back to the dead woman and her child and all the other bodies from her dream. Charlee punched the tree, but without super strength her knuckles cracked. Her hand throbbed. Hopefully no one noticed. "It's my fault she hurt you," she muttered.

Silence fell between them until the morning bell signaled the start of classes.

"Listen, it's going to be all right," Charlee offered.

"I hope so." Sandra wiped away a tear and walked away.

Charlee thought about running to thank her for being such a good friend, a best friend. Sandra was the first to give her a chance at Myron Applebee. She made school fun. In the end, those thoughts went unspoken. Sandra knew it anyway.

When Sandra rounded a corner, Charlee snuck out of the school grounds. She needed to prepare.

§ § §

Charlee checked her phone. 10 a.m. By now, Dad would be at the university, probably in the middle of some boring lecture. Mom would be with Megan at the library. Rising from the bench in the park a block from her house, Charlee slid the hood over her head and crept toward her home.

The dove flew one tree to the next, following her.

Once inside her house, abandoned and dark for the moment, she slunk to the basement door. The medallion waited for her below. Did she really want to do this? Once she stole it from the safe, there'd be no going back. If she was going to face Theodora, she'd have to use that strange disc against her great aunt and then destroy it.

Easier said than done.

According to Cryton, the medallion could only be destroyed if thrown back into a magical fire from the tree from which it was forged, but the *bush* blazed in a labyrinth enchanted by the dark arts. No one knew how or when the hidden lair shifted. Of course, that was all lore.

If the time came, would she be willing to destroy the medallion? "I have to. I can't keep it for myself." But she wanted it. Charlee shook away that thought. Already, the mysterious object infected her. Separation from it made her ill as if a fever burned across her forehead. "No, I'm still in control."

Charlee opened the door and crossed the threshold into the basement. With heavy steps, she trudged down the steps and slithered to the safe. Like the day before, she turned the combination until the bolt unlatched.

Fear of the face she might see in the medallion caused her hands to recoil. Sweat formed across her brow. Her heart thumped so loud it echoed up to her ears. "There's still time to turn back. No, there's no choice at this point. I have to take it. I must possess it." Cautiously, she opened the door of the safe and found herself staring at nothing.

"What?" Charlee nearly screamed.

The medallion wasn't there. The safe was empty. She reached inside and felt all around as if her eyes might be playing a trick on her. Nothing. Blood rushed from her face. She slumped into a sitting position, glaring into the empty safe.

"How could this be? Who could have taken it? Could Theodora already have it?"

"Cryton has the medallion." Her dad's voice was laced with anger.

Charlee jumped to her feet. He was supposed to be at work. How could he know she'd be here...today? A stabbing pain exploded through her chest like her heart burst into a million pieces.

Her dad stood at the base of the steps, his hands hidden inside his tweed jacket. He frowned, and deep ridges lined his forehead. "Why are you—"

"Why'd he take it?" she blurted, clutching her chest. "It's mine."

"What was that?" He stepped toward her.

Charlee paused. "Uh, I mean...uh...I don't know. Dad, just tell me when he took it? Why?"

"Shortly after you left for school this morning, Cryton came to ask for the medallion." Her dad stopped inches away from her. "He told us what you were planning—not that we needed him to tell us. Your mother and I knew you had no intention of opening a portal for us. Teenagers think their parents will fall for anything. I guess you think the same even with a mother who's strong in magic."

"Dad, no." Charlee shook her head. She had to get that medallion back. Somehow. How could Cryton betray her like this? Could she trust him anymore? Could she trust anyone? Even the changeling? Or was that magical beast in on it, too?

"Charlee, we've been gentle with you up to this point," her dad continued. "Didn't want to scare you away from us. Your mother and I wanted you to flex your powers a bit. Learn from Cryton. We hoped you might see things our way.

But I see that's impossible now, so the medallion will remain with Cryton until such time as you open a portal for us."

"Then I'll get it back?" She spit out angrily.

"No, Charlee." Her mom stormed into the basement, Megan in her arms. Her hair was done up in a ponytail, making her high cheek bones even more pronounced. "We will take the medallion and destroy it."

Charlee lowered her head into her hands. "What are you guys even doing home right now? How'd you know I'd be here?"

"I can sense you, remember," her mom answered.

"And we got a call from the school," her dad added.

Charlee lifted her head and bit a fingernail. "Stupid school." She sighed deeply before speaking again. "This is dumb, Mom. I'm the guardian. I should use the medallion to stop Theodora. If I wanted to, I could open a portal to Janasara right now. You couldn't stop me."

"You want to bet?" Her dad crossed his arms. "We're still your parents."

Her mom glided father into the room. "Charlee, did you ever think that maybe Earth needs you more? Maybe you can use your powers to help this world when you are older and truly ready?"

Charlee shrugged. "Maybe."

Maybe she would return to Earth and become a real hero, but for now the people of Janasara needed their guardian. How could her parents not understand that? "Mom, you said it yourself. I'm supposed to be the future queen or something. Shouldn't the queen fight for her people? Isn't that my duty?"

"I've thought a great deal about that." Her mom handed Megan to her dad. "You don't have to be queen. You don't even have to be a guardian. You can choose to be Charlee and just explore who Charlee wants to be in this world. For now, I am still the rightful queen, and I will guide our people to a better future until one day when it is safe for a new queen to take my place."

Charlee shook her head. "I don't know. It's all so confusing. What am I supposed to do?"

Her mom placed a hand on her shoulder. "Open a gateway for us, so that we may stop Theodora. Stay here and help Cryton to protect your sister. Care for Megan in our absence. Do your best to be a normal teenager. I know that won't be easy anymore, but try. Go to school. Make a life for yourself. You have so much ahead of you. When you are more mature then use your power to help this world."

Under her breath, Charlee cursed. Normal teenager? School? Make a life? Was her mom joking? None of that was possible now. She had a destiny. To be a guardian. To stop Theodora. Her parents couldn't stop her. They should know her life could never be the same. Not now. Not ever.

"Fine, whatever, Mom." Charlee threw up her arms. "You want me to open a portal for you, I'll do it. I'll stay here and watch over Megan. When she's old enough I'll tell her why you left her. Maybe she'll understand."

"When things are safe, I'll call to you through your thoughts to open a portal so that we can return to you and Megan." Her mom's eyes reddened. "I promise."

"Sure." Charlee marched past her parents, clomping up the basement stairs to the living room. From there, she sulked into the kitchen where she grabbed a bottle of soda from the refrigerator and took a long drink. Had the angry teen bit worked? Would they believe she'd given in to their demands? It didn't matter. The time to talk had ended.

After swallowing the first gulp, her lips parted in a grin. "Well played, Cryton. I should have known you'd pull something like this. Did the bike help? Doesn't matter. I'll see you soon."

The old man hadn't taken the medallion to hold it for her parents. He wanted to stop her from facing Theodora without him. If Cryton had the medallion, she would have no choice but to cross over with him.

"All right, Cryton. It's you and me. You, me, and the bike."

CHAPTER 8

The Time Nears

A S HER FAMILY slept, Charlee tiptoed through the dark house, the sword at her side in a leather scabbard. She would need the weapon, even if she still wasn't very good with it. *Hope I'm better with it than I think I am.*

She crept to her sister's room and gently pushed open the door. A nightlight bathed Megan in a soft orange haze. The clock on the nightstand blazed 12:01 a.m. in a glowing digital display. Her sister breathed rhythmically in bed, her pink lips parted in a smile.

"Looks like a happy dream. Good," Charlee whispered.

Kneeling by Megan's bed, she blinked away a tear. Would she ever see her sister again? Megan would never understand why her big *sis* suddenly disappeared, but someday she'd learn the truth and maybe be proud of her older sister.

She leaned over and kissed Megan gently on her forehead. "I'm sorry, Megan," she uttered. "I know it sucks for me to leave like this, but I don't have a choice. I'll be back. At least, I'll try to come back to you. I love you, little sis." Charlee removed her cell phone from her jeans' pocket and placed it on the bed beside Megan. A photo displayed on the phone of the two of them together at the beach. "I won't need the phone where I'm going, so you keep it. Maybe it will remind you of me." She also removed her glasses and left them on the nightstand. *Probably won't need these either thanks to the changeling.*

"Take care of them till I come back." Wiping away more tears, she snuck from her sister's room and down the stairs to the kitchen. She could still turn back. Do what her parents wanted her to do. Stay behind. Let them face Theodora. No, it had to be her. She couldn't be scared. Couldn't worry about what Mom and Dad thought. She was a guardian. The time had come to finish her fight with Theodora.

Charlee retrieved a soda from the refrigerator. She let the bubbles tickle her nose before she gulped down half the bottle. Who knows when she might get another chance to savor a carbonated sweet delight?

"Probably don't have too many convenience stores on Janasara."

With a deep breath, she marched through the kitchen door into the backyard where the changeling—in bike form—waited for her.

"It's time."

Charlee glanced up to the second floor. "Sorry, guys." She climbed onto the banana-shaped seat, placed her purple sweatshirt hood over her head and silently urged the bike to take flight. Just as quietly, the changeling spread its wings and obeyed. "Mom…Dad, forgive me. Keep Megan safe. Sandra, too."

They flew into the night. The sky was a patchwork of clouds and twinkling stars. Below, neighborhood streets basked in the quiet of calm nocturnal hours. Cool air brushed against her cheeks and blew off the hood as they raced toward Cryton. What would the air feel like across the dimensional divide? What would she find there when they crossed over? Would the death in her dreams become a reality? Charlee shivered. The answers would come soon enough.

She brushed away strands of brown hair from her eyes. *Maybe we can make one more stop before we leave.*

"Bike, I know this is stupid, but can we do one fly-over at Sandra's?" She sensed the bike didn't approve. The changeling's response came slow, but her winged protector eventually changed course. "I promise I'm not going to wake her up. I just…I just want to say bye one more time."

The bike shot forward toward their new destination. In no time, they soared over Sandra's home, circling the house once, twice, then a third time. Charlee wrestled with the idea of flying over to Sandra's window and waking her to say a proper good-bye. "No, that's stupid. What would I say? Sandra would urge me to stay. I'd vow to return." It was better if no more words passed between them… for now.

"Thanks for being my friend," Charlee spoke in a hushed voice. She lowered her head close to the handlebars. *I hope Sandra knows she's my best friend.*

"All right, bike. That's enough." Her eyes lingered on Sandra's darkened window. "Let's go."

"You'd better come home."

The words carried through the night air, detectable with Charlee's superior hearing, a power bestowed through contact with the bike.

"I'll try." A smile breached her lips. Sandra saw her. In the solitude of the night, they had that one final moment…at least. A comforting warmth radiated to each of her limbs. "I will come back."

Gripping the handlebars, Charlee and the bike jetted toward Cryton's loft above the pizza shop.

The bike landed in the alley behind the shop. Charlee wasn't sure if Cryton would be expecting her, but the old man had little choice but to get ready to make his way with Charlee through the gateway. She wanted to go by herself, but now that wasn't possible thanks to the clever old man. By taking the medallion before she could cross over on her own, Cryton made it impossible for her to leave without him. The old dude has a bone to pick with the witch, too.

Jumping from the bike, she crept to the back door of his restaurant. A white mist floated around her from the early morning San Francisco chill. Shadows danced off the concrete walls. An unseen cat meowed somewhere close.

At the door, Charlee stopped and placed her ear to the thick wood. Silence greeted her. No sound of movement inside the restaurant, at least nothing she could detect even with super hearing. "Guess I'll just knock. Cryton's a light sleeper. He'll hear," Charlee said to the bike. She raised her knuckle to strike the door.

"Why don't you try the doorknob?"

Charlee flinched, retreating to the bike. The muffled voice on the other side of the door stole her breath. She clutched her chest to slow her fast-beating heart. "What the heck?"

"Come on in," Cryton beckoned. "It's open."

"I should have known he'd be waiting for me." Taking a deep breath, she put a hand on the knob and cracked it open just enough to peek inside. Cryton stood a few feet beyond with his arms crossed over his chest. He frowned at her.

He wore his familiar white slacks and white button-down shirt covered by a grease-strained apron. One side of his shirt was untucked. His long white mustache bristled.

She smiled—for an instant. "Cryton, you're—"

"Not alone, Charlee," he interrupted.

Her dad rose from a black vinyl booth and stood next to the old man on the pizza shop's checkered linoleum floor. Lips pursed, he removed his glasses with one hand and motioned her farther inside with the other.

"Dad!" Charlee threw open the door and stepped into the doorway. Her legs nearly buckled. Seeing Cryton awake was bad enough. Facing her dad…well, she was busted. *Oh no! What am I supposed to do now?* She lowered her head into her hands. How could she have let this happen?

"Fancy meeting you here, Charlee." With slow deliberate strides, her dad walked around Cryton.

"How did—?"

"I knew you would sneak out tonight and head here. Besides, you know your mom uses her magic to watch over you. We agreed I'd come alone to talk some sense into you since you and her seem to be bumping heads right now. I have to admit, I didn't think I could get here before you." Her dad, his voice stern, wrapped an arm around her shoulders and ushered her into the pizza shop to a booth, then motioned her to sit.

Charlee rolled her eyes. She had to think of something, couldn't let him change her plans. She scanned the restaurant. *Where would Cryton hide the medallion?* She had to find it…now. Take it. Get out of here with the bike.

"Dad, come on." Her hands balled into fists on the table.

"No, Charlee. This is our—"

Cryton cleared this throat loudly. "Look, you two. Why don't we discuss this over a few slices of pizza and some soda? I'll go warm the pizza up." The old man rose from the booth and strode to the kitchen.

Charlee's dad followed Cryton with his eyes and then returned his gaze to his daughter. "Charlee, I know how you feel."

"How do you know?" She fought the urge to pound on the table.

"Because I want to strike Theodora down as much as you do…maybe more." His nostrils flared. The veins in the side of his receding hairline bulged. "That woman has caused our family so much pain. It's enough, and it needs to end. But running off on your own to Janasara to face her…well, it can't end well. Your mother and I must deal with her. Believe me, we are ready."

"Dad, I won't be alone," Charlee's voice cracked. How could she make him understand? She was leaving tonight, and he couldn't stop her. Not because she wanted to disobey him. Couldn't he understand she was doing this for her family? To protect them. "Cryton and the bike…they'll both be there."

"Pizza's up!" Cryton sang out. He emerged from the kitchen and walked up to the booth carrying a tray loaded with three steaming slices of cheese pizza and three orange sodas. "Listen, folks, it's late. Let's eat a little something and relax. Then you two will go home and get some sleep. In the morning, we'll all have a fresh perspective on this."

Her dad took a deep breath and nodded. "Well, the pizza does look good. I don't think a slice could hurt. And Cryton's right. Maybe the morning will be a better time to discuss this."

Charlee sat back in her chair, ripping a napkin into pieces. Were these two men serious? What more could she say? Did Cryton really think pizza could make everything all right? She threw up her hands as they bit into their pizzas and took long swallows of orange soda.

"Come on, Charlee," her dad urged. "Let it go. Have a slice…of… pizz…"

Before he could finish, his eyes narrowed. His head slumped and landed on the table with a thud. Her father laid there, eyes closed.

Charlee leaped from the table, hands covering her mouth. "Dad? What happened to him?" Had Theodora somehow attacked him from across the divide? "No, it can't be. She couldn't." The blood pumping through her veins turned to ice. She reached for her sword.

"Relax." Cryton chuckled softly. "Just a little concoction I put in your father's drink." He laughed harder. "I may not be a magic conjurer, but a good warrior always knows how to use the elements when he needs to take out an enemy."

Her blood thawing, Charlee slumped back into the booth next to her dad and leaned in close, forehead to forehead. He breathed softly. This isn't what she wanted. "What am I doing?"

Pushing away from the booth, she grabbed Cryton by the arm. "Dad's not the enemy!"

The old man patted her hand. "Don't worry. He'll be fine. He may have a slight headache when he wakes up, but otherwise he'll be uninjured. Now we have the chance to do what you came here to do." Cryton moved off to the back room. He returned with a pillow, which he handed to her.

Carefully, she lifted her dad's head and placed the pillow underneath him. "Sorry, Dad. I'm sorry for everything. I know you'll be mad, but try to forgive me." Charlee never expected the old man to drug her dad. There must have been another choice, right? Maybe not. They reached a stalemate. Still, this seemed wrong.

She tried to ignore her thoughts. "You have the medallion?"

He nodded.

"Uh, can you give it to me and let me go on my own...with the bike?"

"I can't do that." Cryton clasped his fingers together underneath his chin. "You're stuck with me."

"I'm super strong right now, you know." She strolled to the lunch counter and pressed both hands against the porcelain surface. "I could smash up this place until I found it."

Cryton nodded. "You could, but you still wouldn't find it."

She kicked the ground. "Oh come on. Can't you see I just don't want anyone else getting hurt because of me? Just let me go on my own."

He crossed over and wrapped her in an embrace. "I know, Charlee, but I'm a warrior who has faced more battles than you will ever know. You need me, and I need to do this, so we will go together."

Charlee lingered in the hug for a heartbeat and then pushed away. "Then I guess it's time to go."

Cryton started toward the kitchen. "All right then. I have some supplies gathered. I'll get them."

When he was out of sight, Charlee bent and kissed her dad on the forehead. "Sorry, Dad. I really am."

For a long time, she'd been so angry at him for moving the family to the city until she discovered he did it for her safety to keep her hidden in suburbia should Theodora ever find a way to Earth. And even though he wasn't from Janasara, her father trained in swordplay to protect his wife, the rightful Queen of Latara, and his children should they ever be in danger.

He was a good—

"*Charlee, stay put. Don't do this.*" Her mom's voice blared like an alarm deep within her mind.

"She knows and is coming to stop me. Cryton, you better hurry. Mom's coming!"

CHAPTER 9

The Gateway Opens

CRYTON BURST THROUGH the kitchen's swinging door. In place of his grease-stained apron, he wore a brown tunic made of leather or maybe some kind of animal hide—like something early explorers might wear, and cinched by a brown belt around his waist. Long sleeves woven together with lace covered his arms. Pants, made of the same material as the shirt, clung loosely to his aged cracked boots.

He held a carved wooden staff. In this getup, he seemed ready to hike a mountain trail rather than journey through a portal to do battle with a sorceress.

The one sign he readied for a fight was a sword handle peeking out from a scabbard hung over his shoulder. A tan pouch hung from his other shoulder just large enough to hold…the medallion.

It was there. She could feel it calling to her. She needed to touch it. Charlee extended a hand toward the pouch but recoiled. "Control yourself."

Cryton placed a hand over the pouch. "You'll get the medallion back when we cross together."

Stomping her feet, she paced the restaurant. "You're so difficult, old man. We don't have time to argue. Mom knows. She's coming."

"Then stop arguing and let's be on our way." He slid a finger over a button in the center of his staff. Blades, the size of daggers, rose from either end. "You do not need to worry about this gray fox." He pressed the button again and the blades slid back inside the staff.

Charlee reached for the weapon. "How did you make that?"

He didn't answer. Instead, he placed the weapon on the lunch counter and then retrieved a box. "This is for you." He handed it to her. "Go ahead and change. We need to blend in when we arrive in Janasara. Look like outcasts, not warriors."

Out of the box Charlee pulled a beige tunic and pants just like Cryton wore.

"I stitched it myself." He turned away from her. "Now go on and change."

Charlee slipped into the girl's bathroom to change. Lighter than expected, the material fit her well—even better than most pairs of jeans and blouses. A bit baggy, the shirt hid her rounded stomach. A pair of gray boots, cracked like Cryton's, rose up to her knees.

Once dressed, she emerged from the bathroom and fastened her sword to her waist with a thick black belt.

"One final step." Cryton winked at her and then lifted a hood over her heard. "There. You look humble enough."

"Thank you." She meant that. Having him along for this journey would be comforting. Yet, could she keep him safe? Not that he needed protection. But what if something happened to him? What would I do without him?

Cryton placed a hand on her shoulder. "You're welcome. Now, let's get that bike of yours and open the gateway before your mom kills both of us."

Charlee started to follow him toward the doorway that led to the alley but stopped and glanced at her dad. Would she see him again? Her sister…mom? She loved them all so much. That's why she had to go. To protect them.

"I'll bring you back to him, Charlee. You will come home." Cryton uttered over her shoulder. "Now open that portal for us."

"I'm ready," she declared, but was she really? Had she really thought this through? What happened to that scared fourteen-year-old girl? What if the old Charlee returned? The one frightened of almost everything. *No, that girl wouldn't come back. I'm a guardian.* Maybe this was always her destiny. "Let's do this."

Cryton extended his hand to Charlee. She grasped it, and they marched into the alley. A ring of soft light spread around them from a lamp over the doorway.

"You know, I can't be sure the portal I open will even get us to Janasara." Still holding Cryton's hand, she gripped the bike's handlebar with her other. "We could end up on the moon or something."

Cryton grinned. "Get on with it, Guardian. It will be good to get home. I've missed it."

Swallowing a load of saliva, she closed her eyes. "Think of Janasara," she whispered to herself. "I've been there before, even if only in my dreams. Forests of trees with talking leaves. Streams that defy gravity. The castle built into a mountain. Emerald skies. I've seen them all. Get us there."

In a pulsating frenzy, blood rushed to her head. Sparks erupted in her brain as if she touched a live wire. Her arms and legs tensed. *Focus, Charlee.* "Open… a doorway…to Janasara."

"You're doing it," Cryton blurted.

Charlee blinked her eyes open. Before her, the gateway grew into a spinning blue vortex filled with images of Janasara. Corkscrew shaped trees reaching to the skies. Water spouts rising in massive columns over an endless sea. An island mountaintop carved into the shape of a dragon. What was she seeing? None of these sites appeared in her dreams before. Never mind. This had to be Janasara. Just had to be.

"It's time." Charlee shouted over the howling wind swirling around them, flinging old newspapers and trash in every direction.

As the portal enveloped her, the urge to retreat tugged at her like invisible fingers latched onto the back of her tunic. What was she doing? She was just some kid. I'm going to blow it. Let everyone down.

As if Cryton could hear her thoughts, the old man tightened his grip on her hand. His touch helped. Knowing the bike was there too helped. They would defeat Theodora together.

Behind her, the portal shrunk as the doorway to Earth began to close. Ahead, the gateway stretched into a long glimmering hallway with reflections of Janasara spinning in a dizzying array.

"Don't do this!" Her mom's voice boomed from the disappearing alley.

Charlee glanced back. For a heartbeat, her mom stood just beyond the portal, Megan in her arms. Her mom reached out to her and then she was gone. The doorway shut.

Earth and her mom vanished.

"Mom… sorry."

Cryton leaned toward her ear. "You'll see her again."

"I hope you're—"

A blast of lightning inside the portal forced Charlee to close her eyes. Then, for a long pause, there was no sound save the whistling of a slight breeze.

Then came the screams.

CHAPTER 10

Into Battle

THE PORTAL STRETCHED out like a swirling tunnel, propelling them toward a brilliant white light. Faint, muffled screams echoed around them as if terrified beings pleaded for help just outside the passageway. But that couldn't be real. Charlee had to be hearing things as she focused her mind on keeping the gateway open. The cries were nothing more than the wind generated inside this magical subway to Janasara. Had to be, right?

She leaned closer to Cryton, whose skin sparkled like a diamond within the portal. "Do year hear it?"

He nodded. "Perhaps through this dimensional highway, we can hear the cries of the past."

"I have a bad feeling." She tightened her grip on his hand.

Like a slingshot, the portal shot them into the white light. They emerged from the gateway into wilderness.

The screams were real.

A mass of trees with spiraling trunks surrounded Charlee and her companions, masking what lay beyond. Charlee whirled around, ears twitching. Men and women shouted, their cries matched by the growls and barks of wild beasts and the crackle of fire.

Charlee let go of Cryton's hand and removed her hood. She gazed up to a canopy of interlaced branches covered by star-shaped leaves pulsating—like hearts—with yellow, orange, and purple colors. Rays of sunlight zigzagged through cracks, leaving a polka dot pattern along the undergrowth. Shadows crept at her through the streaming light. Covering her ears, she shrunk away. Where had she delivered them? If this was Janasara, they should jump back into a portal and escape to a safer entry point. She wasn't ready for whatever unseen battle unfolded beyond this pocket of alien trees.

Cryton lifted his staff. "Let's go."

Charlee retreated farther. "What? No!"

"We have to Charlee. There are beings out there in trouble. I don't know what's going on, but this is the path you chose, Guardian." He extended a hand to her.

"I don't know if I can do this." She pressed harder against her ears.

He grinned. "Trust me. I've seen the hero inside of you. I know what you can do. Believe in yourself."

This is what she feared…letting that scared little girl take over. Cryton was right. She chose to do this. Whatever was out there, she had to face it. She'd done it before. Back home against Theodora she'd been brave. "I can be brave again."

With a sigh, she grasped his hand. They took off running, dodging branches, which seemed to bend out of her way, weaving through shrubbery shaped like giant spiders. Beside her the changeling shifted form. The bike vanished, replaced by the winged unicorn that helped her fight Theodora on Alcatraz Island.

The roars of vicious beats slid through the brush and pierced her ears. Screams echoed around them. She fought the urge to break away from Cryton and flee. No, she couldn't do that. A guardian wouldn't run from those who needed help. Charlee wished she wasn't a guardian, but she was.

Cryton slid to a stop at the edge of a tree line. He motioned her down to her knees. Tall corkscrew grass as thick as rope and as long as a sword's blade provided cover. The unicorn stayed a few steps back hidden by a web of branches.

"Look, Charlee." Cryton slammed his fist into the ground.

She peaked through the growth. In a clearing maybe half the size of a football field, walled in by a grove of spiraling trees, men, women, and children dressed in little more than rags fought for their lives against a band of Theodora's dark army, the Horeng.

Adorned in dark armor, wielding double-headed battle axes, the wolf-like beasts slashed at their prey without mercy. Some of the monsters lumbered toward their victims on muscular hind legs; others rode atop massive wind horses, which towered over Earth's steeds.

The dead spread across the meadow, turning the dirt crimson.

Charlee covered her mouth to muffle her own shrieks. This couldn't be real. It was a nightmare. She needed to wake up. They hadn't really made the leap yet to Janasara. But it wasn't a dream. They had crossed over into a massacre.

Children cried out, clinging to their fallen mothers and fathers. Women wielded swords, defending the little ones. Men with bows and arrows fired wildly at the wolf beasts, but the enemy was too strong. The Horengs' axes sliced through flesh, tearing through one man's back and another's mid-section. Their blood splashed against the tree where Charlee hid. She turned away, but their screams and final gurgled gasps etched into her memory.

Other beasts set fire to huts. The flames started small but quickly grew into red hot infernos, engulfing the tiny oval-shaped dwellings. The vicious raiders torched rows of crops, tromping over the burning fields.

Choking black smoke billowed beyond the trees toward an emerald sky, shrouding this world's sun—larger than Earth's—in a bloody haze.

Charlee crawled to the changeling. They had to get out of here now. What could they do to help? Nothing. Except die trying.

Footsteps approached from the clearing. She swung back to look. A woman ran toward the tree line until an axe buried into her back. Arching her head back, crying out, she fell to her knees. Charlee flinched and then froze. Somehow, the woman spotted her through the tall grass. She extended her hands toward Charlee. Blood slid down the sides of her mouth. The woman released one last breath and then crumbled to the ground.

Two young children, a boy and girl, leaped onto the woman. They grabbed at her limp hands, begging her to get up. Charlee gazed into their faces. Tears streaked down their cheeks. Were they alone now? What about their father. Had he already fallen? Her hands formed into fists.

A beast, eyes and snout hidden under a black helmet, marched up to the children, axe held high. The brute was about to strike them down.

"Arm yourself, Charlee!" Cryton leaped from the trees, launching himself at the Horeng. He rammed his staff into the beast's cannonball-sized shoulder, driving it backward away from the children. The monster quickly recovered. A guttural growl rose from underneath its helmet like a rabid dog ready to fight to the death.

Cryton twirled his staff in front of him, his fingers releasing the daggers. "Come on, you foul creation. Come and get me."

The beast lunged at him, swinging its axe at his head. Cryton dodged the blow, and with the speed of a much younger warrior speared the dark creature through its armor into its gut. Ripping his weapon free, he then sliced through the Horeng's unprotected neck.

Black liquid oozed from both wounds. Clawing at its throat, gasping for air, the brute howled once before slumping to the dirt.

Cryton, his hands splattered by the creature's dark blood, twisted back to her. "Wake up, Charlee! Your people need you."

She mashed her body up against a tree. "What are you talking about? We need to escape this carnage." Her head spun and stomach churned. Charlee started to hyperventilate. She wasn't a soldier ready to charge into a war. What was Cryton thinking? Peering from her hiding place, she counted maybe two dozen of the armored beasts. She'd seen Theodora's magic twist those back home into werewolves, ready to devour at her command, but these creatures were different— taller with hulking bodies and deadly claws as long as an eagle's talons. They were killing machines.

Cryton pointed at Charlee and threw himself at another Horeng. His words echoed though her mind. *Wake up!* That's exactly what she wanted to do—wake up—as if this were a bad dream. She slowly stood, pushing away from the tree. The cling of steel clashing against steel, the whiz of arrows zipping through the air, the roar of fire and frenzied shouts of men and woman fighting for their lives all rang in her ears.

"Charlee!" Cryton called to her as he spun his bladed-staff. "Unsheathe that sword!" He sliced through a beast's stomach. "Now!" he ordered.

Run away! Far away! Charlee gripped the handle of her sword. *No! I can't run! Can't be scared.* She wasn't that weak little teenager at Myron Applebee anymore that bullies could push around. And right now, these scum were the bullies that needed to be stopped. She had abilities. Strength. Power. She just needed to call on them. "Come on, Guardian. Now or never."

Charlee crossed to the changeling. "We have to help them." Her body shaking, she climbed onto the unicorn's white-coated back and lifted her sword. "Time to be a guardian!" She drew from her protector's energy. Strength coursed through her limbs. The trembling stopped. Muscles in her arms and legs expanded. Her grip on the sword tightened. The time had come to let the warrior out. Charlee swallowed a load of saliva. "Go!" she shouted.

The unicorn charged through the trees. Charlee gripped his mane with one hand, while the other held the sword. A gray mist from the fires hid much of the battlefield, but through the thick gloom came glimpses of Cryton slashing his bladed staff at two Horeng. Others defended themselves from the advancing beasts. Some fell, their blood soiling the earth.

Charlee nearly dropped her sword. There was too much death all around her. Her stomach turned to ice. "We have to escape!" she told herself. "No. Be brave. Focus. Do this."

Through the blackening haze, two Horeng pushed a man, a woman, and two children inside a hut. Laughing like hyenas, the beasts blocked the door and torched the small dwelling.

Charlee pointed her sword at them. She couldn't let those people die like that. She tightened her grip on the blade. Her own blood flowed hot, breaking through the chill of fear. "Bike—there!"

The changeling pounced on the beasts before they could react. With super strength, Charlee swung the sword wildly at one wolf. By chance, the blade dug into the monster's arm just below the shoulder. The brute howled as black liquid sprayed from the wound. *I hit it. I actually did it!* Ripping the steel from the beast's flesh, she struck a second time, driving the weapon into its neck. A gurgling sound escaped its throat. The Horeng tore away its helmet, revealing yellow bulging eyes. Grasping its neck, the creature dropped to the ground. With one final whimper, the wolf fell silent.

Charlee gazed at the dead Horeng and at the blood dripping from her sword. *Did I really just kill?* She'd never taken a life before. Not even a bug. Never watched anyone die up close like that, either. Numbness spread through her body.

The screams of the family inside the burning hut jolted her from her thoughts. Throwing open the door, she dragged the family outside and pointed toward an outcropping of trees away from the fighting.

"Head for that cover," she commanded in the Lengoron language spoken in the Kingdom of Latara. *Where did that come from?* How was she speaking...? *Never mind.*

Coughing from the smoke, the family did as she directed.

She watched them run until the growl of another enemy, this one without a helmet, came from behind. The beast swung at her with its axe. Her body reacted instinctively. Charlee raised her sword just in time to block the slashing blow. The stinging clang of steel coursed through her limbs like a shockwave, knocking Charlee off the unicorn. She fell back hard. Dazed, her vision blurred. Charlee gasped for a breath. With its weapon held high, the Horeng rushed at her.

"He's going...to kill...me. Move...it!" Charlee rolled away, struggling to her feet, and raised her sword just in time to deflect the attack. The beast drove its axe down on her again. She met the steel with her own, but the monster leaned against her with all of its weight, driving its weapon toward her face. Saliva dripped from the beast's fangs onto her chest. The wolf snapped at her. Clumps of bloodied fur stood at attention.

"Get off of me!" Tapping into what magic still pumped through her veins, she shoved the monster backward.

Charlee gripped the sword handle with both hands. Her chest heaved with each long breath. Heart thudded. Sweat dripped from her forehead and stung her eyes. Despite her powers, Charlee's muscles protested against the weight of the sword. How much longer could she defend herself? The blade dipped toward the ground. *No!* Gritting her teeth, she lifted it higher.

The wolf, standing on its hind legs, loomed over her, its fur bristling underneath a black chest. Drool oozed from yellow fangs at the end of a jagged misshaped snout. The monster had only one red eye. Where the other should be was a gaping, crusty hole. A throaty, wheezing laugh rose from the creature.

Charlee retreated, sword held out in front of her.

The Horeng raised its snout and unleashed a blood curdling howl. Fangs bared, the creature charged, a rampaging wolf ready to tear her apart.

Turning to flee, she tripped over her feet and fell to the ground. She gazed up just in time to see the changeling ram its unicorn body into the wolf. The monster yelped, stumbling into the grass, losing its axe. Twisting its head side to side like a wet dog, the beast slowly rose and grabbed its weapon.

Charlee climbed to her feet, the changeling at her side. Now was their chance to run and hide. All around her people screamed. Arrows whizzed by. Fire roared. Her head pounded against the chaos of battle.

"No, I can't run. Have to stand and fight." She gripped her sword tightly in both hands. "Come and get me," Charlee shouted." What was she saying?

The wolf sprang at her, ready to bury its axe in her head. She dodged the blow then thrust her sword at the beast's chest. Steel again clashed, rattling her hands. The Horeng swung its heavy weapon over and over. She blocked every blow, but each sent her reeling backward. She couldn't keep this up. "It's too... strong!"

She tried to attack, swinging her blade like Cryton taught her, but the fiend easily deflected her blows. More wheezing laughter rose from its mouth. The beast seemed amused.

One powerful swing of the Horeng's axe wrenched the blade from her throbbing hands and flung her backwards. The changeling caught her with a wing, wrapping her in a protective embrace. A wave of energy swept through her body, strengthening each limb.

"Thank you," she whispered.

Stepping away from her protector, Charlee retrieved her weapon and quieted her mind. She studied how the beast moved with clunky steps, wielding its heavy axe. How its fur rippled before the wolf charged. "Yes, I see it. I get it."

The beast attacked again.

Their weapons clashed. Charlee spun around the monster, and swiped her blade across its back. The Horeng cried out and swung for her neck. She dropped to one knee, slicing across one of the beast's legs and then the other. The creature's dark blood covered her weapon and dripped onto her hands. Howling in protest, the wolf angled its axe low at her feet. Charlee leaped up and drove the tip of her blade deep into the beast's back.

Theodora's evil creation shuddered, trying to grasp at the steel. Unable to, it dropped. Charlee tore the weapon from the creature and then kicked the brute to the ground. Writhing in the dirt like a wounded animal, the Horeng spit out blood and stared at her with its one eye. The creature was dying. Did it understand death? Did it care whether it lived or died? She didn't wait for an answer. Charlee plunged her sword into its chest. The brute bared its fangs and went silent.

Charlee had taken two lives—even if they were monsters. Could they have once been human, like the people back home Theodora had transformed? Had they been turned into rampaging killers? She wiped sweat from her forehead and rubbed away blood from her hands. Now was not the time to worry about it. More Horeng had to be stopped.

Off to her right, the unicorn, its white body stained with streaks of blood, added a third dead wolf from Theodora's army. She nodded to her protector, then climbed onto the magical being's back. "We have to get Cryton. Make sure he's okay." The unicorn charged into the thickening mist.

"Cryton, where are you?" Charlee called out.

"Here," he answered.

They found him standing over two children. He wielded his bladed staff at a Horeng, knocking the beast off its legs before slashing through its armor and flesh. The creature tried to rise, but the old man drove his staff through its heart. He didn't wait to watch the creature die.

He turned toward her. "Charlee, they're trying to set the forest on fire! Take to the air and stop them."

She peered around. Flames spread through the trees surrounding the village. The plan was easy to understand. Kill everyone whether they burned or suffocated. Some people escaped past the blaze, but most couldn't. The Horeng slashed at them while others ignited the trees.

A wave of stifling heat blew against Charlee's face. "Oh no! Everyone will die! We have to do something." The unicorn responded, taking flight. Its powerful hooves knocked Horeng off their wind horses as it soared above the battle.

Smoke columns billowed up from the trees. Flames spread like an advancing army from the trees onto the grass along the meadow. Charlee tore at her hair. How long until the fire spread throughout the clearing? If she only had the power to make it rain. Or blow a gust of freezing air. But she couldn't. What use was her magic? If only her mom were here. Maybe her magic could make a difference. "What can I do?"

Hovering just above the tree line in a pocket of air untouched by the rising smoke, she searched for an answer. Below the people huddled together among their huts. A few men and women armed with swords defended the rest. Cryton stood at the head of them all, slashing his staff at the Horeng, but the beasts would soon overpower him. "Bike, any ideas? They're running out of time!"

The unicorn was silent, but its actions swift. Her protector shape shifted. Rays of white energy emanated from the changeling, engulfing the magical being and Charlee. The unicorn's body ballooned like a blow fish. Charlee sheathed her sword and grasped the morphing creature with both hands.

The unicorn's head vanished. A blue exoskeleton formed over the creature, now oval shaped with legs replaced by eight dangling tentacles. Monstrous-sized beetle wings, almost translucent, unfurled from the being's skeletal back. Four black crustacean eyes, like a lobster's, poked out on either side of the body.

"What is this?" The teenager in her wanted to flee from this giant weird bug. Even the hum of its wings made her shudder. Instead, she grasped onto ridges in the changeling's hard shell. "Yuck, this is the nastiest thing I've ever seen. What good is this flying freak going to do?"

The answer seeped into her thoughts as if already embedded deep in her mind. *Nantorata. A sea creature with the ability to fly…and use its appendages like water cannons.* "Yes, I understand. Do it! Save them."

The Nantorata pointed its tentacles at the rising flames. Streams of water gushed from each appendage, as if blasted from a fire hose, dousing the blazing wilderness into smoldering patches.

"Yeah, bike!" Charlee drummed her hands on the creature's hard back like a drummer's solo during a rock concert. "You're amazing. You did it. You saved them all. I can't believe it." She pumped her fists high above her head.

With the flames chased away, the changeling aimed at the Horeng. Water became a weapon, smashing into the beasts, knocking them from their wind horses. Some no longer moved. Others moaned. The people, led by Cryton, did the rest. They gathered their swords and drove their blades into the wolves.

A handful of Horeng fled on horseback. Cryton called out to her from below. "We can't let them get away. We must stop them all."

"What? Why?" Charlee grabbed hold of the changeling as her protector shifted back into its unicorn form. They flew down to Cryton, and he jumped onto the unicorn behind her. Charlee gazed over her shoulder. "I don't get it. Haven't we done enough? There's just a few of those wolf things left."

He leaned closer. "If they escape, they'll report to Theodora."

Charlee closed her eyes and drew in a long breath. Cryton was right. If the Horeng reported what they'd seen, the sorceress would know she was here and more importantly, the medallion as well. Maybe she already knew. A chill rose up her back. "Okay, let's go."

The unicorn charged through the smoldering trees after the fleeing Horeng.

"I counted about six remaining," he declared. "We can't let them live—not a single one."

The unicorn stretched its head forward and picked up speed, its hooves thunderously pounding over wild grass and dirt. Ahead of them, the large horses of the Horeng ran incredibly fast. Their hooves didn't even touch the ground as if they flew above the wilderness floor.

The unicorn was faster. Wind slapped Charlee in the face. She tightened her hold on the mane. Dashing around trees, leaping over brush and rocks, they caught up to the creatures.

Cryton struck first. He slashed at the nearest beast with his sword, ripping through its neck. The beast grabbed its throat and fell from its horse. Before she could swing her sword, he felled another.

Now it was her turn. One hand on the unicorn's mane, she hefted her sword and hacked into the back of a third wolf. The beast wailed, swinging its axe toward her head. She ducked and then attacked again, but missed. Cryton finished the wolf off, hurdling two daggers into the Horeng's back. The creature dropped its axe and fell backward off the horse.

The three remaining beasts separated among the trees. Charlee leaned against the unicorn's neck. "We're going to lose—!"

Arrows ripped through the air. Each one found its target. The Horeng fell, thrashing about in the grass, tugging at the arrows.

The unicorn slid to a stop and circled around to the dying beasts. Charlee gazed with her mouth open. Where had the arrows come from? "Cryton, what's—"

More arrows flew from the sky, smashing into the Horengs' bodies. The beasts flinched and then became silent. They lay dead, hidden by the forest. Their horses bolted out of view.

"Who did this?" Charlee asked, her sword held out in front of her to fend off another attack, her breathing fast and erratic.

"They did." Cryton pointed toward a cropping of trees.

Riders atop their own giant horses, their faces hidden by cloaks, burst through the trees. Five in all, armed with bows and arrows.

"Are they friends?" she whispered.

Cryton placed a hand on her shoulder. "I believe so."

Charlee eased her breathing, however her mind still raced. She fought the urge to cry. *Guardians don't cry*. Her stomach did somersaults. Sweat dripped from her hair. What had just happened? The blood. The death. This wasn't some dream. It had all just happened.

She had killed…to save lives. But whose lives? Who were these people? What were they doing among the trees? She lowered her head into her hands. *I think I'm going to be sick*. No, not in front of everyone.

"You did well." Cryton patted her on the shoulder. "You are a warrior. Perhaps you truly are the Last Guardian."

She turned to glare into the old man's graying eyes. "What do you mean… perhaps?"

CHAPTER II

The Remnants

THE FIVE CLOAKED riders approached, nothing visible—no eyes, mouths, not one strand of hair—under their hoods. Their horses stepped over the Horeng bodies as if the beasts weren't even there. Two held bows in a firing position taught with arrows.

Charlee leaned against Cryton. "Are you sure they're friends?"

"We'll see soon enough," he answered.

No more than a car's length away, the riders stopped. One removed the hood to reveal a young man with long black hair, a bronzed face, and eyes seemingly made of coal. A patchy beard, like one a high school teenager might try to grow, spotted his cheeks and chin.

Charlee gawked at him and stared at the ground. There was no denying he was handsome. The kind of brooding type teen girls, including herself, are drawn to. Her gaze shifted back and forth among the riders but returned to him more than once.

The young rider guided his horse closer to them. "You will come with us." He spoke in the Lengoron language, unsheathing a sword and pointing it at Cryton. "Do not attempt to flee. Our bowmen are quite accurate, as you have seen."

Charlee's knowledge of the language, somehow magically embedded in her mind, was still weak. When spoken fast, she missed some words. But the threat was clear. The arrows left little doubt.

"Hey, what is this?" she asked in her best Lengoron, blowing a strand of sweaty hair away from her face. Her flaring temper caused her to forget his good looks, for the moment. "Who do you think you are? In case you didn't notice, we just risked our lives back there to stop those monsters. Now you threaten us?"

The young man glared at her. "Those are our countrymen. We were out hunting when we saw the black smoke. We arrived just as you started to pursue the beasts."

Charlee raised her arms. "So you saw us attack the Horeng. You know we're friends."

He nodded at her. "That remains to be seen. I will say it one more time." He maneuvered the tip of his blade to point at her. "Come with us now."

Charlee fingered the handle of the sword at her side. "Don't—"

Cryton, his hands scratched and bloodied, held up a finger to quiet her.

"Son, we are not your enemy." He bowed to the young man.

"That's right." Charlee eased her hand away from the sheathed weapon. *Don't they know who I am,* she mused. *Stupid, of course they don't.* "You should know that I'm a—"

"We are friends." Cryton shook his head at her.

She studied the old man's face. He cocked one eyebrow. Deep lines formed across his forehead. Bathed in sunlight that penetrated the tree branches above, his pale skin glowed. Why didn't he want her to tell them a guardian had come? Why keep it a secret?

"That may be," the young man challenged, "but we will let the elders decide if you are to be trusted. Now ride." His lips pursed into a frown. One that might be permanent. He probably never smiled—probably had nothing to smile about. Covered by their brown cloaks, they would be invisible in this woodland if not so close to Charlee.

"As you wish." Cryton offered a slight smile.

She leaned toward her mentor and whispered, "Why'd you stop me from telling him who I am?"

"Now's not the time." He held his staff close to his chest. The blades were gone. "From this point on, follow my lead before you speak."

The changeling, in its unicorn form, walked with a slow gait past the armed riders. They lowered their bows and followed close behind. Silence filled their journey back. Eerie after the chaos moments ago. It was as if the land wanted to forget the bloodshed. But the signs lingered. The stench of smoldering wood and foliage spread through the trees. Ashes rained down on them.

All around her a thousand voices cried out in pain and sadness, audible only to her. The cry of the leaf creatures. Rage laced their voices. Charlee sensed they wanted revenge against the Horeng. Against Theodora.

In the distance, mournful human cries mixed with the lamenting voices of the leaf creatures.

She didn't want to go back to the clearing—didn't want to see the death and suffering left behind by the attack. How easy it would be to open a portal and escape. They'd done their part and helped these people. What more could they do?

Through trees looming overhead, the spotty sunlight softened. Was dusk coming? When they left home it was nighttime, but when they emerged from the portal into this world, the larger sun cast an oppressive heat even under the cover of dense vegetation. Her tunic clung to her body as if plastered to her skin. An endless sweat dripped from her hair. Now a warm—but slightly cooler—breeze brushed through the leaves, offering some relief. What would nighttime on Janasara bring?

Charlee glanced over her shoulder at the five riders. They had removed their hoods. Three men; two women. She couldn't tell their ages, especially the women. They looked older, with gaunt cheeks and weathered skin. Hair, stiff and flattened, clung to rigid faces. So different than the mall-loving popular girls at school. *Different even from me,* Charlee thought.

From their solemn expressions, their lives were more about survival, not worrying about whether a cute boy would like them. How much loss had they faced versus kids who cry if they don't get the latest smart phone? She'd seen images on TV of starving children in foreign countries and not taken it to heart. "How petty I've been in my own little life."

The exhaustion edged into their faces reminded Charlee how much her own body ached from the battle. Energy from the changeling enhanced her strength, but she had never swung a sword in battle. Her palms, the skin reddened and rough, ached and shook from the clash of steel. This must be what a boxer's hands feel like after a fight. She craved her mom's healing touch. Sleep would be nice, too. Maybe a slurp of water. Her head drooped under the unicorn's rhythmic trot.

She blinked away weariness and turned back to Cryton. "Is this Janasara? Are we in the right place?"

"What does your heart tell you?" He spoke low. On the battlefield, he fought like a young warrior. Now he looked his age. The wrinkles under his eyes deepened. His mustache hung low. The few strands of hair on the sides of his head blew out of place in the gentle wind.

"This is Janasara. I'm actually here. I can't believe it. Another world. A different dimension." So far away from home. She couldn't feel her mom inside her head anymore. Watching. Protecting. Loneliness pressed against her shoulders. A tear slid down her cheek. *I miss her already. What have I gotten myself into?* she wondered in silence. *This is worse than I imagined. Worse than the first time I faced Theodora. No one died then. But now…*

A song from the Leaf creatures interrupted her thoughts. They did not sing for their brethren burned in the fires. They sang for her.

"The Guardian returns to save The Our. She shall bring peace. Oh let all We rejoice. Guardian. Guardian. Guardian."

Their tiny voices chanted among the branches. The star-shaped leaves communicated through telepathy, just like in her dreams. Hundreds, thousands of them on each tree, though they spoke as if one being. The We. Their trees…part of The Our, the world of Janasara. They had their own language, yet—like Lengoron—she recognized it.

How did the leaves know she was a guardian? She shuddered. What if she failed them? Failed everyone. "I won't. Can't."

The song refocused her attention on the land. Trees with spiraling trunks arched overhead. Short blue grass, glowing like a neon sign, covered the ground along with the taller corkscrew-shaped growth. From somewhere in the distance came the gurgling of a flowing stream…maybe a lake.

Amid the undergrowth, they encountered a dead Horeng with six arrows in its back. The beast's long tongue hung from its snout, while blood pooled around the creature.

The little hairs prickled on Charlee's arms. She held her breath and gripped her sword handle until they passed. Even in death, the monster made her tremble from her legs to her neck. These werewolves in black armor didn't care who they slaughtered. Men. Women. Children. Armed…unarmed. They struck without mercy. How many more from the sorceress' dark army would she face before this ended? How many hunted her right now?

Charlee stopped herself from biting a fingernail. "Cryton, is there any chance the Horeng we've killed were really people Theodora changed just like she did back home?"

"No. The Horeng are different from those poor souls." He rested his deadly staff on the unicorn's back. "They are soulless creations of the darkest magic, bred for war in Theodora's factories. They serve her will—nothing more. Unfortunately, she also has the power to mutate people into the half-wolf, half-human creatures you saw in your earlier battle with her. By now, I'm sure thousands of our people have suffered such—"

Cryton's voice cracked, and he paused before continuing. "Anyone Theodora mutates is considered too weak to serve in her army. Instead, they become slaves. They build her fortifications. Forge her weapons. Feed the Horeng. Within months of their transformation—they die, the change too much for their hearts."

Her face grew hot, and she squeezed the unicorn's mane. "We're going to stop her, Cryton. I promise we will."

"I know, Guardian."

She grasped his arm. "I get why we chased down and killed these Horeng, but don't you think Theodora already knows I'm here. I mean, she's so powerful. She has to know."

A smile crossed the old man's face. "I'm not so sure. Yes, she is powerful. And it may be that she already senses your presence. But it may also be that you have more power than you realize, and we are protected by that power. It may be that she can't sense you as clearly as you think."

"Maybe." She rubbed her sweaty palms together. Her head pounded just like when Theodora touched her thoughts. Was the sorceress watching her now? Or could she block the witch's magic? Thinking about it added to the pain sitting like a weight on her forehead. She tried to ignore it. "One more question. These people—are they…"

"Yes," Cryton responded. "They are the remnants of Latara. Your mother's kingdom. They are your people."

She took a long breath of the damp dusk air. What would *her people* think when they learn the truth? That she is a guardian who let this world suffer. She unleashed Theodora back on Janasara when she had the power to stop her. Charlee shook her head. No reason to worry what they might think. She wouldn't be staying. Theodora was out there somewhere. Charlee had to face the sorceress soon.

"I believe this belongs to you, Guardian, for the time being." Cryton placed the pouch with the medallion over her shoulder.

She touched the strap, following it with her fingertips down to the pouch now at her side.

A wave of excitement swept through her like a child about to open a present on Christmas morning. Her body tingled with anticipation. Her pulse sped up. The black object was hers again. She'd never let anyone take it away from her—ever. She held the pouch close to her body. Her lips parted in a wide grin.

Yet, at the same time, the strap hung heavy over her shoulder like a backpack stuffed with textbooks. As much as she craved the medallion, the burden of carrying it sapped her strength.

Cryton whispered into her ear. "You know what you have to do with it."

She reached her hand inside the pouch. "Kill Theodora."

CHAPTER 12

The Village

UNDER A SUPERHIGHWAY of interlocked branches, Charlee, Cryton, and the unicorn rode surrounded by their five escorts. A purple haze settled over the woods. The air became less sticky, though still not quite cool. No one spoke, but the riders didn't need words to express their distrust toward her.

They headed back to the settlement at a slow, steady trot, but the journey seemed endless. Had they chased the Horeng that far into this forest? She couldn't tell. It all happened so fast, but the pursuit could have covered a mile. Maybe more.

Not far up ahead came the cries of grief. Charlee covered her ears. She didn't want to return to the survivors, to face that much death again, but they didn't have much choice unless Cryton gave the go-ahead to open a gateway.

Right now he didn't seem inclined to escape. Rubbing his mustache over and over, he blinked his eyes rapidly. Was he holding back tears?

They emerged through a thicket into the clearing where the village, if that's what you could call it, lay in ruins. It seemed more like those images on the news of people living in tents as they escaped war-torn countries. These refugees of Latara, living in huts of wood and straw, had that same look of despair and defeat in their bone-thin faces.

The darkening skies could not hide the destruction. White smoke billowed up from dozens of charred huts. Most of their field crops were a trampled or burned mess. Blood stained the blue grass throughout the meadow.

Charlee gulped. How many died? How many lost everything? Would they blame her when they learned she was a guardian? Their guardian. Even worse, she was the granddaughter of their queen. Would they think her family abandoned them? Cryton was right not to say anything…yet.

When they arrived, they weren't exactly greeted like heroes.

Men and women with swords, some barely able to hold the weapons up with scrawny arms, surrounded them. There were no cheers. No applause. No offers of thanks. The remnants of Latara stared at the three strangers. Some whispered while others pointed. They wouldn't recognize her, but what about Cryton? Among the onlookers were those clearly old enough to have known him before he was sent to Earth.

More cries spread through the village. Mothers chanted as they huddled over the bodies of little children. Their sorrowful songs mixed with the crackling of burnt trees as embers still flamed. Charlee's eyes watered from the reek of charred wood, the hovering gray mist, and for the dead.

Her stomach churned. She peered over her shoulder at the tree line. How easy it would be to order the unicorn to spread its wings and fly away. Charlee was there for Theodora, not them. Stopping the witch was the only way to help these poor souls, anyway.

"I'm sorry," Charlee whispered to Cryton.

"You're not to blame." He held her shoulder.

She pushed away Cryton's hand. "I let Theodora live. I sent her back here."

"And saved San Francisco...for that matter, Earth." He spoke like a grandfather, but his words didn't help.

The five riders led them through the huddled crowd, who parted to clear a narrow path. They glared at her with their tired, sunken eyes. Tears crusted to their smudged faces.

Charlee and the others marched to the center of the village to a wood cabin, larger than the other dwellings yet untouched by fire. They stopped in front of the arched entryway. Two young men—their hands bloodied from helping the wounded—approached from the fields. One of the men, a cut across his forehead, stepped forward. "You are to enter and wait inside. The elders will join you shortly after they have tended to our people." The man who spoke nodded to his counterpart, a short stocky warrior with a shaved head. "Remain here and guard them."

"I promise you that will not be necessary." Cryton bowed to them. "Please let us help your injured."

The man with the bleeding forehead held up his sword. "You are to wait inside." With that, he nodded and hurried away.

"Cryton, what's happening?" She held his arm.

"You heard him. We are to meet the elders. I suggest we do as he says and wait inside. Damned fools. They should let us help." He held his staff like a walking stick, the deadly blades no longer visible.

Together, Charlee and Cryton started through the entrance. The unicorn, unable to fit through the doorway, fluttered its wings. Charlee stopped and patted the creature's neck. "It'll be all right. Wait out here."

Their guard, sword held close to his chest, stood by the entryway and motioned them inside. Cryton nodded and they crossed into a dimly lighted room with a dirt floor.

"What am I supposed to say?" Charlee asked once alone with the old man.

"Do nothing. Say nothing until I tell you," he answered.

Charlee bit her upper lip. "Cryton, I have a bad feeling about this. Let's get—"

From the door came the sound of feet. A group of older men and women, their clothes torn and bloodied, entered and walked by Charlee and Cryton without uttering a word. She counted ten in all. They marched in a line to a rectangular table, then sat in unison in wooden chairs. One lighted a torch on the wall behind them.

The dancing yellow flame revealed the oldest men with long, graying beards and leathery skin. Their faces were tired, but they sat straight, heads held high. Four women, their hands streaked in blood, took their places at the table. Three of them appeared to be Cryton's age. One younger woman could easily have been Charlee's mom—maybe in her forties. Glaring at her, some of the elders folded their arms across their chests. Others whispered to those next to them. One man with the longest, whitest beard shook his head. A woman, her sleeves cut away—no doubt used as bandages—bowed her head.

Charlee fidgeted and peered away.

The torch's blaze shed more light on their surroundings. Banners, all the colors of a rainbow with different emblems—some with swords, others with crowns and trees—draped along the walls. *The Ten Unified Kingdoms!* Just like her mom told her. Could the people outside be all that's left of each of those kingdoms? There had to be more, just had to be.

How long had these exiles been living in the wilderness? Too long. Charlee grasped the pouch with the medallion. She would make Theodora pay for this. She'd find a way to return these people to their home.

One woman stood. "Welcome," she said in a throaty voice.

The fire light danced across her wrinkled faced. A trail of blood slid from her nose down to her chin. Her long brown hair, with stands of gray, gathered around her shoulders. She stood tall. A torn robe covered her body, hiding her frame, but the bones protruding from her cheeks showed her waif form. She had thick eyebrows and a pronounced chin. Still, there was something ruggedly beautiful about her. A strength that made her plain features striking.

"We welcome such brave strangers among us." She spoke Lengoron, holding up her arms as if greeting old friends.

Charlee rocked back and forth on her heels like a child called to the principal's office after getting caught breaking a rule. She didn't want to be here to meet the elders. Just outside the entrance the changeling waited for her. They could take flight together with or without Cryton. Right now she'd rather go off with her magical protector after Theodora than face these survivors who would probably condemn her for not coming sooner.

Motioning her not to follow, Cryton approached the table. "I thank you for welcoming us, but I am no stranger."

As he stepped into the light, the elders jumped to their feet.

"Cryton," the woman declared. "Can it really be you…after all these years?"

"It is I." He bowed. "I have returned with my very young companion here to free this world from Theodora's tyranny. You have suffered long enough."

Charlee bit her thumbnail. Was he going to tell them about her? Maybe he shouldn't. Their discussion lowered to whispers. Some of the elders studied her while Cryton spoke. Her face grew hot. One hand clutched the collar of her tunic; the other grasped the pouch tighter. "Why do I feel like I'm about to be grounded?" she mouthed.

Finally, he waved her to the table.

Mouth dry, heat racing, she approached the group. No one smiled. The raised eyebrows and pursed lips revealed anger, sadness, and most of all…doubt.

"Young Guardian." Cryton reached out to her and pulled her closer to the table. "I would like to introduce you to the elders of this community."

Charlee glared at him. Why was he referring to her so formally in front of the elders? She twisted a strand of her hair between her fingers. What was she supposed to say? Without uttering a word, she nodded a few times. She felt like a clumsy little girl, not a guardian.

Who would be the first to speak? Something told her it would be the woman who greeted them. Cryton taught her in Latara the queen led the government and had no king unless she chose to bestow such a title.

"Greetings, Guardian." The woman in the robe spoke softly. She wore a stony expression that gave no hint of her emotions and pointed to a free chair. "Please, sit with us."

Charlee did as directed. "Uh…thank you." Her gaze shifted from the woman to Cryton.

"I am Penaiya, once aide to Queen Assara." The woman's fingers intertwined on the table. "I serve as leader of what remains of the people of her realm…the Kingdom of Latara. It is a position I hold until, one day, the true Queen of Latara returns to claim her crown. And if I should die before that happens, it will fall upon my daughter, Leyan, to lead the people until our queen returns."

Penaiya pointed to the younger woman at the table. Leyan had the same dark brown eyes—the same resolute expression—as her mother.

"I understand." Charlee rubbed her sweaty palms and realized her feet were tapping on the floor.

"The men and women gathered around this table have been called upon to serve as tribal leaders to help me keep order and maintain a sense of hope among our people." Penaiya leaned forward. "Hope is all we have."

Charlee strummed on the table. "Like Cryton said, we—"

Penaiya continued, "For years, we roamed to keep ourselves concealed from Empress Theodora and her armies. We have been successful until today. I do not know if we will be able to recover from this attack. Too much pain and loss to overcome. Their strength is nearly lost. And there are so few of us now. Only three hundred."

Once more, Charlee nodded quietly. *Do I speak?*

"Cryton, once a general to the Guardian Michala, informed us you are of the bloodline of Michala and you have the power of the guardians." Penaiya never once blinked. "Does he speak the truth?"

"Yes!" She started to rise from her seat but Cryton gripped her hand.

"Forgive me, young Guardian, if I question the truth of Cryton's words." Penaiya folded her arms. "But you do not look much like a guardian."

Charlee frowned. "What?"

"The ancients taught the Last Guardian—a young hero—would rise in the darkest of times, and it is true the teachings are unclear as to whether that guardian would be male or female. That said, I would not have expected a guardian to be…well…so fat."

"Hey!" Charlee turned to Cryton for help.

This time, the old man stood. "Penaiya—"

"And you, Cryton. We have not seen or heard from you in nearly the span of a lifetime. Then you miraculously appear with this plump girl you call a guardian to face a small scouting party of Horeng. She belongs in a comfortable palace kitchen, not leading an army. How do we know you are not one of Theodora's creations? How do we know this is not a ploy to trap us?"

Charlee's mouth fell open. *I can't believe what I'm hearing.* "We just fought for you. Doesn't that mean anything?"

Cryton bent over the table toward the elders. "Penaiya, you have every reason to doubt and question. But if this girl was one of Theodora's creations, would the sorceress have generated such an imperfect guardian?"

Charlee gasped. "Hey!" She didn't need this. Bad enough a woman she didn't know made fun of her weight, but now Cryton insulted her, too. She threw up her arms. Jetting off with the changeling to face Theodora seemed better and better.

"Penaiya, as the aide to Queen Assara, you know where I have been all these years." Cryton's hand trembled as he gripped his walking stick. "You know the task placed upon me by Michala. I have come back now because this young lady is ready to be a guardian."

Charlee pushed away from the table. "Look, I don't know if I am the Last Guardian, but I have faced Theodora once and beat her. I am here to finish the job. I can help if you give me a chance. You don't have to believe me. That doesn't matter. I…uh…just want to do what I came here to do. I just want to make sure that Theodora never hurts anyone again."

Penaiya's expression softened. "If that is the case, Guardian, perhaps you can indeed offer our people new hope."

For the first time, she offered Charlee a slight smile and then rose from the table. "We must tend to the families of those we have lost. For your bravery today, please accept a little food and drink. It is all we have to offer. Rest and wait for my return. We have much to discuss." She bowed to Charlee and left the cabin. The others followed.

"Thanks for that 'imperfect guardian' crap." Charlee punched Cryton in the arm after the last elder passed through the entryway.

"I had to say something." Cryton tried to smile, but instead tears formed and he turned away.

She could only imagine the jumble of emotions he must be dealing with to face so much death again. It had to be too much. She placed a hand on his shoulder. Cryton grasped her hands and they embraced.

He broke away and cleared his throat. "Sorry I did not do more to defend you."

She shook her head. "Don't give it another thought, but it didn't seem like you told her about my mother—that she is the rightful queen and that I am—"

"Not the right time." He held a finger to his lips. "They can probably surmise on their own that if you are the bloodline of Michala that you also have Queen Assara's blood in you as well. But give them time. These people see Penaiya as their leader. We don't want to look like we are trying to take her place. For now, let them focus on their dead."

Charlee paced the cabin. "Cryton, I don't want to replace her. I don't even want to be here. We can't stay here. We have to move on. We have a job to do."

He twisted his white mustache, bushy eyebrows narrowed in a frown. "I think Penaiya has more to say, and you need to hear it. Besides, I don't believe in accidents. We were meant to be here—now in these woods—to find the people of Latara. There's a reason for it. I'm sure of that. This is where you need to be. I think you need these people as much as they need you."

"I don't know."

"I do." Cryton managed a smile.

"And what if you're wrong?" She raked her fingers through her greasy hair.

"It wouldn't be the first time." He placed an arm around her shoulders.

§ § §

Janasara's three moons, arranged in a triangle formation, climbed over the tree line by the time Penaiya returned. Darkness settled over the wilderness. Small campfires spread throughout the clearing as the grim task of burying the dead continued. People chanted sorrowful hymns, hushed but loud at the same time. Charlee watched from the cabin, wiping away her own tears. What if her mom or dad or even Megan had been among the dead? How would she deal with that kind of loss? How could these people deal with it?

Penaiya strolled up to them, seeming to glide over the land as her robe hid her feet. She stood a bit hunched over as if she carried a heavy sandbag on her shoulders.

Charlee stood with the unicorn and Cryton, who leaned on his staff, outside the cabin. She had wanted to leave, but the old man insisted they wait. This was a mistake. She had the medallion. Now was the time to find Theodora and use it.

"I am sorry to have kept you waiting." Penaiya tried to manage a smile but her chin quivered. A single tear fell. "The task of burying the dead is never an easy one. I trust you have had food and drink and are sufficiently revived."

Charlee's eyes drooped. She just wanted sleep but didn't dare say so, not after everything these lost souls faced. Death. Pain. Anguish. Doubt filled her thoughts like a constant drip in a sink, getting louder and louder. Their journey to Theodora hadn't even begun, and already blood had been spilled.

"Yes." Cryton answered. "Thank you for your kindness. I know this is a difficult time. I feel it more than you know."

Penaiya grasped his hand. "Please, walk with me."

She led them on a path among the Latarans. A hundred or so wooden huts, many consumed by fire, spread out in a circular formation, like the strands of a spinning galaxy. People in rags huddled together. Parents held their children. Some stared at her as they passed. Whispers filled the night. With her enhanced hearing, she listened to their quiet conversations. Some declared she might be a guardian. Others wanted to believe but weren't ready. How could a young girl, a plump girl at that who did not look like a warrior, be the one sent to help them?

Penaiya held her hands out to her people as they passed by, touching shoulders, arms, even faces. Her gestures were met by smiles. She was more than their leader…a mother reassuring her children they would be safe. A few extended their hands to Charlee. She avoided their touch until Cryton glared at her.

"They need to know that you are real," he uttered.

She didn't respond but stopped flinching when fingers touched her arms or patted her shoulders.

Penaiya led them beyond the village into the towering trees where arching branches blocked the moonlight. The leaf creatures, emitting a pulsating white glow, beckoned to her, their voices filling her mind like a constant wringing in the ear. Could the others hear the leaves at all? Was it the guardian abilities that allowed her to hear their telepathic words?

"We are pleased to see you, Guardian." The leaves buzzed with energy, like power lines sometimes do overhead. "We will stand with you to save The Our."

"*Thank you*," she responded without words.

The tree branches lowered, allowing the moonlight to reach the wilderness floor. Sapphire-colored undergrowth, shimmering under the illuminated night sky, led them farther into the woods.

Penaiya stopped by the spiraling trunk of one massive tree whose branches disappeared into the night. "Guardian, your coming has already generated excitement among the people."

Charlee leaned against the tree. A balmy evening breeze, thick with moisture, tossed her hair. She swept away a few wet strands stuck to her forehead. "I can hear them whispering about me. They don't know what to think of me."

Cryton hobbled on his staff like an old man, not the agile knight he'd been earlier. Was he just tired? She hoped that's all it was. With some effort, he lumbered around the tree once before sitting on top of a fallen log. The changeling, still a unicorn, clomped in a wider circle.

"They know, Charlee." Her mentor grinned. "They know you are a guardian."

Penaiya sighed. "Young one, long our people have waited for a leader to guide them to sanctuary from Theodora until the rightful queen comes who can help us win back our great kingdom."

Charlee adjusted the pouch strap over her shoulder. "You said there are three hundred in your village. Are they the only survivors of Latara—of all the kingdoms? So few? I can't believe it."

The Lataran leader lowered her head. "Our people were slaughtered or imprisoned. There may be pockets out there, like us. Other survivors, but our paths have not crossed. It is possible the Horeng found the others and killed them all. Two beasts found us a year ago at a different site where we set up a home for ourselves. They killed many before we stopped them. Then we fled here. I just don't know what lies beyond these few lives whose welfare has been my responsibility." Penaiya lifted her head. The wrinkles around her eyes softened. "I hope there are more—that our kind will not be erased from Janasara. Maybe you will guide us to a new future."

Charlee stared at her cracked boots. What was Penaiya suggesting? "I could never do what you've done. Never be the leader you are. You've kept them safe. You're their future."

The aging woman shook her head. "I am no leader. At least not the one they need. If you are a guardian, you can open a gateway and deliver them to a new home…a new beginning."

Charlee stepped closer to her. "Penaiya, I…uh…well…I don't have that much power. Not yet, anyway. I can feel it when I open a gateway. I cannot keep it open for long. I really can't open anything big enough to move all three hundred people. I just…I can't handle anything that big. I'm sorry."

Penaiya's gaze shifted to Cryton. "I do not understand."

He stood and gripped her hand. "She has only begun to tap into her abilities. She grows stronger every day, but is not yet ready for anything that big. Perhaps someday soon, but not now. That said, you should not doubt her ability to help. I've seen her courage. I've witnessed her splendid actions. She is a guardian."

I don't like where this conversation is going, Charlee thought. She glared at the three golden moons. "I crossed into this world for one reason—to face Theodora and kill her. If I can stop her, your people will be safe. You have to understand."

"I do." Penaiya tugged her hand away from Cryton's. "I do not wish to keep you from your quest. You must do what you believe to be right. But I wish to correct you, if I may. You refer to the people you see in this forest as my people. If you are truly of the bloodline of the Guardian Michala, then they are your people as well."

"I…I know." Charlee swung back toward them. "I'm sorry I let this happen to them, but I'm not the one they need. It's you…and Cryton. Not me."

"Well," Penaiya turned back to the huts. "I must gather the people. We will have to search for a new home now. You may have killed the Horeng, but it is possible Empress Theodora saw us through her dark arts. She will come for us, just as she came for the others. We will not be her slaves. This I swear."

Charlee's heart pounded faster. Penaiya's voice was resolute. Was she prepared to die? Were they all ready to die rather than fall to Theodora? Her chest ached. What was she supposed to do? Abandon them? How could she? She glanced to Cryton for guidance, but the old man offered none. There must be some safe place for them to go. Then a name came to her. One that might offer hope to the people of Latara. "Cryton, you once told me about the Dragon Lord."

He stroked his mustache roughly and raised an eyebrow. "Yes, I told you the coward refused to help."

She stepped toward him. "If he still lives, maybe he could help now. Maybe I could convince him."

"What?" He slammed his staff against the ground.

She crossed her arms. "The Dragon Lord may be these people's only hope."

CHAPTER 13

The Guide

PENAIYA'S JAW DROPPED. Her hair whipped side to side as she shook her head. She then stormed off toward the village, uttering over and over again, "We cannot seek asylum among the dragons. I will not ask for their help. Ever!"

Charlee sighed and ran after her. "Why?"

"Long ago, the dragons turned a blind eye to Theodora and the threat she posed," Penaiya said, her lips trembling. "The Dragon Lord could have stood with Michala, but the cowardly beast decided our destruction was of no concern to the dragons." Her eyes widened, hands clenched into fists. "No hope is to be found among the dragons."

Charlee exchanged glances with Cryton. He'd been silent too long.

He maneuvered behind Penaiya, driving his staff into the ground with such force it kicked up dirt. "She's right. In our time of need, when Michala sought help, the Dragon Lord shunned him. As far as I'm concerned, the dragons are as much my enemy as Theodora is."

Siding with her over me. Really? Charlee thought. She kicked a rock. "Cryton, tell me why."

He raised a gray eyebrow. "The Dragon Lord stayed out of the Unified Kingdoms' war with Theodora. We might have had a chance with the dragons' help, but they never came. They left us to die. In my book, that makes them the enemy."

Charlee crossed her arms. "That was a long time ago. Things change. If the dragons' realm is free from Theodora, maybe they'll help now." She grasped Penaiya's arm. "Look, I understand what you're saying, but there's no other way. People change...maybe even dragons change. We have to try."

Charlee couldn't believe what she was about to say. "I'll lead your... our... people to the dragons' realm and convince the Dragon Lord to accept us. That's all I can think to do."

"And what if we are turned away?" Penaiya asked. "What then?"

"I don't know," Charlee answered. "But you can't stay here, and you can't keep running with Theodora always two steps behind."

Cryton leaned on his staff. "What if Theodora has enslaved the dragons?"

How could she know? Jeez, she just offered to lead these people on a crazy journey when it's the last thing she wanted to do. "We'll figure that out when the time comes. The way I see it, we'll face bigger problems long before we reach the dragons. Theodora probably already knows I'm here, and she's going to come for me. We'll have to move fast to stay ahead of her and the Horeng."

She gripped her sword's handle with one hand, the other clutching the pouch with the medallion. "If you want me to stay, you have to do things my way. Follow me to the Dragon Lord."

"All right, Guardian." The old man placed a hand on her shoulder. "Perhaps you can do what your grandfather was unable to—win over the Dragon Lord." He gazed east toward mountains barely visible through the foliage but highlighted by the glow of the three moons. They loomed like giants standing watch over the land. "I hope you know how to get us there. The dragons' realm is somewhere beyond those peaks. It's a land of magic where no man or woman has ever been, not even your grandfather. The one time they met it was among those very mountains."

Charlee gulped. She had no idea how to reach the dragons, but somehow she'd figure it out. "I will find a way to get us there."

Penaiya maintained a frown. "Young Guardian, I will heed your words. We will seek out the dragons. Our people will follow you. I will make sure of that. They will believe, for the first time in a long while, that they and their children have a future even if you are leading them to certain death."

Charlee lumbered to the unicorn and leaned against the steed to keep from falling. She really stepped in it this time. How was she supposed to lead so many people to the dragons? This was a huge mistake. *What have I done?*

Bile rose up her stomach into her throat. She waited for Penaiya and Cryton to head back to the village and then the vomit came.

After throwing up for the second time, Charlee reached up to the unicorn to steady herself. "Bike, what have I gotten myself into? How many more people will die because they think I know what I'm doing?"

She spit out a last bit of hurl and patted her changeling protector. "I can't let these people down, but I shouldn't be leading them. I should be going off on my own to face Theodora."

The unicorn stomped its front hoof and rubbed its snout against her face.

Charlee patted the unicorn's muscular neck. "You're trying to comfort me, aren't you? Thanks. You think I can do this, don't you?"

The unicorn stomped its hoof a second time.

She smiled. "I hope you're right."

Leaves rustled behind her. Expecting to see Cryton, she spun around, wiping her mouth. A slime-green mist twisted through the grass. Formless, like fog in the Bay back home, the vapor inched toward her. She retreated behind the unicorn. The air around her froze as if a winter frost cocooned her. Charlee wrapped her arms around her body but couldn't stop shivering. She tried to call out to Cryton, but her breath turned to ice, her voice reduced to a teeth-chattering whisper.

She pressed against the changeling's body. "It…it's her…bi….bike. Theodora. I… can…fe…feel it."

The mist stopped a few feet away from the changeling. The green muck glowed brighter with each pulse. Peering underneath the unicorn, Charlee lifted her sword. "We should…get out…of—"

A gust blew through the trees, kicking up fallen leaves. The wind whipped up the mist, swirling it into a dust devil. Charlee gasped. The radiating vortex morphed until it took a human form, one she expected but feared just the same.

She grasped the medallion inside the pouch and stepped in front of the unicorn. "Theodora."

The squall quieted. Her great aunt, more apparition than solid form, floated before her as the young princess of her dreams.

"Welcome, child." Theodora's voice was gentle and sweet as it had been when they met in Charlee's dreams. "Welcome to your home."

Though a useless gesture, Charlee hefted her sword and slashed. The blade passed through air, striking nothing.

"Is that any way to greet your great aunt?"

Charlee swung her sword a second time. A third. And a fourth. "If you know I'm here, why don't you come and fight me?" she uttered, breathing heavy.

"Oh, we will meet in due time, and I will have what is mine." The sorceress circled her. "But first, I thought I would have some enjoyment at your expense."

"What do you mean?" Charlee gazed toward the village. What was she going to do now? She had to get back to the others.

"I am well aware of all that has transpired since you crossed into my world." Theodora's image morphed from young princess to an aging woman with graying hair and long bony fingers. "I saw you through the eyes of my Horeng. In fact, I took great pride in watching how easily you killed—how quickly evil penetrated your veins."

"What?" Charlee's body grew rigid.

"You enjoyed slaughtering my minions, didn't you?"

"What? No!"

"Yes, you did. That's why I know you will join me before long. I shall have great fun helping you discover your true self—just as you did when you saw the image on the medallion. Do you remember the face you saw?" Theodora laughed.

Charlee released her grip on the medallion. Her legs weakened as the weight of the black object caused her knees to buckle. She drove the tip of the sword into the ground to balance herself. *It's not heavy*, she reasoned with herself. *It's just in your mind. Stay strong.*

"I have been in your head, child," Theodora's ghostly form floated next to her, close enough to touch. "And part of me remains lodged in the darkest corners of your mind. I am always with you."

"No," Charlee shouted.

"Yes." Theodora's ghostly fingers caressed her cheek like a frosty draft. "Now heed my warning. My armies are already on the move, heading in your direction. All these useless creatures you are now protecting—this trash from Latara—will die unless you come to me now. Bring me what is rightfully mine. Join me."

Theodora took a long breath before speaking again. "I have a surprise for you…an old friend waiting to see you again."

"Tribon!" Charlee's teeth clenched.

The giant knight had pretended to be her mentor, only to betray her. He had been a general under her grandfather but, through dark magic, surrendered his heart to become Theodora's slave.

"Perhaps." The sorceress' lips parted in a twisted grin. "We await you."

"You won't have to wait long!" Charlee punched at Theodora, but her fist passed through the apparition. She stumbled forward, falling to the ground. Her great aunt erupted in laughter then slowly faded into the night. Charlee climbed to her feet. "When I see you again, aunty, I'll end this."

§ § §

Astride the unicorn, Charlee raced back to the village, dodging low-hanging branches. Though the leaf-creatures tried to move out of her way, some branches scratched her cheeks, like tiny daggers scraping her skin. "I have to tell Cryton. We can't stay here. We have to go after Theodora. There's no other way."

Her thoughts spun out of control as the changeling leaped over a boulder. How could she lead them to the dragons' realm with no idea how to find it? But if they went after Theodora, they'd be walking into a trap. If she failed, these people wouldn't stand a chance against the Horeng army. What was the right thing to do?

"Think, Charlee. I'm supposed to be—"

A blinding flash exploded before her like a firework. She turned away, shielding her eyes with her hands, but the searing white light penetrated her fingers and closed eyelids.

"It burns!" Charlee tumbled from the unicorn but never struck the ground. *What the…?*

Slowly opening her eyes, Charlee hovered over the trees, only without her body. No hands or feet. No torso. No sword or medallion. Nothing, as if her spirit had separated from her physical form, existing on an otherworldly domain.

Gone, too, was the changeling.

This couldn't be real. What was this? Cryton…bike—?

As if catapulted on the world's fastest roller coaster, she launched away from the wilderness. The forest gave way to open prairies of blue grass. She screamed in silence. *Can't…stop.*

From the fields, she rocketed to mountains as massive as the Coastal Range back home, then passed into a ravine, weaving through a pathway between two rocky goliaths. Faster and faster she soared, emerging from the rocky passage to a beach of white sands. The journey accelerated to a sprawling city built along a horseshoe-shaped cove. Wooden sailing vessels anchored to a harbor that stretched into a vast blue sea.

What was she seeing?

At dizzying speeds, she passed onto a sea unlike any body of water back home. Water spouts climbed from the depths, rising toward the sky. At their peaks, they arched like a canopy of leaves in the forest. These towering columns, like waterfalls flowing upward, stretched toward the horizon. What was this place? Where was her vision leading her?

Charlee zoomed to a group of islands. Maybe twenty. She flew by them all until arriving at the last—and the largest. Crashing waves gave way to a jungle and a single mountain with a peak hidden by a cover of white clouds.

Passing through that misty barrier, a chill washed over her like the feel of the early morning fog blowing along the shore of the San Francisco Bay. Still, she climbed, the air growing thicker as she gained altitude. At such heights, she labored for each breath against the pressure mounting on her invisible chest.

Finally, Charlee reached the summit. As if someone slammed on the breaks, she came to a jarring halt. Before her stood a golden statue of a massive dragon. Could this be the dragons' realm? Was it possible? Was this a dream?

"I have watched you, Guardian," a deep guttural voice declared in English.

"Who said that?"

"Do you know who I am?" The statue's eyes glowed orange.

"Dragon Lord?"

"Yes."

"I'm dreaming, right? This isn't real." This couldn't be. She fell from the unicorn, bumped her head, and was losing it.

"Do not doubt your senses." The statue's eyes pulsated. "I have tapped into your subconscious, so that we might communicate."

"You know I'm getting tired of people and creatures invading my thoughts." She raised her voice. "You're not just some statue, are you? Show yourself."

"I have no desire to reveal my true being."

"How is it you can speak my—"

"Young human, I have not summoned you to answer questions." Black smoke poured from the statue's snout. "I have but one message for you. I know of what you contemplate. To bring your people to my realm."

"Right."

"I will not permit it. You will find no sanctuary here. You will bring nothing but death upon your people. This is the one warning I offer to you. Stay away or suffer my wrath."

"But why? How can you be so cruel?"

"We shall communicate no further."

"Wait…please!" Though she had no visible body, her heart pounded in her ears. Ice spread through her stomach. She had to find a way to convince the Dragon Lord. He had to understand. To help them. But how? "I'll do anything you ask. Just help my people. I'm begging you."

Fire spewed from the dragon statue, engulfing her in an inferno. Orange and yellow flames danced around her, mocking her, but she felt nothing—no heat nor any sensation at all other than a sense of numbness. She imagined it might be the same feeling her grandfather had when the Dragon Lord refused to help him. What was she supposed to do now? Lie to everyone? What choice did she have?

When the inferno disappeared, she was back in the wilderness riding atop the unicorn, her sword belted at her waist, the medallion at her side. Charlee lowered her head into her hands and released a lungful of air.

"Bike, did that just happen? Did the Dragon Lord just warn me not to come? Or was it a Theodora trick? I didn't sense evil like I do when she's around. It felt real, and he is refusing to help."

Charlee shook her fist toward the sky. "Why, Dragon Lord? Tell me why you'd keep us out. Talk to me. What are you…a coward? Is that why you wouldn't help my grandfather?"

She peered through the trees in the direction of the village. Yes, she would lie to them. Her vision revealed the way to the dragons, and she would lead them there and face the Dragon Lord. Make him change his mind.

Lifting her head toward the mountains, she proclaimed, "Guess what, dude. We're coming. You owe my people."

CHAPTER 14

A Guardian's Lie

Y AH," CHARLEE SHOUTED, her legs pressing against the unicorn's body, urging the changeling to race back to Latara's refugees. Branches lifted away as the trees made way for her. Wind brushed against her cheeks and whipped her hair across her face.

She rode with an ominous message. Theodora knew she was here, and the sorceress would be coming. The question was…how long did they have?

A pair of trees up ahead parted, and the unicorn leaped past them into the clearing. Flickering lights poured through makeshift windows in the huts still standing, giving them the appearance of large fireflies in an open field. The survivors huddled together outside by a scattering of campfires. Most climbed to their feet when the unicorn slid to a halt. Some lifted swords. Parents grabbed their children. All eyes fell on her.

In the changeling's haste, the magical beast rushed past Cryton who stood at the edge of the forest, staff gripped in both hands. As she and the unicorn doubled back, he folded his arms across his chest, mustache bristling. "Where have you—?"

"She knows I'm here." Charlee leapt off the unicorn and grabbed him by his tunic's collar.

"What?" He grasped her hands.

"She knows I'm here." Charlee tugged her hands free. "She's sending her entire Horeng army after us. If we're going to save these people, we have to run… now. And the only place we can go is the dragons' realm."

Cryton glared past her at Latara's remnants. Many left the warmth of their fires and pressed closer to them. Penaiya gathered with the other elders outside the cabin in the village's center. The five young hunters who had killed the Horeng with their bows and arrows stood silhouetted by orange flames.

Her aging mentor lowered his voice. "This is madness."

Charlee shook her head. "No, the Dragon Lord reached out to me, Cryton. He told me we're welcome in his realm. He showed me the way. It'll be a hard journey, but I think I can get us there."

She only half lied. The path to the dragons' realm lay etched in her mind like a Google map. She could lead her people to the islands. Would the dragons devour them once there? The Dragon Lord made it clear. *You will bring nothing but death.*

What choice did she have but to risk it? Somehow, if they survived the trek, she'd have to convince the Dragon Lord to spare them.

"How did he reach out to you?" Cryton leaned on his staff. "Through a portal? Did you try to reach the dragons' realm by opening a gateway?"

"I didn't have to." Beads of sweat tickled her upper lip. *Stay calm.* She had to make him believe. "He spoke to me telepathically like Mom sometimes does. In my mind, I traveled to a group of islands across a sea just beyond the mountains to the east. Those islands belong to the dragons."

Cryton stroked his mustache. "How could the Dragon Lord know your idea? How does he even know you're here?"

She shrugged. "How does Theodora know I'm here? It's magic. He said he's been watching me. I don't know for how long. Who cares? These people have a chance if we can get there."

He rubbed his head. "Why would the Dragon Lord choose now to help?"

"People change."

"He's a dragon."

Charlee threw up her hands. "Then dragons change."

"How do you know this isn't all some trick?" He waved a finger at her like her mom sometimes did. "How do you know the Dragon Lord and Theodora aren't scheming together to stop you and kill us all?"

"I don't." She leaned against the unicorn. "I just sense the Dragon Lord isn't evil."

He scoffed. "A sense, huh?"

"Yeah." Charlee had to make him believe because then the others would, too.

A familiar smile returned to Cryton's face. "So you say the dragons' realm is across a sea. How do you suppose we get there?"

"On the other side of those eastern mountains there's a city along the shore. It has a harbor filled with large sailed boats kind of like pirate ships." She pointed beyond the trees. "I don't know if people live there, but we can use those boats."

Cryton's fingers strummed his staff. "You speak of the port town of Balayian. It was under the control of a rogue band of shipping traders, led by a man—Polantro Meor—who called himself a lord. Because of its distance beyond the Great Temora Mountains, Balayian never joined the Unified Kingdoms. Meor preferred it that way. I don't know if he still lives."

Penaiya joined them, her fingers interlocked at her waist, dark shadows under her eyes. "The man you speak of does not live. He was killed by his own people. They feared Theodora and wanted to abandon the port. He refused to let anyone leave, so they killed him and then took their sailing vessels into the sea. They were never heard from again. Balayian is abandoned. The craft you saw must be what remains. I doubt they would be seaworthy, but if what you say is true, and the Horeng army pursues us, we must head east."

Thank you, Penaiya. Charlee fought the urge to embrace the woman. "Listen to her, Cryton."

Penaiya frowned. "You forget one point, Guardian. There is no way our people can climb the Temoras. The mountains divide this world and rise to the heavens."

"That's right," Cryton added. "It would be like trying to climb the Himalayas on Earth."

Charlee forced a slight grin. "No, there's a ravine that cuts all the way through the mountains. I saw it. Trust me. It's wide enough for us to pass through."

Her gaze shifted back and forth between Cryton and Penaiya. They became quiet. Charlee bit her upper lip. What were they thinking? Why didn't they say something?

Cryton broke the silence. "Guardian, I will follow your lead." He bowed to her.

Penaiya lowered her head and sighed deeply. "I will prepare our people for the journey ahead. Guardian, for all our sakes, I hope you are right." She motioned to her fellow elders and hurried to the villagers.

Charlee swallowed saliva. Did she make a mistake by lying about the Dragon Lord? No, she had to.

Placing an arm around her shoulder, Cryton ushered Charlee away from the stares of those who now seemed ready to put their trust in her, even if it wasn't deserved. They stopped at the edge of the tree line where the clearing gave way to forest. Peering over his shoulder once, he bent down on one knee. His body creaked. "How bad is our situation, Charlee?" he asked. "How long do we have until the Horeng overtake us? I fear we will not be able to move quickly enough to reach the Temoras."

Charlee traced the edges of the medallion inside the pouch with her fingers. She couldn't believe what she was about to suggest. "What if I open a portal to the Kingdom of Latara? Theodora's there. I know it. If that's where her army is marching from, we could get a look at its size. See how far the Horeng are from us. Then jump back before being caught. At least we'll know what we're up against."

Cryton patted her on the shoulder. "Look at you…thinking like a guardian. Your grandfather would be proud. I'm proud of you."

She nodded but avoided eye contact. What kind of a guardian told lies to give false hope? No, her grandfather wouldn't be proud. He'd be ashamed. She was gambling with the lives of everyone and didn't have a clue what she was doing.

CHAPTER 15

An Army Rises

THEY STEPPED FROM the gateway's shimmering blue light into the cover of a raven black night, their presence hidden by a formation of boulders. Latara stood maybe a football field away. An orange glow rose from inside its protective walls. Black smoke billowed into the sky from somewhere inside the kingdom, casting the three moons in a blood-red shade.

Even the gloom of the midnight hour couldn't disguise the devastated countryside. In her visions of Latara, Charlee had seen spiraling trees and grass fields. Here the land was barren—a bleak desert that no longer sustained life. Uprooted tree stumps were the only reminder of what once flourished throughout the land.

Dust swept up from the cracked earth irritated her eyes. She breathed it in, the soot coating her throat. The tiny grains felt like little slivers of glass sliding down her windpipe. Charlee held her hand to her mouth to muffle a cough. Beside her, the changeling shape shifted from a unicorn into a white snake, probably to stay hidden but also to avoid the gritty air.

Cryton reached down and scooped up a handful of sand. He watched it slide between his fingers. "As a child I played all over this countryside, climbing trees that stretched to the clouds. Now look at it. Look what that witch has done."

Charlee placed a hand on his shoulder. "Maybe it's not too late to save it. If we kill her, maybe things can return back the way they were. Maybe my mom's magic will be strong enough to fix this."

"I hope, Guardian." His lips parted in a slight smile, but it quickly faded. "But you did not bring us to Latara to listen to an old man babble over his youth. Let's see what we're facing."

He glanced over the boulders. Charlee crouched, peering around the edge. The Horeng army filed through the arched gates of the kingdom, stomping over the land with enough force to shake the ground. They sent dust clouds into the sky. Their rhythmic pace boomed like thunder rolling in from the distance.

She covered her mouth. Adrenaline pumped through her veins; panic stole her breath. Charlee studied the army with her super vision, enhanced by the changeling. In columns, the wolves—trudging on their hind legs, massive shoulders hunched, poured through the kingdom's towering entryway, fifty feet tall. Just like her dreams, two giant carvings of Lataran warriors, one on either side of the entrance, guarded the kingdom. Now, their faces were scorched, replaced by Theodora's image.

The sorceress' monsters traveled shoulder to shoulder twenty wide. They carried torches, axes and banners. Some rode atop massive horses. They journeyed east, those farthest ahead disappearing into the night. The beasts, covered in dark armor, snapped their jaws and howled to the moons, excited to kill the prey they pursued. Charlee covered her ears, but the Horeng's cries of delight pierced her mind.

"Look at that!" Cryton whispered. "I haven't seen an army that large since the Battle for the Kingdom of Menara. That was the last of the Ten Unified Kingdoms to fall before Latara. I was there. I fought alongside Michala before he sent me to Earth."

Her heart thrashing in her chest, Charlee inched behind the boulders. "There's too many of them. We have to get away. We have to get home. This was a mistake."

Cryton lowered down to her. "Don't despair, Guardian."

She barely listened. She sat cross-legged in the dirt and buried her head in her hands. She'd seen enough. Her lips quivered. It was worse than she could have imagined. "I was wrong. We can't escape that horde. We'll get everyone killed."

"Charlee, we can succeed because you have your grandfather's blood flowing through you." With his finger, Cryton lifted her chin. "Have faith in yourself. I believe in you."

The changeling slid onto her lap and twisted around her arm. Its tongue flicked against her cheek. Her fingers caressed the scaly skin. She grinned at the changeling. "I know. Don't give up, right?" she whispered. "That's what you're trying to tell me, isn't it? I still have the both of you with me…and the medallion."

She peered around the boulders one more time. The realm looked so different than her dreams. The gleaming white outer walls from her visions crumbled. Some sections caved in. Black filth coated the sides. The castle chiseled from the mountainside overlooking Latara no longer sparkled like quartz. The sections she could see beyond the outer wall resembled the old abandoned warehouses along the waterfront back home. Cold. Abandoned. Rickety. A ramshackle mess of eroding stone. "What have you done, Theodora?"

The orange glow behind the deteriorating outer fortress brightened. More smoke rose into the skies.

Cryton crept beside her. "Do you see her factories burning into the night, forging weapons for her army? She's taken all that was good and made it part of her evil machine. I promise you I'll have my revenge for all she's taken from our people."

Charlee wanted revenge, too. That's why she journeyed to Janasara, but now, seeing what they were up against, she shuddered. They'd be lucky to survive. "We should get out of here. Theodora might already know we're here. What if she senses the medallion is close? We've stayed too long."

Hugging the pouch close, she climbed to her feet. A new thought crossed her mind, one that caused the hairs of the back of her neck to stiffen and bubbles to dance inside her stomach. What would happen if they did stop Theodora? She hadn't told Cryton about the vision of her face on the medallion. What if she was doomed to be Theodora's evil replacement? Should she tell him? No…Charlee just couldn't let it happen.

She gazed once more at the Horeng, pushing hair from her eyes, but something…or someone else…atop the wall caught her attention.

"Cryton, look!" She pointed to a figure clad in armor standing over the entryway. "Is it Tribon?"

The old man slowly climbed to his feet. "Could be. Hard to tell from here. This one doesn't seem quite as large as him."

"Then who—?"

Something worse rose from behind the armored being. A beast with a long neck and massive head. Fangs protruded from a snout. Yellow eyes stared into the distance. The shadowy outline of wings spread behind the towering monster.

She grasped the old man around the waist like a frightened child. The changeling hissed.

"Cryton, is that—?"

"Looks like it." The old man stroked his mustache. "A dragon."

Her insides turned to ice. It couldn't be! "Does this mean the dragons are fighting on Theodora's side?"

"I don't know." He placed an arm around her. "Before, when the Dragon Lord refused to help us, he stayed out of it. He never actually fought with Theodora. Maybe now he has taken her side. Like I said, maybe when he reached out to you, it was a trick."

Scratching her hair, now gritty with dust, she whirled away from the beast. "No, he's not evil. Something's—"

"Charlee, don't despair. This dragon may not even have ties to the Dragon Lord. It's a mystery we'll deal with later. For now, stick with your plan—and we don't tell anyone else."

"How fast can a dragon fly?" she asked.

"Much too fast," Cryton uttered. "We must make our exit now. Be careful. If that is a real dragon, it can detect the slightest movement. We need to slip away and create some distance from it before you can open another gateway."

Charlee, Cryton, and the white snake crawled from their vantage point. Her mind fumbled over the image of the armored being and the dragon. Bad times lay ahead. How could they outrun a dragon?

Before she opened a gateway, the beast unleashed a terrible cry into the night. Perhaps a warning. Death came for them.

§ § §

89

Charlee was back on Alcatraz Island under a dim midnight sky. Behind her stood a mournful prison barracks wall. In front of her, a car's length away, Theodora sneered, wrinkles embedded deep in her aging face. At the sorceress's side, Sandra. A gray void replaced her best friend's warm brown eyes.

Theodora hurled red energy in the form of cannonballs at her. Charlee blocked each with her hands. The blasts scorched her palms, but nothing stopped her. She would make Theodora pay for kidnapping her friend.

Charlee pushed toward the witch until Sandra stepped in front of her. With an empty stare, her friend drove a stinging punch into her face. She fell to the ground, rubbing her cheek.

"Sandra, please wake up."

"What's a matter, Charlee? Still afraid to fight, like at school?" Sandra spoke, but Theodora's voice replaced hers.

Charlee screamed.

"Guardian, wake up. You're safe." Cryton's words cut through the dream.

Her eyes flickered open. Cryton leaned over her, a weary smile across his face. Above him, darkness gave way to a soft green haze. Streaks of sunlight crossed the sky, breaking through high puffy clouds. Daybreak came much too quickly after a restless sleep. Her head felt heavy, eyelids even heavier. If Charlee was home, she'd beg her mom for another fifteen minutes in bed, but this wasn't home. Her mom was a dimension away. Then again, more sleep meant reliving the day Theodora kidnapped and twisted Sandra's mind. Such memories haunted her dreams. Probably always would.

Charlee shook her head as she blinked away the last bit of sleep. She shouldn't have listened to Cryton. After they returned to the village through the portal, her mentor ordered her to get some sleep, saying their journey could wait till daybreak. She reluctantly agreed, lying in a bed of fallen leaves with the changeling, back in unicorn form, standing over her.

She climbed to her feet, rubbing her eyes. A crisp morning breeze, a respite from the heat, rustled her hair. A scent of pine tickled her nose, a welcome change from the stench of charred wood. Behind Cryton, Latara's refugees labored like a well-disciplined army, breaking down the camp in preparation for a long march. Even the children helped. Some Latarans glanced her way. A few smiled and nodded toward her when she stood.

Charlee adjusted the strap to the pouch over her shoulder and reached inside, running her fingers over the black object. She breathed a sigh of relief. Still there. As long as she had the medallion, she had a chance to defeat Theodora. "You let me sleep too long."

"You needed a couple of hours." Cryton gripped his staff. "I did, too. Are you all right? You were tossing and turning, speaking your friend's name."

"I'm fine." She snatched up her sword from the ground. Grime covered her hands and wrists. A shower would be so nice. Charlee could only imagine what she looked like. Her smell must be even worse, but there was no time to clean. Where would she rinse off anyway?

Penaiya, her hair loosely draped around her face, hurried toward Charlee after directing a group of children where to place armfuls of clothing. "Good morning, Guardian."

Her daughter, Leyan, also approached. The younger woman said nothing. She just stood with her arms crossed, lips bent in a frown.

Charlee cleared her throat. "Sorry I slept so long. I shouldn't—"

Penaiya held up a hand. "You do not need to apologize. Sleep was due. I have been in consultation with Cryton this morning. He informed me of your travels back to Latara during the night and the vastness of the enemy that marches toward us. He says we may have a few days of lead time on the Horeng, but they will quickly make up the distance."

"That's right." Her gaze shifted to Cryton. How much had he told her? About the mysterious dark figure? The dragon?

"Young Guardian, I realize the journey we are about to begin is dangerous and may not succeed, but our people are strong." Penaiya gestured to the men, women, and children preparing for their path ahead. "I have shared with them my belief that you are a guardian sent here to guide us where we will be safe. Most believe. They need to believe. I guess I am starting to as well."

"I understand." Charlee eyed the three hundred or so people with a sense of admiration. These people didn't squabble. They knew their lives depended on each other. Everyone toiled hastily, many hunched over, a sign they'd been working for hours while she slept.

Cursing herself, Charlee's hands formed into fists. How could she sleep while these people raced against an advancing army?

Penaiya crossed to her. "There is more you must know. After yesterday's losses, there are some who do not wish to make the journey. They will stay here with the fallen. They have lost so much already."

Charlee lowered her head. "I understand, but—"

"I will not leave them," Penaiya went on, gesturing to her daughter. "I will remain with them. Leyan will take my place as the leader of our people."

"No!" Charlee stomped her foot. "You can't do that. You...they...have to come."

If they stayed behind, the Horeng would slaughter them. What kind of guardian would she be if she allowed that? No, everyone had to come. They had to stick together. She had to make them understand.

Charlee leaped onto the unicorn's back. The changeling's energy flowed into her body. She used it to strengthen her voice, raising it to a pitch all could hear.

"People of Latara! Gather around…please." She hoped her Lengoron was strong enough to make the people understand, and that her magically enhanced voice would make them listen. "I know life has been hard for you. I know you've suffered and lost so much. I know you have every reason to want to give up."

She hesitated. The eyes of these lost souls focused on her. Cold sweat dripped from her forehead. *Breathe through each word*, she reminded herself. Easier said than done.

"Look, I don't know what the right thing to say is. Truthfully, I don't know if I'm the Last Guardian. I'm not even sure how to be a leader. And I will completely understand if anyone chooses not to come with me. But I'm asking you to give me a chance. I think I can get you to a place where you'll be safe. And I am ready to give my life to get you there." As Charlee heard herself utter the words "give my life," her stomach tightened.

She wet her lips, searching for the next thing to say. Her mouth had gone bone dry from piecing this speech together. She pulled herself up tall on the unicorn's back, took a breath, and continued

"I believe that you…uh, we…can rebuild this world. But it will take all of you to make it happen. And I will stay with you. I promise I will be by your side. Will you stay…er…stand …with me today?"

Silence met her final words.

She held her palms together as if in prayer.

Could these people tell how scared she was? Could they see her as a leader… as a guardian? More importantly, did she see herself as one? The old Charlee, the frightened loner from school, was no leader, but she wasn't that girl anymore. She couldn't be. So why was she trembling? Why did her heart race? Maybe because a bit of her old self remained. Hopefully, Charlee the Guardian would be strong enough for the journey ahead; otherwise all these people would die because of her. Then again, they might die anyway.

The stillness pressed against her like a weight on her chest. She struggled to hold her gaze firmly on the crowd.

From within the congregation, cheers started quietly. Growing to a soft roar, the mothers and fathers, brothers and sisters, sons and daughters of Latara joined in a chant.

"Ana Latara…ana tal garandian! Ana Latara…ana tal garandian!"

"For Latara…for the guardian! For Latara…for the guardian!"

Charlee looked down from the unicorn and saw Cryton at her side. The old man was beaming.

"Well done, Guardian!" Cryton mouthed. His voice was lost amidst the chanting.

CHAPTER 16

Underway

THE SUN BEGAN its slow climb, peaking from behind the eastern mountain peaks. Warmth brushed against Charlee's face. It was time. She could do this. Guide these people to the dragons' realm and convince the Dragon Lord to accept them.

She stood before the people of Latara, breathing in the sweet air of a new day. They lined up across the clearing like a wagon train from the Old West about to depart on a cross-country journey. Ahead of them, the protective cover of the forest, but eventually their path would lead them to open fields, like she saw in her vision, and then the race would be on to reach the mountains before Theodora's army hunted them down.

The refugees, most with their few belonging strapped to their backs, watched her for a command to begin their trek. Some kept peering over their shoulders as if expecting the Horeng to burst through the trees and slaughter them. Charlee, walking beside the unicorn, crossed a few yards to Cryton who placed his sword and staff into a pack on a wind horse.

"What do you think you're doing?" He spoke with a stern voice. After checking to ensure his weapons were secure, he looked at her with one bushy eyebrow raised, and his mustache hanging low in an exaggerated frown.

She furrowed her brow. "What?"

"Why aren't you on top of your mount?" He motioned for her to climb onto the unicorn's back.

Was he crazy? How could he ask that question? "Cryton, come on. How can I ride when so many others have to walk? I'm not going to ride when old women are walking. That wouldn't be right."

He shook his head. "You don't understand. This is not about giving up your seat on the subway because you see some old lady standing up. This is not about chivalry."

"But what am I supposed to do?" Charlee gestured to the crowd of homeless wanderers. "I'm trying to lead these people."

"Then lead." Cryton grasped her arm. He winked a gray eye. "Get on the unicorn. These people need to be able to see you at all times if they are to maintain faith. They need to see their leader atop her great beast, sword in hand, ready to do battle to protect them. That is what they expect from a guardian. That is what you must deliver."

She glared at her mentor for several heartbeats. He might be right, but it felt wrong. The changeling could transform into some giant beast and give a ride to children or the elderly. She would prefer that, but maybe the people did need to see her riding out front, like a leader. She would do as he suggested for now. "And what about you, Cryton?"

"I'm not a guardian."

"What does that mean?"

He smirked. "The people do not need to see me as a leader. In fact, they do not need to see this old man amongst them at all. I shall stay back about half a mile and keep watch from the rear. It will allow me to keep an eye out for the Horeng. I can be the first warning of danger."

Charlee grabbed the top of his staff. How could he abandon her? He belonged next to her. She still had so much to learn. "Cryton, I need you with me."

"No, you don't. But I will be with you—always. Now, go do your duty and let me do mine." The old man reached up and grasped both of Charlee's hands. "You'll do good things. I know it. I believe in you, Charlee Smelton. You have it in you to be a greater guardian than even your grandfather. Remember that."

He released her hands and winked. "Now leave me to prepare."

Charlee blinked back tears. Climbing onto the unicorn, she trotted away, glancing back at her mentor. Her stomach felt queasy, like she was going to lose him. That rotten pizza maker was planning on sacrificing himself, and she definitely was not ready for that.

Grinding her teeth together, Charlee pushed away that thought. She refocused on the scared travelers depending on her. *Can't let my fears get in the way,* she thought. *He's right. He has his duty and I have mine.* Guiding the unicorn among the people, she waved to them as they cleared a path and cheered for her.

She rode into the crowd to ensure everyone saw her and then galloped to the front. Penaiya and Leyan, both atop wind horses, joined her. Penaiya smiled. The Lataran matriarch sat high in her saddle, her dark robe-like cape over her shoulders. Leyan, her hair flowing freely, wore a brown animal skin outfit resembling a rough-cut jumpsuit with a canvas belt around her waist. A dagger hung from her side. Leyan bowed her head slightly, her face rigid. Charlee nodded in return. Penaiya's daughter didn't like her, but why? She'd have to worry about that later.

"Are you ready, Guardian?" Penaiya asked.

"Yes." *I hope so.*

"Then lead your people."

Charlee unsheathed her sword and whirled around on the unicorn to the three hundred faces who looked to her for hope. They stared at her with grim determination. No longer would they hide in their forest village, waiting for death to find them. They would march toward a new life led by a guardian they believed could guide them to a sanctuary. The weight of her lie caused her shoulders to droop. What would happen if the Dragon Lord turned them away? Of course if they didn't outrun the Horeng, her lie wouldn't matter anyway.

The morning breeze blew a little harder, drifting across the clearing and through the abandoned huts and fire pits. How long would it take the wilderness to swallow this makeshift village as if these people had never been here? Maybe someday, if peace ever returned to this world, this would become a holy place where people would come to remember how they survived the dark times. If they survived.

Two of the Lataran warriors she and Cryton encountered while chasing the Horeng broke from the crowd and walked up to her. They each carried a bow over their shoulder and a bag of arrows across their backs. Charlee immediately recognized the young man, the cute one with the long dark hair and brooding eyes.

He bowed. "Guardian, I am Aryean. This is Miramay." He motioned to the young woman at his side. Her bare arms were lean and muscular, nothing like Charlee's. "We wish to help. Is there anything we can do?"

She tried not to blush as he called her guardian. Why would she react like that? "Uh, yes." Charlee avoided his gaze as she spoke Lengoron. "We need someone to ride ahead. You know, like a scout, to make sure our way is safe. Take two of the wind horses. Uh, that would be a big help, but be safe."

Aryean glanced at Miramay. "It would be our honor." They bolted over to a pair of wind horses by one of the supply wagons, nimbly leaped onto the steeds' backs, and rode off into the forest.

Charlee watched them disappear into the foliage then lifted her sword for the remnants of Latara to see. "Everyone, follow me!"

From the rear of the group, across the clearing, Cryton held up a fist and raced away on his own horse to ensure no one could sneak up on them from behind.

"Goodbye, old friend," she whispered.

§ § §

Charlee led her refugees east along a path overgrown with plants and wild grass under the cover of towering trees. A heavy canopy of leaves blocked all but the merest strands of sunlight. For the first time in a while the tension in her shoulders eased. The shade comforted her like her mom's warm embrace. "I miss you, Mom," she uttered. "Can you hear me across the divide? No, probably not. Sorry I left you."

The leaf creatures above chanted a comforting chorus, signaling safe passage ahead. From behind, the rhythmic advance of her people, like students pouring into school in the morning, assured her for the moment all remained calm.

How long would it last? Was Theodora watching from afar? Was this some twisted game to the sorceress? If so, when would she strike? Charlee gripped the pouch at her side. She'd rather gallop away from everyone and face Theodora in a final battle. End this quick. But she'd chosen to be a leader; to have these lives depend on her. *Why couldn't she have been a normal teenager?* No point thinking about that now. Her life was a long way off from normal.

Penaiya and Leyan rode on either side of her. Should she tell them about her lie? That the Dragon Lord warned them to stay away. That she was a fake. No, that'd be stupid. Leyan already doubted her. It would just prove her right. No, Charlee was too deep into this now and had to see it through. Make the Dragon Lord take them in…if they made it to the reptiles' home.

Her heart started pounding. She placed her palm over her chest to quiet her pulse. *Mom, I need you,* she thought. *I was dumb to think I could do this without you.*

Up ahead, a doorway of sunlight drove back the shadows. Another clearing? Charlee raised her sword. With the same authoritative voice used to rally the people, she called out, "Everyone, stop!"

From the light, Miramay rode up to her. The young woman breathed heavy as if she'd run a race. Charlee's body tensed. "Miramay, what is it? Where's Aryean?" She tightened her grip on the unicorn's mane. If anything happened to him…

The scout pointed toward the light. "Guardian, we've reached the edge of the wilderness. The flatlands lay ahead. There is no sign of the Horeng. Aryean stayed behind to keep watch."

Charlee eased her grip. *Thank goodness.*

"Good," Penaiya responded first. "Then we can continue."

"Guardian, there is something else." Miramay breathed deeply. A strand of her curled hair fell over one eye. "Something difficult to explain."

"What?" Charlee clutched the pouch, pressing against the medallion inside.

Miramay turned her wind horse toward the light. "You have to see it for yourself. The sky. The land. Something is very wrong. I've never seen the like. Please, Guardian. Come with me."

Willing her hands not to tremble, she leaned toward Penaiya. "Uh…if I'm not back within ten minutes, you'll know there's danger. Lead the people back deeper into the forest. And if I don't return at all…" She let the thought trail off.

"Perhaps I should go with you," Leyan offered.

"No," Charlee responded abruptly. "I mean, I can handle this."

"As you wish." Leyan scowled.

"If it's safe, I'll signal you." She clicked the sides of the unicorn to follow Miramay. "When you see my signal, move everyone forward. If you don't, you know what to do."

She and her unicorn trotted forward with a slow gait. Miramay rode ahead. As each step brought the sunlit clearing closer, she squeezed the pouch. Drawing energy from the trees and the leaf creatures, Charlee bolstered her strength. Her vision sharpened, hearing enhanced, and limbs gained muscle. Tinges of weariness drifted away.

"Courage," a thousand leaves declared in unison. "We see no danger ahead."

"Thank you," Charlee uttered in their language. *Steady yourself.*

Sunlight reached out to her like giant fingers. The shadowy layer underneath the overgrowth shielded her from the heat, but inching closer to the light was like moving toward a furnace. That might be an overstatement. More like a stifling summer day after a rain when the air feels like a hot, damp blanket wrapped around your body. Sweat dripped between her shoulder blades. "Geez, this world is hot," she whispered." Cryton hadn't warned her about that.

Finally, they passed from the shadows into the blinding beams that broke through the tree line. The rays should have been comforting. She preferred day to night, but leaving behind the cool, protective cover of the wilderness made her want to shrink back into the darkness.

Miramay was the first to climb from her wind horse. She joined Aryean who crouched behind a trunk.

"Guardian, you have to see this." He motioned to her.

Sliding off the unicorn, Charlee crept into the open sunlight. At first, the brightness burned her eyes. For a fearful moment, she couldn't focus her gaze. She was vulnerable and didn't like it. Blinking rapidly, she quickly adjusted, and the world beyond the trees became clear.

An emerald green day spread across open fields stretching toward the Temora mountains. For a heartbeat it was just like her dreams. Grass in hues of purple and blue covered the ground. Corkscrew-shaped trees the size of skyscrapers spiraled into the sky. The Temoras stretched as far as she could see, their peaks disappearing into silver clouds circling above the mountain range. Meandering across the countryside, a river flowed with glassy water alternating between shades of green, blue, yellow and red, like the flavors of the Slurpee dispenser at 7-Eleven.

She turned to the two scouts. "This is amazingly—"

A low rumbling issued from deep inside the earth followed by a gentle movement of the land. An earthquake?

The ground beyond the trees shook with great force. She struggled to maintain balance. As the land shifted, so did her view of the world. The sun disappeared. So did the emerald-colored sky, purple and blue grass, and the great corkscrew trees. All of it faded away. Even the river dried up. Charlee gasped, one hand over her mouth, the other wrapped around the pouch. What was happening? Was the world ending? The grass dried and withered, giving way to a rocky, sand-swept plain covered with stumps instead of trees. Even the mountains looked ominous. Thunder clouds swept over the land, enveloping everything in an overwhelming sense of death.

Charlee dropped to one knee and pulled the two scouts toward her. "Wh… what's….going….on? Never…seen…this." Was she imagining this transformation?

Charlee closed her eyes, then reopened them and peered at the desolate land-scape. Nope, it was still there. The air chilled to the point her own breath turned to mist. She shivered, rubbing her hands over her arms.

Penaiya rode up to her and dismounted her wind horse. Kneeling beside Charlee, she offered an answer. "The good magic that sustains Janasara is giving way to Theodora's evil. Whatever noble enchantment remains is struggling to maintain its grasp on the world, but it is losing ground quickly."

Before Charlee could reply, the landscape shifted back to life—full of light and color. "So time is running out for everything?" Charlee steadied herself and stood. Her head spun. That was just great.

"Yes." Penaiya climbed onto her horse.

Charlee leaped onto the unicorn. The situation was worse than she'd thought. Not only was an army headed for them, the entire world was dying as Theodora's magic spread. She had to get these people to safety and then have her showdown with the sorceress. "Let's move out, now!"

§ § §

The rest of the day's journey passed without incident.

From time to time, the land shifted from open grasslands illuminated by sun and clear emerald skies to a shady, rocky plain where light was snuffed out by a ceiling of gray storm clouds. Frigid conditions, the kind which stung Charlee's face like hundreds of needle pricks, abruptly replaced the thick tropical heat, leaving sweat glued to her forehead. She wasn't sure which was worse. The meta-morphosis made the trek difficult and confusing, but the people moved forward. Charlee's head ached from the dizzying effect as if someone hammered a blunt nail between her eyes.

Rubbing her forehead, she scanned their surroundings. No matter how the world shifted, no creatures flew overhead, nor did beasts of any kind roam across the open plain. The sounds of life—a bird's call or the buzz of a bug—were silenced. The only sound was the crunch of grass underfoot as her people hiked toward the mountains.

"Where are all the creatures of this world?" Charlee asked Penaiya, who rode beside her. The afternoon sun hung overhead, but for how long?

"Many have been destroyed. Like us, some are in hiding, waiting to rise again." The older woman gazed up. Lines covered her forehead, and strands of graying hair fluttered around her face.

"I don't understand. There have to be some mighty creatures in this world." Charlee patted the unicorn. "Can't they unite against Theodora?"

"They see even the great Dragon Lord will not challenge Theodora." Penaiya shook her head. "And those who challenged her—even the mightiest of creatures—

paid a terrible price. So they wait for someone who can bring them hope. Perhaps you are that someone."

Charlee did not respond. *Can I rally an entire world against Theodora,* she wondered? She peered back at the people of Latara following her lead. Their determination astounded her. They walked on thin legs, carrying their belongings on weary backs or pushing carts. Those too weak leaned against their fellow Latarans with more strength. They ate what little food they had during the journey and shared water but never stopped moving. They traveled with more speed than she expected. Fear must have kept them plodding forward. How much of a lead did they have over Theodora's army? Would it be enough?

Charlee wiped her damp brow. Penaiya, on the other hand, was free of sweat. Her skin, tanned and wrinkled, didn't glisten at all. "By the way, how do you handle the heat so well? I'm dripping here."

The Lataran leader smiled. "Yes, I could see how it would bother someone unaccustomed to it, but we have naturally adapted. When needed we can emit cool air through our skin, which blankets our bodies. Do not distress, Janasara does not move around the sun in a perfect circle, but rather moves up and down like the waves of an ocean. We are close to the sun for two days at a time, then farther away for two days through each cycle. The weather will become more comfortable. The challenge will be this unnatural shift as the land grows increasingly sick from the disease Theodora spreads."

Penaiya untied an animal skin pouch from the side of her horse and handed it to Charlee. "For now, drink as much as you need."

Charlee gripped it, removing a band that cinched the top. The liquid swished around inside. "Is it water?"

"Yes, infused with Janasara's magical nutrients. It will help." Penaiya motioned for her to drink.

Charlee shook her head. "No, save it for the others."

Penaiya frowned. "We can go longer without such fluids. Please, you must take care of yourself if you are to lead us."

Reluctantly, Charlee sipped the water. A sweet aroma wafted up to her nose. The liquid reminded her of peach tea. She took a long swig, allowing some to spill from the sides of her mouth. Forcing herself to stop, licking the last droplets from her lips, Charlee offered the pouch back to Penaiya. "Thank you."

"You keep it," the Lataran declared.

They continued their march, but by dusk, enough was enough. They had to rest. Charlee lifted her sword and called on her people to make camp for a few precious hours. They gathered in circles, breaking bread together. Parents tended to their children first, making sure they ate and drank. Some found a quiet place to sleep, using their packs as pillows. Charlee called upon the young warriors armed with bows and arrows to keep watch.

While they rested, the land shifted, rumbling in protest. Blackened thunderclouds rolled in, a shroud across the night sky. Children cried despite the efforts of their families to ensure them the world was not ending, but even adults shielded their eyes and uttered prayers. Theodora's dark magic caused a frigid chill to spread across the desolated crusty landscape.

Shivering, Charlee blew on her fingers and rubbed her palms together. Together with Penaiya, she walked among the people, shaking hands and patting shoulders to try to quiet fears. The changeling trailed behind her.

"We need some campfires. They're freezing." Charlee wrapped her arms around her shoulders.

"The flames' glow could give away our position." Penaiya, shoulders draped under her robe, shook her head.

"I don't think it matters." Charlee tightened her jaw to keep her teeth from chattering.

Penaiya frowned but lamented. "I'll spread the word. In the meantime, you should eat something."

Charlee gazed to the west. A barren desert stretched to the horizon. The forest they traveled through earlier in the day had succumbed to the taint. Cryton was back there somewhere. Why hadn't he checked in with her? He should have by now. Unless...

"Guardian, did you hear me?" Penaiya asked. "Please eat something."

"Uh...I can't right now." She tripped over her words. "I...uh...need to check on Cryton. I'm worried about him."

"I'm sure he's fine. You need to take care of you right now."

Charlee shook her head. No, her mentor wasn't fine. Something didn't feel right. "The people need to rest a bit more. Get those fires going. I'm going to go search for him quickly. When I return, we need to break camp and continue on our way. We can't stay here all night."

"Do what you must, but be careful." Penaiya bowed and then walked away, leaving her alone with the unicorn.

"Bike, let's go find him." She grabbed hold of the changeling's mane to hoist herself onto the magical beast.

From behind a hand gripped her arm. Swinging around, Charlee reached for her sword. "Who—?"

Penaiya's daughter faced her. Leyan, head tilted down, hair draped over her face, held a finger to her mouth and leaned in close to Charlee. "Guardian, I must speak with you," she uttered just above a whisper. "I fear you are wrong to trust my mother."

CHAPTER 17

A Daughter's Choice

LEYAN TRULY WAS her mother's daughter, with the same high cheek bones, pronounced chin, and thick eyebrows. More rugged than beautiful yet striking. A dark robe, like her mother's, cloaked her body. What was it she had said—*I fear you are wrong to trust my mother.* The words rang in Charlee's ears. How could Leyan challenge her own mother? A woman who kept her people alive.

Charlee didn't have time to talk right now. What could Leyan tell her that would be more important than finding Cryton? What if the Horeng got to him? She shuddered at that thought, trying to push it away.

"Can this wait?" Charlee kept a hand on the unicorn. The other held the pouch with the medallion.

"I think not." Leyan's gaze shifted to the camps as if watching for her mother or anyone else who might wander too close. She kept her voice low. Mist poured from her mouth. "It has to do with the safety of our people and lack of leadership my mother has shown."

"What are you talking about?" Charlee's fingers tightened around the pouch.

"Please, Guardian." Leyan grasped her arm.

"All…all right," Charlee gently tugged herself free. "Tell me what's wrong, because so far all I see is your mother is a great leader."

"Not here." Leyan slid next to her so that they stood side by side. Penaiya's daughter was about a foot taller. "We must speak in private."

Charlee frowned. "Then where?"

"There." Leyan pointed toward a circle of tall bushes not far from where they set up camp. Like a small oasis, the shrubbery rose above the cracked, rocky land. From there, Charlee would be able to keep watch over the people of Latara and any conversation she had with Leyan would be private enough.

"Okay, let's go." Charlee took a step.

Leyan seized her by the shoulder. "Wait. We should not be seen walking there together. I'll go first. Give me time. Pretend to rest. Then follow me."

"Fine." She brushed away Leyan's chilled hand.

Something about this clandestine meeting didn't feel right. Leyan hadn't liked her from the start. Why come to her now? But what if she was wrong about Penaiya? Charlee trusted Tribon, and he turned out to be Theodora's evil sidekick. She scanned freshly lit campfires for Penaiya, but she disappeared behind the dancing flames.

Charlee bit her thumbnail. If Leyan had something to say, she'd listen…cautiously. An icy sensation pierced her shoulder blades, but that could be caused by the frosty air. When would the land transform back to a prairie of grass and trees, bringing the warmth?

Rocking back and forth on her heels, she leaned against the unicorn. "Bike, can you go on your own to check on Cryton?"

The unicorn did not respond. Or budge.

"Listen, I'll be fine. I'm worried Cryton might need you more than I do. Will you go?" After a moment's hesitation, the unicorn gave one mighty flap of its wings and took to the sky. Soon it was out of sight. "Find him, please," Charlee said just loud enough for her own ears. "Bring him back safe. I just have this bad feeling inside."

Standing alone half way between the camps and the bushes where she was to meet Leyan, Charlee began to pace. Her thoughts spun like a crazy dream, thinking about the parents and little sister she left behind on Earth to her fear for Cryton. Pinpricks of self-doubt struck like tiny electric shocks across her forehead. Could she actually lead these people? Would she get them all killed? Had she made a mistake coming here? Was it all just one big trap set by Theodora?

She placed her hands over her head to quiet those thoughts. Leyan would be waiting. Charlee surveyed the meeting place. Under looming storm clouds, a gloom settled over the bushes. The wild growth—alone in this wasteland—looked like a gathering of hairy beasts hunched over in prayer. No sign of Leyan. She must have been hiding. A skin-numbing breeze swept past her, pushing her back.

Wiping hair from her face, she slipped away from the Latarans. A quick glance over her shoulder revealed no one followed. They hovered around their small fires, little more than silhouettes under the nightfall.

It took just a few heartbeats to reach the outgrowth site of the covert gathering. Up close, the vegetation appeared as long strands of raven black silk. Taking a deep breath, Charlee gripped the sword's handle at her side but kept the weapon sheathed. She wished Cryton was here. He'd know exactly what to do. He'd probably tell her to turn around. That this was a mistake. He'd be right. She should—

"Guardian, I'm here," Leyan whispered from behind the plants. "Join me"

Knuckles white from squeezing the sword handle, Charlee pushed through the bushes. Leyan stood in the center of the outgrowth, her face covered by the hood of her robe. She appeared more like an apparition than a physical being.

"All right. I'm here." Charlee kept an arm's-length distance away. "But I can't be gone long. Besides, I'm not sure I like meeting secretly like this to talk about your mom. She seems like a—"

"This is not about my mother." Leyan inched closer. Anger tinged her voice. She pushed back the hood.

"I thought—"

"Quiet!" Penaiya's daughter stomped her foot.

Charlee flinched. "Look, I don't know what's going on, but I have to get back to the others."

"No, you don't." Leyan wrung her hands like a mad scientist. "They are no longer your concern."

This is bad. Charlee retreated, lifting her sword. "What's going on here?"

"Silence, Guardian." Leyan reached behind her back and brought forward a long dagger. She waved the weapon over her head. From behind Charlee came footsteps. She spun around. Two young Lataran men, maybe teens, joined them, each wielding blunt swords with cracked handles. Ragged clothing hung off thin frames. They fidgeted like wild animals ready to attack.

Shuffling feet warned her two more approached. They crashed through the bushes and stood behind Leyan—teen boys armed with blades. The musty scent of their sweat spread thick through the tiny space they all shared.

"Leyan, what are you doing?" Charlee held her own weapon with both hands, the tip pointed at the woman. She cursed under her breath. How could she be so stupid to fall for a trap? After Tribon's betrayal, she should know better. What did Leyan plan to do? How could she get out of this?

Bike, I need you. Come back. If they had a telepathic link, now was the time for the changeling to hear her. *Please hurry.*

Penaiya's daughter twirled the dagger between her fingers. Deep frown lines formed around her mouth. "Guardian, for far too long our people have suffered. You cannot understand it. You have not lived it. You have not seen them die. You have not seen the brutality with which our magic conjurers were ripped from our lives. Men, women and children just disappeared. Those who struggled were killed instantly."

"I...kn...know!" Charlee fumbled over her words then took a deep breath. *Have to remain calm. Like Cryton taught.* "That's why I want to help. I can lead you to freedom. I can destroy Theodora."

Leyan sneered. "You are a fat child. You may be a guardian, but you don't have the power to stop Theodora. You know it. I know it. Mother suspects it, but she is a fool. She allows you to lead us even though, deep in her heart, she knows the fate that awaits her people."

"No! You're wrong." Charlee sidestepped the men behind her. "If you let me out of here...if you give me time...I'll prove it. I'll pretend like this never happened. No one will know."

"There is only one way you can save your people." Leyan's voice was hushed. "You must die here—tonight. Then we can deliver your body to Theodora. We will ask her to grant us peace as a reward for taking your life. She will have to listen."

She wants to kill me! The blood rushed from Charlee's head, and her arms wobbled. The blade dipped. Pain radiated from her stomach as if she'd been punched in the gut. She drew in energy from the surrounding plant life. Even from Leyan's little gang. Her body vibrated. Strength returned to her limbs. She raised the tip of her sword.

"You're crazy!" Charlee spat out. "Theodora doesn't care whether I'm alive or dead. She'll never stop her attack. You should know that. You can't do this. You'll only bring more pain."

Leyan pointed the dagger at her. "I think not. And I am willing to wager your life, or rather, your death, to prove myself correct."

The four hoods hefted their swords ready to strike at Charlee.

Do something! She instinctively willed an invisible protective energy shield to surround her, just as she'd done when she entered the burning house. A white glow pulsated from her body, spilling light inside the circle of bushes.

"Does the great guardian fear common men?" Leyan grinned.

"If you believe I'm a guardian, you know I have the power to open a gateway. I could easily escape. You couldn't do anything about it."

Leyan shook her head and then motioned behind her. "I have thought of that."

A fifth hooligan stepped into the circle. He held a child, a girl not more than four years old. She slept unaware of the danger.

Charlee's heart sank. She could defend herself, but not the girl. Not against so many swords. "Leyan, this is between you and me. No one else. Leave her—"

"You are right. You could escape us." Leyan stroked the girl's cheek. "But the moment you open a gateway, this child dies. No matter how quickly you wield your sword, trust me—our steel is faster."

"How can you do this? Where are her parents?"

"Dead…killed a year ago when a band of Horeng stumbled upon our hidden dwellings, once again causing us to flee and find a new place to hide like animals."

Charlee took a step toward the child. Two of the young men stepped in front of her, blocking her path. She lowered her sword. What was she supposed to do, kill them? They didn't know what they were doing. Could they be under some spell? "How can you threaten this child?"

"She is just one life… an orphan who will not be missed," Leyan reasoned. "But she will live because you will do the right thing. Lay down your life for her and all the rest."

One hand still on the sword, Charlee rubbed her forehead with the other. She allowed the magical layer protecting her to vanish. Leyan was right. Without fully realizing her powers—without having absolute confidence in her abilities— she couldn't react fast enough to save her own life and that of the little girl. *Cryton, what do I do?*

A low rumbling voice filled her thoughts.

Use the medallion. Feel its power. Let it guide your actions. It is the only way.

Whose words bounced around her mind? Her own? Was she telling herself to use the medallion? Had someone else reached out to her? Theodora maybe? No, the voice sounded different. Not her own. Not Theodora's. Who then?

I should use the medallion. It's time. She reached toward the pouch, but stopped herself. *No, I can't...not now.* What if she lost herself to the medallion's evil? She couldn't let that happen.

Charlee's gaze shifted from Leyan, to the men, to the child. There had to be a way out of this. Cryton's teachings replaced thoughts of the medallion. *Once you decide to act, you must commit yourself fully, or all is already lost. Reach the point where your movements are no longer a reflection of your enemy's or an answer to his. Rather, you are a step ahead of the enemy and cannot be defeated.*

She relaxed her muscles and focused on breathing. Slowed her heart. Envisioned the battle. Charlee would take Leyan's legs out from under her. Then use her enhanced strength. Ram into the two closest warriors. Before anyone could react, she'd grab the child. Wrap her in a protective energy shield. And run. All without killing anyone. It would work. Had to.

"Lay down your weapon, Guardian, and open your heart to our steel," Leyan's eyes bulged.

"All right." Charlee let go of her sword. *Get ready!* "This is wrong, but I understand why you're doing it."

"Thank you, Guar—"

Now! Charlee dropped to her knees then spun like a top, sweeping Leyan's legs. Penaiya's daughter fell on her back with a yelp. Charlee leaped to her feet. With all her strength, she rammed her shoulder into one of Leyan's rogues. The strike knocked him off his feet into another attacker. Their heads collided and they crumbled onto the dirt.

Grabbing her sword from the ground, she slashed wildly at the other two. They cowered, running off into the night.

That left the one holding the child. Awake, she squirmed in his arms. He held a hand over her mouth and a dagger to her throat.

Charlee crept toward him. "Enough. Let her go. You don't want to hurt her."

His eyes shifted to the girl. That was her chance. Charlee pounced on him, grabbing his arm and ripping the blade from his hand. Driving an elbow into his gut, the young man hunched over, releasing the girl. Charlee slammed a fist into his face. Either his cheek or her knuckles cracked. He collapsed to the ground.

Charlee hoisted the girl to her feet. "Run."

The child heeded her command, slipping away through the brush. Charlee turned back to Leyan. "It's over, Ley—"

A blade sliced into her shoulder, tearing through skin and muscle. A wave of blinding pain sent her sprawling along the ground. She cried out when hot blood seeped from the wound, running down her arm, pooling around her torso.

Blinking away tears, she gazed at Leyan, who stood over her, dagger in hand. Blood dripped from the weapon.

"Good bye, Guardian." Leyan knelt over her. The dagger just over her heart.

Charlee closed her eyes. I have to get out of this. I have to fight. Get up! She tried to lift her body but couldn't. Something whizzed through the air. Leyan screamed. Her blade never struck again.

Charlee opened her eyes. A gasp escaped her lips.

An arrow ripped through Leyan's hand, the tip covered in blood. More red ooze dripped from the shaft. She grasped her wounded hand, eyes bulging. Her dagger lay at her feet.

Charlee stared unblinkingly. What's happening?

Leyan slumped to her knees just an arm's length from Charlee. Her chest heaved. Tears streaked down her cheeks. She breathed through clenched teeth. With her good hand, she hefted the blade. Another arrow slammed into her arm, splitting through flesh. Leyan's blood splashed against Charlee's face. The woman shrieked and then fell on her side.

"It was the only way," Leyan whispered. "Now we are doomed."

"No." Charlee shivered as she tried to speak. "I...pro...promise you...you... you're wrong."

High above, lightning cracked. The zigzag spark of light revealed Cryton atop the winged unicorn. He gripped a bow in one hand, an arrow in the other.

Charlee smiled.

Then her eyes dimmed.

CHAPTER 18

No Time to Heal

S HE WAS BACK at home, seated at the dining table. Dad read the newspaper beside her. Megan played with a bowl of cereal. Mom, her back to Charlee, prepared breakfast. The familiar scent of coffee and scrambling eggs settled over the kitchen.

"You were right, Charlee." Her mom turned from the stove and slid eggs from a pan onto her plate.

"Mom, is that you?" Charlee studied her face. Laugh lines accentuated the sides of her mouth. But…

"Who else would it be?" Her mom placed a hand on her shoulder. "Now eat your eggs before they get cold."

"What…how…how did I get here?" She scanned the kitchen. Everything seemed normal. Family photos covered the refrigerator. Her mom's spices sat on a wooden shelf to the right of the sink. A decorative plate with Megan's hand print hung on the wall by the kitchen window.

"What a strange question. Did you have another one of those dreams?" her mom asked.

"Dreams?"

"You know, about some flying bike, fighting an evil empress, and all that crazy magic."

"Mom, you know it's not a dream." Her fingers tapped the table. Her stomach pitched.

"Isn't it?" Her mom swung back to the stove. Her words were more a statement than a question. "To be honest, Charlee, I've had enough of this foolishness."

"What?" Charlee stood.

It couldn't have been a dream. Hadn't she just been in the other dimension, in the world of her ancestry? Hadn't the people of Latara asked her to lead them on a journey? Weren't they being pursued by the Horeng and by Theodora?

Something was very wrong.

"Mom?" This time, her mom did not respond.

"Mom?" When again there was no response, Charlee placed a hand on her mom's shoulder. It was like touching ice. Charlee's fingers froze. A stinging sensation of pins and needles climbed her arm.

"Mom?"

Slowly, her mom turned. Her normally blue eyes were bright red. Blood flowed from them like tears.

Charlee stumbled back against the table. "No!"

Her dad showed no reaction. He just read his newspaper. Same with Megan. She played with her cereal. Were they even there? What kind of nightmare was this? Yes, it had to be a nightmare.

Her mom lunged for her, grabbing Charlee by the neck, and flung her across the room. Charlee slammed against a cabinet, grunting as air exploded from her lungs, then fell to the tiled floor. Gasping for a breath, she glanced up. Her mom casually crossed the room. With each step, her face distorted, growing young and then old, stretching and shrinking until...

Theodora stood before Charlee.

"It is so easy to play with your mind, young Guardian. When you are my slave, I will enjoy doing so for all eternity." Theodora smiled wildly.

Charlee painfully climbed to her feet. She wheezed, trying desperately to move air in and out of her lungs. Each breath burned, the lingering effect of Theodora's icy grip. Once on her feet, Charlee steadied herself. "A moment ago, you said I was right. Right about what?"

Theodora's face stopped morphing. She now appeared as the beautiful princess with long flowing golden hair and a white gown. The sorceress chanted a response. "It wouldn't have mattered if that creature, Leyan, killed you and delivered your lifeless body to me. I would still destroy her people. I will kill them all. And it's because you led me to them."

"Leave them alone." Charlee grabbed Theodora's dress with both hands and pulled the sorceress close. "It's me you want."

Theodora tugged Charlee's hair. "Remember, Guardian, I am with you always. There is no escape for you. I know where you are running. Do you think the Dragon Lord will protect you from me? The Dragon Lord—like all the creatures in this world—is mine. Run all you like. I am enjoying the chase. But know that it will end in defeat for you. You and the people you are leading will fall. My army—my general—will soon reach you."

What did she mean, "my general"? Did she mean Tribon? Was he the dark figure Charlee saw standing on the wall beside the dragon, overlooking Theodora's vast army?

It didn't matter.

"If you know so much, Aunty Theodora, come and get me now."

With a last look of hate in her eyes, Theodora vanished, as did the image of Charlee's home and family.

Everything went gray. Yes, it had been a nightmare.

Or a vision.

§ § §

Her eyes fluttered open. Cryton knelt over her. The unicorn stood behind him. Penaiya crouched on one knee opposite the old man, head bowed, shoulders hunched.

"You're back!" Cryton stroked her hair.

"W…where…I mean…what happened?"

"You almost allowed yourself to be killed." Concern laced his voice. "Damn fool thing, too. If your changeling friend and I had not reached you in time…well I don't want to think about what would have happened."

She blinked. Her surroundings came into focus. She lay on a blanket beside a campfire. Flames swayed in a soft breeze. White smoke billowed into a purple sky dotted by glowing stars. How long had she been unconscious? How long till morning? How could she have let this happen?

She lifted her head. "Leyan! That little girl!"

"Do not worry, Guardian." Penaiya rested a hand on her arm. The Lataran's normally high cheeks sagged. A loose strand of hair hung across her face. "The little girl is resting with friends. She is young and resilient. As for my daughter and the others, they will be dealt with. I am truly saddened I did not foresee her actions. I should have known."

Charlee's mind cleared as the remnants of sleep and her nightmare drifted away. She became aware of the faint ache in her shoulder where Leyan's blade penetrated. The pain should be worse. *I must already be healing. Probably have my shape shifting protector to thank for that.* She smiled at the unicorn. Charlee missed seeing the changeling in the form of a bike.

She placed a hand over Penaiya's. "Please don't punish Leyan and those with her. She was only doing what she thought best for her people. Or Theodora might have her under some mind control."

"The elders and I will decide the punishment." Penaiya stood. "I will need to speak with Leyan first."

Charlee tried for a second time to rise but Cryton motioned her to remain on the blanket. "You need your rest," he said.

"There's no time." She grabbed onto his arm and lifted herself to her feet. She breathed easier than in her dream encounter with Theodora, if that's what it was, but her throat was still sore, as if the sorceress' touch had been real.

"You may be right," Cryton admitted. "I fell farther and farther behind to keep watch for the Horeng. I could see the flames from their torches lighting the horizon. And there's something else. We are being trailed by the knight in dark armor atop the dragon."

"The dragon we saw?" Charlee asked.

"Must be." Cryton peered toward the dark sky. "Maybe the dragon rider is a spotter and has orders not to attack until the full army reaches us. Then again, the rider could be more than that."

Charlee nodded. Theodora spoke of her general. Who was this mysterious leader of the sorceress' army? Dismissing the thought for now, she eyed Penaiya. How would the woman who led the people of Latara for so long, and warned about the Dragon Lord, react to a reptile on Theodora's side?

Cryton must have noticed. "Don't worry. She knows about the dragon rider already. I felt it best to inform her."

Charlee shifted her gaze from Penaiya to Cryton. "When the time comes, I'll deal with the rider and the dragon. For now, we must move on. How long have I been out? How many hours have we lost?"

"Maybe an hour. That's all," he answered.

With a slight smile, Charlee patted the unicorn. Its energy continued to seep into her muscles, speeding her recovery. She flexed her arms and legs. Opened and closed her hands. Her limbs responded stiffly, like a day after a fitness test at school when her whole body was sore, but strength returned.

"Well, let's get our people ready and continue on our way."

"If you don't mind, I will go and consult with my daughter," Penaiya's voice was little more than a whisper. "Perhaps I can determine if she can be saved. Or if she has become too twisted by Theodora."

"Don't give up on her." Charlee slid next to Cryton. "In the meantime, we'll help get everyone ready to move again."

Penaiya offered a slight bow and slipped away, head hung low. Her dark robe became a shadow amid the campfires.

Charlee watched her leave, wondering where Leyan and her helpers were being held. Why worry about that right now? Her concern was more for Penaiya. "She's broken, isn't she?"

"For now. But she may recover." Cryton grabbed his staff from the ground. "I hope so. Now, we—"

"Wait a second." He leaned in close to her. "Following Leyan was stupid. Unless you start thinking like a guardian, you will not survive. Then all will truly be lost."

"I know."

"Do you?" The old man spoke gravely, grasping her hand. The wrinkles in his forehead deepened. "What kind of guardian allows herself to walk into a trap and then surrenders herself so easily?"

"Never again!" Charlee's hands tightened into fists. He was right. She had to be smarter.

"I hope so." Cryton's voice softened. "I won't always be there to protect you."

What did that mean? She didn't ask the question out loud.

He twisted his mustache. "Now, what were you going to say before I interrupted?"

Charlee took a deep breath. "We are going to have to walk throughout the night without stopping. This time, I need you to stay at the front of the group. Come morning, I'm going to disappear."

"Dare I ask where to?"

"I think the changeling and I need to meet that dragon rider."

"No!" He struck the ground with his staff.

"Cryton, yes. I have to do this. Without you. Away from our people."

"You don't have to."

"Yeah, I do." Charlee raked her fingers through greasy hair. Her stench must be worsening by the moment. "I think the rider hasn't attacked us because that's not his plan. The dark knight wants to face me alone."

"That doesn't mean you should face him." Cryton paced in front of her. "It's too dangerous. You are too important. I cannot accept this decision."

"Cryton, you have to trust me."

"And if you don't make it back?"

"I'll come back. I'll outsmart him. Get a sense of who or what he is. Then… well, I'll take him out of the picture somehow. Meanwhile, you'll lead everyone on a run to the mountains."

Cryton sighed, his hands twisting around the staff. He stared at the ground for much too long before he spoke again. Finally, he lifted his head. "You must be careful. Your life is more important than you can possibly imagine."

"I will, and I'll have the bike…er…the unicorn." She leaned against the great beast. The animal wrapped a wing around her.

Shaking his head, Cryton rested his staff on his shoulders. "You know, if I survive this, your parents are going to kill me for letting you cross over to Janasara."

"They'll kill us both," Charlee shot back.

Before they moved on, Charlee noticed her shoulders felt lighter like a weight had been lifted. That could only mean….*Where's the medallion?*

"Looking for this?" the old man asked, holding up the pouch. "I removed it, so you could rest more comfortably. It is safe."

Almost wildly, Charlee snatched away the pouch and peered inside. *Yes, it's there!* Then she slung it over her shoulder with an embarrassed chuckle.

"Sorry, Cryton. It's just that…"

"I know, Guardian."

If only he truly did know. If only she could tell him her terrible secret…that because of this medallion, someday she could become just like Theodora.

But Charlee couldn't bring herself to utter those words. Not yet…not ever.

CHAPTER 19

Out of the Clouds

CHARLEE AND HER unicorn emerged from the swirling portal into the cover of mushrooming clouds. There they remained. Motionless. Listening. Below, the people of Latara marched to the eastern mountain ranges toward the pathway to the dragons' realm based on her lie. Their only hope depended on Charlee convincing the Dragon Lord to open his land to them. If the dragons didn't already serve Theodora.

A big if.

Just a few heartbeats ago, she and the changeling had been on land at the head of the Lataran survivors. The uneasy bleakness of the shifting night gave way to the first glimpses of morning light. Above the rugged mountain peaks, a pale lime green glow licked the horizon. She had been waiting for daybreak. Dreading it. That's when she would put her plan in motion. Fly with the unicorn to a showdown with the mysterious dragon and its rider. She had to stop them or her people were doomed. Worse, if this dragon's service to Theodora meant the Dragon Lord sided with the witch, all was lost. Charlee didn't believe that. When she spoke in her vision with the great beast, he didn't seem evil. Just angry and maybe scared.

When the sun began its march skyward, she signaled to Cryton, Penaiya, and four elders riding wind horses. They moved in close and surrounded her. The old men, their graying beards rustled by the morning breeze, glared at her. Did they fear the dragon or her magic? Maybe they still didn't believe she was a guardian. No time to worry about that now. Dismounting the unicorn, she knelt and drew lines in the earth with her finger, pretending to give directions, a ruse to mislead anyone—or any beast—who might be spying on them.

Under the cover of the wind horses' massive bodies, she squeezed her eyelids shut and focused on opening a portal. A slight tug pulled at her mind as if an unseen rope connected her thoughts to the gateway. Blood surged like a wave rushing toward shore. Her eyes shot open. A ball of blue energy popped into existence, hovering before her, at first a pinhole doorway to lead her anyway she chose. Even home. She shook that thought away.

The gateway expanded into a manhole-sized circle. The wind horses stirred and the elders gasped. When it grew large enough, Charlee and her unicorn dropped into a tunnel where the world of Janasara vanished. Inside the portal, clouds whirled and lightning flashed. By now, Charlee was used to it.

Within the gateway, she concentrated on a bank of towering clouds to the east. Like plugging in coordinates on an Internet map, she zeroed in on them before making the jump. Though now out of sight inside the blue tunnel, she fought to maintain her mind's lock on the destination. "Come on, Charlee, don't blow this," she uttered, clutching her forehead with both hands. Would her powers work right? Would the portal open in the right spot? Or somewhere else? Like Timbuktu back on Earth.

She crossed her fingers. The portal spit them out into a pocket of moist atmosphere surrounded by layers of puff. *Yes!* Charlee took a relieved breath. They arrived deep within the misty veil. Safe for the moment.

Now they waited, silence broken only by the unicorn's fluttering wings and Charlee's shallow breathing. The sky was at peace, the murky thunderclouds from the night replaced by silvery formations. Perhaps a sign a bit of good magic remained to hold Theodora's diseased grasp on the world at bay.

Would the dragon give itself away? How long would they have to wait? Maybe the beast…

An ominous whoosh suggested they wouldn't have to wait long.

The blood in her veins froze. Like a scared child hugging a teddy bear to ward off scary noises in the night, she wrapped her arms around the unicorn's neck. Her heart beat loudly in her ears. Charlee buried her face in the unicorn's mane to muffle her racing breaths. The flying monster was close! Did the beast see her already? What was she thinking? How could she face a dragon?

"Bike, did you hear it?" she whispered to the changeling.

The unicorn's ears twitched.

Charlee scanned the inside of the cloud bank, but the fog proved too thick. Even with her superior vision, the dragon eluded her. "I know it's here. We have to lead it—"

A large shadow passed overhead. Chilled air swept over her. The gust brushed against her face and hair. Pricks of pins and needles spread through her limbs.

Instinctively, she reached back to feel the medallion.

The voice she'd heard while facing Leyan returned. *Take hold of the medallion! Unleash its power!*

She tapped her forehead. "No! Not yet. Not until I face Theodora!"

Charlee jerked her hand away from the pouch. She instead grabbed as much of the unicorn's white flowing mane as she could. Strength and courage from the unicorn's energy flowed through her. The ice in her veins thawed. Her blood pumped faster. Muscles expanded. She sat taller on the unicorn's back.

"Steady," she whispered. "Let's wait for the right time to make our move."

What did that mean? It wasn't much of a plan. She shook her head in disgust. *That was her problem. She never thought things through. What the heck was she going to do when the beast tried to eat her?* She forced her mind to listen again.

114

Silence, until…

From behind, hot breath grazed her neck. Beads of sweat ran down her shirt, tickling her back. Charlee didn't have to look behind her. Didn't want to. Didn't dare.

"Bike, fly! Fast!"

With one mighty thrust of its wings, the unicorn ascended higher into the thick cover. A terrible roar shook the clouds like crashing thunder. A wall of fire lit up the sky and scorched the air. Charlee stared down as the hellish orange dragon-fire rushed beneath her.

Her entire body flinched. "Jeez!"

The dragon soared into view, ghostlike within the mist. Scaly armor covered the beast's back. A long narrow neck led to its massive spiked head and snout. Wings, as large as an airliner's, stretched across the sky.

Riding on the beast's neck—the mysterious knight shrouded in dark armor.

Her stomach became queasy. Charlee couldn't stop her hands from shaking. Her breath lodged in her throat. The dragon was big. Very big. Like skyscraper big. She clung to the unicorn as the changeling raced even higher.

Below, the dragon arched its neck and glowered at her with eyes glowing yellow. The giant creature seemed to grin, baring huge white fangs.

Her knees trembled. Courage slipped away. Her grip on the unicorn weakened. She should open another portal. Get out of there. And leave the people unguarded? *I can't*, she argued with herself. *What do I—*

The dragon's rider hefted a sword and pointed it at her as if to order a charge. The dragon threw back its wings and climbed after them.

"Fly faster!" Her fight-or-flight instinct kicked in. Right now it screamed run. "They're coming after us! Go! Go!"

Like a rocket, the unicorn soared deeper into the morning clouds, creating as much distance as possible between them and the dragon.

Under the expanding grip of dark magic, the sky shifted. Tranquil clouds exploded with the rumble of thunder and a blinding crack of lightning as they morphed back into dark storm clouds. Charlee flinched, almost losing hold of the changeling. Gail-force winds slammed into her, but she clung tighter to the unicorn. Then, like someone turning the channel on the TV, daylight stabbed through the dimness again. Calm skies returned. The winds vanished. Why such a fast fluctuation? Was the world fighting back against the sorceress?

Charlee shook her head to block out the dizzying transformation. She had to concentrate. Focus. That thing was coming after them.

The unicorn blasted through the cloud ceiling into the morning sunlight, then swerved into a sharp turn, nearly throwing her. She squeezed the changeling's neck, pressing her heels into its body. Her magical protector raced above the mist.

She glanced over her shoulder. The dragon breached the clouds and spread its wings wide to brake. Charlee lowered her head. As powerful as the unicorn was, they couldn't out fly a dragon. They were going to die. Burned alive. Eaten. Either way…they were dead.

"Bike, we're in big trouble! Any ideas?" Air slashed at her face.

A horrifying cry from the dragon stole her breath. She didn't need to look back to know the beast closed the distance. The stench of its breath, like charred wood, washed over her. Any minute, the fire-breathing creature would be close enough to scorch them.

"Bike, dive!" she yelled. The unicorn swung back into the clouds. Her body tensed. Chest tightened. *Hold on!*

They zipped through layers of the silvery barrier, tears streaking from her eyes. Bursting through the clouds, they plunged faster toward a stitched-together patchwork of grasslands and rocky terrain like skydivers without parachutes. Charlee screamed, though barely audible against the crying wind. Inside the cloud bank, her view was boxed in. Now exposed, death spun toward them. Her mind swooned. Vision blurred. She could blackout at any moment.

She gritted her teeth, forcing blood back into her head. "Have…to…stay… alert." A glance over her shoulder revealed the dragon still chased, ripping through the clouds, carving a line toward them. Her heart sank. Either the fall would kill them or the winged monster. They had just one chance. "Mom…be… with…me."

The ground rushed at them like a steep roller coaster mercilessly plummeting her toward a jolting stop. The dive rattled her senses. The world spun. She buried her head in the unicorn's mane. How could they pull up? They'd smash into the earth for sure. Nothing would be left. Just a pile of twisted bone and flesh.

"Bike! Now!"

Seconds from collision, the unicorn jerked upward, skimming above the land. Its hooves struck dirt before it launched skyward again. Charlee grunted through clenched teeth. The jarring shift jostled her brain. Her vision tunneled. Bile rose up her throat. *Going to be sick.* She forced the puke back down. She couldn't allow herself to be sick. She strained to maintain her grip on the unicorn. Sweat poured off her forehead. She gasped for air.

Gazing back, Charlee desperately wanted to see the dragon crash into the ground, its rider crushed under the beast's weight.

Nothing. The dragon and its rider vanished. An icy tremor rumbled through her body.

"What…How…?"

The unicorn slowed. Brightening daylight turned the morning sky to a deeper shade of emerald. Charlee scanned for any sign of the dragon. All was quiet. Too quiet. She blinked rapidly, chewing on a nail. They couldn't just disappear. Something was wrong.

They were not that far from her people, which meant everyone witnessed her battle with the dragon. Mouth dry, stomach churning, her mind lingered on one thought. This wasn't over. She needed to get that dragon as far away as possible.

Charlee laced her fingers around the unicorn's mane. "Bike, there's some bad magic at work here. That dragon and its rider are still close. They must be. Let's lead them away. Take off toward the mountains."

The unicorn did as directed. With a thrust of its wings, the changeling soared toward the Temora goliaths, which stretched to both the northern and southern horizons. They stood as solid stone walls towering over the land as if to divide Janasara in half. As they approached the mountain ranges, Charlee breathed easier. Her pounding heart, beating like a sledgehammer, calmed.

Blossoming sunrays touched the mountaintops. Trees spotted the peaks. Boulders lay in bundles. A swirl of colors—mostly shades of purple and green—mixed along the face of the jagged rock, creating a marbled appearance.

She nudged the changeling toward one peak bathed in the morning light. A row of trees would hide them from the dragon. Unless the beast already watched them. The goose bumps on her arms told her the dragon had them in its sights. Why couldn't she see it? Or sense it?

"Let's land there. Watch for the dragon. And that knight. Let them come to us. Maybe the knight has something to say."

With a few quick sweeps of its wings, the unicorn came to a gentle landing.

Beyond the mountains, a great sea merged with the horizon. Just like her vision! Water spouts, like enormous trees growing from the depths, rose toward the sky. "Yes, just like I saw."

Along the shore, green water danced calmly, glimmering like golden coins reflecting the morning sunlight. The sun cast a brilliant white line across the vast waterway like an arrow pointing to the dragons' realm.

"At least, I hope that's where it's pointing," she told the unicorn.

Charlee filled her lungs. Sweet. Fresh. Alive. Different from the lands to the west where Theodora's evil cast a wide shadow, one that pressed against her chest with a constant sense of doom. Here, she lifted her shoulders; even with the weight of the medallion, Charlee breathed deeper.

The sun appeared smaller than a day ago, just like Penaiya promised. That's why cooler air wafted around Charlee instead of the intolerable heat.

There was something else. This place seemed free of the sorceress' spells. Maybe her vile magic hadn't yet taken a hold this far east.

Scanning once more for the dragon revealed nothing. The monster could be hiding in the mushrooming clouds to the west. Only one way to find out. They had to fly back into them. That thought made her shudder, but what choice was there? She had to keep her people safe, and that meant solving the mystery of the dragon. So far the creature and its rider only seemed interested in her. Why else hadn't they attacked the Latarans?

"Bike—"

"I never thought a guardian could be such a flabby coward." A young female voice bounced off the trees.

Charlee whipped around, but large trunks and shrubbery hid the stranger. Her heart dropped into her stomach. Could it be the—

Once again, the hot breath of something big washed over her. The stench of burning charcoal made her eyes water.

The dragon!

From deep within the foliage came the thunderous crack of trees toppling to the ground, one after the other. The earth shook. She ducked under the unicorn, covering her head, trying to keep her balance.

The dragon roared. Charlee covered her ears. She retreated farther under the unicorn. A whimper escaped her throat. They were going to die.

"Look at how the guardian cowers." The female voice mocked her.

When the ground stopped shaking, Charlee slowly lifted her head. The dragon towered high above, perched on splintered tree trunks. Standing underneath the beast, the knight, in black armor, chuckled. A cackle reminiscent of that bully Tina Lomeli back in school.

From where she crouched, Charlee's hands balled into fists. On trembling legs, she forced herself to stand up straight.

"Wh...who are you?" With a shaky, sweaty hand, she clutched the medallion at her side. The other gripped the handle of her sheathed sword.

"You think you have the right to question me? You do not, Guardian." The knight strolled forward. Though the helmet gave her voice a metallic quality, something about the tone sounded familiar. Could the knight really be a girl? The stranger wasn't much taller than Charlee. Maybe even an inch or two shorter.

Charlee pressed her body against the unicorn. The comforting touch gave her access to the changeling's energy. Was she ready? She had to be.

For a heartbeat, her attention shifted to the dragon. A towering creature standing four, maybe five, stories tall. Charlee gulped. What power could stop such a creature? No sword could. The medallion? Deep purple scales covered the beast's armored back. A bronzed armor protected its stomach.

Like a snake, a line of orange divided each glowing eye down the center. Charlee avoided eye contact as if the dragon could peer into her soul and sense fear. Black smoke rose from two cavernous nostrils on either side of its snout.

Did such a creature have any weakness at all?

Trying to disguise a terror that squeezed her body, Charlee thrust out her chest and repeated her question. "Ans...answer the question. Wh...who are you?"

The knight paced in front of her. "You will know in time."

I know that voice? But how? Who is she?

The knight lifted a sword from behind her back. The blade was long and curved with a raven black handle.

"Let's see what kind of guardian you are." The knight spun her blade. "I think it best if you take your sword in hand. I mean to strike at you."

Charlee backed up a step, unsheathing her blade. She held the weapon low and to her side, like Cryton taught her in his alley, to disguise her first blow. Sweat dripped down her arms. How could she fight her? The only duals she had were with the old man. And she never won. *Calm down, Charlee. Breathe. Like he taught.*

With a war cry, the knight rushed her, slashing her blade in a downward angle.

Charlee answered with an upward block. Steel met steel. Her hands shook from the collision. The cling of their weapons echoed throughout the mountain range. Her eyes shifted from the knight to the dragon and back again. The beast growled, lowering its long neck.

After the first blow, the knight retreated. "That was a standard block, Guardian. Do you have nothing better to offer?"

Charlee tightened her grip. "Bring it."

The knight lunged. Her blade whined as it struck from every direction.

Blocking and parrying, Charlee did everything she could to keep pace. With each crash of steel, she gasped for air. Her muscles burned. Chest ached. *I... can't... hold on. Tiring!*

The knight again broke off the attack and backed up—then laughed.

"Out of breath already, Guardian?" she taunted, circling Charlee. "Maybe it's because of your roundness. We've only just begun."

"Round or not...I'll kick...your butt." A surge of strength flowed into her arms. They tingled. Her protector fed her its energy.

Charlee needed to absorb more. She had to keep the knight talking. That may give her more time. "Show me who you are. Take off your helmet. Let me see your face."

"Before I kill you, you will know the truth." With these words, the knight attacked once more. This time, she drove the tip of her sword directly at Charlee's heart.

Sidestepping, Charlee blocked the attack and then, spinning backward, launched the edge of her steel at the knight's head.

With nimble footwork, her foe stopped the blade and then threw a kick to Charlee's chest.

Charlee yelped and fell backward onto the peak's rough surface. Coughing. Unable to suck in air. The sword slipped from her fingers. She clawed at her chest. Searing pain radiated down into her bones. *Can't...breathe!* She tried to stand.

The knight shoved her back down.

A guttural rumbling rose from the dragon's throat. *Laughter?*

Charlee rolled onto her back. She forced air into her lungs. Gazing up, the tip of a weapon danced inches from her face.

"Guardian, I could kill you now and all would be done," the knight declared. "But your death now would be too easy." The mysterious female slid her sword behind her back. "You see, Guardian, I was not here to kill you this day, but to test your skills."

"And?" Charlee slid away.

"You are weak." The knight backed up to the dragon. "Sad, really. I expected more. But then, I thought Empress Theodora was underestimating you when she made light of your abilities."

Charlee climbed to her feet. "Why are you serving Theodora? She's evil. Call me crazy, but I sense you're not like her. There's something familiar about you."

"Oh, but I am, Guardian. I am like her. You see, I am her daughter."

Charlee tried to comprehend what she heard. Theodora's daughter? How?

The knight leaned against the dragon, "Today, Guardian, I am going to let you live, but only so you may see the people of Latara die one by one when my mother's army reaches them. And the Horeng will reach them soon. Mark my words, your people will not pass through this mountain range. Once they are all dead, I will see to it you die along with them. And then, in that last moment of your life, you will know who bested you."

"Why wait for the Horeng?" Charlee asked. "You have a dragon. Kill those poor people now. Kill me. Don't wait. Do——"

The voice in her heard interrupted. *She cannot kill you, for you possess the medallion. She knows it. Theodora knows it. They fear your power. Use it now. It can bring dragons to their knees.*

Could the voice be right? She clenched her teeth. *Get out of my head. Whoever you are. I decide when to use it.*

The knight hesitated before she spoke. "If mother were to give me the order, I would kill every one of them with joy. She does not yet wish it. But soon. They will die. And you."

Without a further word, the knight climbed onto the dragon's back.

The beast fluttered its wing, kicking up wind and dust that nearly knocked Charlee off her feet. Together the beast and the knight flew away, vanishing into a row of clouds.

Charlee slumped to her knees.

"Theodora has a daughter?" she wondered aloud. "How is that possible? Bike, it just can't be. Can it?"

CHAPTER 20

A Hopeless Dash

THE UNICORN CIRCLED above the gathering of refugees. The land below them transformed. Barren desert again replaced lush grasslands, the earth dried and cracked. Storm clouds loomed above, blocking the sun. How long until the mountains and beyond fell under the sorceress' spell?

She didn't have an answer.

Charlee waved to her people who pointed to her and called out the title, "guardian." They spread across the dusty plain like a herd of lost animals. Their only strength came from what little hope they had left. What was she supposed to tell them? That they were fools to believe in her? That they would all likely die?

"Let's get down there." She patted the unicorn's neck. They swooped to a soft landing. Once she slid off the unicorn, the Latarans surrounded her like a frenzied group of fans trying to get a selfie photo with a celebrity.

Cryton emerged from the crowd, his eyes glistening. He grabbed her shoulders. "Are you all right?"

"Yeah," she answered. Not really. She had her butt kicked and failed to stop the dragon.

"Everyone, she's all right," Cryton called out as more surged forward to greet her. They chanted for her, declaring her their champion. Charlee whirled around as hands reached out, touching her arms and shoulders. She wanted to run. Cryton wrapped an arm around her. "People, please, give her space."

He ushered Charlee away from the mob, stopping when they stood clear of the others. Throwing his hands in the air, Cryton paced in front of her. "Most full hearty thing I've ever seen. You could have been killed. I never should have allowed it." He roughly twisted his mustache. Was he angry, concerned, or both? "We lost sight of you as you flew to the mountains. Thought we'd...I'd...lost you. What happened out there? Are you sure you're okay?"

"Yes, Cryton."

He held her hand. "Sorry, I know I' not your grandfather, but to me, you're—"

She hugged him. "I know. I'm really okay, but you need to teach me more about using a sword. I...I blew it." That was hard for her to admit. A guardian wasn't supposed to lose fights.

His mouth dropped open. "What do you—?"

Charlee ended the embrace and peered past him to the congregation of exiles

121

who now whispered amongst each other. Thunder exploded high above, and lightning flashed inside the darkening clouds. Charlee blinked away dust and returned her attention to Cryton.

"I…spoke to…the knight." She struggled to get out the words. "She's a girl. Says…she's Theodora's daughter. Is that possible? I didn't see her face or anything. She never removed her helmet, but she sounds young, and she's about my height."

He rubbed his chin. "Anything is possible, Charlee. The question is how did she come to have a daughter? Naturally? Through magic? I guess time will tell. What about the dragon? You said the Dragon Lord will welcome us to his realm, but why would a dragon serve Theodora? Are we heading into a trap?"

Charlee shrugged. How much longer could she keep up her lie about the Dragon Lord? He warned her to stay away. This whole journey was based on her lie. Still, she never had the sense the Dragon Lord sided with Theodora. There had to be another reason he refused to help. As for this mystery beast...

"I don't know, Cryton." She brushed wind-whipped hair away from her face. "I didn't learn anything about this dragon, except it's big. Really big. This one may be on Theodora's side, but I still don't think The Dragon Lord serves her. Searching for his realm is still the right thing to do. Trust me."

He gently lifted her chin with his forefinger. "I do trust you. I don't trust those giant winged lizards. But we will continue on the path you've set for us."

"There's more to say." She nudged his hand away. "I couldn't stop the knight or the dragon. They're still out there. The only reason they're not attacking is so Theodora can enjoy watching us run from the Horeng. This is all some joke to her. We'll never make it to the mountains." Charlee crumbled back into his arms.

Cryton gently pushed her away. "Yes we will. Once again, Theodora has failed to realize the kind of leader you are. Guardian, you are going to get us to the dragons' realm. Believe that. Believe in yourself. Make your people believe. They need to hear from you. Lead your people."

She gazed at the remnants of Latara. Fear and uncertainty etched deeply into their faces. What could she tell them? How could she give them hope when dread chilled her insides and weakened her own resolve? "I don't know what to tell them."

Cryton grinned. "I know it's not fair for one so young to be in this position—to face this kind of burden—but I have seen you grow from a child to a young woman with the kind of bravery only a true leader can possess. You are here for a reason, and if you believe in yourself nothing—no one—will stand in your way."

Her stomach growled. "I wish we were back in your pizza shop. I could really use a cheese pizza right now and a large soda."

Cryton patted her shoulder. "When this is over, I promise you free pizzas as long as I live. Now go lead your people."

"I'll hold you to it." Charlee chuckled, then turned and walked back to the

Latarans. What would she tell them? What could she tell them? For now, continue the lie. False hope was better than no hope. They gathered around her in a circle. All three hundred of them grew quiet. A hush fell across the land, except for the cry of the wind and the rumbling thunder.

"Listen, everyone!" She amplified her voice. "You don't have to worry about the dragon you just saw me fight."

"So you destroyed it?" a woman in the crowd shouted.

Charlee hesitated. "Not exactly."

"Then it is still out there," a man groaned.

"It will not harm us." She lied. "I…I…" She searched for the right word in the Lengoron language. "I vanquished it." Another lie.

The congregation cheered. Then another woman spoke out. "But you want to take us to the dragons' realm. If they fight for Theodora, why should we go there?"

Charlee swallowed hard, shifted her gaze to Cryton, then back to the crowd. Men stood side by side with women. Children huddled close to their parents. Those with swords fingered the handles. Elders stood with their arms crossed. "The dragon I fought is Theodora's creation," she answered. "Not from the dragons' realm. The true dragons are not evil."

Maybe that wasn't a lie.

"Listen to me. We must travel now, and we must travel fast," Charlee continued. "Behind us—moving quickly—is Theodora's army. We must reach the mountains before they reach us."

She let the thought linger. Some gasped. A few whimpered. More whispers spread through the travelers.

"We can do this," she went on. "Are you ready to march on—with me?" She held her breath.

After a moment of silence…a moment that lasted forever…a man shouted, "We stand with our guardian!"

Everyone else—men, women and children—chanted their support in a chorus that spread over the dry land. Charlee climbed atop the unicorn and raised her sword. *I wish we never found these people,* she thought. *We did, and there's nothing I can do now but hope the Dragon Lord turns out not to be a jerk.* She pointed her sword toward the Temoras. The unicorn plodded forward.

The race was on.

Lightning lit the clouds on fire. Thunder bellowed. Charlee gazed skyward. Somewhere close by the dragon and its rider trailed them. How could she possibly stop them if they decided to attack? How could she stop an entire army of Horeng?

Was Cryton right? Had Theodora underestimated her?

"I'd better be stronger than she thinks I am," Charlee told herself out loud. "Stronger than I think I am."

§ § §

They traveled non-stop for the entire day. The scenery shifted around them as magic battled for control of the land. A parched desert morphed back into grassland and trees with the sun and emerald sky above. Even Charlee rejoiced in the change as if the signs of life offered hope. Her heart dashed when the grass and trees again wilted away, and the murky clouds hid the light. How much worse must the Latarans feel. Still, they marched on. When night fell, the mountains were no more than two days' journey away. They wouldn't make it.

Riding the unicorn, Charlee separated from the others and gazed west. An orange haze licked at the horizon. The Horeng. Flames from their torches signaled their approach. "They're going to catch us," she uttered. "Time is running out. We have to do something. I have to do something. But what? I'm not some Moses from the Bible. I have no sea to part. No way to crush the Horeng."

Cryton and Penaiya, on their wind horses, joined her. In silence, they watched over the weary travelers who walked without complaint. But Charlee's super hearing registered their hushed conversations and whispers of fear.

Charlee rubbed her burning eyes. She blinked away drowsiness. The people were right to be scared. She'd led them out here to die. "No, don't think like that," she whispered. "Don't give up. There has to be a way."

Above, Janasara's three moons began their trek across the sky, beams of light pushing through the clouds. The Latarans slowed.

"They're tired." Charlee nodded to the families as they passed by. Each person smiled. "We have to stop for at least a little while."

Cryton pointed to the west. "Look out there. You can bet the Horeng will not stop until they have us."

Penaiya glared at Charlee. "It doesn't matter whether we stop now or continue. At this pace, we won't make it."

"Then we have to double our efforts." Cryton held up a fist. "This will be a sprint to the finish line—the mountains."

Charlee reached into the pouch and slid her fingers over the medallion. "Even if we make it to the mountains, then what? Are the Horeng just going to stop? No. And what about that dragon out there? Cryton, we have to figure something else out and fast."

He sighed. "You're right, Guardian. We have to make a stand. We must fight. It's the only way."

"What are you thinking?" Charlee gulped.

"How does that saying go…sometimes the best defense is a strong offense? Is that right?" He twisted his mustache.

"I think so," she answered.

"I don't understand." Penaiya raised an eyebrow. "Are you suggesting we fight an army? Look at our people? They cannot fight."

"Yes, they...we...can." Cryton climbed from his mount and then drew circles in the sand. "Not all of us. Just a few dozen strong enough to wield a sword and a bow. We'll break off from the group and march back to confront the Horeng. Trick them. Make it look like we're a massive army. Attack from hiding places, break off and attack again from a new location. They're dumb beasts. They'll be easily fooled. Meanwhile the rest will continue on their way toward the mountains."

"That's right," Charlee jumped in. "We can be like the Minutemen in the Revolutionary War. We studied about them in school. Small groups carried out attacks on the British army and then escaped, to attack again. Cryton, you know what I'm talking about. With a little luck, we can hold them off long enough for the rest to reach the mountains. Maybe we can even draw that dragon's attention away from our people. Maybe on the battlefield I can find a way to kill it."

"I don't know about this Revolutionary War from your world, but I do know you would all be going off to your death." Penaiya slid from her steed, lips pursed. Her pronounced jaw line became rigid.

"It's the only way to give the rest of the people the chance they need." Cryton rested his hand on Penaiya's shoulder. "Our sacrifice is necessary."

He turned to Charlee. "But I agree with Penaiya. Many could die. You cannot be among them. You must stay and lead our people to safety. I will lead this mission."

Charlee climbed from the unicorn. "No! I will. I'm the only one with a chance to stop that dragon."

The old man stretched out a hand to the people walking by. "You must lead them to the dragons."

"Cryton, I'm the guardian." She grabbed his hand. "If we're talking about a small group of warriors, I can open a gateway right on top of the Horeng. I know my powers haven't really been tested, but I think I can open a gateway big enough for a group for a short time."

"We cannot risk your life—not when there is so much at stake," he protested.

Charlee slightly smiled. "You need me there."

He did not respond.

She took his silence as a victory and turned to Penaiya. "You'll have to lead the people to the mountains. Don't stop for anything. You must move quickly, no matter what."

"I shall," Penaiya said, "but there is a flaw in your plan."

"What?" Charlee asked.

"I can answer that one," Cryton explained before Penaiya could speak. "We don't have the weapons necessary to carry out an attack on the Horeng. We need stronger swords. Bows with large enough arrows to cut through armor from long distances. I've seen the kind of weapons we have. Most of our arrows are fashioned from the forest and made for hunting. They may kill up close, but won't do in this kind of battle."

Charlee frowned at her mentor. "So what can we do?"

Cryton scratched his chin. "The answer might lie buried underneath the Kingdom of Excersa.

"I don't understand." Charlee raised an eyebrow. What did he have up his sleeve? Her pulse quickened. Goose bumps formed along her arms.

A smile crossed Penaiya's face. "He's right."

"What are you two talking about?" Charlee studied them both, contemplating what revelation they were about to share. "Tell me."

Cryton gazed in the distance as if looking back in time. A sullen expression washed over his face. "The Kingdom of Excersa was on a hilltop east of Latara. As Theodora rose to power, before your grandfather sent me and your mother to Earth with the changeling, I was part of a mission to hide weapons in a hidden labyrinth far beneath the castle grounds. Theodora had already begun her conquests, defeating the armies of the Unified Kingdoms on each battlefield. We hid the weapons with the idea should our generation fail to stop the sorceress, future generations might one day rise up to challenge her with the armaments we left behind. The entrance to the lair was magically sealed, the secret known only by a few who would pass word down to new warriors when the time was right."

Charlee's stomach churned. Was it because she hadn't eaten in who knows how long or excitement for the story he told? Did she dare hope the weapons would still be in Excersa guarded all this time by magic? "Come on, they can't still be there. Theodora would have found them."

"Maybe, maybe not. But it's worth a look. Maybe she couldn't get past the enchanted lock. Perhaps the only way in is through a portal." Cryton took a long breath then placed a hand on her shoulder. "Guardian, with your powers, you can open a gateway into the labyrinth. We can gather as many weapons as possible and be out of there. Even if the Horeng are still inside the Kingdom of Excersa, they'll never know we were there, if we are lucky."

"I think I can do that if my powers work right," Charlee answered. "You'll have to help me plot a course for Excersa. Cryton, I'll need to probe your mind. You know, telepathically or whatever."

He nodded. "So it's agreed. Tonight, we gather weapons. Tomorrow, upon the next nightfall, we do battle with the Horeng."

"There's one point we have to think about," Charlee reasoned. "If Theodora is really in my mind, she'll know what we're planning. She'll be ready."

126

"I'm willing to gamble if she's in there somewhere, you can keep her locked away." He tapped her head gently with his staff. "Use your mind. Send her false information. Confuse her. Have faith in yourself—the way I do."

She gulped loudly. "I'll try."

§ § §

Under a pitch-black sky shrouded by looming thunder clouds, Charlee tried to quiet her doubts. She stood apart from the Latarans as Cryton gathered a dozen men and women for their mission.

The enemy's torches cast an orange haze across the western horizon. Could they really do this? Could she really do this?

Despite the chill of night, sweat dripped from her forehead. Her body trembled. "You can do this," Charlee whispered. "You have to do this."

But a voice she heard more and more invaded her mind. *You can't succeed without the medallion. Why do you ignore it?*

"Who are you?" An uneasy feeling grumbled inside her gut like the time the rich-kid bullies at school pretended to be her friend.

Just reach for the medallion, and give yourself over to its power. Then you will know what to do with it, the voice continued.

"How?" She gingerly gripped the pouch at her side. Could the voice be right? Should she give in and try to use its power? Maybe it wouldn't affect her. She was strong and could fight off the medallion's evil.

She started to reach inside…

"Charlee, what are you doing?"

She recoiled and swung to face Cryton. "Nothing! I wasn't doing anything." He stood silently, an eyebrow lifted.

"Well, your warriors await you." The old man motioned for her to follow. "Let's go."

With heavy legs, she lumbered alongside him without speaking a word. A few campfires cast a crimson radiance across their gaunt faces, the crackle of the flames the only sound among the hushed onlookers. Above, lightning streaked across the sky followed by the loudest crack of thunder yet. Children cringed, clinging to their parents. Their fear was a weight on her shoulders, making each stride difficult.

Charlee avoided eye contact. Her hand stroked the pouch. Why shouldn't she listen to the voice in her head and use the medallion? No! She would decide the right time to tap into the medallion's power, if she could even figure out how to use it. Not because some voice told her to. Besides, was the voice a friend or an enemy?

She, Cryton and the unicorn emerged from the crowd to a gathering of volunteers for the mission. They stood tall, surrounded by the rest of the refugees.

Penaiya, arms folded across her chest, lined up with the elders to the right of the team, and introduced this ragtag ensemble.

The Lataran leader started with a pair of teens, a boy, Cortain, and girl, Tornea, who smiled broadly and bowed to Charlee. Next to them a gray-haired woman, Yellan, taller and more fit than most. Beside her a balding man, Orteno, with a patch over his right eye. Four more men, Lorten, Moro, Parran, and Usan, stood like stone statues, lean but strong looking with broad shoulders. Two women, Illian and Adana, joined the group, each young, maybe in their twenties, with long hair twisted into tails running down their backs. They had long, thin legs, like distance runners.

The scouts, Aryean and Miramay, were the last introduced. Aryean tipped his sword to Charlee, a slight grin across his chiseled face. Charlee, her cheeks burning, looked away.

Penaiya took a long breath after the introductions. "Guardian, these twelve have answered the call to carry out this vital mission. Their names will forever hold a place of honor in our hearts."

Cryton ushered Charlee closer to the mismatched band. He was the first to speak, lifting his head and raising his voice. "Warriors of Latara, what we are about to embark on is of critical importance."

Then he nodded at her.

Try as she might to focus, Charlee's mind still toyed with thoughts of the medallion. She cleared her throat. "Uh, yes. Thank you…uh…for volunteering. You are all very brave, and it means a lot to me to stand with you tonight."

She gazed back at Cryton.

"Not your best speech." He leaned in closer. "Don't be nervous. You can do this."

Charlee shrugged. If only the old man knew her thoughts. She struggled to keep her hands from shaking. Her hair matted against her forehead from the sweat gathered along her brow.

"Guardian, are you ready?" Cryton asked.

"Yes," she responded. She rubbed her sweaty palms together. *I hope I'm ready.*

"Warriors of Latara, are you ready?" He cried out.

"Yes," they shouted. The rest of the Latarans closed the circle around them, their shouts and cheers echoing across the desert landscape. The praise soon quieted, replaced by the cries of family members who embraced the warriors.

Cryton held up his staff and then pointed at a mound of canvas sacks on the ground. "It is time. Grab one. Tonight we will gather the very weapons to stand our ground against the Horeng."

The warriors broke away from their friends and family and gathered up the sacks. Wide smiles crossed their faces as if they looked forward to the mission ahead. Charlee blinked away tears. What a brave group. She hoped they would all return. If any of them died…

"All right, Guardian, it is now up to you." Cryton interrupted her thoughts.

I hope this works. Charlee closed her eyes and grabbed onto his shoulders. Her body trembled. The pounding of her heart, and his, echoed in her ears. They beat separately at first and then slowly fell into synch. An image formed deep within her mind of a castle on a mountain peak with towers extending skyward. Inside its walls, statues of past kings and queens filled the courtyard. Caverns bathed in darkness far beneath their feet. Hidden. Forgotten.

Her head throbbed like the feeling of pressure when swimming deep underwater. Charlee released Cryton and rubbed her temples. Instead of drinking in energy, she felt her strength siphoning away, limbs weakening, shoulders hunching over.

She blinked and then opened her eyes. In front of the warriors, a blue circle of energy formed. It grew in size until they all could enter at once.

Teeth clenched, Charlee pushed her powers beyond their limits. She trembled as if seizures overtook her.

"Quickly!" she called out. All twelve hesitated.

"Follow me," Cryton ordered. He jumped into the gateway, and the squad followed.

Come on…Charlee. Just… a little…longer. Hands in front of her as if breaking though the gateway, she staggered into the blue light, the unicorn by her side.

For an instant, all became peaceful as the swirling blue energy engulfed her in protective warmth. But almost as quickly as she stepped into the gateway, she jumped out…into the wrong place.

The Horeng surrounded them! What had she done?

CHAPTER 21

The Discovery

ER GATEWAY SHOULD have opened into a labyrinth underneath Excersa. Instead, Charlee delivered her raiders into the middle of a Horeng horde perched along the walls of a castle.

"Charlee, this is Excersa's courtyard. Get us out of here!" Cryton unsheathed his sword.

The beasts' barks and howls nearly eclipsed his words. They swung around to face the intruders, bringing their bows and arrows to bare on the invaders. Their rage-filled growls signaled more of the wolf army. Monsters poured from hidden corners, surrounding Charlee and her team.

Huddling together, the Latarans lifted their blades in a meaningless gesture. Any second, they'd be cut down by a barrage of arrows. Charlee's head spun. How could she have blown it so bad?

The Horengs' roars and the cries of her squad flooded her mind. She grasped her head, whirling around in search of an escape route. Nothing! Archers stood on a terrace above them. Infantry armed with battle axes boxed them in. They were going to die! *My…fault!*

Cryton grabbed her shoulders. "Do something—now! Charlee…Charlee!"

His words, distant at first, became like a lighthouse beacon ushering through the fog of her own fear. She had to open another gateway.

Charlee knelt to the ground and pressed her hands against the cold damp stones of the courtyard. She willed another gateway to form. Her head pounded in protest. Drops of blood fell from her nose, pooling around her fingers. Could she open a second gateway this fast? "Come on! Powers work!"

The stone underneath her vanished. She and the others fell into a swirling blue tunnel. As if in slow motion, the courtyard slipped from view, but not before the archers launched their attack. Dozens of arrows rained down upon them. No! She had to stop them! Careening into the portal's abyss, Charlee waved her hands, calling on her magic to seal the doorway.

Not fast enough. Some arrows made it through. They whizzed by her, one grazing her arm. Charlee cried out.

Thrashing wildly, she plummeted deeper into the portal. When would this end? Where would the gateway dump her and the others? "Cryton, where—"

Charlee burst through the swirling passageway into pitch black. She shrieked until she slammed into solid ground, shoulder first. Gasping for a breath, she tried to push air in and out of burning lungs.

The moans of others echoed around her.

Where were they? Charlee slowly lifted herself on shaky arms. Warm blood dripped down her arm to her wrist and hand. She ignored the stabbing pain radiating from the wound. She had to find Cryton and the others. A palpable darkness limited her view to just a few feet in each direction. She drew in long breaths of thick air. The earthy stench of moss and mud seeped into her nostrils.

Charlee crawled along a damp rocky surface, reaching out into the gloom. "Cryton, where are you?"

No response came, but the moans continued. She struggled to her feet on unsteady legs. "Anyone, speak to me. Is anyone hurt?" Charlee wandered through the darkness, nearly stumbling to her knees.

"Concentrate." She eased her breathing and slowed her thumping heart. "Use your power."

She closed her eyes, then opened them again. This time, the world around her lit up as if gazing through night-vision goggles—in an eerie green glow, revealing a cavern. The others lay on all sides of her, slowly stirring. But where was Cryton? Why hadn't he answered?

There! In a corner by a rock wall. He didn't move. Charlee started toward him until something fluttered onto her shoulder. Screaming, she slapped it away, then gazed up. A glowing bird—a dove—hovered over her.

"Bike, is that you?" she whispered.

The creature landed on her shoulder a second time. She held out a finger and the being jumped onto it. The changeling had shifted forms from the unicorn to the same dove that watched her from the skies during school.

She placed the changeling onto her shoulder. "We have to get to Cryton."

"I'm okay," he finally said. Slowly rising, he leaned on his staff. He spoke softly. "Is everyone accounted for?" He lifted a torch from his satchel and ignited it with a little device from Earth—a lighter. The flame crackled to life, its orange radiance pushing back the darkness.

Charlee lumbered to Cryton, throwing her arms around him. "Are you hurt?"

He winced, rubbing his side. Blood dripped from his lip. "I've been hurt worse." He touched her arm. "You were hit."

"It's nothing." Charlee backed away from him. "We have to help the others."

"Guardian, over here," One warrior called. She recognized the voice. Aryean's. "It's Miramay. She's...." His voice trailed off.

"No." Charlee swung around. The lighted torch revealed the Latarans leaning over one of their own. Her heart jack hammered inside her chest. "Please, no."

Reaching them, she dropped to her knees. Miramay lay sprawled on the stone ground, her head cradled in Aryean's lap. Two arrows struck her. One in her chest, the other in her stomach. Blood flowed from the wounds. Miramay coughed. Tears slid down her cheeks.

Charlee's hands trembled. Her stomach rolled. What had she done? She grasped the brave young woman's hand. It was so cold.

"Miramay, breathe. I'll get you out of here." Charlee gazed back at Cryton who followed her. "We have to get her away. Help her. Maybe I can get to Mom. She can heal her."

The old man shook his head and glanced at the ground. "It's too late."

"Don't say that!" Charlee shouted. There had to be a way. Miramay couldn't die. She just couldn't.

"It's…okay, Guardian," Miramay whispered. She pulled Charlee closer. "I… lived to fight…at your side. A…guardian's…side. I am…proud." She coughed again. Blood oozed from her mouth.

Charlee squeezed her hand. "I'm so sorry."

"Don't…be." Miramay took a long breath. It was her last. Her eyes stared off blankly. One last tear slid down her cheek. Aryean gently slid his fingers over her eyes and lowered her head to the ground.

Silence filled the darkened chamber.

Rising to her feet, Charlee slunk away. Her chest heaved and the tears came. How could she have let this happen? She had seen the Latarans die when the Horeng attacked their village. She lived with it, telling herself it wasn't her fault. This death was her fault. How could she go on?

The changeling, back in unicorn form, rested its snout on her shoulder. She pushed him away,

"What did I do?" She slumped to the ground.

"Shake it off, Charlee." Cryton took hold of her shoulders, lifting Charlee to her feet. "I know how you feel. I know what it is to lose people serving under you. In my younger years, I faced it far too often. I know it hurts, but we don't have time to mourn right now. We're in the right place. We have to move. The Horeng army has claimed Excersa. They may know a way into this labyrinth. We still need you."

He spoke loud enough for everyone to hear. "You must all stay focused. We still have work to do. You want to honor Miramay. Complete the mission."

Aryean spoke up. "He's right. It's what Miramay would want."

The others voiced their support, some sniffing back tears, calling out, "For Miramay."

Charlee ignored them. Her blood boiled. She wanted to scream., to pound her chest and rip out her hair. She whirled away from everyone.

"Pull yourself together, Guardian." Cryton swung her around to face him. "You got us here. We're in the labyrinth. You're giving us a fighting chance. You have not failed us. You did not fail Miramay. She knew the danger. Accepted it. We must move."

Cryton waved the torch over his head; the fire brightened, chiseling away at more of the shadowy lair. Enough to hint at the sheer size of the cavern. As big as the New York subway she'd traveled through with her family on vacation.

The ceiling disappeared into the murkiness above. Beyond the reach of the torch, the labyrinth stretched lengthwise into obscurity. Charlee shuddered. They were too vulnerable. The Horeng could sneak up at any time.

Cryton's long strides suggested he could have moved through the labyrinth blindfolded. He quickly found what he was searching for—a set of torches lining one of the walls—and lit them.

As each burned, the cavern's secrets were revealed.

"Look at that!" Aryean pronounced.

"I can't believe it!" Tornea added. She had a gash above her forehead and walked with a limp.

Charlee bit her upper lip and scanned everyone. Most had injuries. Orteno bled from his leg. His blood pooled around his foot. An arrow with a crimson-soaked tip lay next to him. Cortain had scratches across his young face. He gripped his own wrist, grimacing. Could it be broken? The others hobbled around the chamber, ignoring cuts on their hands, arms and faces.

She turned away from them. "Dammit. How could I be so stupid?"

Cryton pulled her aside and leaned in close, a scowl across his face. "Guardian, look around you," he muttered. "These people need you. Be their leader. Stop pitying yourself. There is enough of an arsenal here to serve a small army. Maybe there is hope after all."

"But—"

"Sometimes all it takes is a little belief to beat impossible odds." He winked at her. "Just sometimes."

Wiping her eyes, taking a deep breath, Charlee nodded. She would never forgive herself, but right now she needed to get off her butt and act like a guardian.

She peered at the weapons. Long swords and short blades, staffs with daggers attached, large bows and strong arrows, and stacks of armor surrounded them. They glowed under the orange flame of the torches. Ominous looking armament, in the right hands more deadly than the crude gear the Latarans wore. The only problem, the people they left behind were not soldiers. They were weak, hungry and tired. Would they be able to fight? Charlee took a long breath of the moist air. There simply was no other choice.

There is a choice. The voice inside her head returned as if it could read her thoughts. *Take up the medallion. With its power you will be unstoppable. Without it you will fail and more blood will be on your hands.*

Charlee grasped the pouch, which clung to her as if magically attached. She started to reach inside but recoiled. "Get out of my head," she mouthed. "Leave me alone." Her body tensed. When the time was right, she'd have to have a showdown with the voice. That didn't change the fact the voice was right. Sooner or later, she'd have to learn the secret of the medallion to fight Theodora. Just not yet.

From behind, the unicorn nudged her with its snout.

She relaxed her muscles. "I'm all right." It was a lie, but for now she'd be the guardian everyone needed her to be.

"All right, load up," she commanded. "Fill your sacks with as much as you can hold. I don't know how long until the Horeng figure out where we've gone. We won't have time to grab it all, but we need to take as much as we can."

Cryton smiled so wide not even his thick mustache could hide his lips. "You heard the guardian."

The group moved quickly despite their injuries, bolting in different directions. Steel clanged together. Shields rattled as they were stacked together.

Cortain, the teenager, hefted a sword nearly his size but it quickly drooped. "I claim this one for myself," he declared.

Aryean handed him a much smaller blade. "I think you should stick with this one."

The teenager swung the large sword wildly, almost dropping it. "Nope, I'll stick with this one."

Charlee marveled at them all. So brave. So willing to sacrifice. They were ready to become soldiers even if she wasn't. She grabbed two sacks. She would fill an extra sack for Miramay.

She trudged toward the weapons until tiny voices whispered to her in a language no one else seemed to hear. The leaf creatures! They beckoned her. But how could they be down here?

"Guardian, the We has something to show you here by the Our," a thousand wispy voices declared in unison. "Hear the We and come to the Our."

She started to call out to Cryton, but he was busy wrapping Orteno's injuries. Charlee followed the leaves' voices. What did they want her to see? Could this be a trick? A Theodora scheme to separate her from the others? She lifted her sword and clutched the pouch.

"Can you see the We now, Guardian?" the voices asked.

She peered deeper into the labyrinth, tapping into the changeling's energy to strengthen her sight. In the distance, a lone tree flourished in the dark. Its thick trunk rose from the labyrinth's stone floor. Thick branches stretched high above, covered by star-shaped leaves, pulsating with a faint white glow. How was this possible? Magic?

"Yes, I see," she whispered in their language.

Dropping the sacks and her sword, Charlee glided toward the tree as if hypnotized. When she reached it, she ran her fingers over the rough bark. Despite the cool damp atmosphere, warmth rose from the trunk. She embraced it with both arms. Tears formed. She felt a connection with this tree. But why?

"The We welcomes you, Guardian. You were meant to find the Our."

What did they mean? Her mind swirled. She glanced down. At her feet lay a gathering of fallen leaves. A stray dancing light from the torches picked up a gleam from underneath the foliage.

She dropped to her knees and brushed away the leaves. A sword lay hidden there with a long blade as clean and sharp as the day it was forged. The silvery handle had the graceful shape of a bird with wings extended.

More tears flowed down her cheeks. This sword meant something. She reached for it but stopped. She didn't have the right to touch it. Somehow, deep in her mind, she knew the blade belonged to...

"What have you found, Guardian?" Cryton stood just behind her. The unicorn beside him.

"I saw this tree, and I had to come to it. I couldn't help myself. I mean, what's a tree doing down here?"

"I don't know, but we have to get out of here."

"Wait, Cryton, look at this." She wiped away her tears and pointed at the blade." Her mentor dropped beside her.

"Cryton?"

He gently slid his fingers over the steel then placed his lips to the blade. Slowly, he stood and backed away from the tree, his eyes watering.

"Say something?" Charlee demanded.

"I can't believe it, but Charlee, this is your grandfather's weapon... Michala's blade. This can only mean."

He stopped then retreated.

"What?"

"Guardian, this is Michala's burial place." His voice cracked. Is it possible even in death, his power for good could manifest in this tree? How else could it grow alone here without sunlight?"

Charlee scrambled to her feet, handing the sword to Cryton. Her heart stopped.

He held her grandfather's sword close to his chest. "After his death, his body must have been secreted here. Those who brought him must have labored to hide his body under stone, but why not lay his sword with him?"

"The old one is correct," the leaves answered, though only Charlee could hear them. "Your grandfather is here with the We. His sword was placed with him but as the Our grew, the sword rose with it. Your grandfather wanted it to be found. He would want you to wield it."

Charlee couldn't hold back her tears. She was about to tell Cryton, but the leaves continued to speak. "There's more, Guardian. Your grandmother, Queen Assara, is here as well. Together with her husband. For all time."

Charlee collapsed onto her knees. "Cryton, my grandmother is here, too."

"What?" He slid next to her. "How do you know?"

"I just do."

He reached out and touched the trunk. With his other hand, he handed her the blade. "Your grandfather's sword was meant to be wielded by a leader… by a guardian. You were meant to find this place, and you have."

She grasped the handle with both hands, but the sword sagged, tipping to the ground. Heavy. Longer than the one Cryton gave her. "Give me strength." With a grunt, she hefted the sword, holding the tip high.

"Guardian, you will wield this sword in your grandfather's name." Cryton placed his hands over hers.

"What? No!"

"You must! It belongs to your family. Your grandfather would want you to have it."

Charlee shook her head. Breaking away from his grip, she handed him the blade. How could he suggest she take the sword? She didn't deserve it. Not yet anyway. "Cryton, I can't."

"Yes, Guardian—you can." He pushed the sword back to her.

With a deep breath, Charlee held the weapon close to her face, studying the powerful steel.

Cryton winked at her. "Use that weapon proudly, as your grandfather did."

"I don't know if I can. All I do is screw up, and now because of me Miramay is dead. I—"

He raised a finger to his lips. "Someday you will know—just as I do—that you deserve to carry that sword. It is the true sword of a guardian."

The blade revealed her reflection. Her face. In all its imperfections. Her greasy hair. Shallow skin. But not evil. Not like the vision of her face on the medallion.

She lowered her head to the fallen leaves. "Grandfather… grandmother, I'll try to make you proud. I promise."

CHAPTER 22

The Battle Begins

UNDER A GRIM early-morning sky, sunrise still several hours away, Charlee knelt on one knee before the family of the fallen warrior. With her head bowed, she asked for their forgiveness. Miramay's body was at rest on the changeling's back, protected by its wings. Cryton and Penaiya knelt with Charlee.

Three hundred Latarans circled them, joining in a sorrowful chant. Charlee tried to shut out their tears but couldn't. She understood. This death added to the pain from the Horeng attack on their village.

"I'm so sorry I let this happen," Charlee offered in her best Lengoron. "If I could take her place—"

Miramay's mother grasped her hand and lifted her chin gently with a forefinger. She had her daughter's strong face but with cracked skin ravaged from sun exposure. The woman smiled as tears dripped down wrinkled cheeks. "We are grateful to you, Guardian. You gave my daughter a purpose—to serve her people with honor. Her sacrifice will give us strength."

Charlee nodded. *Grateful to me? I'm the reason your daughter is dead. Me! I screwed up.*

The woman kissed her hand and turned away. She and the other members of Miramay's family removed the body from the unicorn and carried her away followed by others who joined in the mourning.

Penaiya placed an arm around Charlee, then followed the others. Wiping away tears, Charlee climbed to her feet and stormed past Cryton. The old man reached out to her but she shoved his hand away.

"She wouldn't be dead if I just faced Theodora alone." She glared at the old man. He leaned heavily on his staff as if it were the only thing keeping him on his feet. His shoulders slouched, head tilted to one side. "Now more are going to die in this plan to attack the Horeng. I can't do it, Cryton. I can't deal with people dying because of me. Just let me go off and face Theodora on my own."

He rubbed his head in silence with a shaky hand before he spoke. His mustache drooped. "That's just the point, Charlee," he finally responded. "If you went after Theodora unprepared and failed, these people would have no hope of survival. Theodora would slaughter them. By leading them to the dragons, you give them hope of protection."

The Dragon Lord will probably torch them and eat them for lunch. Should she tell Cryton the truth about the dragon's warning to stay away? No, she couldn't. Wait, what did he mean...*went after Theodora unprepared?*

She stomped up to him, stopping a foot away. "You don't think I can beat Theodora, do you?"

"I didn't say that." He scowled at her.

"Good to know what you really think." She grasped the pouch.

"Char—" Cryton reached for her.

She backed away. "I'll show you, old man. I'll show everyone."

She gritted her teeth. Wait, what was she saying? What was she doing? Why was she so angry? "I...I'm sorry. I don't know...." She let go of the pouch.

"It's all right, Guardian," His expression softened. He reached to her but pulled his hand back. It still quivered. "You're right. I shouldn't—"

"No, it's me. Something's happening to me. I feel...different." She let out a slow breath of air. *Tell him about the medallion*, she thought. Tell him about the vision of your face on it. Tell him about the voice urging you to use it. No, not now. He doesn't need to know. No one does.

"You're just tired like all of us." His lips curled up in a slight smile that quickly faded. "Rest for a bit. You deserve it. Our mission was a success because of you. Remember that."

He formed a fist with his trembling hand and stared toward the orange haze in the west, a harbinger of the advancing Horeng. "You're right, Guardian," he continued. "When we attack Theodora's army, some of us will die. It is a fact of war, and this is a war for our survival. I know it's hard for you. After all, you're only fourteen. But we must do this. You could go off to face Theodora, and you might be victorious, but the truth is you could fall. I believe your guardian abilities delivered us to our people for a reason. Sure, it changed our plans, but we must follow this course. In the end, this new path will lead us to victory. Of that I am sure."

"I hope you're right." She gripped his hand. "Cryton, are you all right? Maybe it's you who needs rest."

He slid his hand away from her. "Just age. I'll be fine. Don't worry about me. Just ready yourself for what's to come."

Charlee pulled Michala's sword from a scabbard at her waist. With her arms outstretched, she held the blade up to the sky. "I hope he'll be with me."

"He is always with you." Cryton lifted himself, no longer leaning on his staff. "You know, I see your grandfather when I look at you. I know he's proud of you. I am proud of you. Now, what about getting some sleep for a while?"

Charlee lowered the sword. "No time. We have to keep moving."

Cryton sighed but nodded. "Lead the way, Charlee."

Once Miramay was laid to rest, they marched through the remaining night and into the new day. They never stopped. They ate as they walked. Prepared for battle on the move. She strode alongside the unicorn and Cryton at the head of the three hundred or so people depending on her.

The weight of their hopes and fears pressed against her shoulders, which made each step heavy even as the changeling fed her energy to strengthen her limbs. Concern for the warriors who would soon go off to battle didn't help. She rotated her neck to try to loosen stiff muscles.

Their plan was simple but required her to do something with her power she had never done before—open two separate gateways at once.

Gather a group of Latarans strong enough to wield weapons and fire arrows. Split the warriors into two groups. Charlee would lead one; Cryton the other. The two gateways would deliver them to positions north and south of the Horeng army if her powers worked right.

They'd have to find cover and, armed with bows, arrows, and slings, attack. The goal—stop the army's forward march—at least temporarily. Divide the beasts in two. Make them give chase in the wrong directions. This might just give the group led by Penaiya time to reach the mountains.

Charlee shuddered. It was a crazy plan.

Soon, dusk settled over the land. Cryton gathered the warriors together. Men and women. Fathers and mothers, sisters and brothers, grandfathers and grandmothers. They numbered fifty in all. They stood tall in gleaming metal armor like a real army. Only they weren't.

Charlee, her tunic covered by a golden chest plate, light weight but sturdy, was leading them to certain death.

How was she supposed to do that? Was she strong enough? Charlee bit a nail. She would have to keep a mental lock on Cryton and his team. Without it, she couldn't bring his group back. They'd be stranded alone with the Horeng.

She shook off the thought. "I have to remain positive for them all."

Cryton's words broke through her thoughts. "Guardian, take this." Adorned in his own silver chest plate, he handed her a spiraling ram's horn. Unpolished, rough and cracked, it looked like it could crumble into pieces at any moment.

"What's this for?" she asked.

"It is the horn of the Grensera, a very proud mountain beast. In the olden days, generals used these to signal their knights that the time for courage had come. Michala used one just like this. Today you are the guardian. Use it as he did."

"Where did you get this?"

"Penaiya kept one as a symbol for the people. Now, it is your time to signal Latarans to fight once more, as we did in days' past."

Charlee carefully took the horn, climbed onto the unicorn's back, and blew. At first, she produced nothing but a cough and sputter from the horn. *Come on, stupid.* With a deep breath, she tried once more. The song blared fourth on her second try and sounded over the land. She lifted her head and thrust out her chest, sucking in her rounded stomach. It was time.

"Uh, my friends," she called out. "What you are about to do will be remembered forever by our people. They'll know this day as the day you gave them a chance to survive. I can't tell you for sure what's going to happen when we meet the enemy tonight, but I can tell you that we'll all stand together."

Cheers followed her words.

She raised the ram's horn. The people grew silent.

"One more thing," she bellowed. "Let this moment go down in history as the day the people of Latara said, 'Back off, Theodora! We will not run anymore.'"

Beside her, Cryton nodded his approval.

More cheers exploded.

"Now, follow me!"

Charlee slid off the unicorn. She dug her feet into the dirt and tightened her body, willing herself to use the power she barely understood—in a way she had never done before. Each muscle of her body quivered from the effort. Her head was so heavy she thought she might fall.

Two circles of light formed in front of her. The swirling blue gateways increased in size until five people could walk through them at one time, side by side. She struggled to keep the gateways open. When she couldn't speak, Cryton spoke for her.

"Warriors of Latara, march forward in the name of our kinsmen. Earn your place among the greatest knights our people have ever known. March on with me—and with our guardian."

With that, he strode forward into the light, followed by two separate lines of warriors who disappeared into the portals.

Head burning like a fever swept across her brow, Charlee fought to keep the gateways open. She clenched her teeth as if straining against the super G-forces of a massive roller coaster. *Just…a little…longer*, she urged herself.

When the last of the Latarans vanished into the light, Charlee, holding her head to keep her skull from splitting open, limped inside the portal. The unicorn entered beside her. Then both doorways collapsed.

§ § §

Inside, Charlee's vision grayed as she slipped near unconsciousness, drained from the effort to control these magical pathways. No! she had to stay awake. Alert. The others were depending on her. She shook her head to break the foggy layer. It worked. Light broke through the dimness.

Warm liquid dripped from her nose down her lips. She wiped it away. *Blood!*

Beads of sweat dotted her forehead and slid down the side of her face. "Don't freak out. Keep it together."

Reaching up to grasp the unicorn's neck, Charlee tapped into the changeling's life force. Energy rushed into her muscles like a surging river. Her lungs filled with air. Pulse quickened.

Up ahead, was an opening to the spiraling tunnel. "Going to make—"

She burst through the portal into the shadows of nightfall, falling to one knee. Her warriors surrounded her.

"Guardian, are you hurt?" Aryean leaned in close, his warm lips inches from hers. He placed a hand on the side of her head, his touch strangely soothing.

"I'm all right," Charlee reassured him, wiping more blood from her nose. Gripping his strong shoulder, she climbed to her feet, then backed away from him. Her face felt flushed. If this were high school, he'd be the jock and she the clumsy, shy nerd afraid to make eye contact. Here, she was a guardian. This was not the time nor the place for any of those teenage feelings.

Scanning their surroundings, she breathed a sigh of relief. Perhaps by mere luck, she delivered her fighters into a place of relative safety. An outcropping of trees concealed their presence from the Horeng…for now. If the land shifted, their momentary good fortune might run out.

Charlee patted her grandfather's sword and offered a moment of silent thanks. Her grandfather must have intervened on her behalf and placed the sheltering trees here. The foliage was so thick, she couldn't see past the rows of spiraling trunks, arching branches and glowing leaves, which formed a ceiling overhead.

She didn't need to see the Horeng army to know it was out there beyond the woodlands. The thunder of Theodora's beasts tromping over the earth froze the blood pumping through her veins. Charlee forced herself not to shiver. A guardian shouldn't show fear.

Grasping the handle of her grandfather's sword, she rested the blade against her forehead. Warmth flowed from the weapon, radiating through her body. "I can do this." She started to slink forward but was stopped by the voice in her head. *Crude steel is not the answer. Take the medallion.* She gazed at the pouch. "Shut up."

Charlee pushed on, creeping like a lion on prowl, motioning for her team to follow. Short shallow breaths escaped her lips. Too loud. She had to be quiet.

Reaching the edge of the tree line, she crouched in tall grass. The twenty-five warriors with her settled into hiding places behind tree trunks. The changeling hung farther back.

Charlee covered her mouth to muffle a gasp. Beyond the trees, the massive army trudged toward the Temora mountains in the east—and the fleeing Latarans led by Penaiya. Flaming war banners cast the hordes in a blood-bathed glow. Their yellow eyes shined under a darkening sky.

143

These wolf-creatures grunted and barked. Some laughed like hyenas. Others lifted their snouts to sniff the air. Could they smell her hidden warriors? Or the fear of the people they pursued?

No reason to worry about that now. Somewhere beyond the Horeng, hopefully safe for the moment, Cryton and his force waited for her to act. Lifting her grandfather's sword, she uttered, "Give me strength. Courage. Be with me."

Ready or not, this battle—one they had no chance of winning—was about to begin. Deep in her mind, she grappled with the fact she was only fourteen and had no business leading anyone into a war. The voice added to her internal struggle. *You can't win without the medallion. Use its power before it's too late and anyone else dies.*

Quieting her thoughts, she swung back to her warriors. "Archers! Get ready."

The men and women lined up in a tight formation just behind the tree line. They armed their bows with long, silver tipped arrows, then waited for Charlee's next order.

"Remember, this is for your people." She held her sword over her head. "Make sure your arrows find their targets."

If all went right...if the Horeng were as bloodthirsty and stupid as Cryton believed they were...they'd break rank and seek their attackers. The beasts would lose control and forget any leadership that kept them in order. Fight like wild, confused dogs.

Disorder would follow. For as long as possible. Long enough, she hoped, to draw the attention of Theodora's daughter and the dragon she rode. If they showed up, she'd find a way to destroy that winged threat...somehow.

At some point in the battle, she'd open two gateways for the warriors to escape and rejoin their people. This stand would hopefully give them all the few precious hours necessary to reach the mountains.

A good plan but plans fail. She had to be positive.

Again Charlee steadied her thoughts. *The time is now. It begins.* In one heartbeat, she slashed the sword down.

"Fire!"

CHAPTER 23

The First Strike

HER ARCHERS LAUNCHED arrows into the night sky. Without hesitating, they fired a second round. A third. A fourth. Creating the impression of a much greater force than the mere twenty-five who stood with her. The arrows cut through the air, landing in the midst of the Horeng with vicious precision. Each arrow struck a dumb beast with a thud. Cries rose from the wounded and dying. Howls and roars spread among their ranks. Those closest to the attack swung in every direction, battle axes raised high. Like a domino effect, the army slowed and then stopped their march.

"Yes!" Charlee proclaimed.

She marveled at the aim of the archers. Years of hunting had honed their skill, preparing them for this night.

As the final wave of arrows landed, ripping through more of Theodora's dark creations, the savages scrambled, like confused animals.

"We're doing it!" Charlee waved a fist in the air, but the moment cut short as the beasts glared at the trees where she and her warriors hid. The unnatural fiends lumbered toward their position. "Come on, Cryton, it's your—"

Another rain of arrows fell on the Horeng—this time from Cryton's archers across the battlefield.

"Here we go," Charlee called to her squad. "Move down the tree line and prepare to fire your arrows again."

Now came her time to strike. She signaled her archers to let their arrows fly. Again they shot one round. Then another. And a third.

The arrows raced to their targets, like tiny jets screaming across the skies. They tore into the scum, burying into flesh. More beasts dropped to the ground, moaning and writhing in pain.

The plan worked...so far...but she couldn't celebrate. The battle had just begun. She and her band were vastly outnumbered. Theodora's forces stretched before them. Her heart did somersaults inside her chest. "Keep it together, Charlee."

With a wave of her hand, she motioned the Latarans to dash along the tree line to new positions. From there, they launch one more wave of arrows. But the sinister enemy regrouped faster than she expected. Barks came from their lines that had to be commands.

Charlee fought off the queasy feeling of fear building in her stomach. *"They're going to—"*

In full battle gear, waving their swords, battle axes, and spears, hundreds of the creatures stampeded toward the trees. The ground shook under their assault. This is what she wanted. Keep them away from the rest of the Latarans escaping to the mountains. The monstrous charge was terrifying nevertheless.

"Retreat!" Charlee shouted. "Use the trees, bushes—anything to remain hidden. Then let your arrows and slingshots fly. We have to keep this up. Pull as many of them as possible into the trees."

She paused just long enough to take a breath.

"Good luck!" she sang out. "Now, move!"

Bravely and without question, her warriors disappeared into the protective cover—to which they had become so accustomed during their exile—as though they were one with the woods.

Charlee crouched behind a thick trunk, holding her breath, waiting for the upright wolves to burst through the foliage. "Bike, in case I fall…." She stopped and glanced around. The changeling disappeared. *What? Bike? Where are you?* She scanned the trees. Maybe the unicorn morphed into a dove. Nothing. Her protector left her alone. No, there had to be a reason.

From above came a thousand tinkling voices. The leaf creatures!

"We are with you, Guardian," they declared.

She peered at a low-hanging branch. "Thank—"

The brutes crashed through the trees, threatening growls rising from their snouts. Charlee flinched, fumbling with her grandfather's sword, nearly dropping it. She had to flee. Run far away. No, she couldn't. Lives depended on her.

The Horeng hacked at the trees, but the leaves struck back. Branches swept downward, smashing into the beasts. One wolf hurtled backward with a yelp until it collided against another tree trunk. A second monster was lifted off the ground, then body slammed. The trees pummeled more brutes, striking them over and over as if wielding branches like clubs. Some of the wolves were silenced for good, their bodies twisted and mangled.

Another wave approached more cautiously than the first, slashing at the branches with their weapons. The leaves cried out but kept up their fight. Charlee cringed. Their pain echoed in her ears. So much death. She had to save the brave trees. Lead her warriors. Bring steel against steel. Absorbing the energy of the trees into herself, the muscles in her arms and legs bulged. She gripped her sword in both hands. *Strike now!* She leaped from her hiding place.

Charlee swung at one creature. Her blade pierced the enemy's armor and hacked into flesh. Warm, sticky blood coated her hands and splashed across her face. She shrieked, slashing wildly. "Die…beasts!"

146

In seconds, she disabled four wolves.

Arrows whizzed by her head, striking the advancing Horeng. Panting, she glanced over her shoulders. Her archers fired endlessly. More arrows zipped through the air. The howls of pain from Theodora's army surrounded her—but even as they fell, more kept coming.

How long could they keep up the fight. How many Latara warriors would fall? What about the dragon and Theodora's daughter? They had to appear. When they did, she'd cut the giant lizard's wings—anything to keep it away from her people.

Charlee reached for the Grensera horn, hung on her waist. She was about to signal the call for retreat, but a woman's cry stopped her. One of her warriors was about to be killed by a Horeng standing over her with a spear.

Crossing the distance, Charlee brought her sword down just in time to cut the spear in two. Before the wild animal had a chance to react, she sliced through it. The foul creation slumped to the ground.

She reached for the woman. "Are you all—"

Another beast growled above her. Charlee gasped. An axe swooshed toward her head. She raised her sword to meet the steel. Their weapons clanged. Before the wolf could deliver another blow, a second axe hacked at its shoulder. It yelped and tried to slink away only to be struck again.

One more Horeng stood over the fallen one. Charlee lifted her sword to defend herself yet again, but before she could strike, the new beast bowed.

"Bike?" Charlee uttered.

The brute, whose fur—different from the others—was white, nodded. Her changeling protector transformed into one of Theodora's wolf soldiers. A perfect disguise. "I knew you wouldn't leave me. I just knew it."

Charlee grinned and blew on the Grensera horn, signaling retreat.

Horn in one hand, sword in the other, she gestured for the woman and changeling to follow, then sprinted through the trees. Low branches bent away to clear a path for her. The wolves, though slowed by their heavy armor and massive weapons, chased close behind. Charlee glanced back. One beast leaped at her, but a tree snagged it around the waist, hurling the animal into the darkness.

The rest of the Latara warriors gathered behind a giant fallen tree. It would provide the perfect cover from which they could make their last stand.

Charlee scrambled over the wooden goliath with the changeling, returned to unicorn form, at her side. Surrounded again by her fighters, she swallowed hard and took a deep breath. She still had to be their leader.

"All right." She raised her sword. "Here they come. Fire your arrows and slings one more time. Then run with all your might. We can't do much more."

"We can't stop now," Aryean, his face bloodied, countered. "We need to give our people more time."

Charlee pointed at him. "If we don't, you're all going to die."

"But—" another warrior began.

"As you run," Charlee interrupted. "I'll create a gateway back. Jump through. I'll only be able to keep it open for a minute. Can't let these bastards through."

"What about you?" a third warrior, a young man with a dirt-streaked face and gash along his forearm, asked.

"I'm going to join Cryton and the others. Open a gateway for them. Trust me. I'll be right behind you." That wasn't true. She had to find the dragon first and wage her own fight against Theodora. Even if that meant using the medallion.

"No!" Aryean protested. "We will stay with you and fight."

With no time to argue, Charlee nodded in agreement. Another lie. "All right, then, we fight together. Get ready. Launch your arrows and slings—now."

Once more, they fired their arrows and slung their rocks at the advancing army, whose progress slowed because of the leaves and trees. The Horeng fell quickly—but more charged.

"Retreat once more!" She had to act quickly. Charlee strained her muscles. Blood rushed to her head. *Focus*, she urged herself.

Her team did as ordered. As soon as they turned to run, a swirling tunnel of energy swallowed them up. The Latara warriors disappeared from the battle—back to safety. Charlee quickly closed the gateway behind them.

She slumped against the tree, relieved all survived, but now she sat alone in the gloom. *Well...not alone.* The changeling remained at her side.

Opening the gateway tapped her strength. Her head drooped. Arms collapsed at her side. Charlee couldn't even bring herself to lift her sword. *At least she saved those warriors from certain death.*

Now the task would fall on Penaiya to lead on to the dragons and convince the Dragon Lord to change his mind. Hopefully this little war had given them time to reach safety. "It probably hasn't."

Suddenly, her body tingled as if jolted by an electric shock. Her blood pumped faster, and her tired arms swelled as the muscle underneath her skin grew. Lifting her head, she slid next to the unicorn and grasped a leg. The bike...the unicorn... was funneling as much of its energy as possible into her, sparking her back to life.

One thought raced through her mind. What was she doing? This wasn't over. She had to save Cryton and find a way to stop the dragon.

Charlee reached out to her mentor with her mind, trying to get a sense of Cryton's location, but her mental lock on him had broken.

"Damn!" she muttered. She had to find him. *Please don't be too late.*

She lifted herself off the ground and climbed onto the unicorn. "Bike, fly!"

The unicorn thrust its wings hard against the ground and lifted off—just as a pack of Theodora's monsters reached the old fallen tree.

Spears flew through the air after them.

"Hang on, Cryton!" she called.

The unicorn flew over the whole freaking army, which halted its march to focus on the battle at hand—a battle that looked larger than it really was.

She scanned beyond to another outcropping of trees. At first, no sign of Cryton or the others. Where was he? Even with her enhanced vision, the old man and his team alluded her. Then…

"Bike, look." Cryton's warriors were scattered throughout trees—and they were not alone. The mindless killers surrounded them, fighting sword to sword. Some of the Lataran warriors had already fallen.

"No!" Charlee wailed. Her heart sank. She nearly lost her grip on the unicorn's mane.

You see. You should have used the medallion, the voice inside her head proclaimed.

CHAPTER 24

It Can't Be True

THE WARRIORS BELOW wouldn't last long.

Brave though they may be, they lacked strength to stand against the beasts in close-range combat. The Latarans, whose armor hung off their slim bodies, were like a high school freshman football squad standing up to a varsity team full of bulked up seniors. Theodora's army had them surrounded, squeezing them in for a quick slaughter.

Steel clanged together. Axe-wielding wolves howled in delight. Warriors grunted with each blow. More Horeng rushed toward them from the legions across the battlefield. The images all swirled together in a dizzying display. Charlee's stomach lurched. Bile rose up her throat.

"No!" she screamed. Tightening her grip on the unicorn's mane and pointing her sword at the chaos, she called out, "Bike, we've got to save them!"

The unicorn threw back its wings, forcing itself into a fast dive toward the trees. The tree branches parted, clearing a path. Their whispery voices declared in unison, "We stand with you, Guardian."

Charlee's protector skimmed over the heads of Theodora's vile creations. She waved her grandfather's blade wildly. The aged steel slashed through necks, cut across snouts, and sliced off ears. Blood spewed from the wounds, coating her weapon. The beasts crumbled into the tall grass, gurgling, whimpering and thrashing about.

After one pass, the unicorn soared into the sky then swung around for another attack. Charlee leaned forward, teeth clenched, hair soaked from sweat and the enemy's blood. "Let's get—"

She spotted Cryton. The old man fought beside a group of Latarans separated from the rest in a small pocket surrounded by the Horeng. He swung his bladed staff, fending off two of the savages. The warriors fought on both sides of him. An axe smashed through the skull of one man, nearly splitting him in half. He never had the chance to cry out.

"Bastards! I'll kill you all!" Charlee banged her heels against the unicorn. "Bike go! Save Cryton!"

With one mighty thrust of its wings, the unicorn raced forward, plowing into the chaos. Three of the monsters fell. Charlee leaped to the ground next to her old mentor. She held her sword in front of her. "Cryton!"

"About time…young…lady." His chest heaved. Claw marks ripped across his shoulder and leg. A gash across his forehead bled. He struggled to catch his breath and still managed a slight grin.

Charlee cursed herself. She left him alone too long. What was she thinking?

"Cryton, we have to get you all out of here—now."

A wolf swung an axe at her. Cryton blocked it and then sliced through the creature's midsection. The beast dropped its weapon, clutching its innards pouring through the gaping wound. Charlee plunged her own blade through the belly of a second. She kicked it in the stomach to free her weapon.

"Lead…the…way." The old man spun his staff as more of Theodora's army burst through the trees, chopping off branches. The leaf creatures bellowed, striking back, but were no match for the onslaught. Trees toppled as the Horeng advanced like a tidal wave crushing everything in its path.

"Everyone, follow me!" Charlee grasped the ram's horn tied to her waist and blew. Its deep soulful cry called to the scattered warriors.

As they retreated, she counted them. Only twelve! Not enough. There had to be more. Could so many have died? Time had run out. She had to open a gateway now to save Cryton and the others.

Not for herself. She couldn't abandon any warriors still fighting…somewhere. Drawing all the energy she could from the unicorn, trees, and leaves, Charlee opened a portal. The blue energy appeared instantaneously.

"All of you, jump into the light!" Her sword slipped from her hands as she concentrated on holding open the portal. Her shoulders slouched. Legs wobbled. *Don't let up.*

One after another, the warriors of Latara disappeared into the swirling tunnel.

From behind her came a threatening growl. A Horeng! She spun around as the beast's axe hacked through the air toward her head. *Move!* She dropped to the ground and rolled. By the time she climbed to her feet the beast crumbled to the earth. Cryton stood over it, blood dripping from one side of his weapon.

Just then, the portal shrunk from a spinning circle of light to a marble and then puffed out of existence.

"Cryton, you were supposed to go." Charlee stumbled to him.

"Can't," he uttered. "More of my warriors are here. I have to find them."

She shook her head. "I'll find them. Let me open a new portal for you."

Cryton wielded his staff at a charging Horeng, cutting through the monster. "No. I'm staying." He took off running in search of his lost fighters, disappearing into a thick grove of trees.

"Wait for me." She reached out for the unicorn to once again tap into the changeling's energy. Strength quickly returned to her tired limbs. She picked up her sword. "Why couldn't he just listen to me?"

Charlee bolted after Cryton into the dense hardwood, more beasts giving chase.

From behind came a crack as if a whip slapped against skin. Wolves yelped. She glanced back. Theodora's fiends moaned in the undergrowth, victims of another strike by the leaf creatures.

With her enhanced vision, Charlee peered ahead through the narrow passages between the dense foliage. The remaining Latarans huddled just beyond the trees on the bank of a dry creek bed, their shields held high to protect them from what?

Charlee scanned deeper and gasped. Across the channel stood the dragon and its mysterious rider who called herself the daughter of Theodora. The reptile roared and spit fire into the night sky, casting the land in an orange glow.

"No!" Charlee dodged through the trees, barely aware of the unicorn running at her side. Without waiting for the old man to keep up, she burst through the trees and came face to face with the winged beast and its rider.

The daughter of Empress Theodora, her head still covered by a black helmet, leaped the narrow creek. Unleashing an ear-shattering war cry, she unsheathed her sword and attacked three fighters at once. She effortlessly slashed one bearded man across the chest. He shrieked, then fell silent. The two others back-stepped away from the dark knight, stumbling over each other.

Four others had fallen, charred by dragon fire. Steam rose from their bodies. The stench of burnt flesh hung heavy over the battleground.

Charlee clutched her chest to slow her thudding heart. The dragon had to be stopped, but how? She gritted her teeth. *Cut its neck.* She'd make the dragon and Theodora's daughter pay for the men and women they killed.

She motioned to the unicorn. "Protect the warriors. I'll get the dragon. Find a soft spot. Ram Grandfather's sword into the beast."

She might not kill the towering beast, but hurting it might gain the time needed to open a gateway for everyone to escape. She'd stay behind. Use the medallion on the giant reptile. Or die trying.

Charlee charged the dragon, screaming, the tip of her blade aimed at the creature's stomach. One chance. That's all she'd have. Her fingers squeezed the handle. Legs tensed, ready to bound over the creek at the fire-breather's underbelly. *Let this work!* But before she could reach the behemoth, the dragon reared its head. Fire shot from its snout, racing toward Cryton and the others like a giant flaming net.

"No!" she cried.

From nowhere, a gushing stream of water smashed into the fire with a thunderous explosion that shook the ground. Charlee lowered to her knees, covering her ears. "What the?" It was as if someone had opened a massive waterline, the raging flow creating a barrier against the inferno. Heated vapor sizzled into the sky, the steam spreading over the land, searing her skin. "It burns!" She buried her head into the grass. The battle raged on for several heartbeats before the dragon's firestorm vanished in a hiss of white smoke.

"What the heck was that?" Charlee lifted her head and whirled around. In the air, hovering above Cryton was the half-beetle, half-octopus creature with long tentacles from which water flowed. The Nantorata! That's what the changeling morphed into when the Horeng set fire to the wilderness. Her magical protector had once again transformed and saved everyone. "Yes, you did—"

The Nantorata's wings, buzzing much like a humming bird's, slowed and then stopped. The changeling crashed to the ground with a thump, kicking up mud from the soaked ground. Its tentacles thrashed about wildly until they, too, dropped into the muck. Her protector lay in silence.

Charlee's body numbed. She'd lost the changeling once before. On Alcatraz Island back home. The creature, in unicorn form, was stabbed by Theodora's crony, Tribon, then flung into the ocean. Somehow, the changeling survived and returned to her. She couldn't lose her defender again. "Please, don't—"

She started toward her champion but stopped when the dragon coughed and then wheezed as though the unexpected blast of water had stung it.

Her chance had come. She had to take it. But the changeling? *He'd understand*, Charlee told herself. Tapping into what super strength was left in her legs, she sprung at the dragon, leaping onto the beast's long, muscular neck.

Violently, the dragon tried to shake her off. Legs clamped against its neck, Charlee lifted her grandfather's sword over the dragon. *One…chance! Do it…now!* With both hands grasping the handle, she drove the blade into the dragon's flesh.

The steel failed. Instead of piercing the beast, her grandfather's blade shattered upon impact, exploding into shards that rose into the night and disappeared.

"It can't be! What have I done?" Charlee lifted the sword handle and the jagged remains of the blade to her face.

From beneath her came metallic laughter. Theodora's daughter chuckled, clapping gloved hands together to mock her.

Charlee eyed the broken blade in her quivering hands. This wasn't over. It couldn't be. She had to try again. Strike down the beast with all her strength. Then shut that girl up. Her nails dug into the handle.

She lifted the splintered weapon over her head, but the dragon's tail smashed into her chest plate. Jarring her neck, the strike sent blinding white hot flashes of pain throughout her body. She flew off the dragon, losing her grip on the remains of her grandfather's sword. The destroyed blade lost to the darkness.

Like a bird slamming against a windowpane, she crashed onto a grassy mound, face down in dirt and mud. Her golden armor, cracked down the middle, fell from her body. Air spilled from her lungs. She grunted, trying to force a breath but couldn't. *Can't…breathe! Help…me!* Finally, she coughed then wheezed, managing a few shallow breaths. It was just enough to keep her alive. Liquid oozed from her mouth. Blood!

"Have…to…get…up." She gurgled out the words.

Charlee tried to lift herself but her limbs didn't budge. A tingling sensation radiated from her back, spreading to her arms and legs. This wasn't the sensation she had when the changeling fed her energy and made her stronger. This time, her body numbed until she could no longer feel her limbs. She couldn't wiggle her fingers, her toes or flex a single muscle. Nothing worked. "Oh… please… no!" Charlee lay in the muck like a puppet whose strings were cut, blood rushing to her head, sweat pouring from her brow. "This…can't be…happening."

"Charlee, no, hang on!" Cryton, his voice shaky, scrambled toward her, his remaining team following.

This was her one chance to save them. "Concentrate. Block out everything else." She retreated into her mind, tapping into her magic to open a gateway. Her temples pounded, cheeks shook. A groan escaped her lips, but the swirling portal flashed into existence in front of Cryton and the others, like a vacuum sucking them inside.

Those closest plunged in immediately, shouting in protest, their voices swallowed up by the tunnel. The warriors a couple of steps back slid to a stop, twisting around to avoid being dragged into the light.

"Guardian…no!" One Lataran fighter bellowed, inching away from the gateway but disappeared into the churning doorway. All the rest were tugged through the opening, their arms, legs, torsos and heads vanishing. Then the entryway shut, like a black hole closing in on itself.

For a heartbeat, silence spread over the field.

Charlee spit blood from her mouth. Each raspy breath wet with phlegm. She closed her eyes, head buried in the muck. Whatever happened now, at least they were safe for the moment. She tried again to lift her arms, but they wouldn't cooperate. "Mom, I need your healing powers. Can't go out like this," she screamed but it came out as barely a whimper. She hadn't done enough yet. Hadn't killed the dragon or stopped the Horeng. "Move it, dammit!"

With some effort, she managed to rotate her neck. Not far away, a yellow glowing mass, like an amoeba, floundered in the grass where the changeling, in Nantorata form, had fallen. Was that the changeling in its true form? It looked… hurt. "No, what's happening to you? Stay with me. I need you. I need—"

The dark knight erupted in laughter. Theodora's daughter strolled toward her. "Valiant effort, even for a weak guardian like you," she said as her twisted cackling subsided. "No, I mean it. You fought well and even saved those who fought by your side. Well, most of them."

Charlee, still on the ground, balled her stiff hands into fists. She could move them! What else could she do? "What are you laughing for? How many of your freak army died tonight? Go ahead and count them."

Theodora's daughter stopped just above her. She rested her sword on her shoulders. "Do you think mother cares how many die for her cause? She'll conjure up more. As many as she needs."

Huffing, spit and blood dripping between her clenched teeth, Charlee slid her quivering arms underneath her body and rolled onto her back. She couldn't stand, much less fight, but if she could keep the knight talking perhaps the fleeing Latarans could reach the mountains.

"Why don't you take off that helmet now and show yourself." Charlee glared at the knight. The metal facemask staring back at her was emotionless…empty. "You've won anyway."

"Yes, the time has come, but first I think I will have you taste my steel and in your dying breath you will come to know me. My face will be the last you ever see." Theodora's daughter lifted her sword.

"No…wait! Don't do this." Charlee's gaze shifted from the knight to the pouch at her side. If only she could reach for the medallion. She had to try. Just a little more time. "I'm begging you."

"So the guardian pleads for mercy." Theodora's daughter glanced back at the dragon. The beast, curled up across the creek like a dog at rest, thumped its tail on the ground and snorted as if amused. "Do you hear this pathetic girl? She's no leader. Just a coward. Mother will be so pleased when I deliver your body."

"To get to her, you must face me." Cryton leaped from the shadows, his bladed staff in hand. He stood tall, shoulders squared, eyes narrowed. His lips curled up in a confident grin.

What? He didn't leave? Charlee lifted herself onto her elbows but her strength failed. She slumped back into the mud. "Cryton, get away."

"I think I'd rather send a little knight back to her mommy." He twirled his staff.

"Brave words." Theodora's daughter circled them, holding her sword with one hand in front of her body. "Just as well. I can kill two as easily as one."

"You have the voice of someone very young." Cryton raised a bushy eyebrow. "You might just learn a lesson this night."

"From one so old?" the girl behind the dark helmet placed both hands on her weapon's handle.

"You might find this old man has some fight in him yet," he answered.

Charlee pounded the ground. "*Come on,*" she ordered her limbs. "*Move!*" More blood dripped from her mouth.

She reached out with her mind to tap into the power of any living creature but her abilities were short-circuited. Her only hope was the medallion. She had to use it now—had to figure out how to make it work. If only her arms would obey. "Reach for it!" Her limbs slid to it much too slowly.

Cryton swung his staff at the knight's torso. Despite the swiftness of the attack, Theodora's daughter evaded the blow. She pivoted and brought her sword down in a swift motion, trying to slice through him.

"Stop!" Charlee cried. Her hands reached the pouch.

Her mentor blocked the young knight's attack. Rotating his staff like the blades of a helicopter, he lunged forward, ready to cut her with both sharp ends of the weapon. Temporarily driven back, the knight quickly recovered. Nimbly, she launched another assault, slashing her sword wildly at Cryton.

Charlee's fingers crept inside the pouch and curled around the medallion. *Use it! Now! Before it's too late!*

A lesser swordsman might have fallen already to Theodora's daughter, but Cryton would not succumb that easily. Capitalizing on a moment when she overstepped her strike, he drove his blade forward and upward. Clang. The weapon struck the knight's helmet, knocking it off her head. It crashed against a tree trunk into the grass.

The young woman dropped to one knee, squealing with rage. A gloved hand covered her face; the other still grasped her sword. Long brown hair spilled around her fingers and flowed over her armored shoulders.

Charlee peered at Cryton; the old man frowned back at her.

"This fight is over," he declared.

"Is it?" She slowly rose, removing her hand from her face. "I think not."

Charlee gasped, her mouth opened wide. The face staring at them, lips parted in an evil smirk, was Sandra's. The voice belonged to her best friend. Blood seeped from a cut across her cheek. This Sandra, shroud in dark armor, smeared the crimson liquid across her face with the back of her hand and laughed harder.

Charlee let go of the medallion. *It can't be.* How could her best friend be here? What had the sorceress done? She studied the face. The deep brown eyes and long hair. High cheeks. Strong chin. All the same. This was the face of the girl who introduced herself to Charlee in the cafeteria at school. Stood up for Charlee against the bully Tina. Came to Charlee's rescue the first time she'd faced Theodora. Become her best friend.

Cryton lowered his weapon.

Sandra struck.

The old man, suddenly fumbling with his staff, did his best to defend himself against the onslaught of blows she rained down on him.

Wake up, Charlee. She grasped the medallion with both hands and slowly climbed to her feet on wobbly legs.

"Sandra, face—"

Something tackled her from the side, throwing her to the grass. A wall of dragon fire shot past her, baking the air. Head spinning, she scrambled to her knees. To the left, the changeling, in its unicorn form, thrashed about in the grass, its hind

157

side scorched. For the first time, the creature cried out, a high-pitched neigh. The magical being's skin sizzled. Black smoke rose from the shape shifter's body. Charlee swung to the dragon, it's fangs bared in a wide smile. The changeling had saved her from the reptile's hellfire.

"No!" Charlee crawled toward the unicorn until the cling of steel clashing stopped her. Cryton's bladed staff clashed with Sandra's sword. Charlee scrounged for the medallion. Grasping it, she stood and hefted the magical object, her body braced for an explosion of magic. Nothing happened. Not one spark rose from the black metal. How could this be? "Do some—"

Sandra's sword cut Cryton's staff in two. Then, as if in slow motion, this girl who had Sandra's face drove her weapon into his stomach. The old man's eyes swelled. He placed his hands on Sandra's face and shook his head. "You…will…lose."

Sandra tore her blade from him, a wide smile across her face. His blood dripped from the blade. "Good night, old one."

He fell motionless to the ground, landing on his side. Shallow breaths flowed from his mouth. The ground underneath him turned red.

"Cryton!" Charlee dropped. Her eyes shifted to the two beings in this world who had given her strength, Cryton and the changeling. Life bled out of both of them and all she could do was watch. She slammed a fist into the ground, then stood with the medallion pressed against her chest. "Damn you. What have you done?"

"Hurt you." Theodora's daughter grinned with the same warm brown eyes of the girl Charlee remembered. Now those eyes mocked her.

Tears streamed down Charlee's face. She thrust the medallion in front of her. Nothing happened. No magical burst of power. No ray of energy to strike down her enemies. If she couldn't make it work, maybe she could bluff this girl. "Do you know what this is? Do you know what I can do with it?"

Sandra, her skin pale, retreated to the dragon as if she feared the object. She jumped onto its neck and together they rose into the air. "When we next meet, Guardian, I will kill you."

With that, the dragon disappeared into the night sky.

Charlee glared at the medallion. "What happened? Why didn't you work, stupid thing." She threw it into the grass.

"Guardian," Her mentor spit blood, wheezing, struggling for each breath. His hands covered his gut wound.

She ran to him. "Cryton! Cryton!"

"No need…to shout." He coughed between words.

"Why did you fight her? I opened a gateway. You were supposed to go back and lead our people." She grasped his hands, leaning close to his face.

Cryton smiled softly. "That, young one, is your job."

"No! I need you." She wrapped her arms around him.

"No…you…don't." He lifted her away.

"Cryton, you're going to be all right. I have to get you home to mom. She can heal you." Charlee placed an arm around his shoulder to lift him.

"No!" He forced his voice to be strong. His eyes fluttered. "You have…a job… to finish. Finish it!"

"But…Sandra?"

"Listen…to me. That was not…your friend." His voice grew faint. His eyes closed and then slowly opened.

"Cryton!"

"Go now. Back to…our people."

"No!"

"You are…Guardian." Blood dripped down the side of his mouth. "Grandfather's…legacy. I am…proud of y…"

Before he could finish, Cryton exhaled his last breath. His eyes closed. The old man who had been Charlee's mentor and in so many ways her true grandfather died.

She held him tight. *I can bring him back. Use my energy. Heal him.* She clutched his chest but nothing happened. "Come on! Please! Don't leave me!" When magic didn't work, she pressed her palms into his chest. He lay still.

More tears fell from her eyes. "Damn you, Theodora. Damn you!" She spotted the medallion and pummeled it with her fists until she was out of breath.

"Useless thing." She slumped into the grass next to Cryton. All around her came the growls of advancing Horeng. She no longer cared. It was over. She let him die. She failed.

Charlee felt a brush against her cheek. It was the wing of her protector. The unicorn stood over her—wounded, burned—but still with her. She stared into the unicorn's eyes.

"Just go. Leave me."

The changeling refused. Stomping its hooves against the ground, the winged creature grabbed her with its teeth and lifted Charlee to her feet.

She mashed her body against the unicorn. "Don't you get it. He's dead."

The unicorn whinnied, arching its head back. She understood. Her protector was telling her not to give up. To fight on. That's what Cryton would want, but how could she go on without him?

Charlee gripped his cold hand. "Tell me what to do." She didn't need an answer. Her priority was clear. Get the people of Latara to safety, quickly. Then, make Theodora pay…for everything.

Wiping away tears, she picked up the medallion and shoved it inside the pouch. She reached for Cryton's body, but Theodora's fiends charged. The unicorn bit down on her shirt and flung her onto its back as if she were as light as a feather. Her protector then lifted into the sky, dodging the wolves' claws and weapons.

"No, we can't leave him." She tugged on the changeling's mane. "No. Cryton. I'm sorry." Soaring skyward, she screamed into the night. When she quieted, she willed opened a gateway.

The portal formed just ahead, a glowing escape route for her and the unicorn. Before entering, she glanced far below at the land swarming with Theodora's army. Lost were the bodies of the fallen warriors and Cryton. Charlee pulled her hair as if to tear it out strand by strand. "I'm so sorry," she sobbed. They all deserved better. If she survived, she'd return for them all and bring them home. Where ever that might be.

Charlee and the unicorn entered the light and disappeared. The thunderous sound of the Horeng on the march followed her into the vortex.

CHAPTER 25

A Race Through the Temoras

INSIDE THE MAGICAL pathway, Charlee reached out to the Latarans, her abilities acting like a sonar. Once locked in, her gateway stretched across the cracked landscape to the base of the Temora mountain range. Was it possible? Could her people have traversed such great distance during the night? Had the battle with the Horeng lasted longer than she thought?

She grasped the unicorn's mane with one hand. Images of Cryton falling after the blade pierced him played over and over in her head like a movie. Closing her eyes didn't help. The darkness only made the pictures more vivid. "I just abandoned you. Forgive me, Cryton. Forgive me."

High winds inside the enchanted corridor whipped her hair. She'd never felt such speed inside the portal. Why this time? Maybe because she tried to reach a moving target. Maybe because her mind rumbled like a volcano about to erupt from the hate building inside—for Theodora, for that evil version of Sandra, for herself. Her forehead pounded.

They shot out of the portal, zipping over Latara's refugees on a collision course with the mountains. If they didn't stop, they'd splatter against the nearly vertical jagged face. "Hit the brakes!" Charlee leaned against the unicorn. Spreading its wings to slow them down, the changeling arched its head and flapped furiously.

Clutching her chest to slow her speeding heart, she directed the unicorn back to the fleeing exiles.

When they landed, her quivering arms turned to jelly. Deprived of strength, she slid from the unicorn and dropped to her knees. Penaiya rushed to her, bending down and embracing her. "Guardian, you've returned to—"

"He's dead," Charlee uttered. "Cryton's dead. It's my fault."

Penaiya's body shook. Her hot tears dripped onto Charlee's shoulder. "Oh, child, it's not your fault."

Charlee broke from the embrace. "He died defending me."

Penaiya stroked her cheek. "No, he died defending all of us."

Slowly climbing to her feet, Charlee shook her head. "I wasn't strong enough to save him. My magic was useless. And too many others died out there. I didn't even have a chance to bring them back. I'm so sorry."

"Take heart, Guardian." Penaiya grasped her hand. "You have given us a fighting chance to survive. All of you have."

161

Around Charlee echoed the cries of those just coming to grips with the loss of their loved ones. She covered her ears but couldn't muffle the sound. "How many returned?" she asked.

"Thirty-five," Penaiya responded. "Fifteen did not. Their sacrifice will be remembered, but now we must ensure they did not die in vain. Look to the west. The skies burn with flames from Theodora's army. Guardian, we must hurry to the mountains. There will be time to mourn later."

Charlee turned west. A thunderous rumbling in the distance warned of the enemy's approach. The land shuddered under the massive horde's march. She'd bought these poor people a little time—but not enough. Death came for them like a tidal wave they couldn't escape. What was the point of even trying?

"I never wanted this." Charlee grumbled. "Remember that. I wanted to face Theodora alone. But I listened to Cryton and now he's dead. You're all going to die because—"

Penaiya slapped Charlee across the face. "Guardian, you must finish this. Save our people. Look at them. The children—all of us—we need you."

Charlee rubbed her cheek, her gaze shifting from the terrified faces of the Latarans to the fiery western skies. What was she doing? Giving in to fear? When these refugees needed her the most? "I'm sorry. You're right. We have to get to the mountains, now. Drop everything. All belongings. And run."

§ § §

Charlee pointed to the mountain. "This way! Move as quickly as you can."

Beams of early sunlight spread across the sky, parting gray clouds over the Temoras. The remnants of Latara charged toward the west face of one towering goliath. A vertical wall thousands of feet high with no way around. Looming peaks stretched to the northern and southern horizons. Only, this is where Charlee's vision revealed a passage.

Riding the unicorn, her thoughts shifted to the medallion. Why hadn't it worked during the battle?

A cold voice responded. *You did not give yourself over to the medallion. You had too much doubt and fear. You did not hate your enemy enough. You were not ready to accept the gift of power.*

She grasped her head and whispered, "What does that mean? Who are you? Why do you keep talking to me?"

The voice silenced.

"Come on! Don't abandon me now." She tugged on her hair but got no response. "I said—"

The changeling staggered on its hind legs, nearly falling backward. Charlee wrapped a hand around the animal's neck to keep from sliding off until the magical being steadied. The burns had vanished, but the shape-shifting creature was far from healed. "Are you okay?"

The unicorn ignored her.

Charlee's stomach ached at the thought of the changeling suffering, but she needed the creature for the task ahead. "Please, hang in there."

Reaching the base of the mountain ahead of her people, Charlee gasped. A chunk of granite as tall as her two-story house blocked the path through the Temora range. Her stomach churned. She leaped from the unicorn, cursing under her breath. The jagged boulder stood like a towering door.

"No!" She pommeled the rock with her fists. Chips of granite fractured, but the blockade held. Charlee glared at her hands, reddened from the collision but otherwise uninjured. What was she supposed to do? Had she led her people all this way to die at the base of the mountain?

Penaiya joined her. "Guardian, where is the passage you spoke of?"

Charlee pushed away from the obstacle. "It's here. I mean on the other side of this rock. It must have tumbled over the entryway. Or been pushed. I know the passage is here."

She banged on the rock once more. Did Theodora do this? Was this the witch's way of playing with her?

"What do we do?" Penaiya frowned.

In the distance, the Horeng boomed powerful drums.

Panic spread among her people. They pushed forward, scrambling to get as close to the guardian as possible. Stumbling, their bodies mashing together. Cries spread through the crowd. Parents scooped up their children and ran aimlessly.

"They're coming!" a woman shouted.

"We aren't going to make it!" a man moaned.

"No…no…no!" Charlee again pounded against the rock. There had to be a way. She had to do something with her abilities. It couldn't end like this. But what? "Cryton, show me the way."

Just then, the unicorn's life force pumped through her veins, giving her strength. It felt like a lightning bolt struck her. A jolt of hot energy coursed through her, nearly knocking her off her feet.

Charlee needed more. She reached out magically to her people, borrowing their strength.

A fire burned deep within her chest, spreading to her limbs. What was happening to her? She cried out as her insides scorched. A yellow glow pulsated from her fingers and slid up her arms.

"Feeling strong. Like I could…"

She braced her hands against the mammoth boulder and shoved. At first nothing happened. Then a crack sounded from within the granite. The two-story chunk budged. Her hands glowing bright as the morning sun, she strode forward, one tiny step at a time. The rock bellowed in protest but slid away, revealing the path through the mountains.

"Guardian!" Penaiya declared. "From where does such power come?"

Gasping for each breath, Charlee slumped against the unicorn. Her arms shook. Legs wobbled. The glow emanating from her hands vanished. She chose not to respond to Penaiya. Better to keep some of her magic abilities a secret. "Just get moving. We don't have much time."

Penaiya raised her own sword and waved the Latarans to follow. "My brothers and sisters, we are not defeated yet. This child guardian has shown us the way. Hurry now."

Everyone poured into the ravine after Penaiya, reaching out to touch Charlee as they rushed into the mountain.

One set of hands in particular gripped hers. Aryean's. Charlee stared into his dark eyes, and he kissed her forehead. His lips were rough but warm. Without saying a word, he slid his hands out of hers and led others into the passage. Charlee watched him go, her brow tingling where his lips brushed against her.

Would she ever know what it was to fall in—

The changeling stomped the ground next to Charlee, and she shifted her gaze to the unicorn. Was her protector scolding her for that lingering moment? She shook off those feelings and focused.

What was the power surge she just experienced?

"I don't know how," she whispered to the magical creature, "probably thanks to you, but a few moments ago—when I moved that massive rock—I felt like I could draw in an endless amount of energy from you...them...any living creature on this planet. How?"

Charlee contemplated that question. Was it because her abilities were growing stronger? If that were the case, how powerful could she become? And would it be a help or make her dangerous?

The unicorn remained silent.

"I wish you could talk." She grinned at her protector. The smile quickly faded.

In the distance, a dust cloud rolled over the land like a tidal wave. Theodora's army had arrived. Their shouts and howls echoed across the mountains.

"We're all going to die," one woman cried.

The refugees scurried like frightened mice into the ravine, crushing each other to enter. A child fell underneath the screaming crowd. Charlee grabbed him by the arm and lifted him before he could be trampled. She had to do something.

She climbed onto the unicorn, swinging her sword. "Everyone, just keep moving. I'll find a way to stop those beasts. Don't lose—"

A cold breeze swept across her face. A familiar laugh echoed in the wind. A cruel laugh. Theodora's. Charlee shivered. The sorceress was close. Her cheek stung as if frozen lips offered an unwelcome kiss.

"We have to slow the Horeng down." She gazed up at the rock she'd just moved. "I have to seal the entrance to the ravine." Charlee threw her arms around the unicorn. "I need your energy one more time."

The roar of the pursuing monsters rose. They were so close now.

"Hurry inside," she called to the remaining Latarans. She held her breath. Would they make it? Would there be time to stop the beasts or would blood be shed right here at the entrance?

The last to enter the ravine were Leyan, Penaiya's daughter, and her youthful cohorts. Their hands were bound, and two broad-chested men armed with swords escorted them. Leyan said nothing when she passed, but spat at the ground near Charlee's feet.

Ignoring the gesture, Charlee glanced once at the massive wall of dust almost upon them then sprinted into the passageway with the changeling. "Here we go." Sparking her powers back to life, she grasped the rock once again with glowing hands. With her super strength returned, Charlee slammed her shoulder against the granite and gave one mighty shove. The rock slid back, rumbling like an avalanche.

Her chest heaving from the effort, she stepped back to the unicorn. "Not sure how long this will hold, but it will slow them down. Maybe give us a chance to reach the other side."

With the changeling following, Charlee ran to catch up with the others, following the twists and turns of a passageway no wider than a neighborhood street back home. Shadows darkened their path. Not even the sun's rays penetrated deep within the mountains.

Up ahead, the Latarans continued their desperate charge, the rough sides of the Temoras rising above them like skyscrapers. Their cries reverberated off the sharp, winding walls. Would they win this race? Even if they did, what would they find on the other side? One thing was for sure, those beasts behind them would find their way into the ravine. She had to do more to slow them down. But what?

She slid to a stop, the unicorn beside her. "We have to come up with something else to block those freaking things. Cryton, if you can hear me, I need a sign. Show me what to do."

Charlee scanned the gorge. A few dead trees extended from the sides, like bony fingers reaching out to snag her. A hardened crust covered the floor of the rift. Fallen rocks bunched up in corners. "Come on, there has to be something I can use."

From behind came a boom that rattled the ground. A second explosion, louder than the first, followed. "Oh no, they're trying to breakthrough."

Small rocks bounced down the mountainsides.

Peering up, the passage narrowed high above. Her enhanced vision revealed a series of boulders teetering on stone terraces high above. If she pushed hard enough, maybe she'd force them into the ravine, creating another barrier against the army.

"That's it!" Charlee allowed herself a slight smile and stroked the unicorn's snout. "We have to force those big rocks to fall. We have to try. Do you think you can fly? I know you're hurting."

The unicorn spread its wings. She took that as her cue to climb on the magical creature's back. Her protector flapped wildly and, although it seemed to struggle at first to lift off, they slowly rose. But the changeling was weakening. Charlee had to help, but how? She couldn't lose the changeling, too. Not after Cryton's death.

They landed on a rocky overhang beside one boulder. Sliding from the unicorn, Charlee closed her eyes and concentrated on tapping into the life energy flowing around her, but not from the *bike*. Bracing her glowing hands on the rough surface, she summoned as much strength as she could…and pushed.

The unicorn did as well. Together they strained. A grunt escaped her lips. Her arms trembled. The first crack sounded like music. It was followed by another. The boulder pitched back and forth.

"Push harder," Charlee ordered her own muscles.

The boulder gave way, tumbling into the passage. She raised her hands then grabbed the unicorn. "We did it." The rock careened off the ravine's walls, picking up speed, until it smashed against the chasm's floor with a thunderous explosion.

"We need more," Charlee declared. She and the unicorn rushed to another giant rock. Digging her fingers into its crevices, she shoved with tiring arms. Somewhere inside her chest came a rip as if muscle tore away from bone, but the massive chunk of granite dislodged. Like the first, it plunged into the passage.

Next to her, the unicorn struck a third piece of the mountain with its hind legs until it jostled free and joined the others far below.

"Bike, this is—"

The changeling legs wobbled, then gave out. Her protector dropped into a sitting position, head drooped against its chest. The creature panted. A clear liquid spilled from its mouth.

"No!" Charlee grabbed her protector's snout and leaned in close. The creature showed no outward signs of the injury caused by the dragon's fire, but something must be wrong inside. "Don't you give up. Stand up. You're not going to die. I'm not going to let you."

The magical beast snorted and neighed. She placed her shoulder underneath the changeling and lifted. The creature slowly climbed to its hooves, flapping its wings to balance itself.

"That's it. You're done." She patted the unicorn's neck. "You need time to rest. Get out of here. Fly away and heal yourself."

The unicorn shook its snout, lowering a wing to her.

Charlee backed away and sighed. "You are so stubborn." Truth is, she still needed the changeling. She couldn't do any of this without her protector. Down below, the passageway was blocked, but it wasn't enough. They needed more rocks to build up the barrier and make it secure. Time was running out. The howls of the enemy echoed throughout the mountains. How long until they broke through?

"Okay, we'll do this together a little longer, but the first chance you get, you're out of here. We need to break off more rocks. Any ideas how we do that?"

The unicorn extended its wing farther.

Reluctantly, Charlee climbed onto its back. They took to the air, floating down to a section of the mountain where smaller boulders teetered on ledges and loose rocks gathered in piles.

Charlee studied her hands, opening and closing her fingers. Their glow dimmed. Her strength faded. With what power she had left, she swung her fists at the face of the mountainside. As though her hands were made of iron, they smashed through the stone, sending debris tumbling down onto the barrier below.

The unicorn hovered from one rocky section of the mountainside to another. Again and again she swung, jabbing through granite. When finished, her lungs heaved, desperate for air. Her heart pounded, fists burned.

Charlee eyed the solid wall of boulders, rocks and gravel. High enough to delay the Horeng. To advance, they'd have to either break the wall down or climb over it. Either way, it would give them more time.

Gulping mouthfuls of air, she declared, "Let's get…out of…this mountain."

Charlee and her protector swooped down to the Latarans.

"People, move!" she urged them. "They're close behind us. We must get clear of the mountains and reach the boats."

§ § §

Snaking their way through the passage under the shadow of the Temoras, the refugees hurried to stay ahead of the beast army. Their muffled cries spread through the gulley. Some called out that they wouldn't make it—that they'd be massacred under the mountains. The ravine would become their tomb.

At their head, Charlee marched beside Penaiya, who turned her wind horse over to a group of children.

"The Horeng are nearly upon us," Penaiya stared ahead stone-faced, raking her fingers through her hair.

"Yes," Charlee answered. "I don't know if we can—"

"We will, Guardian," Penaiya clutched her sword. "We will make it. We have to. Our children and grandchildren will live on and rebuild. You have given us hope."

Charlee nodded. She thought about bringing up Theodora's dragon—the fact it was still out there, but what was the point now? If the dragon showed up, she'd destroy the winged creature with the medallion or her own newfound strength.

But she needed to know what laid ahead of them and behind. Charlee cupped her ears for any sound of pursuit. No howls or barks or pounding of their claws over the rocky path. Something wasn't right.

"You need to keep the people moving forward. We'll reach the end of the ravine soon, and the sea is not far from the edge of the mountains." Charlee swung around. "I'm going to gather a few warriors and try to fend off those ugly dogs."

Penaiya nodded, lifting her sword. "Everyone, follow me."

Charlee ran back through the crowd, the changeling alongside her, dodging past the terrified Latarans. Through the rush, Charlee spotted Aryean. He had a child on top of his shoulders. Two others held onto his hands.

Charlee stopped him. "Aryean, I need your help." His kiss still burned along her brow, but she did her best to ignore it.

He handed the children to two women passing by. Sweat dripped from his brow. Dirt smudged his tanned face. "What is it, Guardian?"

"You need to scout to the other side of the ravine." She pointed ahead. "Find out what we're facing out there. If our way is clear."

Aryean bowed. "On my way."

Running ahead, he quickly disappeared through the mass. Charlee jumped onto the unicorn. Together, they galloped through the throngs who parted way for them. "Warriors of Latara," she called to those hastening by. "I need you one more time. Follow me."

Over twenty-five men and women brought their swords, spears, slings, bows and arrows and gathered in a circle around their guardian at the rear. They were thin. Tired. Hungry.

Charlee sighed. "I'm sorry to ask for your help again, but I think we might have one more battle ahead of us. Those damn wolves will soon break through the barriers. When they do, they'll reach us. I need you to fight with me against them. We must stand between them and our people. Will you join me once again?"

All raised their weapons and shouted their support.

Her eyes welled up. Tears for Cryton and for the fallen. For the support she didn't deserve and those about to fall. They were twenty-five against an army. It was hopeless, but they marched forward in an arrow formation behind her. They held their weapons high. One woman chanted what sounded like a battle hymn. A man joined her. Soon they all recited together, their voices low but proud.

They silenced their song when they rounded a corner and neared the barrier. Charlee held up her hand to stop them. She held her breath, listening for the army. By now, they should have been trying to crash through the blockade. Instead, silence filled the passage. No howling brutes enraged to find their way blocked. All was quiet.

Charlee trembled. The enemy was up to something.

Suddenly, shouts and screams rang out from behind. She cringed, all the blood rushing from her head. Had Theodora struck? Or the dragon? Charlee bit her lip, steeling herself to whatever was to come. "We've got to get back to the others." Clicking her heals against the sides of the unicorn, she urged the steed, "Fly, if you can. Fast!"

The unicorn blasted into the air, tearing through the ravine back to the main group. Dead branches from the sides of the gorge slashed at her. She dodged one but another grazed her cheek. Charlee leaned forward, urging the changeling to fly faster. The Latarans' cries grew louder, becoming pleas for mercy. Whatever it was, she'd protect them. She had to. *Finish it*, Cryton had said.

Up ahead, her followers came to a halt. Some retreated back the way they'd come. When they saw her, they fell on their knees.

"You've led us to them," one bearded elder claimed, shaking his fist at her.

"What have we done?" a woman grasping a child bellowed.

Charlee flew to the head, landing beside Penaiya who stared ahead without uttering a word.

Aryean ran up from behind, panting. "All...all is...lost!"

Charlee gritted her teeth. *Stay strong.* She climbed from the unicorn and ran toward the ravine's opening with Aryean at her side. The changeling trailed behind. She reached the edge and covered her mouth.

Legions of the beast army awaited them.

Her heart sank. Stomach iced over. What had she done? How could she protect them from this? She couldn't. No one could. The people had good reason to lose hope. The warrior's words rang true. *All is lost.*

CHAPTER 26

In the Hands of the Enemy

LIKE SOME TWISTED version of an ancient Roman army about to crush a rebellion, the Horeng blocked the path to the sea. They lined the shore, shoulder to shoulder, row after row, pounding battle axes against chest armor, the clank of steel echoing up and down the coast. Kicking the dirt like dogs, they howled and barked, bearing fangs covered in drool.

Behind them rose the gates to the abandoned seaport township, Balayian. Archers gathered on top of the stone entryway and an array of guard towers all along the outer defense walls.

Charlee stepped out from the ravine onto an open plain between the Latarans and Theodora's forces, motioning the changeling to follow. She lowered her head, gripping the handle of the sword at her side. Theodora knew her plans all along. The witch had let them run probably for her own amusement. Now the game was over. There'd be no defeating the overwhelming line of axe-wielding fiends before them. Her heart raced; vomit rose up her throat, but she swallowed it.

She glanced back at the refugees quivering under the shadow of the mountains. Everyone looked to her for a way out, but she had nothing to offer. The sobs of mothers cradling their children filled her ears. Elders herded the rest deeper into the rift, arguing the only chance was to go back the way they'd come.

Charlee hunched over, covering her ears with her hands. She couldn't breathe or think. Was this how her grandfather felt before he took his own life in one final act of defiance against Theodora?

More howls rose from the army. Charlee lifted her head. Several beasts stepped forward. They each carried something. Her mouth fell open, eyes bulged. The beasts held the bodies of the dead warriors, only now they'd been decapitated.

Laughing like hyenas, the monsters hurled the bodies. Then more of the cackling animals stepped from the line holding staffs. On each was a head of the fallen fighters.

"No!" Charlee screamed. "Damn you!"

Cries came from behind her.

Heat radiated from the medallion at her side. Was the dark object beckoning her to use its magic against the Horeng? Or was it calling to Theodora. The sorceress had to be close. She wouldn't miss the moment she'd led Charlee toward—the moment of her ultimate failure.

The beasts exploded in a chorus of grunts and growls.

One heavily armored being marched from their ranks, crossing half the distance to Charlee on legs the size of tree trunks. The figure held a staff with a head on it, the face turned away. Though a dark helmet hid the being's face, a red beard peaked out from underneath. Charlee shivered.

The being spoke.

"You, the survivors of Latara, have been led to your demise by this so-called guardian." The voice echoed over the land from the sea to the mountains.

"Tribon!" Charlee uttered.

Back on Earth, the giant man pretended to be her friend. Tricked her into believing she transported his spirit to Earth through her mind and told her he would prepare her to face Theodora. In reality, Tribon had been preparing her to serve.

Long ago, he had given his soul to Theodora. Now he was nothing more than her slave—her zombie. Theodora removed the heart of Tribon from his chest, only to give him new life as her servant.

Charlee bit her lip. She wanted to end his life almost as much as Theodora's. But how do you kill a zombie when the sorceress used her magic to keep his gray, cold heart pumping in the palm of her hand?

The voice inside her head returned. *Strike now. You have but one chance. Give yourself over to the medallion. Let all doubt subside. It is the only way.*

Her fingers inched toward the pouch.

Tribon raised his voice, speaking like a stern but loving father. "People of Latara, hear me. You do not need to die today. Join Empress Theodora, and all shall be forgiven. Forsake this girl who pretends to be a guardian, and give yourselves over to your empress. If you do not, your fate will be the same as his." He twisted the staff so that all could see the face of their beheaded countryman. "Behold."

"Cryton!" Charlee dropped to her knees. The face of her mentor, eyes open but vacant, glared back at her from atop the post. "Cryton, no!" She plunged her hands into the sand and squeezed as if choking the life out of Tribon. How could she have let this happen? How could she make the bastard pay?

Tribon removed his helmet. The dark eyes that had once looked so protectively at her now mocked her. His fiery red hair, tinged in gray, framed a chiseled ghostly pale face. "Look how your guardian falls before me. If you continue this rebellion against Empress Theodora, you shall die needlessly, all because of a girl...a stranger...who misled you."

Charlee's fingers tightened around the grip of her sword. Her free hand clutched the medallion inside the pouch. Its warmth spread up her arm. Her skin boiled. She wanted to rush at Tribon to strike him down. *Kill him! Kill them all! Then rule. That is your destiny.*

She shook her head. Was that idea hers...or the voice's?

Murmurs behind her suggested her people were considering Tribon's words. She had to do something now. *Take hold of the medallion.* From deeper in the mountains came a ground-rattling explosion. Charlee flinched.

"The army has broken through your barrier, Guardian," someone cried out from inside the ravine. "We have nowhere to—"

In the sun-bleached emerald skies over the Temoras a creature unleashed an ear-piercing cry. Charlee threw her arms around the unicorn's neck, gazing skyward. The dragon skimmed the tops of the mountains, then dove to the land below. The knight who looked like Sandra clung to the winged reptile. This time, she did nothing to conceal her identity. Long brown hair flowed behind her as she and the dragon swept overhead.

Charlee's magically-strengthened eyes followed Sandra. The girl who called herself Theodora's daughter smiled.

The dragon roared, swooping out over the sea—above the sailing vessels Charlee hoped would carry her people to the dragons' realm. With a mighty gust of fire, the dragon engulfed one of the ships in flames. Then it flew to a second vessel and blasted it with another wall of fire.

The crackling blaze quickly became an unforgiving inferno swallowing everything in its path. Black smoke billowed into the morning sky. Masts crashed into the sea, and decks collapsed into the depths. The ocean itself seemed to burn as orange streaks and steam rose from the water.

As each vessel gave way, Charlee's heart sank lower. "Stop it." She ripped the medallion from the pouch. *I will give myself over—*

Commotion caused her to whirl around. Leyan dashed out from the crowd. With her ran the young men who tried to kill Charlee. They must have seized the moment of chaos and found a way to escape.

Penaiya's daughter and her henchmen ran to Tribon. She stopped half way to the giant man, then turned to face the Latarans.

"My friends," she shouted, "don't you see that this is the only way for us? We can be reborn as a people. We can return to our homes and live without fear. All is possible under Empress Theodora."

Penaiya rode up to Charlee, sadness written in her face.

"I'm sorry," Charlee again reached into the pouch, caressing the round object. Her head drooped against her chest. She apologized both for Penaiya's loss and for the terrible end they all faced.

Penaiya placed her hands against Charlee's cheeks, lifting her head. "This is your hour, Guardian."

Charlee peered at the others. Some had already taken a few steps forward, ready to follow Leyan. She couldn't let that happen.

"Join us and be free," Leyan declared.

Tribon embraced her as if to welcome her.

Charlee shuddered. Leyan would face the same fate as him.

"You see, good people, all are welcome," Tribon bellowed. His voice was laughing, friendly and warm. "You have nothing to fear. Join us. I await your answer, but do not take too long to decide."

The voice echoed in her mind. *If you doubt, the medallion shall not work. Only the faithful can*—

"No, there's another way." Charlee shoved the pouch behind her back. She was a guardian with her own powers. It was time to really use them. Not hold back. She flexed her arms. "Be strong."

Charlee took a deep breath then retreated back among the refugees, who quickly encircled her. Penaiya followed her.

"Guardian, what do we do?" a young woman asked?

"Show us the way," another woman, her face covered with dry tears, pleaded.

Charlee nodded to them but did not answer, instead searching through the crowd of people for Aryean and any man or woman still armed with a weapon. Many of the fighters gathered to the rear of the larger group, swords held up to hold off any advancing beast from the other end of the ravine.

"Aryean, everyone else, gather to me," she called, pushing past others, evading hands that reached for her.

"You have formed a plan?" Penaiya trailed behind her.

"I think so," Charlee grabbed Penaiya by the hand and together they dodged more Latarans until they reached Aryean and the others. They stared into the darkened abyss of the mountain gorge waiting for the beast army advancing through the ravine to charge through the shadows.

"What is it, Guardian?" Aryean rocked back and forth on his heels, his long hair tied back into a ponytail.

She placed a hand on his shoulder and smiled. If only they were normal teens back on Earth where maybe they could go on a date. Not too young people about to sacrifice their lives. "We've come so far. I want to thank you for standing by me. I'm not sure I deserve it, but all I can say is thank you…again."

"We are with you, Guardian," declared a young boy probably no older than twelve who could barely hold his sword. "Just give the word, and we will fight at your side."

Charlee nodded. "I'm not sure if I'm strong enough, but I will try to open a large gateway—one that will lead all of our people to the Dragon Lord."

She interlaced her fingers under her chin. "I'll do all I can to keep it open as long as possible. But we'll need diversions at both the front and the rear of our group. In other words, we'll have to attack. We'll keep the beasts occupied as long as we can so our people can get through the gateway."

Those gathered at her side exchanged glances. Penaiya crossed her arms, raising one eyebrow.

"When I can't hold the gateway open anymore," she continued, "we'll be left here. Others will be, too. I'm sorry, but I don't think I can keep a big gateway open for a long time. Get it. This morning will be our last."

Charlee held back her own tears. At fourteen, she wasn't ready to die, but what choice was there?

She waited for everyone to react. They had every right to curse her. How Charlee wished things were different, but what was the point of thinking about that now? They had to make a stand.

The young woman Charlee saved in the assault against the Horeng was the first to speak. She grinned, brushing away sandy hair from her face, revealing dried blood by her right eye. "As we have said, we are with you, Guardian—to the end."

"Thank you." Charlee wiped her eyes. If she had to die today, it would be an honor to meet her end fighting alongside these warriors. Hopefully, somehow her parents and little sister would know what she did. And they'd be proud. "Now, I need you to go among our people and let them know what is about to happen. Make sure they know as soon as they see the blue light appear, they need to get through as fast as they can."

The warriors left to deliver the message.

Charlee turned to Penaiya. "You must be the first to enter the gateway. You have to live. You have to find a way to make the Dragon Lord understand we need him—and he needs us, too."

"Guardian—" Penaiya started to say.

"There's something else." Charlee raised her voice. Secrecy was no longer an option. Penaiya has to know the truth. Charlee swallowed a load of saliva before speaking again. "I need to tell you something. I lied. The Dragon Lord didn't say he'd welcome us. He told me to stay away, but I think there's a reason for it. He's not evil. I'm sorry for lying, but it was the only way. Make him help us. And help him. I think he needs it."

Penaiya lowered her head. What would she do with this revelation? She rubbed her chin and then lifted her head. Lips curled up in a faint smile.

"I shall do as you command, Guardian," Penaiya agreed. "And Guardian, I... I want you to know, no matter what happens, you shall be remembered by our people as a great leader. With whatever life I have left in me, I will make sure of that."

Penaiya pulled Charlee to her. The embrace felt like clinging to a buoy in the midst of a raging storm. Her head nestled against the rough fabric over Penaiya's chest. The older woman's heart beat rhythmically, the vibration almost comforting, drowning her fears of failure and death. If Charlee closed her eyes, the arms around her could have been her mom's.

175

She took a deep breath and slowly released it, holding back tears. She squeezed tighter as if somehow her family would be able to feel her arms around them across dimensions.

Finally, Charlee gently pushed Penaiya away. "All right, be ready. When you see the portal, lead everyone into it. I will keep it open as long as I can."

Together, they maneuvered back through the crowd to the edge of the ravine. Hands touched her shoulders, her arms, her hair. This time, she allowed the contact, even smiling despite her fear.

At the opening to the beach, Charlee climbed atop the unicorn. "Just you and me, bike." She patted the changeling's neck then urged the steed to slowly trot toward Tribon and Theodora's army.

As she rode, she summoned every bit of energy she could from the land, from her people—from every living creature around her. Even the changeling despite the magical being's weakened state. Each heart beat pulsated through her body like an electric shock. Her head throbbed as if her brain pushed against her skull. Yet she couldn't let Tribon realize the power she amassed. Couldn't let him see her hands shaking. Temples thumping. Veins popping out.

"Where did you disappear to, Guardian?" Tribon held the staff with Cryton's head like a spear. "Did you think you could escape back into the mountains? You cannot. We are everywhere." He hurled the staff at her. It landed in the sand mere feet away. She closed her eyes. Her hands formed into fists. She would hurt the giant man…somehow…when she had the chance. For now, she had to keep him distracted.

"Tribon, how does it feel to be a traitor? How does it feel to be a slave to Theodora? You're nothing but the walking dead. You're just a tool she's using. How could you betray your people?"

"What are you doing, girl?" he shouted back. "What game do you play? You had your chance to join Empress Theodora, but you chose death instead. And, while death didn't find you before, it will now. The people you have led into disaster will see how quickly their false guardian falls. Then they will know the truth. They will join in the new world Empress Theodora is building."

"Kiss my butt, traitor." Once again, the image of the dragons' realm flashed into her mind. The stretch of sea that led to a distant gathering of islands. A mountain towering above one shore. A great statue of a dragon atop the peak. The Dragon Lord's home.

Holding this picture in her mind, she caused a gateway to form inside the mountain ravine hidden from Tribon's view.

The gateway began as a ball of energy no bigger than a marble then grew in length and height until it extended across the narrow corridor.

Blood poured from her nose. She hid the crimson ooze with her hand. Her head boiled as if on fire. She held back a scream.

Though Charlee could no longer see Penaiya, she felt her enter the gateway. The people scurried after her. Charlee's shoulders hunched from the weight of maintaining the portal, and it got heavier as each person crossed over.

"Hold... on!" Her strength faded. Muscles trembled. Heart beat dangerously fast. More blood flowed from her nose. Even her ears. The warm liquid slid down her neck.

"Why have you suddenly grown quiet, Guardian?" Tribon asked.

He received no answer.

Tribon took a few steps forward—then froze. "Clever girl. I know what you are doing." With Charlee silently absorbed in her task, Tribon issued a command to the beast army. "Attack!"

She closed her eyes. The roar of Horeng charging her was deafening. *Just a little longer. So many not safe yet.* Charlee lifted her head, trying to hold on, but her body started to spasm. Limbs shook uncontrollably. Chest heaved. Another fever drowned her in sweat. "Burning up! Can't keep it open!"

A dizzying haze overtook Charlee. She slid off the changeling, crashing to the ground. Her mental grip on the portal severed.

The gateway faded. Whoever hadn't made it across was doomed to death at the hands of Tribon, Theodora, and her hordes of howling monsters.

§ § §

Charlee tried to stand, but slumped into the sand. Her head swirled. Images of charging, ax-wielding wolves melted with a winged unicorn standing over her, wings spread, and Lataran warriors rushing to their deaths. She couldn't hear the growls of the beasts and the stomping hooves of the changeling as it fended off any fiends who dared come near her. Silence surrounded Charlee despite the screaming of those who hadn't reached the portal before it closed.

Aryean and the other fighters made their final stand in this hopeless battle, and she could do nothing but watch it unfold and wait for the darkness of unconsciousness to envelop her.

There was only one voice she could hear. *The medallion is your only hope,* the voice declared from the deepest regions of her mind. *Take it now.*

"Yes," Charlee mouthed.

Finding the strength to roll onto her side, she shakily reached into the pouch. Even as her eyes darkened, her fingers probed the outlines of the dark object.

That's when a shadow passed overhead. She recoiled her hand. *What was that?* Immediately, another giant shadow glided above her. Then a third. A fourth. And even more. Charlee willed herself to stay conscious a little longer. *The shadow looked like...*

Voices echoed around her. They were muffled and seemingly distant. Charlee tried to make out what they said but couldn't. She tried to shake apart the whirlwind of clouds in her head that swallowed her hearing. The silence remained.

The Latara warriors surrounded her, screaming and pointing skyward. Aryean knelt close to her face and shouted. She still could not hear it. She narrowed her eyes and concentrated on the movement of his lips. Finally, she recognized a word.

"Dragons!"

The clouds in her mind shattered. The sunlight of clarity shone inside her. Hearing returned.

"Guardian, look!" Aryean lifted his sword to the sky. "It's the dragons—and they are fighting off the Horeng!"

The Latarans who surrounded Charlee helped her to stand and held her up, protecting their guardian. Charlee hardly allowed herself to believe what she saw. At least ten dragons with wingspans as large as an airliner's circled high above. The sun glinted off these giants of the skies, casting their reptilian scales in a neon glow.

The winged creatures seemed to study the chaos below. Then, they attacked.

Unleashing terrible roars, the dragons dove at the Horeng, spewing fire at Theodora's dark army. The assault was devastating. Her legions were being wiped out. Other dragons swooped down and extended their long wings to remaining Latarans. Reluctantly at first, her people climbed onto the backs of the dragons. Then the creatures rose into the sky and flew the refugees out to sea. But why?

Charlee gazed over the battlefield. *What's…happening?* The army was fleeing. Behind her, the wolves were under attack. Trapped in the ravine, the once unified force dissolved into nothing more than a bunch of clumsy, bewildered creatures scrambling for a piece of open ground where they might have a chance to put up a fight. The battle raged on. Fire swept through the ranks. In the middle of the inferno stood Tribon. He didn't flinch even as the dragons spit their fiery breath at him.

She locked eyes with him. They held their wordless stare until a blaze engulfed him, and the giant disappeared in a sea of orange flames and black smoke.

Tribon would survive this. As long as Theodora held his heart, their paths would cross again.

What about the impostor Sandra and her dragon? Had they burned or escaped? Cryton's killer deserved a fiery death for what she'd done, but the pair had probably fled. Charlee saw no sign of them…roasted or alive.

She didn't have long to think about this. A dragon—smaller than the others, though still as big as a two-story house—landed in front of her. The reptile stood on all fours, its muscles rippling under dark green tear-shaped scales. A brown exoskeleton, extended from the top of the monster's head, like a Mohawk, over its back to a barbed tail. The creature tucked its leathery wings, fixed atop broad shoulders and a hulking chest, against its body.

The dragon took one step toward her, slowly lowering its massive snout until a few feet away. For a moment, the creature stared at her, head tilted. Its yellow eyes with a line down the middle—like a cat's—blinked several times. Long triangular ears fluttered. Cavernous nostrils sniffed her, then the massive lizard lifted its head and snorted as if somehow disgusted by her odor. Not a surprise since she hadn't showered in—forever.

One more time, the dragon lowered to her, its hot breath blowing across her face. Charlee didn't twitch a muscle or blink her eyes. She didn't dare breathe, waiting for whatever terrible death awaited her.

Aryean and the other fighters stood just as still but didn't leave her side. Nor did the changeling. The unicorn's head hovered just above her shoulder.

The dragon blinked and snorted again. Dark lips parted, revealing dagger-like fangs. Charlee retreated a step, mashing her body against the unicorn's. She wanted to ask the creature what it had done with the others. To tell the creature whatever it was going to do to her to just get on with it. But Charlee couldn't find her voice.

With a flick of a long red tongue, the dragon spoke in a language only Charlee could understand. English. A teen's version of English, at that. "Dude! Took you, like, long enough to get here," the reptile hissed. "I am at your service."

Then the world around Charlee went dark.

CHAPTER 27

A Dragon's Choice

I'M DROWNING, CHARLEE thought desperately. She was sinking into the depths of an icy sea. The surface…just out of reach. Beads of light beckoned to her from above. Unable to breathe, lungs burning, she clutched at her throat.

Reach a little farther. Stretch a bit more. Swim up. Charlee couldn't give into the shadowy depths. Breathe! Live! There is more to be done.

And, just like that, she broke through the surface. Charlee awoke, gasping for air as if she had been drowning instead of lost in a murky layer of an unrestful sleep.

At first, her vision blurred, limiting her view to a few hazy feet in every direction. Curled up like a baby, she lay on a bed of what felt like soft cut grass. It reminded her of the alfalfa fields in the country before her family moved to the city. After the crop was cut, she would jump into the loose piles.

Blinking her way to clarity, she struggled to remember what happened. Everything went dark in the wake of…

Faces and images flashed across her mind, like a bomb exploding in her head. She grasped her forehead and held back a scream. It hurt so much. The pictures played like a movie. Tribon and the Horeng bathed in flames. The evil Sandra and her dragon destroying the boats meant to provide passage for her people to the dragons' realm. A gateway opened for the people of Latara.

A phantom sensation of fire had scorched her from within as she struggled to keep the gateway open. She expected to die but didn't.

Death couldn't hurt this bad.

Her mind continued its replay. Shadows appeared overhead—massive winged shadows. "The dragons!" Charlee nearly shouted.

With that, she became fully aware of her surroundings. She was in a vast chamber or cave. The stone walls were engraved with unfamiliar script, kind of like Egyptian hieroglyphics, and rose into darkness above her. Shadows hid the ceiling. What was this place?

Strands of daylight angled in from points unknown and converged overhead into a triangular chandelier. An eerie yellow glow radiated throughout the chamber. A moist, cool air blew across her skin, and she shivered.

Dizzy from the strange environment, she willed her body to move. Slowly, Charlee stood.

Was she in the Dragon Lord's lair?

A reptile had spoken to her before she blacked out on the battlefield. What had the creature said? It had been waiting for her. What did that mean? The creature even used the word...dude.

"*Weird,*" she said just loud enough for her own ears. How would a dragon know English and be familiar with the ways teens speak?

Nausea overcame her. Charlee bent over and spewed, the yellow mucous-filled bile burning her throat. Spitting out the last bit, she collapsed to her knees, her chest heaving with each breath. How pathetic it must look for a guardian to lose her lunch, especially with nothing in her stomach.

Suddenly, her pulse quickened; the pressure on her head tightened. All those poor souls! Dragons had swooped down, picked up the remaining people, and flew them out to sea. But why? To save them? To eat them? What? She needed answers.

"Where is everyone?" she shouted, climbing to her feet.

Nothing but her own echo greeted her. Charlee spun around. Wait a second! Where was her bike...or the unicorn...her protector? It never left her side, yet now she was very much alone. She placed her hand against her chest to quiet her heart. It didn't work.

"Anyone there?" she called out.

An angry roar—ferocious and thundering—echoed off the cavern walls. She cowered, covering her ears with her hands. Where had it come from? She might be a guardian, but fear of the Dragon Lord made her whimper like a child.

She disobeyed him. What would he do?

The terrible roar returned. This time followed by what sounded like words... more barked and growled than spoken, in a language she couldn't understand.

"Raaa-croriannnn ... errrrrnaaaaroooo ... orrrrriiinoooo ... srrrrrennnoooo."

The guttural sounds grew louder with each indistinguishable syllable, rattling the cavern. Charlee shuddered. Whatever creature spoke did so in a voice full of anger. She pictured her father scolding her before she made the jump to this world. Still, Charlee could not understand its language.

"Strange," she whispered. "I've been able to understand every language I've heard spoken in this world."

Even if she could decipher the words, Charlee would rather flee than face the thing out there, but running wasn't an option. Not now. Not when the Latarans were in danger. She had to figure out where everyone had been taken, find the changeling and the dragon that offered its services. Charlee rubbed her head to stop the pounding. The answer to all her questions most likely rested with the beast that produced such terrifying sounds.

Then another thought crashed through her mind like a tidal wave.

"*The medallion!*"

She frantically searched her bed of grass. Nothing.

"Please be here." She crawled around, but the round object eluded her. "It's not here. They've taken it from me. They can't do that. It's mine." She shook her fists. "If the dragons have taken it, I'll make them suffer." Charlee stood and paced, running fingers through her hair over and over. What was happening to her? Was she becoming evil already? "I can't let that happen. I have to destroy Theodora and then the medallion. Before it takes control of my mind."

She first had to find the Dragon Lord. As if on cue, another roar, louder than the earlier ones, caused rocks and dust to drop from the cavern ceiling around her.

Blowing out a nervous breath, Charlee took sluggish steps in the direction of the bellowing creature, but a ground-shaking explosion stopped her, followed by another. "What the heck is that?" She embraced herself to keep from trembling, and continued through the chamber. "You can do this. You have to do this."

Charlee ran her eyes over the cavern. She passed under a vaulted archway high above. Carved dragons guarded both sides, chiseled from glimmering stone reflecting the strands of daylight. Whatever this place was, she sensed it was ancient, like walking upon holy ground. The tiny hairs on the back of her neck stood straight. She was a trespasser here.

But a dragon presumably brought her here. Why should she be scared? Because it wasn't the Dragon Lord himself who rescued her. At least, the smallish reptile didn't seem like the leader of the dragons. Who then? And why help her?

She reached another archway covered with engravings. One displayed two winged creatures lifting up the stars in the sky. In another, a large beast held a smaller one aloft, like a parent helping its child to fly. For a moment, Charlee became lost in her study of the etchings.

Thundering outbursts shook the ground. Charlee lost her footing, stumbling to one knee. More chunks of ceiling fell beside her.

Charlee froze. She couldn't will her legs to continue their journey. *The Dragon Lord's going to roast me alive.*

A different softer voice followed as if to argue with the angrier one. She still couldn't understand the language.

"Sheorrriaaaan… sssrrroooannn… jorraaaaannnn," the second voice uttered in a less commanding—less threatening—manner than the first.

Charlee strained her ears. "I think that's the dragon that spoke to me before I blacked out. I'm almost sure it is."

A savage growl rumbled through the lair. "Nooorrrrrr…noorrrrrr…noorrrrrr," the first creature protested. Now the harsh tone sounded much like her dad's when he became frustrated. Thinking of him comforted Charlee. Oh, how she wished her parents were here to fix everything.

But, she reminded herself, *I made my choice. Too late to turn back now.* Too late to want Mommy and Daddy by her side.

"Come on, Guardian," she muttered. "Get moving. You faced the Horeng army. A few dragons shouldn't be too hard." Charlee entered a long hallway, still cavernous but narrower than the other chambers.

On either side of the hallway the rocky walls were studded by gems glowing in a brilliant mix of reds, blues, greens, oranges and yellows. The rainbow of color they caused in the hallway confused her senses.

The gems glittered in the refracted light. In another time, Charlee would have been awed by the beauty, but the guttural roars from the beast made her teeth rattle. If she kept going, was she going to become a dragon's fire roasted lunch? The simple truth was she had no choice. Charlee forced herself deeper into the lair. Each step drove her perilously onwards.

Another archway towered up ahead. Beyond it, the dragon's bellowing tantrum boomed the loudest. Two creatures seemed deep in an argument. She crouched to the ground, holding her breath inside her bone-dry mouth. Her stomach felt as fragile as a thin sheet of glass. Common sense told her to back away, like a scared mouse, rather than face the wrath of a dragon, but since she learned of her true identity had she ever shown sense?

She crawled behind one side of the archway, then peered into the space beyond. Two dragons faced each other in a labyrinth, soaked in crimson light. Rays of sunlight streamed in, reflecting off a boulder-sized ruby gemstone hung from the ceiling. Charlee's insides felt hollow, her limbs like jelly.

One dragon towered over the other. The larger reptile stood on its hind legs at least four stories tall. At full height, its head became a silhouette against the sunbeams slicing across the ceiling of this goliath chamber. Light bounced off blue scales, and it wasn't just one hue. Teal, turquoise, and royal shades blended together almost like the coloring of the ocean from the shallows to the deep. A tan shell covered the creature's underbelly.

Charlee began to mouth, "So beauti—"

The monster whacked its barbed tail against the ground. The lair trembled, throwing Charlee around like a paper bag. She rolled onto her side, then scrambled back to her hiding place. Smashing its tail one more time, the giant creature extended its massive bat-like wings, then slapped them against its hulking body. That really reminded Charlee of her mom when she'd bang her hands together to end an argument.

Bending its long, muscular neck, the beast's head finally became visible. Large eyes glowed green, with a line of blue through the center. Spikes rose from the head, stretching along the neck. Hanging from the dragon's snout, unless she was mistaken, was a white goatee. Perhaps it was an elder. Fangs the size of swords extended from a mouth so wide the beast could easily devour her in one bite.

Dragon Lord?

When she turned her attention to the smaller dragon, Charlee nearly jumped with excitement. The one on the seashore! The one that talked to her! This one had the same noble look and proud eyes as the larger reptile, but was clearly younger. Its green scales stood at attention, shifting in color. At first, they glimmered like emerald gemstones but dimmed as the larger dragon thrashed its tail.

The smaller creature raised its neck as if to challenge the larger beast. Was this the Dragon Lord's son?

From her hiding place behind the carved rock pillar, she tried to reason what occurred on the seashore.

Cryton and Penaiya had told her how years ago the Dragon Lord chose not to stand with her grandfather, Michala. Yet the Dragon Lord's son—if that's what the smaller dragon was—rescued Charlee and the refugees—maybe to feast on them—but she didn't think so.

But why would the young creature defy his dad just to rescue them?

She had to speak up—now. Face the Dragon Lord. Make him understand.

Behind her, the damp, hot breath of yet another beast ruffled her hair. "Oh no!" Before she could spin around, a huge tail wrapped itself around her waist and lifted her into the air.

Charlee wrestled against the beast, but the tail tightened, like a huge anaconda squeezing her to death. The rough reptilian skin shredded the long sleeves of her tunic and tore into her flesh. She cried out until the lizard's grip stole her breath. The creature could easily crush her, but eased off. Pressure released from her chest, and Charlee drank in the moist air. What happened? Why didn't the dragon strangler her?

The monster, draped in red scales clinking together as if metal armor, lifted her until she was inches away from its snout. A black pointed horn affixed to the end resembled a rhino's. The beast examined her with white crystalline eyes, then opened its mouth and hissed. She flinched—both at the heat and at the almost gasoline-like aroma of its breath.

"Let go of me!" Charlee wiggled her arms free and struck the tail. Was this a guard? What was it going to do with her? How could she be so stupid to get caught? She forced herself not to shiver. Best not to show fear for whatever was to come, but the icy grip of terror clamped down on her heart.

The dragon did not utter a word. Instead, it lumbered into the cavern with the Dragon Lord and the younger reptile. Waving its tail, the guard flung her around like she was nothing more than a toy tied to a rope. Charlee's head jerked in every direction, shaking her brain.

"Stop!" she cried.

Finally, the beast lowered her to the ground in front of the dragon leader and released her. Bowing its massive head, the sentry stomped to a far off corner and stood at attention, stiff as a stone statue.

Charlee held her head to stop it from spinning then did the only thing she could think of. "Uh...er...hi there." She gazed back and forth from the Dragon Lord to the one she suspected was his son.

The two dragons lowered their heads and stared at her.

"Uh, I'm Charlee." She spoke in English, not sure what to expect, and refrained from calling herself a guardian.

Hot air poured from the great nostrils at the end of their snouts. Beads of sweat dripped down the sides of her face. Charlee retreated a few steps, not that distance would make much of a difference. The dragons proved themselves fire breathers. There'd be no escaping them if they decided to toast her.

"Um—"

"You should not be here," the larger reptile hissed. The creature...the Dragon Lord, if that's what he was... spoke in perfect English. His deep voice held a seething, barely contained anger. He thrashed his long tail against the ground. Charlee stumbled but quickly rose.

"You must leave," the beast continued. "You must leave now, before it is too late. And you must take your countrymen with you."

Charlee tried to connect her thoughts into a clear sentence. "Wait...how... I don't understand—"

"Father, please!," the younger one interrupted. "Her people have been through so much to get here."

"No!" roared the elder beast. "You acted rashly. You and your rebellious bunch of winged friends had no authority to help these...these two-legged beings."

Charlee pointed to the blue-scaled beast. "Are you the Dragon Lord?"

"I am." He fixed his green eyes on her. The blue line in the center of each grew thin.

Ignoring the relentless pain in her head and her own anger at the Dragon Lord's sentiment, she asked, "Can you tell me how is it that you know the language I speak back home?"

He sighed. Black smoke rose from his mouth. "Ever since you entered the world your people call Janasara, I have maintained a mental lock on you. That has enabled me to learn your language."

"I have, as well," the younger dragon piped in. "Cool, huh?"

Charlee couldn't get over his teen way of speaking. In some ways it was off-putting for such a majestic creature to speak like one of her friends, but then again it was kind of cool. *How could he know how I speak back home?* She stopped herself from voicing the question. It wasn't important to figure things out right now. "I have more questions," she continued. "Where is my unicorn? And where are my—?"

The Dragon Lord maneuvered his snout within inches of her face. "I warned you not to come here, child."

Charlee fought the urge to duck. She stood her ground in defiance, wrinkling her nose at the sulfurous stench. Sweat covered her palms. "What choice did I have? Answer my questions."

The younger creature spoke again. "Your unicorn was badly hurt by a dragon's fire."

"Yes," the Dragon Lord said. "Your unicorn...your changeling...has great magical ability, but it could not withstand the poison inflicted by that evil coward, Noorrennn."

"Who is Noorrennn?" Charlee asked. "Is that the stupid dragon that fights for Theodora?"

"Yes," the Dragon Lord answered. "When Noorrennn wounded your protector, the changeling did not wish to leave your side, but finally it lost consciousness. Do not fear. Our healers are treating its wounds. It should survive."

Charlee thought back to when the unicorn pushed her out of the way of the beast's fire when she tried to run to Cryton. She never knew how badly the changeling was hurt. *That's a lie,* she told herself. She'd seen the unicorn growing weaker but ignored it. The changeling was slowly dying and as always it was willing to lay down its life for her.

And what did she do for the unicorn?

Nothing.

Charlee tried to fight these thoughts, but they were the truth. If they survived, she would never take her protector for granted again.

But, she reminded herself, there are other lives at stake right now as well—the lives of the people of Latara.

"And my people?" she asked.

"They are being kept at the base of my mountain." The Dragon Lord rushed his words as if impatient. "Neither they nor you should have come to this land. And you would not have made it here if not for the actions of my son." He swiveled his head away from Charlee. "I can do nothing for your people, nor for you."

"Then you are a coward just like Noorrennn." Charlee's teeth clenched.

With a speed amazing for a creature that size, the Dragon Lord spun back around to her, snapping its jaws. "Careful, Guardian!" Lava-like drool dripped from its fangs, pooling by her feet. White smoke rose when each droplet struck the ground. Searing fumes rose from his nostrils. The skin on her fingers popped under the intense heat. She winced from the agony. Tears streaked down her red hot cheeks, but she did not cry out or retreat.

"Father, stop hurting her," the younger dragon roared.

The Dragon Lord raised its head. "Next time this child guardian should hold her tongue."

Charlee lowered to one knee, blowing on her fingers. Her hair, wet with sweat, clung to her forehead, cheeks and neck. She tugged at the tunic, which stuck to her body like a damp towel on a boiling summer day. She climbed to her feet, eying her blistered fingers. The stench of her own burnt skin made her stomach churn.

"Help her," the young dragon demanded.

The Dragon Lord sighed. "Do not move, child." He then opened his snout and a green mist seeped from his throat, flowing over her like a waterfall.

"What the…?" The vapor, which had the distinct odor of menthol, engulfed her. Immediately, her skin cooled. Whatever this spray was, it healed her hands. The blisters vanished. What kind of magic was this? What were these creatures capable of?

Though healed her mind still burned with one thought. *The Dragon Lord knew her identity. He'd been watching her from the time she arrived in this world. And, by the seashore, his son called her…guardian.* No reason to hide her true self now. She needed answers, and that meant revealing her bloodline.

She lifted her head to the Dragon Lord. "You know who I am, and I know how you failed by grandfather, Michala. You didn't help when he faced Theodora. If you had, maybe together you could have stopped her. But you turned your back on him—like a coward."

The Dragon Lord hissed but said nothing.

"Why, Father?" his son asked. "I have always wondered why you did not stand with Michala in their time of need. And why, now, do you turn your back on them?"

The Dragon Lord stared down at his son with eyes meant to send a message. The Dragon Lord was not to be questioned by anyone, not even his son. "What I have done or not done is my concern. That is all you need to know—ever."

He returned his attention to Charlee. "I have boats ready to take you and your people away from here. You will find no safe shore in my land. Leave now or become my next meal. You look like you have some meat on your bones. You would make a fine snack."

Before she could respond, the younger dragon spoke up. "Father, your cowardice brings shame to our kind. That is why I acted on my own."

The next time the son spoke, it was to Charlee.

"I regret that I did not seek you sooner. Perhaps I could have prevented some of the losses your people suffered. I am sorry. I let the fear of my father's wrath slow my actions. Never again will I allow that to happen."

The Dragon Lord unleashed his loudest roar yet. It sent Charlee toppling. Even the Dragon Lord's son took a few steps back.

"It was an act of betrayal!" the Dragon Lord snarled.

"No, Father! Your failure to help is the betrayal. You betrayed these people, and you betrayed the ancients…our true heroes and lords." The young dragon turned away from his father in protest.

Charlee sat on the ground motionless, unsure what her next move or words should be. Her eyes shifted around the cavernous chamber. On a side wall hung a familiar object. *My pouch!* Was the medallion inside?

She slowly stood and crossed toward the wall, but the Dragon Lord's tail slid in front of her, blocking her path. She glared up at the beast. When the Dragon Lord next spoke, pain filled his voice.

"Kraannaannn," he said to his son, "you are right. But there is much you do not know. There is much I have not told you."

"Then tell me now, Father," Kraannaannn demanded.

The Dragon Lord hesitated. *Here's my chance!* Charlee leaped over his tail and then dashed to her pouch. She tugged it free from the wall.

Before she could reach inside, the room exploded in a blinding flash of light. Charlee covered her eyes.

CHAPTER 28

A Father's Pain

PEERING THROUGH HER fingers, Charlee's jaw dropped. Theodora, more specter than physical, hovered high above. Her body, draped in a form-fitting dress, glowed fluorescent green, bathing the dragons' lair in a slime-colored haze. Why was she here?

"Let me provide the answers your son seeks, Sheorrriaaaan, great Lord of the Dragons." Theodora, appearing as her younger self with long flowing hair outlining her porcelain face, floated over to the Dragon Lord's son. Her voice matronly.

The Dragon Lord's blue scales raised and lowered, like the rushing tide. He side-stepped close to his son. A threatening growl pierced his lips. "Empress Theodora, there is no need for you to—"

"Quiet!" Theodora commanded.

The sentry stationed against a far wall came to life, his red scales glowing bright. The beast stomped its clawed feet and threw itself at Theodora, chomping down on her with razor sharp fangs. Instead, the wild reptile's head passed through her phantom form and crashed to the floor. Agile for such a large monster, the guard quickly perched on its hind legs, tail thrashing, prepared for another attack.

The Dragon Lord barked a command and the enraged servant, chest heaving, dropped to all fours, his blood red scales lowered against his body. The creature roared once at Theodora, its snout twisted in revulsion, then retreated from the cavern.

Charlee placed the pouch over her shoulder and crept to Kraannaannn. What was happening? Something wasn't right. The Dragon Lord appeared scared, but why? She clenched her teeth and pinched her lips. If Theodora could frighten a creature as fierce as the Dragon Lord, the reason had to be terrifying.

The sorceress spoke in the Lengoron language. "I thought we had an understanding, Sheorrriaaaan. I would allow you to rule over your own land as long as you stayed out of my affairs. I thought you understood the consequences of any interference on your part."

Charlee frowned. What was the witch saying? She turned to Kraannaannn. The tilt of his draconic head and his wide eyes revealed the same confusion.

Sheorrriaaaan's long curved neck bent around the sorceress. He lowered on muscular legs like an animal ready to pounce on its prey. The Dragon Lord's coloring shifted from blue to raven black.

"Theodora, I have broken no pact," he answered, his guttural voice reduced to little more than a whisper. "My son acted impetuously. He did not know about our understanding. You cannot blame him. I am now correcting his mistake."

"Father, what is going on?" His son's head shifted back and forth, tail twitching.

"Quiet, Kraannaannn!" the Dragon Lord hissed.

Something bad was going to happen. Charlee lifted the medallion from the pouch. "Theodora, I have the medallion." She held up the rounded object. "Whatever's happening here, forget about it. Come and get me. I'm the one you want."

The sorceress ignored her. Her words focused on the Dragon Lord. "I am sorry, my friend, but the offense has occurred. The price must be paid."

"No!" Sheorrriaaaan stood on his hind legs and lifted his snout. A bright orange glow rose up his neck, then the beast belched flames into the cavern.

A second form took shape and hovered beside Theodora. Tribon! He carried a large transparent case made of glass.

Charlee stepped in front of Kraannaannn. What was Tribon up to? Her heart raced and she breathed in short gasps. She called again to the sorceress. "Theodora, stop this. Here's your medallion."

Tribon held the case out in front of him like a serving tray. Theodora gestured with her hands. The cover rose and drifted a short distance away.

Whatever lay inside floated in a pool of crimson liquid and pulsated rhythmically. About the size of a football, the object gave off an audible *thump… thump* that echoed off the cavern walls. Charlee inched closer to Tribon, puzzling over the mystery in the box. Could it be a heart?

"Theodora, you cannot do this!" the Dragon Lord protested. He cocked his head back and blew a gust of fire at the sorceress and Tribon, but it had no effect on them. Their images became skewed for a moment under the intense heat but quickly took shape again.

Laughing, Theodora produced a long, thin, jewel-encrusted dagger. With both hands, she lifted the blade over the pulsating object and smiled once again at the Dragon Lord.

"No!" Sheorrriaaaan leaped in front of his son, wrapping a wing around him.

"Theodora!" Charlee shouted, waving the medallion. "Take it. It's—"

With one swift motion, the sorceress sunk her blade into the object.

Kraannaannn wailed, digging his claws into his chest. Flames shot from his mouth. He recoiled like a cobra, thrashing his tail and wings in every direction. Chunks of rock from the ceiling fell throughout the lair.

Charlee's whole body numbed. Her face sank and her heart stopped. She nearly dropped the medallion. Why was the young dragon in agony? What had the witch done to him? What kind of dark magic was at work? How could she save the Dragon Lord's son?

Sheorrriaaaan roared, lashing out with his fangs and claws, ripping at the images of Theodora and Tribon, but the attack was useless. His strikes passed through the apparitions like cutting through wind. The sorceress crossed her arms and grinned with satisfaction.

"Father, what's—"

Kraannaannn released a rumbling moan then fell to the ground. He rolled on his side, claws still over his chest. Bright green scales along his reptilian body morphed into a shade of pea soup. His spiked tongue hung between parted lips. Each gurgled breath came slower than the last.

"My son!" Sheorrriaaaan cried out, unleashing a flaming inferno toward the cavern's ceiling. He lowered his head to his son, who gasped and snorted out blood from his nostrils. His yellow eyes dimmed. "Kraannaannn, my son... oh my son."

Charlee bolted to the young dragon and knelt by his head. "What's happening to you?" She stroked his snout. Blood coated her fingers. "What did she do? How can I help you?"

"Get away from him," his father growled. "Don't touch him."

The Dragon Lord nudged his son's head. "Oh my son. Your little heart."

Charlee backed away. It was Kraannaannn's heart. But how? He was not a slave to Theodora like Tribon, who had given up his heart to the witch.

"Sheorrriaaaan, it pained me to do that." Theodora hovered close to the Dragon Lord.

"If my son dies, I will exact a terrible revenge!" He snapped. Flames rose from his nostrils.

"My friend, there is little I can do now." Theodora took delight in the moment. "Your son has only hours to live." She paused as if deep in thought and then continued, "However, there is a way that your son might yet live. Kill the weak beings you are protecting. Kill the sons and daughters of Latara."

Her ghostly image turned to Charlee. "And you, Guardian, you can help save the young dragon as well. Come to me! Return my medallion and swear yourself my slave forever."

Charlee lifted the medallion again. "I offered it to you already. You didn't have to do this."

Theodora's image faded. "Yes, I did. A ruler must punish her subjects when they disobey her. You both have but a short time to act. The sands of time flow, and Kraannaannn's life slips away. Oh, his death would be unfortunate."

With that, the sorceress and Tribon faded away. Their glow vanished.

"Fa...Fa...Father," the young dragon uttered.

"Rest, my son. I will save you," the Dragon Lord reassured him.

The older dragon's massive head swiveled to her. "This is your doing. You brought this on my son, and now you have forced me to do Theodora's bidding. Your people must die."

193

"I'm sorry." She stumbled backward. "I didn't know."

Sheorrriaaaan seethed, snapping his jaw. He stabbed his fangs through his own lips, drawing blood. "I don't need your words now, Guardian." He reached for his son, cradling the younger dragon in his wings. Simmering tears dropped from his eyes. "Oh my only child, how could I have allowed this to befall you? I promise burning death to everyone, especially that witch. Just live, my son. Breathe."

Kraannaannn reached up to his father. "What…is…happening…to me?"

"Don't speak, my son. Rest. I will do what I must to save you." He grabbed Charlee around the waist with a claw, lifting her from the ground. "I will kill all of your kind. When I am finished, all two-legged beasts will no longer exist. I should have unleashed death on you all long before Theodora was even born. Your kind is a disease on this world."

In his rage he was going to kill her…and everyone else. What could she say? What could she do? "If you had helped my grandfather—"

"Shut up, girl." The Dragon Lord lifted her to his mouth.

"Tell…me!" Kraannaannn hissed. He tried to roar but coughed instead. "Release…her…and…give me the truth."

Sheorrriaaaan dropped Charlee. She landed on her feet and rolled away, her death temporarily delayed. She wanted to run but needed the truth as much as Kraannaannn. It might be the only way Charlee could save the dragon and the Latarans.

The Dragon Lord raised his head, gazing at the ceiling or maybe beyond. "I… I cannot bring myself to speak the words." His voice no longer seethed with rage. He spoke barely above a whisper. "I have tried so hard to pretend like it never happened. Like we could go on this way. That the dragons could separate themselves from the rest of the world. That I could somehow protect you, my son, by hiding away. But I knew this day would come. I have been a fool and a coward and now you would have me speak of the greatest failure in my life. I should rather die."

"Father, what are…you…saying?"

Sheorrriaaaan kissed his son on the head. "Very well. I will tell the story, but it won't change what I must do." He took a long breath, smoke rising from his snout. His eyes shifted to Charlee. "Before Theodora rose to power, my Tinnaaashhhiinn… what you would understand as a mate, or wife…gave birth to our child, Kraannaannn, with the help of Noorrennn, the greatest healer among the dragons."

"Theodora's dragon," Charlee interrupted.

"Yes, that is true now. But at one time, he was my trusted advisor and my healer." The large reptile bowed his head. His throat glowed orange, ready to spit more fire.

Charlee thought of Tribon. He had been Michala's trusted general before he, too, betrayed his own people.

The Dragon Lord caressed his son's wings. "Soon after Kraannaannn was born, Theodora began her conquests. She enticed Noorrennn to serve her. As my son, a mere infant, slept, Noorrennn used his healing powers to remove a section of my son's heart. Not enough to kill my son, but enough to weaken him."

He pounded his tail against a cavern wall. Chunks of stone splintered away. His chest heaved and his claws raked the ground. He finally forced himself to speak again. "My wife walked in on Noorrennn and tried to stop him. But, as strong as she was, his abilities were too great. He took her from me that day, and cut my son's heart."

Tears slid down Charlee's cheeks. "I'm so—"

Flames shot from his nostrils, searing the air. She held her breath but couldn't stop herself from coughing as black smoke wafted around her.

"Let me finish," he commanded. "Before I could avenge myself, Theodora appeared and told me that she had Kraannaannn's heart. She said she would spare my son's life if I did not interfere with her rise to power. If I did anything against her, my son would die."

Charlee blinked away more tears. She cleared her throat and stood on wobbly legs. "You should have told my grandfather. He could have helped."

"No one could have helped." Sheorrriaaaan's scales graded together. "So I let your grandfather stand alone, and Theodora destroyed your people. I was a coward, but my son was all I had left. I wanted him to live."

She edged toward him cautiously. "I understand. You never told Kraannaannn."

"I have told no one."

"Father." Kraannaannn tried to stand but fell back into Sheorrriaaaan's wings.

"Don't speak," the Dragon Lord responded. "I am going to save you. I am going to do what I must do to save your life. I will not lose you, as I lost your mother."

"Father," Kraannaannn whispered, his words spoken through gasps for air. "I would have acted to save the guardian even if I had known. Please, Father, help her. You are the Lord of the Dragons. Remember what that means."

Kraannaannn's yellow eyes closed, his life slipping away.

Charlee's hands formed fists. Once again, she had allowed Theodora to hurt someone. "No more!" She gripped the medallion. Hate made her blood boil. She retreated from the two dragons, studying the round object in her hands. She would give herself over to the medallion. Use it to strike down the sorceress.

She glared at the Dragon Lord. "This game ends now. Do what you have to, but I am going to do what I should have done from the start. Your son will live. I'll make sure of that."

With that, she summoned all the strength she could. Her mind shuddered. She touched her forehead. Little veins protruded from the skin, but she strained harder until the familiar blue ball of energy popped into existence in the cavern, hovering in front of her. The doorway increased to the size of a manhole cover. She peered at the Castle of Latara where the sorceress presumably waited for her.

"No, Guardian," the Dragon Lord bellowed.

Charlee ignored him. "Here I come, witch. The doubt in me is gone." She leaped into the portal, medallion clutched to her chest.

A voice in her head responded...*good.*

CHAPTER 29

The Gateway to Nowhere

THE IMAGE OF the castle loomed large across the magical tunnel she'd manifested, like a lighthouse guiding her through a storm toward her destination. Charlee held the medallion in front of her like a shield, prepared for battle. "Theodora, I'm—"

Another picture flashed across Charlee's mind, an unexpected blinding snapshot. The castle vanished, and her magical pathway curved to the right as if detouring to another highway. Another location. But where? She tried to focus on the Kingdom of Latara, but the new image invaded her thoughts. A land of rolling white sand dunes stretched forever in all directions under skies where day and night were sewn together. A giant yellow sun hovered against a sea of pale blue to the east. In the west, distant dots of light marked the darkness as other worlds rose on the horizon.

She squeezed the medallion. "Concentrate, dammit."

Too late. The portal dumped her in the middle of nowhere, then closed. "No... no. This is wrong. I can't be here. I don't have time for this? What's happening?"

Charlee spun around. Her stomach clenched. Like a tiny boat in a vast sea, she stood in an open desert studded with sweeping sand dunes stretching before her in every direction.

"This has to be a Theodora trick. It's not real. She's taken over my...." A staggering sense of loneliness swept her breath away.

Ivory sand covered her cracked boots. Bending down, she brushed her fingers through the soft silt. She'd been in a desert before. Felt the grittiness. This substance flowed like liquid.

Overhead., nebulas swirled like bands of cotton candy, floating in a purple sky. Glowing planets, some so close she could see the ripples in their shimmering oceans and their snow-topped mountains, spread from one horizon to the other. One blue marble in the distance could have been home. Earth!

Was this supposed to be the center of the universe? Was she staring at an endless array of galaxies?

"No, it's not real."

Yet the vastness pressed in on her. Charlee had become an object lost in space... even though her feet were firmly planted on this nowhere land.

"Where are you, witch?"

She received no response. Maybe this wasn't Theodora's game. Her guardian powers didn't always work right. Could her mind have malfunctioned, sending her across the universe?

Charlee shuddered, pressing the medallion against her chest. *"All right, girl. Keep your head straight. Wherever this is, whether Theodora caused this or not, you have to get out of here—now."*

She started to will another gateway into being…one that would take her to the Castle of Latara.

"Guardian, do not leave." A faint female voice beckoned to her from across the sand.

"Who said that?" Charlee peered over her shoulder. "Is anyone out—?"

A glint in one of the white sand dunes caught her attention. She turned toward it. Something shimmered, reflecting the sunlight in the eastern sky. Was the sparkling object tied to the voice? Whatever it was tugged at her for reasons she couldn't explain. An invisible force compelling her to investigate.

No, she had to get out of here. "I'm probably hearing things. Probably just a rock in the sand."

Charlee closed her eyes. She had to open another portal. The Dragon Lord's son was depending on her. His life depended on her facing Theodora. An image of Latara formed in her mind but quickly scrambled. Charlee bit a nail, peering again at the mysterious glimmer.

"Damn, I have to see it." She twisted strands of hair. "What if I'm here for a reason. What if there's something here I can use against Theodora."

Still clutching the medallion, her feet sank into the soft surface up to her ankles at every step. What was she doing? This could still be a trap. Charlee told herself to turn back but slogged forward. She breathed fast as much out of anticipation as for the difficulty of the trek.

Nearing the object, she crouched for a better look. Buried underneath the sand with just an edge visible, she couldn't tell what it was. Sheer, transparent, it seemed glassy or maybe made of ice.

Charlee placed the medallion back inside the pouch and knelt closer. A stinging chill rose from it like an icy barrier warning her of danger.

Her heart boomed inside her chest. Her fingers twitched.

She thrust her hands into the sand and dug feverishly. Outlines of the object took shape. A slab of ice lost in this nowhere land and forgotten in time. "Weird. How could ice form in this desert wasteland?"

Her mind told her to run but the tingling sensation all over her body made her stay. Reaching out, Charlee's fingertips froze on contact with the slick surface. She snapped back and rubbed her hands together. The cold shock didn't stop her.

She swept away more sand, exposing half of the slab.

Though a milk cloud covered the ice, hiding its contents, it soon became clear something lay within. Despite the stinging sensation, she put her face close to the block and peered inside.

"No, it can't be!" Charlee scurried away on all fours. Climbing to her feet, she lumbered through the sand, creating as much distance as possible between herself and what she'd seen inside the block of ice.

"No! That can't be right." Charlee stopped. Breathing heavily, she brushed away some of the silt from her face and hair.

"It can't be real." If it was, then nothing made sense. "I'm going crazy." That was the only explanation. Unable to deal with reality, she'd created this vision.

Trembling, Charlee forced herself to crawl back to the block and gazed inside one more time.

She could only whisper, "Theodora?"

Dry heaves overtook her and Charlee gagged. What was she seeing?

Trapped within this icy coffin, the young version of Theodora—the princess who appeared to Charlee in her dreams—lay draped in a white dress. Golden hair flowed around her face. Thin hands rested on her chest. Eyelids closed, she seemed to be in a deep sleep…or dead.

Charlee's mind raced. She looked skyward to the emptiness of space and the sea of colorful planets. Each one glowed like a full moon on a cloudless night. Was home out there somewhere? If she leaped back to Earth would life make sense again? Charlee lowered her head into her hands. "This has to be a trick. A game. Theodora's playing me like always. Don't fall for it."

She peeked through her fingers.

A motionless Theodora showed no sign of life until…

The blue orbs of her eyes shot open and stared straight at her. Screaming, Charlee backed away. That's when she heard Theodora in her mind.

"*I need you, Guardian.*"

Again, Charlee willed herself to crawl closer to the ice. Theodora's eyes were closed as if they never opened.

"*Free me!*" The words of the young Theodora echoed inside her thoughts. Charlee shook her head in disbelief.

The pleading persisted. "*Save me!*"

"No!" Charlee shouted. "Get out of my head!" She clasped her hands over her ears, trying to quiet the voice. It seemed to work.

Could the figure in the icy coffin be the sorceress? If so, who put her there— and why? If this was Theodora, who was that magical being who proclaimed herself empress and unleashed terror over Janasara?

"It's not real." She gruffly rubbed her eyes. But what if it was real? Charlee couldn't just ignore what she'd seen. There were secrets here. She had to unlock them.

But there was still work to do. The only way to save the Dragon Lord's son and everyone else was to reach the Theodora—real or fake—fortified in Latara.

Could the sorceress she'd done battle with be something else? Some dark creature with the ability to steal identities? Was Charlee its next target? The only way to know was to kill that witch…or whatever the being was…held up in the castle, then return here and try to free this young Theodora.

She had no idea how she'd opened a gateway to this nowhere land. But if she hoped to return, she'd have to figure out how.

That is, if she lived long enough. What kind of being was she about to face? What could be worse than Theodora? "You can't rule out its all some scam," she reminded herself. "Keep a clear head, if that's even possible."

With a last look at the frozen sarcophagus, Charlee concentrated on opening another gateway. Hopefully one that would lead to the Castle of Latara.

CHAPTER 30

The Heart's Beat

BEFORE THE GATEWAY swallowed her, Charlee lifted the medallion from the pouch. The smooth metal burned her fingers. She hissed through gritted teeth, trying to withstand the heat long enough to study both sides. What caused the object to scorch her now? Because of the coming battle? Was it a sign she was about to change to something dark? If her face appeared on the medallion—twisted and scarred—her journey toward evil had begun.

Nothing. Her face did not materialize. Her fate had not yet been decided. Hiding the object in the pouch, Charlee breathed a sigh of relief, but how long until her image did appear? She'd decided to give herself over to the medallion as the voice in her head urged her to do. If that was the only way to use the weapon against the sorceress, there was no other choice. Theodora—or whatever this freak was—had to be stopped. The medallion offered the only hope of destroying her. Charlee had to take the risk.

After killing Theodora, she'd find the tree of fire that gave birth to the dark object and throw it into the flames, saving herself and everyone else who might hear the calling of the medallion and be consumed by it.

"Somehow, if I beat Theodora, I'll have to hold on to my mind long enough to find that hidden tree. Or sacrifice myself."

The portal deposited her on the crusted wasteland outside the Kingdom of Latara. Charlee stood under a dark sky dimmed by swirling storm clouds. High winds cried out, smacking her in the face. Was it day or night? Impossible to tell under a sorrowful sky shrouded magically by Theodora's evil.

Before her the kingdom's shuttered gates stood at least fifty feet high, guarded by the chiseled forms of knights—two tall, looming statutes carved into the stone. Their faces altered into Theodora's likeness. An orange haze from the sorceress' factories hovered over the realm, but all was silent behind the walls. Charlee shivered as if a snowball smacked her across the back, but she stood firm. "Stay ready."

Should she sneak in? Try to surprise Theodora? Charlee shook her head. "Pointless. She knows I'm here. This is what she's been waiting for all along. To hurt everyone I care about. To teach me a lesson. Then take the medallion and kill me."

Charlee reached inside the pouch and grasped the medallion. Sweat rolled down her palm from the heat emanating from the object. "Well, witch, it begins now."

Lifting the medallion over her head, she shouted, "Theodora, I'm here! And look what I have in my hands. Come and get it! Come and get me—if you're not afraid."

The shrieking wind drowned out her voice, but it didn't matter. The image of the young Theodora trapped in ice still hung heavy on her mind. A trick to throw her off? Probably. Charlee held her breath, waiting for a response. When none came, she shouted again. "Hey, crazy lady, you must be scared if you're not coming out to face me."

This time, the gates to Latara creaked slowly open.

Before her lay the way to the castle—lined by Theodora's beast army. They stood shoulder to shoulder on either side of the stone walkway. Growls rose from their throats. Drool slid off yellow fangs. Some slashed the air with their claws, while others struck their chest armor with battle axes. What held them back from ripping her to shreds?

How could one girl stand against an entire army? She couldn't. One thought eclipsed all others. She was about to walk to her death. Raising a shaky hand, Charlee brushed hair from her face. For an instant, her courage drained away and the frightened girl returned. Flee this place. Why should she die?

No, there was no running away from this. Charlee was a guardian and she had to fight. If she died bravely, perhaps it might unite this world against Theodora. Dragons, Latarans, and all beings of Janasara standing together against evil. "I have to do this," she uttered. "Cryton, please be with me."

Charlee stepped forward on wobbly legs.

Placing the medallion underneath her arm, the object cooled but vibrated softly. Charlee glared at the medallion. On one side, the outlines of a tree became visible in the dark stone. A crimson radiance illuminated the engraving. "What the heck?" She tucked it against her chest, and kept walking.

Howls rose among the Horeng ranks as she passed. Those closest snarled, snapping their jaws. Still, none attacked. Theodora's orders probably. The witch wanted to kill Charlee herself.

"No going back now," she murmured.

Charlee passed through the gates and entered the kingdom. Ruins of the once great kingdom surrounded her. The grassland from her dreams burned. Trees felled. Everything natural gone. In its place, factories belched fire and filthy smoke.

Inside the walls, the almost deafening mechanical hum of the factories never ceased. No peace. No quiet. Only the grinding motion of Theodora's war machine.

Charlee walked toward the castle, desperate to pull energy from the surroundings and the beasts. But creatures born from dark magic and land overcome by death gave off no life force for her to absorb. If only a bird would fly by. Or a singular blade of grass grew. Something… anything…alive.

Nothing.

Charlee couldn't even tap into embers of the planet's soul. Somehow, in this place of death, Theodora blocked Janasara's natural energy.

Her strength fading, she trudged forward. "Must stay strong. Can't show weakness." She tightened her grip on the medallion. Pressed against her chest, the tree outline continued to glow, but the object did nothing to heighten her abilities. *Stupid thing, you better work.*

The voice in her head spoke. *Believe and you will soak in its power. It will give you new life. You will be reborn. Are you ready for that gift of power?*

She glared at the magical object. "I am." What choice did she have?

"Oh, Mom, I wish you and Dad were her," Charlee whispered, marching along the stone pathway to the castle. Wolves on either side of her stomped their claws against the stone and gnashed their fangs.

Hate for the monsters swelled inside her. She wanted to strike them all down. Shatter their bones with a wave of her hand. Teach these beasts what it is to feel fear, then silence them forever.

Charlee closed her eyes. She had to concentrate and not let her boiling emotions make her stupid. If only she could talk one more time with her mom. Hear her comforting advice and feel her warm embrace. Just once more.

"Can you hear me, Mom? Across dimensions? No, you can't, can you? I'm on my own. Just me and this medallion."

Behind her, the Horeng followed her to the castle.

Charlee quickened her steps. Pushing out her chest, she called to Theodora. "So, you need an entire army to defeat me?"

The sorceress' laughter rang out over the kingdom, warped church bells calling a congregation to prayer. Then, the witch spoke. "I figured a royal escort was in order for the guardian."

"Whatever," Charlee said aloud. "Just open the gates to the castle. I'm almost there. It's time for you and me to meet face to face."

"You will find the castle open to you," Theodora's disembodied voice answered. "I eagerly await you."

Great, I'm walking into a trap. I have to be careful. Charlee held the medallion close to her mouth. "You better work."

Castle Latara loomed menacingly before her. The waterfall from her dreams still spilled in magical silence from the mountains into the castle's center, but the glimmering blue waters were crimson…like blood. It seemed to ooze, rather than flow, down the mountainside.

She took a deep breath. "It's not real. It's just the sorceress."

When Charlee reached the gated entryway, two guards blocked her entry. Charlee walked up to the beasts, expecting them to move aside. Instead, they pointed their battle axes at her and growled in anger.

Then they howled in agony. Their bones cracked. With nothing more than a gurgle, the creatures fell like lumps to the ground. Charlee eyed the dead creatures.

"My apologies, child," Theodora offered. "My pets should not have tried to stop you. Do you like how I punished them?"

Charlee did not answer. She stepped past them into Theodora's lair.

Sadness filled her heart at the destruction surrounding her. Banners of each of the Ten Unified Kingdoms lay shredded on a stone floor covered with dirt and muck inside the grand hall. Ten pillars—some cracked, others cut in half—lined either side of the chamber. A table in the center was split in two. Upon closer inspection, it once held a miniature replica of the Unified Kingdoms. Black stains covered the walls. Chunks of ceiling had collapsed and shattered across the floor. Her teeth clenched and cheeks became red hot. This had been home to her grandparents, and the sorceress ripped it all away. Now the stale stench of death hung over it.

"Stay sharp," she said aloud.

"Oh yes, do." Theodora's voice sounded louder than ever.

Charlee crept through the hall, but each step echoed off the walls. She cringed but continued to a spiral staircase rising through the castle.

"Climb to me," Theodora called to her like a mother to a child. "I await you high above in your grandmother's throne room."

Rolling her eyes, Charlee threw up her arms. Ascending would be treacherous. The steps were cracked, some missing, leaving gaps she'd have to jump. A gray mist hung over the rising path, hiding the upper sections. She clutched her rumbling stomach. Food would probably just make her sick right now, but a gallon of soda would help. A cold sweat formed across her scalp. "I can do this. I have to do this. For Cryton. Kraannaannn. Everyone." Charlee began the long climb.

"Careful, Guardian, we wouldn't want you to fall," Theodora sang from every corner of the castle.

"Shut your mouth, witch." Charlee leaped past two missing steps.

Each level brought her to a new scene of destruction. Pieces of stone from cracked walls littered passageways. Horeng wandered aimlessly through the different halls, fighting among themselves, eating savagely, howling and snarling. They feasted on bones, some with flesh. A gathering of human skulls lay strewn across the floor. The bones of her people? "They'll pay. All of them." Charlee scrunched her nose. The stench of rot and decay, worse than any trash-filled alley back home, became unbearable.

She shook herself away from the ravenous wolves and climbed until the gray mist blocked the view of the rest of the stairway. Charlee stopped and reached into the chilled murky layer.

"Just do it," she told herself. "The only way to Theodora is through this fog."

A guttural whisper greeted her first step through the gray wall. Unintelligible at first, the voice grew louder. "Why did you let me die?"

Charlee recognized the speaker.

"Cryton?" She peered through the hovering fog. Her heart rate quickened. Mouth opened wide. It couldn't be?

"You were supposed to save me."

"Cryton, is that you?" Tears slid down her cheeks.

A face appeared against the mist. Her mentor's face. The eyes white. Cheeks gaunt. Mustache matted down by dried blood.

"Guardian, you failed."

Charlee shook her head. "This isn't real."

"Guardian, why did you fail me?"

"No! Theodora, get out of my head." She lowered her head. "You're not real."

Glancing up, Cryton's face vanished. He spoke no more. Theodora's laugh pressed against her chest. She pushed on, climbing carefully, watching for missing steps. Charlee climbed until another voice spoke up.

"Give up this hero's game." This voice, too, was familiar to Charlee but in a different way. Raspy. Crusty. Evil. But hers. A larger, heavier, older version of herself greeted her a step above.

Shrouded in the mist, she couldn't make out specific details of the figure before her, but it was unmistakably her own. Round. Heavy. Scarred. The exact image on the medallion in her visions.

"Come on, young one! You don't owe a thing to anybody." Her older-self crossed her arms, lips curled up in a twisted grin.

Charlee took a step back. "Stop this, Theodora!"

She lifted her foot to take another step, but this future version of herself hefted a long, dark blade and swung it at her. "Death to the guardian."

Charlee fell to one knee, expecting to feel the steel blade slice into her, but the death strike never came. The twisted apparition disappeared. Silence engulfed her, save for the pounding of her own heart.

"Enough tricks, Theodora." She slowly stood and willed herself to take a few more steps. "Finally."

At the castle's top level, she peered down a long hallway with vaulted ceilings. No Horeng here. No burn marks on the walls. No bones. Just a long stone walkway that led to a chamber hidden behind double doors.

Torches burned along the walls. Their blood-red glow provided dim lighting. Every step became sluggish. Head felt heavy. Shoulders slouched. The evil enchantment within the castle drained her energy, robbing her of what magically enhanced strength she had left.

"What have I gotten myself into?" Charlee muttered.

Steeling herself against what lay ahead, she crept along the hallway, the little hairs on the back of her neck standing tall as if unseen eyes followed her. "I have to remain strong. The Empress's reign has to stop. It's up to me to end it…now."

Bulky wooden doors blocked entry to the chamber. Charlee reached for an iron handle the size of a cannon ball, but they opened on their own, creaking in protest. Beyond the entryway was a massive throne room, and on the far side a veranda, revealing ferocious, blackening clouds.

Charlee didn't want to enter but destiny brought her here.

Grasping the medallion, she took her first cautious steps inside. A wave of unnatural frosty air wrapped around her like a snake, squeezing her chest until each breath burned. Charlee coughed, mist rising from her mouth, but plodded deeper into the chamber.

In the center sat an enormous throne that nearly reached the ceiling. Charlee inched closer and gasped. Human bones, blackened and coated in dried blood, formed the base of the throne and the seat. Skulls lined the armrests and spines and ribs forged the back. Hand bones, fingers raised high, covered the top of the throne. Were these the remains of her victims?

Dented, crushed crowns were strewn along the stone steps leading up to the throne. Broken swords hovered in a corner and spun in a strange dance.

Charlee bit her lip. The poor souls. They all deserved proper burials.

Theodora remained hidden, but the sorceresses' presence hung heavy over her. "I'm here, Theodora. Let's end this." Charlee's voice bounced off the walls. "You hear me?"

A crack of lightning flashed from the clouds beyond the balcony. A muffled explosion of thunder followed. Charlee flinched at the sudden flood of light. Her gaze rested on an item sitting on a table on the far end of the room. She recognized it. Carefully, she approached, each step making her more certain. There, encased in a shaded glass-like covering, lay the barely-beating section of Kraannaannn's heart, the knife still embedded.

"I have to save him."

Placing the medallion back into the pouch, she gripped the case and tugged but couldn't lift the cover. Her jaw clenched; she tried again. The cover still wouldn't budge. "Come on!" Charlee struck the case with fists that had cut through rock in the ravine. Without her enhanced strength, she couldn't break the glass.

The case withstood each blow, protected by a barrier of dark magic. "Damn!" With shaky hands, she reached for the medallion. *Maybe she could use it to shatter the case.* Worth a try.

Charlee raised the round object over the case and braced herself to bring it down with a crash.

She stopped when a familiar laugh—that of a truly evil being who believed herself unstoppable—resonated through the chamber.

CHAPTER 31

The Medallion's Grip

I T CAME FROM every corner of the chamber. Outside, lightning flashed across the sky, causing shadows to bounce off the chamber's walls. Torches by the entryway burned brighter, shooting flames toward the ceiling. Their crackle matched pitch with the sorceress' laughter.

Charlee spun around, still alone. "Sho...show yourself!"

"Has the guardian grown so weak she cannot lift a simple cover?" Theodora mocked. Her voice flowed from every direction.

"I'm strong enough...to stop...you." Charlee lifted the medallion and the invisible grip around her shattered. Pushing air in and out of her lungs, she uttered, "My abilities stopped you once. I'll do it again."

"That shadow of a victory has long since passed," Theodora answered. Now her voice bristled with irritation. "It is a moment in time that shall not be repeated. In this place, you cannot use my power against me. There is no source from which you can draw strength. In fact, by now I am sure you have noticed this place is consuming your power."

"If you have no fear, face me." Charlee held the medallion in front of her with both hands and sidestepped to the throne. "Here is your immortality. Come and get it. In fact, I'll trade you the medallion for Kraannaannn's heart."

"It touches me so to see how much you care for the child of the Dragon Lord."

Footsteps, as if someone with high heels approached, followed Theodora's words. The clip clop came from the chamber's doorway.

Charlee backed against the throne. Her fingers tightened around the medallion, but her hands shook. She was freaked out but didn't dare show it. "Stay strong."

The slow, rhythmic sound of Theodora's footsteps continued to click toward Charlee. Then the sorceress appeared, popping into existence. At first a faint ghost, the witch's body slowly solidified as she sauntered across the chamber.

Okay, here we go. Beads of sweat ran down the sides of Charlee's face. She steadied her wobbly knees.

Theodora took her younger form, with crystal blue eyes and flowing hair. The sorceress wore a long white gown and a golden crown. *Just like when I first saw her,* Charlee remembered. *When she first fooled me.* On her feet were golden, jewel-encrusted shoes with heels as high as a super model's, as if she had just stepped out of a fashion mall. Razor sharp metal points covered the toes.

"Do you like them?" Theodora glanced at her own shoes. "I discovered high heels in your world and created a pair of my own."

"Theodora, take the knife out of Kraannaannn's heart, and maybe I won't kill you." Charlee tried to sound tough.

"Now, Guardian, is that anyway to greet family?" The sorceress stood an arm's length away from her, grinning. "Why all this talk of death? Forget the dragons. Forget the people of Latara. Let's us have a nice visit and become reacquainted."

Charlee held the medallion like a shield. "I mean it, Theodora."

The sorceress stroked her own hair. "I know that you mean to use my medallion…my source of immortality…against me, but I can assure you that until you learn to use its power, it will do you no good. Instead, all you will accomplish will be to waste time—time the Dragon Lord's son does not have."

"I might surprise you." Charlee shifted her attention from the sorceress to the medallion. *Please, work. I give myself over to you.* She bowed to the object. *I'll do whatever you want as long as you help me stop her.*

Theodora frowned and climbed the marble steps to the throne. Gracefully sliding into the seat, the witch caressed the two skulls at the edges of the armrests. "Tell me, my child. Do you hear the voice of the medallion? Does it call to you?"

What? The voice she'd been hearing was the medallion's? Cryton never told her that. Charlee's grip loosened on the object for a heartbeat, but she quickly recovered and pressed the medallion to her chest.

"Yes, Aunty, the medallion does talk to me." Charlee retreated farther from Theodora. "I guess that makes it mine now, doesn't it? Maybe the medallion has chosen me over you."

Theodora glared at her. "My child, what if we struck an accord? Hand me the medallion and swear yourself to my service for all eternity, and in return I will save the life of the Dragon Lord's son."

Charlee breathed deeply. "What of the people of Latara? What of my world?"

"You worry about trivialities."

"Theodora!"

"Oh, all right. All shall be my slaves—in this world and in yours. But you need not worry. They will live full lives in service to me just as you shall."

Charlee allowed herself a slight smile. "No deal. Before today is over, I'm going to use this medallion to make sure you never hurt anyone again."

"That is a most unkind way to speak to me in my own home." Theodora rose.

"This isn't your home. It belonged to my grandmother and grandfather." Charlee steadied herself for the attack about to come. She wasn't nearly as confident as her words suggested.

"Tribon, dear! Will you join us?" Theodora waved her hand as if calling to an old friend.

Charlee sighed. This was going to be a repeat of their battle on Alcatraz back in San Francisco Bay when she had to fight Tribon before she could reach Theodora. She would have lost to the giant knight, if her dad, her mom and Cryton had not shown up to save her.

But this time, her parents weren't there. Cryton was gone. She didn't even have the changeling at her side. She was on her own, and any strength she had was quickly fading.

Tribon lumbered through the doorway. His armor still smoldered. Steam rose from his metal-covered shoulders, chest plate, and back. Tribon's face was severely burned and scarred from the fire.

Charlee raised an eyebrow. While nothing could kill Tribon—as an undead slave serving Theodora—a dragon's deadly breath still hurt him. The sorceress might be able to heal his injuries, but it would take time.

He walked up to Theodora and stood by her throne.

"Tribon, I grow tired of this piece of art." She carelessly indicated the heart of the Dragon Lord's son, still inside its case. "I wish it to be discarded."

"And how would my Empress like to see it discarded?" His dark eyes focused on Charlee. A smile crossed his scarred, leathery face.

"Incinerate it, just as you were set ablaze," Theodora answered. "Yes, make a fire and throw it in."

"As you wish." Tribon bowed. He went to the case and picked it up.

"No!" Charlee ran at Tribon.

A flash of red energy burst from Theodora's hands and smashed into Charlee's stomach. The blast hurled her back. She crashed against the cold, hard floor, nearly losing the medallion. It was all she could do to hold onto the object. She cried out, searing pain racing through her body. Her charred tunic stuck to her belly. The skin underneath sizzled and popped. Charlee breathed through clenched teeth. "Get up! Can't stay down!"

Climbing onto all fours, Charlee blinked to stay alert. She then slowly rose, each motion agonizing. A whimper slipped through her lips. She staggered to her feet, legs barely able to support her weight. With a final push, Charlee lifted her head and held the medallion against her chest.

"Guardian, this is all so unnecessary. I really have no wish to kill you." Theodora stepped down from the throne and crossed to her.

"Yeah...right." Charlee limped toward the balcony, clutching her scorched stomach with one hand, eyes on Tribon.

He made no move to leave the chamber. Instead, he watched his empress torture the guardian. His lips parted in a warped grin.

Good. Stay. Watch me suffer, Charlee thought. At least Kraannaannn's heart would be safe for the time being.

She swung to Theodora.

The sorceress' face aged. Cheeks caved in. Crevices formed on her forehead. Her golden hair turned thin and gray. But her eyes glowed red hot.

Did she need the medallion—her immortality—to maintain her youthful appearance? Whenever she used her magic, without the aid of the medallion, did the effort age her? Was she even Theodora or some other beast? Was the true Theodora imprisoned in ice in that nowhere realm? Did that even matter right now? The woman before her, whether her great aunt or not, had to be killed.

"Getting tired, Aunty?" Charlee blew damp hair away from her eyes. She flexed tired muscles, kindling a last bit of magic strength. Her blood pumped faster. Limbs stopped shaking.

Theodora unleashed a shriek that could have shattered glass and then fired more dark magic at her.

Ignoring her wounds, Charlee dove onto the stone floor just in time to avoid the blast. The crimson ray soared past her, slamming into a bone table, which shattered into sharp fragments.

Charlee rolled out of her dive, cringing from her smoldering wound. Despite the blistering agony of the rough cloth melted to blackened skin, she scrambled to her feet, then pointed the medallion at Theodora—just as a third bolt of red magic raced toward her.

The voice in her head spoke. *Do you believe?*

"Yes!" She stretched her arms in front of her to their fullest length. "You are the only way. Now strike her down."

Like a switch thrown to light up an entire city, the medallion sparked to life with a blinding flash. Charlee squeezed her eyelids tight but couldn't block the stinging flare. The energy wave expanded to her arms, shoulders, neck, face, and head. Her body convulsed, but she held onto the magical object.

Time itself seemed to slow.

"What's…happening…to…me?" Charlee thrust the medallion farther out in front of her. The object absorbed Theodora's attack and then spit it back. The enchanted discharge struck Theodora in the shoulder, sending her reeling backward. She crashed into the throne and slumped to the ground.

Breathing heavy, Charlee brought the medallion to her face. The tree etching pulsed with a ruby glow. Her own body tingled limb to limb. Blood rushed through her veins. The sensation was more intense than when the changeling siphoned power to her. A yellow radiance engulfed her hands, sparks leaping from her fingertips. Charlee's charred skin healed; the pain in her stomach vanished. Tired muscles hardened as if she were a bodybuilder. "I feel strong."

This was an uninhibited power. Charlee could do anything, and no one would stop her.

Take revenge! Destroy!

The words filled her mind. Were they her thoughts or the medallion's? The object spoke to her as it had done, unbeknownst to her, all along. Only, for the first time, it became hard to separate her thoughts. Charlee started to hyperventilate. Her heart thudded loudly. Had the medallions taken control? Was she already losing herself to its evil? Did she care? The power was so enticing. She thirsted for it.

Charlee waved her head. "I'm already losing my mind! Have to hold on."

Kill the witch now! the voice demanded.

"Yes." Charlee ignored the doubtful thoughts. A smile crossed her face. She hurt Theodora and liked it. "How about that, Theodora? Did it sting?"

The sorceress stood with great effort, face ashen gray, limbs trembling. Theodora grabbed onto the throne to steady herself. A knowing smile crossed her wicked lips. "How does the power of the medallion feel, Guardian? Do you feel it in your mind…in your heart? Is it merging with you? Is it corrupting you? It feels good, doesn't it?"

Theodora's words were lost to the rumbling voice that filled Charlee's head. *Destroy anyone who gets in our way! Together, we can rule.*

But another part of Charlee could hear some of what Theodora said. That part of her understood what was happening. She was becoming more and more willing to give herself over to the power.

Without any thought or direction from her, the medallion fired a scarlet ray at Theodora. The jarring burst of magic vibrated Charlee's hands to the point her wrist bones threatened to shatter. She pressed against the medallion like trying to hold back a charging bull.

"Must…hang…on!"

The sorceress countered by hurling a fiery cannonball of her own sorcery back at Charlee. In a blazing explosion, the two blasts collided. The chamber shook. Chunks of ceiling collapsed.

The medallion's magic engulfed Theodora's, then redirected a beam back at the sorceress. It slammed into her chest, a whip cracking against flesh. With a high-pitched scream, she crashed against a wall with enough force to break every bone in her body. The witch didn't move. Nor groan.

Charlee stood, the medallion pressed close to her chest. "Let the witch be dead." She slowly crossed to Theodora's limp form. No sensation of remorse. No sympathy. Only satisfaction.

If Theodora lay dead, then she *and the medallion* would rule not only in this world but in many others.

Yes, the voice in her head declared—the medallion's voice.

After all, she was a guardian. Why shouldn't she rule? Why shouldn't people bow to her?

Charlee stopped in mid-step. These thoughts weren't hers.

The medallion spoke again. *Yes! They are ours.*

"No!" Charlee banged her head with a fist. "I don't want to rule. I just want to stop Theodora. Just wanted to save—"

You don't have to save a soul.

"I have to save Kraannaannn," she challenged. Charlee tried to focus her mind on the Dragon Lord's son, but the thought was fleeting.

The power can be ours. It can all be ours. I have waited so long for you to accept my gift of power.

She peered at the medallion. What she saw made her tremble. An etching of her face began to form on one side. "It's happening. I was wrong. I don't want this. Mom, what have I done?" She backed away from the sorceress.

Something swooshed through the air from behind.

Charlee whirled around, raising the medallion to block an unseen blow... but not fast enough. The tip of a blade ripped a gash from her right cheek up to her forehead, almost piercing an eye. Blood splashed across her face. Her torn skin flapped loosely. Screaming, one hand clutching her shredded flesh, Charlee collapsed to the floor. The other hand lost its grip on the medallion. She reached once more for it but missed.

Charlee wailed. Though she feared its sway over her, the object created a hunger deep inside nothing would fulfill except re-establishing their contact.

She scrambled for the medallion. She had to have it back! Where was it? It was hers! Charlee didn't even bother gazing up to see who attacked her. Who cares? Nothing else mattered but the dark object.

"Get up, Guardian." Those words, spoken in the Lengoron language, were uttered by Sandra—at least, by Theodora's version of Sandra.

Charlee ignored the command. "The medallion. Where is it?" An icy chill spread across her face. Then, scorching heat rose from the wound. Warm liquid oozed between her fingers and dripped onto the stone floor.

"I said, to your feet." This time, the girl placed the blade next to Charlee's neck.

With a deep breath, placing one hand over her bleeding cheek, Charlee tried to stand, but her strength failed her. A haze drifted over her vision. *Have...to... think. Still...Charlee.* She braced her hands against the floor and lifted her body a second time. She stood, but her head drooped, her arms hung limply at her side.

Sandra held her blade inches from Charlee's chest.

"Sandra...please. You know me." She extended a trembling hand to Theodora's daughter.

"What did you call me?" This Sandra lowered her sword.

"You are...were...my friend," Charlee's blurry gaze shifted around the chamber in search of the medallion.

Sandra again lifted her sword. "I am your enemy, not your friend."

"No, I'm not...your enemy," Charlee uttered. She still didn't see the medallion. Where was it?

Theodora's laugh broke the moment.

Once again, she sat on her throne. Charlee turned. The sorceress and her immortality were reunited. The witch held it in her lap.

"No, it belongs to me!" Charlee stumbled toward the throne, until something blunt clubbed her over the head.

Jolting pain rattled her mind, scrambling her senses. A high-pitched hum deep in her ears deafened her. The only other sound was her own breathing amplified as if by giant speakers placed against her head. Her eyes dimmed and stomach cramped. She crumbled to the floor, fighting against the darkness that surrounded her.

Sandra stood over her, a dab of blood on the bottom of her sword handle. Charlee extended a hand to the back of her head. More blood coated her fingers.

The battle was over.

Through the pulsating ache flowing from her skull, a new thought filled her mind. *Still...a guardian. Must...save...Dragon Lord's son. Must...save...my people. Or die...trying.*

CHAPTER 32

The Edge of Darkness

THEODORA CRADLED THE medallion—her immortality, caressing it with the fingers of her right hand, like a mother tenderly stroking a child's head. Reunited with the dark object, her aging, cracked skin softened and color returned to her cheeks. Flesh reformed around bony fingers and the sorceress' long blond hair flowed over her shoulders. The white dress hugging her body glowed with each lightning strike flashing across the throne room's terrace.

Blood dripped from the open wound on Charlee's face. Holding the split skin together, she blinked away dizziness. The ringing in her ears faded, but the chamber still spun slowly like a carousel. Despite the nausea building in her stomach, her eyes locked on the medallion.

She wanted it back.

No! Theodora needed to be stopped. Charlee had done so before, without the medallion and could do it again. But how? What guardian power did she have left?

"Guardian, your time came, and it has now gone. You touched true power and let it slip through your hands. And now it has returned to me." The sorceress rose from her throne and crossed the chamber to her. "What is truly sad is that you had the medallion in your possession, and you lacked the will...the imagination... to think what could be, if only you would embrace it."

I did embrace it. Look what good it did me. Charlee rolled onto her back, the room rocking back and forth. The warmth of unconsciousness called to her.

"No, Guardian! Do not slip away yet." The sorceress bent down and stroked Charlee's hair. "There is more that you must know."

"Don't touch me." Charlee shook away a gray tunnel beginning to engulf her. Through the fog in her head, Theodora's daughter stood to her right, wiping blood from her blade. Behind her, Tribon still held the case with Kraannaannn's heart.

Theodora bent closer to Charlee, their faces inches apart. "First, I want to formally introduce you to my new daughter, Assara. I'm sure you recognize her striking resemblance to that awful little creature you care about so much. What do you call her? Sandra!"

The sorceress strolled to her daughter then placed an arm around her. "I have you to thank. You see, if I had never known of your Sandra, I never would have taken her. Never been able to harvest some of her hair to create this clone, my lovely daughter. You have blessed me with my new family."

What was she saying? Charlee tightened her hand into a fist. Not only had Theodora hurt Sandra—she'd taken something from the innocent girl and used it to generate this unfortunate creature. Then she had named her Assara! The name of Charlee's grandmother.

Cryton told her how Assara, Theodora's older sister, had been named Queen of Latara. Theodora desired to be queen, turning to the dark arts and to the medallion to steal the throne.

"Why have you done this?" Charlee asked.

"To hurt you," Theodora stomped back to her, stopping an arm's length away.

Charlee forced herself to stand. *Can't give up. Must find a way. Kraannaannn needs me.* "I'll make—"

Assara spoke up. "Mother, what are you talking about? Who is this San... dra? I don't understand your words."

"And now you should know what I plan to do," Theodora went on speaking to Charlee. "I will use this medallion to take your power from you and make it my own. Then I will gain the ability to open a gateway, and I will return to your Earth."

The sorceress circled Charlee. "I will kill your mother, father, and sister. I will claim Earth as my own. It will be the beginning of my conquest of all the universe. One by one, I will possess any world across any dimension."

"No!" Charlee shouted. The single word rang throughout the chamber. "I'll stop you."

Not my family! I can' let this happen. Her stomach tensed. Charlee lumbered to the sorceress, but Theodora slapped her away.

Charlee, more blood flowing from her cheek, crumbled to the floor. "Get up, girl. I have to stand and fight."

Theodora laughed.

"Mother, what of me?" Assara asked, her blade held close to her chest like a child snuggles a teddy bear.

This time, Theodora did not ignore her daughter. "Oh, I shall leave you to rule this world in my place. No one shall stand in your way."

Assara did not respond.

Painfully standing, eyes locked on the medallion, Charlee stumbled to Theodora. *Take it from her. Can't let her out of here with it. Can't let her hurt my family.*

Her own desire for the dark object clouded her thoughts. If I could only have one more chance, I wouldn't blow it. I'd destroy Theodora. Then be the ruler of everyone. Bring peace.

"Guardian, I want to thank you for your gift." Theodora held up the medallion.

Before Charlee could register what Theodora said, a stream of blazing energy poured from the object. It slammed into her shoulder, like a bullet fired at close range, launching Charlee across the chamber until her head struck the base of the throne. Pain flashed before her eyes. Black smoke rose from a gaping hole beneath her shoulder blade. The skin popped. How much of this could she take? When would the final blow come?

The crimson ray did more than simply zap her. The dark object's attack began to drain her guardian powers. Her body became numb, her skin a shell with nothing left inside that made her Charlee. She lay on the floor, her limbs useless. *Don't give up. Get up! Stand! fight!*

Maybe, she could find a way to absorb the medallion's energy, rather than allowing it to consume hers. Perhaps she had enough magic left to create a protective layer to shield herself from Theodora's witchery.

"Let me have…just a little magic…left." With her mind, she scanned her body for any remaining spark of magic. Nothing! Without the changeling to charge her powers, she was defenseless. Alone. "Dig deep. Find the strength."

"Guardian, with your next breath, your power shall be mine." Theodora placed her lips to the medallion, then lifted it over her head.

A lightning bolt leaped from the object, wrapping around Charlee like a lasso. She screamed, but an electric shock cut her voice to a whimper. Her body jerked wildly. Mom, help me! Hurts! Make… it… stop!

Then it ended.

The lightning entangling her vanished. Tears slid down her cheeks. She was powerless. Cold inside. Shivering. Everything that had made her a guardian gone. Now she was just…helpless Charlee.

She clenched her teeth, trying to move her muscles, but her broken body wouldn't respond. Every limb throbbed as if she'd been struck by something big then tossed aside like trash on a corner. Each heartbeat sent pulses of pain, like little dagger strikes, through her chest. Worse was the realization she'd failed everyone. What an idiot to think she could stand up to Theodora on her own. If only she'd listen to her parents. If only Cryton were here…and the changeling. Damn me!

Tribon's throaty laughter mixed with Theodora's, resonating throughout the chamber. Charlee strained to rise, but it felt as though her bones had liquefied.

Theodora knelt beside her. "I could end your life now, Guardian, but I'm not going to kill you. "Instead, you will be sealed into a dungeon in the depths of this castle, with a full legion of my Horeng standing guard to make sure you never escape. There, as I unleash myself on your world, I will open a conduit to your mind so that you can see all that you have caused to befall those you love."

"Someone will…come for me." Charlee managed to ball her hands into fists.

"I think not." Theodora stood. "I will broadcast news you are dead. There will be proof of your demise, of course. Do not expect rescue, for there shall be none. You have no future beyond the dungeon deep under this castle."

Don't let this happen! Enraged, Charlee inched her hands underneath her body and started to lift herself but quickly slumped back to the floor. Her head pounded, vision blurred. Darkness beckoned, but she couldn't give into it.

"Guardian! You lack the strength to face me." Theodora's head tilted in mock concern. "And I think I no longer have any wish for you to serve as my slave. Your life is now meaningless to me. Even if you could escape the dungeon, you would never reach me. I have all your power."

Fear for her family building inside Charlee like a hurricane about to hit shore sparked her muscles back to life. She forced herself up on all fours. "You have the medallion, you witch. Isn't that enough? Stay away from my world...from my family."

Theodora chuckled. With a wave of her hand, she declared, "Take her to the dungeons!"

Two Horeng stormed into the chamber. They yanked her up, holding Charlee roughly by the arms. Her feet dangled above the floor, head drooped against her chest. Raspy breaths slid from her throat.

Do something! Now! She bit her upper lip. Was it already too late? No, it couldn't be.

Lifting her head, she fixed her eyes on Tribon. He still held the case with Kraannaannn's heart.

"Is this funny, traitor?" Charlee whispered

Must save Kraannaannn!

Closing her eyes, Charlee searched deep inside for a last spark of guardian power. At first, she felt nothing. *Look deeper!* Teeth gritted, she focused on her rhythmic heartbeat and each breath, using them as a metronome to focus her thoughts. Still nothing. *Come on!* Like plodding through an endless maze, Charlee plunged farther into the darkest regions of her mind until...

A flicker of light, like a distant star in the blackness of space, ignited inside her brain. *There!* A glimmer of magic the medallion hadn't stolen! But would it be enough. It would have to be.

Even as the Horeng dragged her from the chamber, Charlee's eyes shot open, and she clenched every muscle that would still obey her will. She'd have just one chance before the flame of magic dimmed for good.

Grunting, she envisioned the The Dragon Lord's lair. Her head throbbed. Blood dripped from her nose into her mouth, but a tiny blue circle formed in front of Tribon and quickly grew into a portal.

"Hey, what's...?" Tribon wondered.

Before he could react, Charlee's gateway swallowed his arms and the case with Kraannaannn's heart.

"No!" Theodora shouted.

Tribon yelled, "You little—"

The passageway shuttered, slicing through his forearms. Tribon bellowed in agony. He fell to his knees, glaring at the bloody stumps—cut off at the elbow—where his arms used to be. His own oozing black fluids, rotten and foul smelling, formed a pool around him.

Charlee's head collapsed to her chest, but she allowed herself a slight smile. Hopefully, the rest of Tribon's arms were on their way to the Dragon Lord along with Kraannaannn's heart. If the elder dragon could remove the blade still embedded, maybe he could save his son's life. She'd never know if it worked, but at least she had this moment.

The Horeng released Charlee, and she crashed to the floor. She lay on her stomach, resting her head against the cold stone. Her thoughts swirled. Did she dare hope the Dragon Lord would unleash revenge against Theodora and save her family? She had to believe that.

Theodora's daughter bent down and slapped her head with a gloved hand. "Whatever you did, Guardian, you better undo it now."

Charlee tilted her face just enough to make eye contact. She could only muster a whisper. "Deal…with…it."

Theodora let out a thunderous laugh that overshadowed Tribon's labored breathing and growls of pain.

"Well done, Guardian!" She crossed to Charlee. "You are stronger than I thought, but instead of saving yourself, you wasted your last bit of power on a worthless act." She spoke like a teacher lecturing her pupil. "But it is of no consequence."

Theodora grabbed Charlee's hair in her hand and yanked.

Her head snapped back, but she didn't flinch. Charlee was tired. The edges of darkness tunneled in on her. Better now to give into unconsciousness—even death—than more punishment. How wonderful it would be to stand with Cryton and her grandfather on the other side and watch the dragons destroy Theodora. Wait a second. How could she leave this to the dragons? How could she so easily slip away? No, she had to live. Don't fade away!

"This…isn't…over," Charlee declared

"I think it is." The sorceress shook Charlee's head. "Heed my words. Even if you have saved the Dragon Lord's son, the dragons are no threat to me any longer. I and my immortality have the power of the guardians. I can reach any world I choose. And, since you were the last of your kind—the last Guardian, no one will be able to reach me when I leave this world and all its useless lives behind. Now, remove this little girl from my sight!" she commanded the two wolf guards.

As Theodora strode off, Charlee raised her voice one more time. "You should… kill me…Theodora! I will find a way…to stop you."

Theodora sneered. "As I said, I will not kill you. That would do little to make you suffer for the trouble you have caused me. No, it will hurt you more if I allow you to live with your failure."

Once again, Theodora pointed the medallion at Charlee. It glowed to life, then a beam burst from its center, striking her in the chest. Volts of electricity raced through her body, boiling her insides. *I'm burning alive!* When it was over, steam rose from her reddened skin. She wheezed for a breath. "No…more. Please. Water…I need…water."

"Look how the proud guardian begs for a drink." Theodora strolled around her. "You may have a drop when I feel you are truly sorry for your insolence. Now, take her away!" The sorceress commanded again, gliding from the throne room.

The beasts dragged her to the doorway. Assara watched her mother, lips pinched together, one hand grasping the handle of her sword, the other over her mouth.

Charlee concentrated on Assara's face. Frown lines spread across her forehead just like they did on Sandra's when she was angry or concerned. The familiar expression brought Charlee a moment of comfort, but questions filled her thoughts. What was going through Assara's mind? Could a bit of Sandra have rubbed off on her? Was there a chance to reach her?

Assara sheathed her sword and followed Theodora. The chance to connect passed. The beasts tugged Charlee, her body sliding over wet stone. Her eyes closed. The cold loneliness of unconsciousness embraced Charlee. Darkness overtook her.

CHAPTER 33

The Dungeon

THE SQUEAK OF a tiny creature scurrying by her legs startled Charlee awake. Her eyes fluttered open. She sucked in air too quickly and coughed, a frothy saliva sliding down the sides of her mouth. Charlee's head spun and heart raced. She licked her parched lips, tasting her own salty blood. Was she alive? Must be. Then again, maybe the dead could talk to themselves.

If Charlee were dead, the stench of mold wouldn't sicken her so much. She wouldn't be sitting in wet filth against a cold rocky surface with muck dripping onto her hands. Bleak darkness as a pitch black pit boxed in her vision to a few feet in each direction. A heavy dampness pressed against her chest, making each breath difficult.

Charlee struggled against the sense of panic that overtook her.

They chained her to the wall, hands stretched to the sides, held by rusty shackles cutting into her skin. Charlee tried to wiggler her hands free, but the steel cut deep. Her legs extended out in front of her, ankles in irons.

"So thirsty," she muttered.

Her head, heavy and dizzy, drooped, neck no longer able to support the weight. It would be easy to fall back into the void of sleep and not think about what happened. How she failed everyone and left her family to face Theodora alone. Because of her, Cryton was dead. Easier to drift into another black abyss than feel his loss.

Charlee's face still ached where Assara's sword had cut her. She'd probably wear the scar for life. Just like in her vision of the medallion. Did its evil already course through her even though Theodora ripped the object away?

She wanted the medallion back. Needed it back. Like an addict. Her body quivered. A cold sweat dripped from her forehead. How could she have lost it? How would she ever retrieve it? Wait, that didn't matter. Only her family mattered. She couldn't save them without her powers.

"It's over," she sighed.

"*You cannot give up.*" A ghostly voice drifted toward her through the darkness. Charlee froze. "Who's there?"

At first, she received no response. "I'm hearing things." She watched her own sweat drip onto her leg.

The soft voice returned. "*You are still needed. Your role in these events has not yet ended.*"

"Is someone there?" Her gaze darted in every direction. "Show yourself."

A dim ball of light appeared in a corner of the dungeon. The apparition did little to illuminate the space, but it started to grow...and take shape.

Charlee watched, wide-eyed. Was her mind playing tricks on her?

The light took the form of a woman—the same Charlee had seen encased in glass. Young Theodora. The sorceress, her body transparent, floated before her. Had the witch come to twist her mind? To torture her?

Charlee pressed her back against the wall. "What are you doing here?"

"*You must prevail,*" the phantom said.

"What...what are you talking about?" Charlee wanted to strike at the ghostly form but had no strength to fight against her shackles. "You did this to me."

"*I did not.*" The specter glided closer. "*Do you not remember the place the gateway brought you to—the place where the heavens seemed to touch the world upon which you stood?*"

Charlee remembered that nowhere land she'd unexpectedly jumped to when she first tried to open a portal to the castle. She still didn't know if that place was real or a trick by the sorceress. "Yes, I do."

"*And do you remember what you found there?*" The spirit's golden hair flowed around a thin face. A white gown hugged a bone-thin frame.

"I saw you asleep or dead inside something like ice covered by sand." Charlee spoke with a hoarse voice through clenched teeth. More tricks. That's what this was. She couldn't fall for it.

This Theodora drifted within inches of Charlee. She wanted to back away. The presence had the same crystal blue eyes as the sorceress, but this face revealed no hate. The slight tilt of the head. A heavily furrowed brow. Lips slightly parted as if unsure whether to smile or frown. Was this an expression of compassion? Even remorse?

Theodora extended a bony arm toward her. "*What you saw was real. I am not dead, but imprisoned...kept alive, but forced to sleep for all time.*"

"So?"

"*Young Guardian, your presence in this world has awakened me from my endless sleep. I was able to send for you. I was the reason your gateway opened to the In-Between. I needed you to find me. I needed you to know the truth.*"

Charlee squeezed her eyelids. This wasn't real. Just a dream by a girl drifting in and out of consciousness. She opened her eyes and the ghost was still there. "Just leave me alone. So tired. Let me sleep." Her head drooped to her chest.

"*The person you saw was me...the true Theodora. The one you have done battle with...the one who now threatens all you cherish...is the medallion's creation.*"

"You're lying. Charlee lifted her head and spit at Theodora. "You're playing me. When I get out of this...Her words faded. She took a long breath. "Just let me be," she whispered.

The phantom Theodora backed away. *"If your world and mine are to survive, you must accept what I say as the truth."*

"I..."

"You must return to the In-Between and free me. Together, we must destroy the medallion. I let this happen and I must answer for what I have allowed to come into existence. Please help me to end this."

Charlee shook her head. Was she starting to believe her? No, she couldn't. "You're playing with my mind."

"No!"

At that moment, the click-clack of a locking mechanism interrupted their conversation. A door creaked open, allowing a line of hazy, unnatural orange light to filter into the dungeon. The spirit...or delusion...vanished.

Theodora, in physical form, slithered past the open dungeon door, bathed in a torch's flame. She held the medallion at her side. Assara stood beside her mother.

This Theodora mirrored the ghostly version—young and beautiful—but with eyes laced with red lines and a wide evil grin.

"Well, Guardian. Not dead yet, I see." Theodora stepped closer.

"I need water." Her dry throat burned.

The sorceress held her nose. "Yes...water. I can barely stand your stench." Theodora motioned to the Horeng. The wolves snorted then fetched two large buckets. One monster flung a gritty liquid into Charlee's face. It stunk of filth, but it was cold and revived her. The water splashed against her lips, and though putrid, she slurped as much as she could into her mouth. The second wolf slowly poured the bucket's contents over her head. Chunks of something fell on top of her. Peering at the ground, human fingers—their bones still protruding—lay around her.

Bile rose up her throat. She was going to be sick but with nothing in her stomach, she could only manage dry heaves.

The sorceress leaned down to her. "Is that better, child?"

Charlee lifted her head. "I told you, Theodora...you should have killed me."

"In a way, I have killed you." Theodora stroked Charlee's torn cheek. She was taking delight in the moment. "See for yourself."

Theodora waved her hands in circular fashion, and a picture formed. Like a grainy cell phone video, pictures revealed Theodora blasting her with the medallion, tearing a hole through her chest. The Charlee in the image died on the floor of the throne room.

Theodora closed her hand. "I will make sure to share this with the Dragon Lord and his son. They will believe it. They will think you are dead. There will be no one to save you."

"You're wrong."

The changeling wouldn't believe it.

223

"As I said, Guardian, your life is now meaningless to me. It makes no difference whether you are alive or dead." Theodora held up the medallion. "I have left you powerless. For now, it suits me to let you live, so that you can reflect on how your family, your friends, and your world will pay for your rebellion. Eventually I will kill you."

Charlee sighed. "Leave…my family…alone. I'll…hunt you…down." She couldn't take her eyes off the medallion. It called to her.

Theodora waved it in front of Charlee. "I think you may be more like me than you would let yourself believe. But you are mistaken. The medallion is mine and shall be for all time. Now, I must be off, but I just thought you would like to be present when I use your powers to open a gateway and enter your world… and conquer it. I thought you might like to look into the portal and see Earth for the last time."

Charlee had to warn her mom and dad, but how? If only she could find the strength one more time. "Don't do this…Theodora."

Another voice spoke up inside the dungeon.

"Mother, I have served you well, and I will serve you in any way you think best." Assara, still in her black armor, placed a hand on her mother's shoulder. "But when you leave this world and travel to another, I wish to go with you and stand by your side."

Desperation filled Assara's voice, a child afraid to be separated from her parent. If only she knew Theodora—or whatever this sorceress was—created her as a cruel joke. If only she knew Theodora had no love for her.

Theodora pushed her daughter's hand away. "We have discussed this. I need you to stay here and rule this world in my stead."

"But, Mother, you said the lives of this world were now meaningless to you," Assara responded. "What…what about my life? Is it meaningless as well?"

"Child, I did not mean you." Theodora's voice was soft and motherly—but fake. "I cherish your life. That is why it is important that you remain here to do my will. I could trust no one but you."

"She doesn't care about your life," Charlee asserted.

"Quiet," Assara blurted.

Theodora's daughter paced in front of her mother. "And will you return?" she asked.

"Of course, my child." Theodora slid her fingers through Assara's hair.

Charlee scoffed. "She's…lying. She…does not…care…about you."

Theodora's daughter glided to Charlee. Was she getting through to the girl? Instead, Assara slapped her across the face with a gloved hand. Charlee yelped. Her eyes dimmed. She blinked rapidly, fighting off unconsciousness.

"Silence, Guardian! If my mother asks me to rule this world until she returns, then it shall be done. I will rule it as she has, and the name of Assara will be just as feared as the name of my mother."

"Good, my daughter." Theodora wrapped an arm around Assara and ushered her back to the doorway.

Assara bowed to her mother...but her sunken cheeks, red-streaked eyes, and pursed lips expressed another story. Maybe there was some hope of reaching her. Maybe a little bit of what made Sandra so strong, independent, and kind was buried deep inside her clone.

For now, though, that part of Assara remained hidden. The girl held onto the belief she truly was her mother's daughter.

"My time has come," Theodora declared with delight. "Watch, Guardian, as I use your power to open a gateway."

"Wait." Charlee lifted her shoulders. "Are you...Theodora? Or...something...else."

The sorceress stood silently before answering, face twisted in a scowl. Then, her evil grin returned. "What a silly question." She bent toward Charlee. "I am Empress, conqueror, destroyer...but above all else, I am Theodora. The one who killed your grandmother, defeated your grandfather in battle, and the one who will make sure your world suffers. Now, I take my leave of you."

"No!" Charlee bit her lip until it bled. What could she do? Would her parents be strong enough to stop her? Could Earth fight her? Not while Theodora had the medallion. "Listen to me. Take off these chains and let's fight to the death. That's the only way you can be sure I won't break free and regain my powers."

Theodora ignored her.

Standing in the doorway of the dungeon, holding the medallion close to her chest, Theodora closed her eyes. A blue ball flew out of the medallion. It grew, shedding a bright, pure light throughout the dungeon. The Earth appeared deep inside the portal as if viewing the world from space.

"You can see, can't you?" Theodora said menacingly.

"Yes," Charlee hissed. She struggled once again against her shackles, but it did no good. *If only she could reach out to* her *mom! If only...*

Charlee tried to sense her mom with her mind, but all was silent. She couldn't find her, couldn't warn her.

Theodora stepped into the gateway. She looked back once at Charlee and her daughter and then continued on her journey.

"I'll...find...you!" Charlee mouthed.

But it was too late. In the time it took her to shout her protest, Theodora vanished. The gateway along with her.

She slumped against the wall. Her head dropped against her chest. "No... no...no! I'm so sorry."

She thought of the danger her family was in—and there was no one to protect them. She thought of Sandra. Charlee feared how her friend would react if she ever learned Theodora used her to create a clone.

As these thoughts swirled around her mind, Assara clutched her hair, jerking her head.

Charlee winced. "Let go…of me."

"Guardian, we will see how long you can last without food or water…because I will bring you neither."

"Assara, don't…do this." Charlee took one last chance to convince her to change. "This isn't…right."

"Enough!" Assara released Charlee's hair. The back of Charlee's head slammed against the wall.

She hissed through clenched teeth, trying to ignore the ache. "Assara…listen."

Theodora's daughter turned and walked to the door. Once there, she glanced back at Charlee one more time. "Good-bye, Guardian."

With that, she left.

When the dungeon door closed with a thunderous slam, all was silent. Charlee was left with nothing but the solitude of her own thoughts. Her mind wandered to her protector—the changeling.

"Where…are…you?" she cried out into the darkness. She needed her protector more than ever. He always knew when she needed help. Why hadn't he come? She hoped for a miraculous response, as she'd always gotten from the magical being. But this time, none came.

Charlee breathed deeply. Her thoughts shifted to Cryton.

"I'm so sorry I let you down. You would still be alive if it wasn't for all my mistakes. I miss you."

Then Charlee did something she almost never did.

Prayed.

Looking up to a hidden ceiling—to a sky far from reach—she prayed for the safety of her family. For Sandra. For all the people of Earth. She prayed for forgiveness for failing them all.

When her prayer was finished, Charlee lowered her head and closed her eyes.

CHAPTER 34

The Protector

THE CHANGELING RACED across the darkened sky toward the Castle of Latara in the form of the winged unicorn. How could he have been so stupid as to let the girl out of his sight for even a minute? The guardian was his responsibility, his charge—more importantly his friend—and he failed her.

Weakened from the burns suffered during the battle with Theodora's fire-spewing monster, he submitted to the care of the dragon healers and, grudgingly, allowed Kraannaannn to carry the unconscious guardian to safety. But he lingered too long in a healing state, and now the guardian was alone and hurt. He could feel it in every fiber of his shape-shifting body.

The changeling flew fast. He had to reach her soon—had to recharge her.

In the distance loomed the Kingdom of Latara. Storm clouds hovered above. Lightning zigzagged from the gloom like hands reaching across the heavens. Barren land, once alive with trees and grass, surrounded the realm. Maybe, if they stopped Theodora, life would return.

He was almost there. He just might reach Charlee in time.

Something swooshed overhead. A massive wall of flame rained down just in front of the changeling. He thrust out his wings, sliding to a stop just ahead of the scorched air, then dove toward the ground. No, he didn't have time for this. Not now. He knew where the fire had come from—Theodora's dragon.

Circling away from the flames, the changeling glanced back. The massive beast, its purple scales almost black under a melancholy sky, burst through the graying clouds above.

"You shall not save the girl," the dragon barked. "And you shall not save yourself either, little changeling."

The unicorn had no time to battle this dragon. With a thrust of its wings, he shot forward to the kingdom.

Racing behind, the beast yelled. "You will not reach her. You cannot out-fly a dragon."

His hooves galloping through the air, the changeling stretched his body to make it more streamline, willing himself to fly faster. He had to stay ahead of the dragon. If the flying serpent cut him off, they'd have to fight, and his magic was no match for a dragon.

A flash of orange flickered from behind. The monster had once again spit fire. Heat barreled down on the changing, leaving him no choice but to shift direction. The girl would have to hold on a little longer.

Wings pressed against his unicorn body, he dove back to the ground. Hopefully, the beast would follow.

It did.

At the last second, mere feet above the ground, the changeling tried to pull up but did not succeed. He crashed into the crusty, dying lands outside the castle, tumbling along the dirt and weeds. The collision shattered his form. His body morphed into its natural gelatinous state. *No, not now!* Forcing himself to regain control of his glowing body, the changeling shifted back into a unicorn.

The dragon crashed just as hard into the earth; a plume of dust rose around him. On wobbly legs, the unicorn crept toward the reptile. Had the dragon met its end?

A guttural laugh erupted from the beast.

The towering creature climbed out of the crater. Blood dripped from its deep nostrils. A tear cut across one wing. The reptilian creature looked at the unicorn with a dazed smile.

"You cannot kill me, changeling." The dragon spit blood. "The time has come to end this."

The changeling leaped into the air. The only way it was going to reach the guardian was by destroying this dragon.

With a thrust of its wings, it shot toward the darkening storm clouds. Under their cover, he might have a chance against the dragon. His only chance.

"Very good, changeling. Run!" the dragon mocked. It took flight as well.

The unicorn reached the bank of thick clouds, swinging into a ninety-degree turn, racing out of the dragon's path. If the beast followed, they'd both be blind in the mist. If he found the reptile first, maybe he'd spot a weakness…and attack.

Seconds later, the dragon blasted into the clouds. Yes! The plan worked. The changeling slowed, fluttering his wings just enough to stay aloft. The dragon was close, its ears sensitive to the slightest movement.

From above, the reptile called. "There is no way to hide from a dragon, little changeling. Why play these games? Surrender to me now, and I will make sure your death comes quickly, painlessly. Force me to continue this game, and I will make your end agonizing."

The changeling angled his unicorn ears, waiting for the swish of the dragon's wings, but cracks of lightning and the rumble of thunder cloaked its presence.

He had to locate the—

From the right, the beast's tail slashed at the changeling, smacking his side. Bones cracked. His right wing crushed against his body. The unicorn neighed furiously then fell through the clouds, plunging back to the wasteland below.

No, can't fail the guardian! Thrashing his one good wing, the unicorn struggled to stay aloft. Tapping into his magic, extending strands of energy—like tiny lightning bolts—to the shattered bones and broken appendage, he began to heal his wounds.

When both wings were strong enough, he soared back into the gray muck. He had to hide until he fully recovered.

"Still alive, I see." The dragon's head plowed through the clouds, jaws wide open, revealing fangs as sharp as long blades.

The changeling ducked just in time to avoid becoming lunch.

"I guess you are stronger than I thought." The monster circled him. "Well, that's good. I like to look into the eyes of my victims before I slaughter them. I think we have reached that moment. Your end is here."

The dragon might be right. This might be the final stand. Time to stop running. The changeling arched his back and charged at the winged-lizard. If this was to be their final battle, so be it. If he was to fall, the dragon would, too. Somehow.

Startled, the enemy hesitated, but not for long. It leaped at the changeling, snapping its jaws.

The changeling dodged the dragon's mouth, swept upward, wheeled around in the sky, and dove onto its back.

Enraged, the dragon flew wildly, trying to shake the changeling off. The unicorn steadied himself with his wings. He only needed a moment to accomplish his goal. Closings his eyes, he transformed the spiked horn on his forehead from bone into iron. Then, spotting an area of skin unprotected by the dragon's scaly armor, impaled the creature.

The dragon let out a mighty roar.

With the spike still embedded in the dragon's back, the changeling twisted his own head back and forth, bending the shaft until it cracked. *Finally!* The sound he'd been waiting for. He let out a pained cry as the stem broke free from his head, the lance left deep inside the dragon.

In a frenzy, the dragon snapped its tail. Its barb struck the changeling from behind, swatting him away. Rattled, the unicorn fell hard and fast from the sky.

"You will die for what you have done." The dragon followed just as fast. Plummeting above the unicorn, it reeled its head back to blast another breath of fire.

"Burn, changeling!" the dragon hissed. Flames licked forth. "Burn in—"

A bolt of lightning streaked down from the clouds and struck the iron lodged in the beast's back.

The spike blazed. The dragon roared in agony.

A second slash of lightning caught the giant lizard. Then a third.

The reptile roared once more and was silent.

Spreading his wings, the changeling slowed his fall but still struck the ground with bone-jarring force, rolling over and over until his body came to a stop. Head swirling, he tried to rise on shaky legs but slumped against the dirt.

High above, the burnt body of the dragon dropped from the skies like a falling rock. The monster hit land with a deafening explosion. Dead!

The changeling gazed up where a streak of black smoke lingered. Then he shifted his attention to Latara. Blinking his eyes, he forced himself to stand then took an unsteady step toward the kingdom. He had to reach her.

The guardian's story could not end deep within the castle. She had more to do. More life to live.

CHAPTER 35

A Tiny Spark of Blue

ACROSS THE DIMENSIONAL divide, in a two-story house like any other in a row of Victorians along a San Francisco street, a mother sat at a kitchen table, hands tensed into fists, tears rolling down her cheeks.

She felt a profound loneliness in her chest, making it difficult to breathe. But it wasn't her emotion. It was her daughter's. Somehow, even a world away, Tira Smelton felt her daughter's suffering.

"Joseph, she's hurting." Charlee's mom grabbed her husband's hand. "I can sense her pain."

"It's my fault." Charlee's dad held a picture of her in his other hand. "I should have been able to stop her. I should have been able to prevent all of this. I knew what was possible, and I still let it all happen."

"No, there was nothing you could do about Theodora or preventing our daughter from going after her. It was…destiny."

"Then I should have gone with her." Charlee's dad freed his hand from his wife and pounded the table with his fist. "Cryton should have included me."

As he mentioned Cryton's name, Mr. Smelton saw tears in his wife's eyes. "What is it?" he asked.

"Something…bad…has befallen Cryton," his wife answered. "I… can't…feel his presence any longer. I think…" She let her words trail off.

Mr. Smelton hugged his wife. They embraced for several moments before he let go. "We've got to find a way to reach them," he said. "There has to be another way. I'm no physicist, but if there's some dimensional doorway, there has to be more than one way to open it."

"Joseph, I've tried but don't have the ability. My magic just doesn't work that way. I've tried to reach out to Charlee, and while I can feel her presence, my thoughts can't reach her."

"Well, we can't be out of options. I refuse to believe it. We're her parents. We have to reach her."

At that moment, the Smelton's two-year-old daughter, Megan, started to giggle as she sat in her high chair on one end of the dining table.

Something was in her right hand.

"Joseph?" Tira Smelton asked.

"I don't know," her husband answered.

Both stumbled over to Megan, who stared happily at what looked like a little blue marble.

The Smeltons reached their daughter and realized the ball was not in her hand, but rather was hovering just above.

And it wasn't a ball or a marble.

It was a circle of blue energy!

The Smeltons looked at each other in disbelief…and hope.

Also by Darren Simon

Guardian's Nightmare

Charlee Smelton is an average thirteen-year-old girl struggling to adapt after her family moves to San Francisco. She thinks her biggest obstacle is facing the bullies who brand her a nerd. She's wrong. Can Charlee find the hero inside her, the hero she must become, to save her friends, family, city, and world from an evil only she can defeat, an evil she allows into this world.

Nessie Out of Water
Stacey Wooten

Awkward situations seem to seek out Nessie, a post-college secretary at a portable toilet rental company, like stalkers of a boy-band sensation. She has dealt with unstable roommates and an ever-present toaster salesman, but this one takes the cake. There will be daring escapes, secrets unturned, inspirational pondering, and pointed questions on the quality of her cooking as Nessie comes to understand that God's plan and purpose, though sometimes different than expected, are always best.

Darkest Hour
Tony Russo

After the Great War, a terrifying new enemy conquers much of Europe before turning its sights on Britain. All that stands between the unstoppable Black Legion and invasion is Briley and a handful of brave pilots. With its historical twists, surprising romance and heartfelt tragedy, Darkest Hour is the first of a series of truly unique and epic adventures.

www.ingramcontent.com/pod-product-compliance
Lightning Source LLC
Chambersburg PA
CBHW070818180626
46818CB00001B/319